IGOR

A Novel

Raymond Hunter Pyle

This story is a work of fiction. Names, characters, places, and incidents either are the product of the author's imagination or are used fictitiously, and any resemblance to actual persons, living or dead, business establishments, events, or locations is unintended and entirely coincidental.

Copyright © 2017 Raymond Hunter Pyle

All rights reserved.

ISBN:
ISBN-13: 9781521074480

CONTENTS

Series title List

Chapter 1	1
Chapter 2	8
Chapter 3	22
Chapter 4	38
Chapter 5	47
Chapter 6	55
Chapter 7	60
Chapter 8	68
Chapter 9	76
Chapter 10	86
Chapter 11	94
Chapter 12	100
Chapter 13	108
Chapter 14	118
Chapter 15	125
Chapter 16	132
Chapter 17	138

Raymond Hunter Pyle

Chapter 18	142
Chapter 19	147
Chapter 20	153
Chapter 21	159
Chapter 22	168
Chapter 23	177
Chapter 24	183
Chapter 25	195
Chapter 26	205
Chapter 27	213
Chapter 28	219
Chapter 29	227
Chapter 30	233
Chapter 31	238
Chapter 32	243
Chapter 33	249
Chapter 34	256
Chapter 35	260
Chapter 36	269
Chapter 37	275

IGOR

Chapter 38	281
Chapter 39	293
Chapter 40	299
Chapter 41	304
Chapter 42	313
Chapter 43	322
Chapter 44	328
Chapter 45	338
Chapter 46	343
Chapter 47	348
Chapter 48	354
Chapter 49	359
Chapter 50	366
Chapter 51	373
Chapter 52	378
Chapter 53	383
Chapter 54	390
Chapter 55	396
Chapter 56	404
Chapter 57	410

Raymond Hunter Pyle

Chapter 58	416
Chapter 59	422

VIETNAM SERIES

THE GUNNY
BULLETS AND BANDAGES
MASTER GUNS
THE BEAST
JUMP WINGS AND SECRETS

GLOBAL WAR ON TERROR SERIES

IGOR

CHAPTER 1

Mirrors were nightmares, but children were the worst. He was becoming hardened to those reactions, at least outwardly, but no one can ever become completely immune to an honest and innocent expression of horror when he is the source of the horror.

Navy Lieutenant Junior Grade (LTJG) Lee Toliver was glad to finally be out of the Burn Center at Brooke Army Medical Center in San Antonio and on his way to his new assignment. It had been a tough year, but he was lucky in many ways.

Feeling lucky was as difficult as feeling grateful, but he was both. A lot of the guys in the burn center with more extensive burns hadn't had his luck. Some died, and some faced kidney or lung problems that would last the rest of their lives. Even with his damaged face, he figured he had something to be grateful for. He wasn't pretty, but he had reasonably good health now, and hopefully, his career was waiting for him. He leaned back in the seat and let his breath out slowly.

"Leaving is a bitch for all of us, Mr. Toliver. You'll kick ass. Don't worry about it."

Sergeant First Class Charlie Cross had been a good friend during Lee's year at the center. His scars weren't visible, but under his clothes they were more extensive than Lee's, and his struggle had been longer and more difficult.

"What's with the mister stuff, Charlie?"

"You're back on duty now, sir. Time for you to start acting like an officer again."

"Thanks, buddy. I'll be okay. I'm just dealing with not being able to come back to the center tonight or when it gets too tough out there."

"You're ready. If you can take those showers, you can take anything."

The first weeks at Brooke, nearly a year ago, were hard on a lot of levels. The showers were the worst part. While his brain was still recovering from the shock of the explosion and his burns still raw, the nurses put him in a support contraption and wheeled him into the shower. Pain medicine only helped a little. Over and over he was told to suck it up, in a kind and concerned way, but suck it up was the message. It was part of the process for preventing infection. It had to be done. Those first weeks were a nightmare of pain, fear, and confusion.

"Heard anything about your return to duty?"

Lee asked Charlie.

"Not a damn word. The board meets in a month and I still haven't got a feel for what they will do. The Docs aren't offering much encouragement. Be glad you got your clearance for full duty."

The months he had spent in recovery with surgery after surgery had seemed like they would go on forever, and toward the end, Lee worried he might not have a career to return to. So many of the guys were medically retired. That scared the hell out of him, the thought of being turned lose to start over with his life and looks irreparably changed, an object of pity. So, that was another thing he had to be grateful for. His brain was fine and the Navy still wanted him, and maybe even more important, he might get an overseas tour out of the deal. Maybe it was just a chance to run away. He wasn't sure.

"Are you worried about the crowds in the terminal?" Charlie said. It was like he was reading Lee's mind. But then, the burn group was tight, and they were truthful with each other.

"Yeah, some. Just going to the PX is hard. The kids are the worst."

"Remember the process, Mr. Toliver. You can't change it, so deal with it. Hold your head up. People react to how you feel about yourself."

Lee laughed. "You could give that lecture by yourself."

"I have," Charlie said and chuckled. "There's a

lot of truth there. Don't forget it."

He hated getting caught in public places and an airport was about as public as it gets. He told himself he was getting used to it, but the pain and humiliation caused by those looks of revulsion and shock still dug deep. And each time it happened his hate grew for the bastards who blew people up.

Had his wounds been from war, he could have moved on, maybe not forgiven, but moved on knowing he might have caused someone else the same or worse, but his horror happened in London with an attractive lady. They hadn't been a danger to anyone. He was just trying to get to his hotel.

"The anger eases up when you accept it," Charlie said, reading his mind again.

"Accept it? What choice do I have?"

"It's all a choice. That's the only control we have; how we let it influence us. It takes a while, Lee. Don't let it fuck up your career."

"Yeah. I'm good. Thanks, Charlie."

"You'll get there. Just don't forget your paper bags"

Lee laughed out loud. One day in the burn group therapy circle, Charlie called Lee a two-bagger. He told Lee he could probably get laid if he put a bag over his head, but in his case, he should use two bags in case one split. It was one of the milder forms of dark humor they used with each other.

"I'll use plastic," he said

Charlie grinned and picked up the speed as they entered a four-lane to the airport.

"You're going to do great. Dazzle them with a little French, and they'll melt in your arms. Oh wait. Your specialty is Middle East. Find one in a burka and then you'll both have bags over your head. A match made in heaven."

Lee laughed again, something he hadn't been doing much of lately. "Oh Christ, Charlie. That's worse than the two-bagger joke."

Lee Toliver was a bright guy all around, but like all savants, his talent in one area was truly astonishing. He was a Naval Academy graduate and a gifted linguist and polyglot who was fluent in multiple Middle Eastern languages and dialects. He was a language savant who picked up new languages like most people pick up bad habits. His honors research at Princeton, two papers on a group of five obscure languages called Nuristani spoken only in northeast Afghanistan, caught the attention of Navy Special Warfare Command and led to his second chance for a career.

"Wish I was good at languages," Charlie said. "I'd like to learn Spanish. I can field strip and repair just about any weapon in the armory, but I can't remember a single word of Spanish for ten minutes. How the hell do you learn five or six languages."

"It's just something I was born with. It doesn't make me any smarter than you. I wouldn't know where to begin field stripping a machine gun. It's just something I'm good at."

Like a gifted pianist who reads complete measures of music instead of notes, Lee learned language by the phrase and picked up grammar, intonation and inflection in a single package. Give him two weeks immersed in a language with native speakers, and he could hold a conversation in authentic dialect. He didn't have to work at it. It was just the way his brain was wired.

Several agencies and departments tried to recruit him when he finished at Princeton in near east studies after the Academy, but Office of Naval Intelligence (ONI) had the inside track. Lee was assigned to a select group in ONI dedicated to Naval Special Warfare Command (read SEALs) called Trident and had completed almost a year of specialized training in interrogation, intelligence database management, combat fundamentals with the Marines, and military intelligence at the Navy and Marine Corps Military Intelligence School when it happened.

On the morning of July 7th, 2005, he was met at Heathrow in England by an attractive female British Army Leftenant. He still remembered her name, Abilene Dundee. She was Lee's liaison with MI6, British Military Intelligence, where he was scheduled to receive an intelligence briefing on the Pakistan FATA region before he deployed to Afghanistan supporting a SEAL Team.

On their way to his lodging in London, he and

his escort had the incredibly bad luck of getting caught up in a suicide bombing near Travistock Square just before 10am. As they attempted to get around a double-decker bus, the whole rear of the bus exploded with the roof flying through the air. Her back was broken leaving her crippled and in a wheelchair, and the left side of Lee's head and face was burned and severely scarred.

As Charlie left him at the arrivals gate, Lee shivered at the thought of the crowds inside.

CHAPTER 2

As SEAL Teams preparing for deployment entered the final phase of work-up, they were designated squadrons and began taking in critical support staff, everything from administration and intelligence to Seabees and medical, to support the deployment. The additional staff often ballooned the squadron up to twice or three times the Team's original size depending on the deployment area and responsibilities.

Platoon-sized Detachment Bravo from SEAL Team Two in Little Creek, Virginia would get only a small intel support package consisting of one Trident Intel officer for interpreter and interrogation duties and one Trident enlisted intel computer and communications specialist.

Originally, Trident debated where to put Lee for his return to duty. West Coast Team 3 was deploying to Iraq and East Coast Team 2 was deploying a platoon sized detachment to Afghanistan. His language and intel expertise could be used in both places, but the Afghanistan detachment offered a unique opportunity.

He would embed and fly to Bagram with Detachment Bravo of Team 2, get some low kinetic experience, and then, if he had done well, join a Squadron 3 Task Unit in Iraq later in their deployment, giving him theater-wide experience in one deployment.

Lee had met the Team commander at his interview earlier in the day, so after checking-in with Team Two Command Master Chief, he was assigned quarters with the bachelor officers. He visited all the offices on his check-in sheet and stopped at the building exit. He almost cheered. He was in. He was deploying. The paperwork was out of the way, and he could start his new assignment and get his career back on track. Now to meet the people he would be supporting.

As Lee backed into the room he was assigned, a JG standing in the passageway marked his arrival.

"Attention on deck, new meat arriving!"

A second head poked out of a door.

"A Lew-ten-ant very Junior Grade cherry," the second officer said. "God is good to his faithful children. I am no longer the junior new guy."

Lee had been warned to expect hazing. He wasn't a SEAL, but he was an IA (individual augmentee) new-guy deploying with the platoon. As an IA, he was reasonably safe, but no one escaped new-guy status completely. All, must be humbled. Whether SEAL or support staff, you had to earn your spurs every day. He turned his head slowly to get a better view of his antagonists. The guy in the passageway got bug-eyed.

"Jesus Christ, what happened to you?"

The second officer came into the passageway in his skivvies to see what the fuss was about and just stared when he caught sight of Lee's face.

Lee decided to play the game.

"The wind messed up my hair," he said.

"Bullshit, what did that?"

"What did what?"

"What hell, your face. What happened to your face?"

"Suicide bomber," Lee said, tiring of the game. "I got off light. My partner got a broken back."

He didn't mind the way the SEALs were reacting at all. It was the furtive and covert looks and subtle revulsion he got from most people that bothered him most, as though somehow, he had become a lesser being because of his burns, something that shouldn't be allowed out in public to make people uncomfortable. These guys were about as subtle as a battleship. Instead of being repulsed, they moved in closer for a better look and checked him out openly.

"You already deployed? We were told you're a new guy. Where did it happen?"

"London," Lee said. "I'm not a SEAL."

"London? Geeze! I know you're not a SEAL. Master Chief briefed us. You're a Trident Intelligence geek, right?"

"Right. I'm a linguist and interrogator. This is my first deployment."

"I'm Mike Osborne, and that sorry excuse for a Naval officer is Jerome Washington. You're Toliver?"

"Lee Toliver."

Both the SEALs were quiet for a moment and examined Lee closely.

"What do you think, Jerome?" Mike said. "If he's going to work with the detachment, he needs a handle."

"Igor," Washington said. "It's got to be Igor."

"How about Scarface? Too obvious? Okay, it's Igor. You named him. You own him."

"Screw you," Lee said, and dragged his bag into his room, but he was grinning. These guys held nothing sacred. Everything was fair game. It was like being back in his burn group. He liked it.

"Man up, new guy," Osborne said." You ain't seen nothing yet. Are you going over with us, or are you going ahead?"

"With the platoon."

"Then you are mine as of now," Mike said. "Didn't know we were getting an American Terp. What do you habla?"

"Pashto, Dari, Urdu, and Arabic."

Damn, that's the big four where we're going. Okay, get unpacked, and I'll introduce you to the platoon."

Mike told Lee to go to the team room and told him how

to get there. He said he'd be there as soon as he got changed. Problem was, word of new meat spread ahead of him. When Lee walked through the door to the platoon space, he was ambushed from both sides.

His attackers didn't even talk while they pinned him down and wrapped him up with duct tape. He didn't know what hit him and just struggled wide eyed. This kind of thing just didn't happen to an officer on a Naval base. Who the hell were these guys? Were they a bunch of disgruntled nuts out for revenge on an officer? He was so shocked, he struggled quietly, and finally he found himself bound up in a cocoon of tape and alone. They stood him in a corner and just left him there. Those sons of bitches just left him there.

Everything was silent. Everyone had disappeared. He was in a little bit of a panic by the time Osborne arrived fifteen minutes later. Were they coming back? When would someone find him? He struggled, but you can't beat duct tape. Finally, Osborne came through the door, stopped dead, and started laughing.

"Oh shit, Igor. What was I thinking sending you down here alone? Bravo! Get your asses in here!"

The platoon drifted in one by one with shit eating grins on their faces.

"Somebody cut that crap off him," Osborne shouted between belly laughs.

When he was finally free, Lee glared at his tormentors. With his face, glaring was almost an art form. He wasn't stupid though. This was his new home.

Instead of the offended indignation he felt, he said, "Well, that was something you don't see every day."

They had been watching him closely for his reaction and liked what they heard. There were a few chuckles and everyone relaxed.

"Bravo, listen up," Osborne said." This new meat is Lieutenant Igor. LT Igor is an IA Terp and interrogator from Trident, and as you can see, he's already had one round with the opposition and finished second. He's a walking, talking lesson for you guys. Second place is the first loser. He's embedding with us. Ours is not to question why, etcetera, etcetera. JJ and Snake, take care of our boy and get him set up with a cage, gear, and weapons. Take him to the range, and make sure he knows which end the bullet comes out."

Special Warfare Operator Second Class (SO2) Jason Jones, called JJ, and SO3 Johnny Vhiper (pronounced viper) took their time looking Lee over. JJ looked at Snake and shook his head as if to say, Why me?

"What do you know about weapons, LT?"

"I hit what I aim at," Lee said.

"That's always a good thing," Snake said. "What weapons are you qualified on?"

"Expert badge for the M14, M4, and Sig P226. The Marines qualified me on the M79, M203, Mark 19 and M249 SAW. They gave me familiarization training on the Ma Deuce, M240, and the M60." (SAW-Squad Automatic Weapon)

What Lee didn't tell them was his varsity sport

at the Academy had been marksmanship. He also played intramural Lacrosse, but marksmanship was his primary sport. He was on both the rifle team and the practical shooting team for pistol. He had placed second in a national match with rifle and won a regional practical shooting match for pistol. With the additional weapons training the Marines provided at Lejeune during his combat training, he was probably as good a shot, in his opinion, as any SEAL in the teams—except for trained snipers—and a caveat of shooting at targets, not people.

"We'll start with the M4 and Sig. Is your face going to be a problem on the range?"

"Not to me." Lee said.

"Then it ain't going to be a problem for us either. Draw your weapons, Igor, and meet us back here."

"That's Mr. Igor," Lee said.

JJ laughed. Aye, aye, Mr. Igor, sir."

The SEALs surprised Lee. Before coming to Team Two, he had a mental image of SEALs as big, tall, muscular bruisers obsessed with physical conditioning. The conditioning obsession turned out to be true, but the SEALs themselves were a mixed bag physically. At five-foot, ten inches, Lee was taller than the shortest SEAL he met and could look many of them in the eye without craning his neck, and while muscled physiques were well represented, lean and wiry frames were also common. Well, to flog a dead cliché, you can't tell a book by its cover.

Lee drew an M4 with three magazines and a MK25 Sig P226, 9mm pistol with two extra 15-round magazines. The M4 was equipped with an Aimpoint M68 CCO red dot sight. (CCO- Close Combat Optic)

His SEAL mentors loaded him and his weapons into a beat-up Yukon that looked to be on its last legs and took him to the known distance range. On the outside, the Yukon looked okay, but the inside was trashed. Seats were ripped, floor covering had holes in it, head rests were missing, and one of the door panels was completely gone. When Lee got in he had to slam the door twice to get it to latch. When he sat down in the back, the seat gave way and slid forward. Yet, it was a relatively new vehicle.

"Geeze!" Lee said. "What happened to this piece of crap?"

JJ and Snake laughed. "SEAL crap, Igor. We sometimes get bored and a bit rambunctious on long trips. Here's a tip, new-guy. If you ever ride with the platoon anywhere, sit in the very back and hit the deck when the shit hits the fan." They didn't explain exactly what that shit might be

JJ instructed and tested him on safety and range rules first. Lee expected it. He was an NRA certified range master and firearms instructor himself. Never assume anything about the condition of a gun or the shooter's knowledge. Having established he could handle his weapon safely, and he understood the range rules, JJ let him zero his rifle on the 100-yard target. When he was satisfied with the sights, the SEALs tested his shooting out to 300 yards.

The SEALs didn't expect a lot from him and didn't demand a lot. He was individual augmentee (IA) support staff. He had to be able to defend himself if the occasion arose, and the occasion might arise where the Teams set up operations, so he would be issued weapons. Mostly they wanted to be sure he was safe around weapons and wouldn't kill or injure someone through ignorance.

Lee was comfortable with range procedure and followed Snake's range master commands expertly and put them all center of mass on the torso targets. They had him fire one magazine on automatic just to check him out and to be sure he could control it. Automatic fire wasn't something used often, but for suppressing fire, it was useful.

When he was through on the rifle range, they had him field strip and clean his weapon and stow it in the truck. He breezed through the cleaning and reassembly.

When Lee saw the range for the next exercise, he smiled to himself. The range they took him to for the pistol was essentially a practical shooting set-up, and not a very tough one either. He had competed on set-ups exponentially more difficult and placed high in the rankings while competing for the Academy.

Since he handled his weapons expertly and safely, JJ put him through a move and shoot exercise.

He had to move fast and nail each target twice while on the run. He aced the course without a problem. When he completed the exercise, he sensed he had gained a measure of respect and creds. A small measure. His status moved up one notch to someone who probably wouldn't kill you by mistake.

When they arrived back at the team room, JJ found LT Osborne and gave him a thumbs-up.

"He knows his weapons and hits what he shoots at," JJ said.

"Okay, give him a load-out list and let him draw cruise boxes and his gear. Assign him a cage for his stuff. Check him out and make sure he has what he needs. Maybe this won't be a baby-sitting exercise after all."

Since he wasn't a SEAL, and the platoon didn't want to be slowed down, Lee was excused from their PT and wasn't allowed near their other training. But each morning Lee went to the compound and did eye-opener PT with the detachment anyway and even tried to run with them at the back of the formation. The SEALs tolerated his presence, but mostly ignored him. Both the PT and run were more than he could handle at first, but he tried and did all he could, and his conditioning improved day by day. When they went to the water though, he went home. The SEALs gave him credit for trying and more credit for not acting like a wannabe.

Lee spent most of his days with the team

Master Chief, Operations Chief, Detachment Chief, and platoon LPO (leading Petty Officer) learning about missions and team level intelligence gathering and analysis. He had a school level knowledge of military intelligence, but he needed to understand actionable intelligence at the platoon level, and he needed to understand what was actionable from a SEAL operator's point of view.

The effort was a grind, but he listened well, took advice and direction well, and put out maximum effort at everything he did. Trident trains its analysts well and his database and computer skills were welcomed. The detachment SEALs slowly accepted him and decided he might eventually be more help than trouble.

Just before the detachment deployed, Lee was assigned a most difficult task by the Team Two head shed.

"You want me to what?" Lee said to the Team Command Master Chief.

"I think I made myself clear," Master Chief said.

"Sensitivity training? For a SEAL Platoon?"

"Mr. Toliver, I said cultural sensitivity training. You are the expert on the Middle East. I assume that means you have knowledge of Islamic culture. Put together a half day training class to familiarize our team with the Muslim religion and the Arabic culture in Iraq. This is continuing education. We not only have to fight these people, we also have to work with many of them. Focus on manners and avoiding religious and cultural faux pas. You can do that, can't you?"

"When?" Lee asked

"No hurry. Let's say Thursday morning." It was Tuesday.

"Well," Lee said scratching his head, "I'll give it my best shot."

"Who could ask for any more?" Master Chief said.

Lee worked on his Power Point presentation all day Wednesday and whittled it down most of the evening. He dreaded Thursday morning. The SEALs could be . . . how shall we put it? Mildly sarcastic? Well, that's close enough.

What he didn't know was the class was as much for the platoon to check-out his Middle East expertise as it was to teach them what he could. All of them, except for two new guys, had multiple deployments to Afghanistan and Iraq.

Thursday morning came, and sixteen SEALs from Bravo Platoon filled the classroom. Standing in front of sixteen SEALs with all of them staring at you with skeptical looks was daunting, to say the least.

"Good morning, gentlemen. I want to spend some time talking about Islam this morning to help increase your sensitivity to the cultural norms that will help you as you interact with Muslims. Are any of you familiar with just how much a Muslim's life is influenced by his religion?"

"We've all had Hajj 101, Mr. Toliver," the LPO said. "We've all deployed to the Middle East too. Tell us why we should care. How is it important to the mission?"

Lee swallowed and got his thoughts back on track.

"Will an understanding of what motivates them help you fight them?"

"Okay," the LPO said. "Go on."

The first thing I'll tell you is you can't think of them as just religious. Every facet of their life is influenced by the Qur'an and the Hadith. It's not just a religion. It's a way of life, a way learned from birth."

"So is Christianity. So is Judaism," a man in the back said.

"Christianity is not even in the same ball park," Lee said. "Most of a Christian's life is influenced more by secular society than religion. Diet, law, politics, fashion, government, and manners are good examples. Orthodox Judaism is close. For a Muslim in the Middle East though, religion is society, diet, law, politics, manners, and politics. Even the smallest and most common parts of daily life are touched by Islam."

"Okay, give me a real-life example," the LPO said.

Lee had anticipated this question. SEALs were good at getting right to the heart of a matter.

"Okay. To demonstrate the range of life issues discussed in the Hadith, try this one on.

"Hadith 51. Narrated by Jabir. Let me set the

stage. Muhammad's companions were seeking guidance from the Prophet. A companion says, and this is where the Hadith starts, "The Jews used to say, 'if one has intercourse with his wife from the back, she will deliver a squinty-eyed child.'" So, this verse was revealed by the Prophet, "Your wives are a tilth unto you, so go to your tilth when or how you will."

First there was a snort from the back, and then the whole platoon cracked up. Someone said, "So, I can go home and poke my tilth anyway I want, and I don't have to worry about glasses for my kids? I think I might like this class."

When they settled down Lee continued.

"Sure, not something you'd expect to learn in Sunday school, I guess, but I wanted to help you understand just how broad a swath Islam cuts through a devout Muslim's life."

A man in the back raised his hand. "Mr. Igor, sir, I've got a question."

The wise-ass crap was starting, Lee could see it coming. Trying to keep a straight face, he said, "Yes. What is your question?"

"Does a tilth have hair around it?"

He lost the class again, but he knew he had them.

The rest of pre-deployment went better for him after that class, and tilth became a synonym for . . .well, you know.

CHAPTER 3

The U.S. base at Bagram was huge. Like Denver, it sat a mile high in the middle of a mountain range, high enough where your lungs had to adjust to the lower oxygen when you first got there. His first impression of the base could be summed up in his thought, shack city. Rows and rows of B-huts, 18' x 36' plywood structures designed to hold eight troops each, stretched out as far as he could see. They were better than tents, but not by much. There were hundreds of them.

Late February in the Afghan mountains was the beginning of the thaw and opening of spring hostilities, but it was still cold. Insurgents and supplies were beginning to move through the mountain passes from Pakistan, just a trickle this early in the year due to snow in the high passes, but spring was coming.

The detachment mission was primarily training Afghan National Army (ANA) special forces, but Lee had additional duties. A DEVGRU detachment worked with Army Ranger special forces out of the Joint Special Operations Command (JSOC) compound at Jalalabad (J-bad). Lee would support Detachment Bravo in Bagram and be available to DEVGRU for linguist and interrogation duties on an as needed basis. (DEVGRU is sometimes known as SEAL Team Six and is the Navy's equivalent to the Army's Delta Force)

Lee learned about new-guy status the first day at Bagram. His silver JG bars didn't confer any immunity from grunt work. New-guys got the grunt jobs, even new-guy IAs. First, he helped unload the Detachment's packed gear and weapons and helped transport it to its assigned areas. Then he helped unpack it, unloading Conex boxes, breaking down pallets, and moving everything to its appropriate space. It was exhausting work, but he learned a lot about what it takes to deploy a SEAL platoon and where everything the platoon used was stored.

The new-guy treatment wasn't just harassment or hazing. He recognized the similarities to the way an apprentice in any trade was treated. Most tradesmen started with a broom or a shovel in their hands. You learned to walk before you were taught to run. The tedious and back breaking work of breaking down the platoon's gear and equipment and distributing it to the appropriate work spaces taught the make-up of each element of the detachment's organization, who participated in the element, where it was, what they did and used, and how they fit in the overall task. When he was done, Lee knew where to find anything in camp.

The mission in Afghanistan for SEALs was different than for Iraq deployments. There, SEALs worked with Marine and Army infantry providing sniper over-watch and clearing operations as well as direct action ops in urban environments and did some training for the Iraqi Army. In Afghanistan, SEALs, mostly DEVGRU, hunted for specific high value targets in the mountains, scrambled on rescue missions, did some training, and provided personal security details. The SEAL detachments did selected ops in the mountains, some direct-action ops in more urban areas, but the mission was training ANA troops.

The mountain AOs (areas of operations) were remote and wild. The terrain was mountainous and rugged and populated only sparsely. The target insurgents were elusive and knew the terrain better than the Americans. The process for finding them and then setting up a mission to capture or kill them was so arcane in its use of secret technology, it approached the realms of magic. But intelligence gathering still depended on HUMINT and human judgement. (HUMINT- Human Intelligence-Snitches, eyeballs, and interrogations)

Because of the Pashtun culture, remoteness of the AO, and difficulties with personal communications, local snitches were rare and unreliable. Every piece of information obtained from locals had to be double and triple confirmed. Single source intel was rarely useful.

Too often it turned out to be one Pashtun with a blood vendetta against another clan or family using the Americans to do his dirty work.

The problem could swing from no confirmed intel, to too much information in too many forms, and that's where the detachment's role touched DEVGRU's role. The intel job for the detachment was to develop actionable intelligence for ops within their own capabilities and limited AO.

Their primary source was HUMINT from interrogations at the DIF (Detention and Interrogation Facility) and other intel groups in the Bagram area. Those sources often produced intel on targets out of the area and of little value to the detachment, so whatever intelligence the detachment developed went into the databases DEVGRU intel and targeting cells used. Through interaction on targets of interest to DEVGRU, the detachment intel officer soon became known to the DEVGRU team.

Detachment Bravo in Bagram consisted of one Lieutenant JG officer-in-charge (OIC), an experienced platoon Chief, twelve SEAL operators/trainers, Lee as intel officer, one IA communications/computer Petty Officer from Trident, and one EOD Tech. (EOD-Explosive Ordnance Disposal).

Lee was fitting in well, and LT Osborne and Chief Boyle began to see potential in him for a more active role on direct action ops with SEAL task teams. His language skills could be a valuable addition to ops outside of the wire. With direction from the OIC and detachment Chief, the SEALs started pushing Lee to improve his physical conditioning and worked on his combat skills. He didn't need SEAL level skills, but they wanted him capable of functioning in small unit tactics and able to take his place in a stack when they entered a target building.

His morning and evening physical training took on a new dimension and range time was added to his already demanding schedule. Since working in the mountains often required carrying sixty to seventy pounds of gear up and down steep slopes, squats in the weight room with heavy weight were added. Physical and weapons training became a daily duty.

Lee's first intel new-guy work-task was working with the detachment Chief to organize the intel files into a system for analyzing and cross-checking data coming in from ops, DEVGRU, interrogations, OGAs (other government agencies) and Army and Marine Corps S2 and G2 in Bagram. The amount of material; intelligence reports, summaries, incident reports, interrogation records, and single source tips, was astonishing, and most of it wasn't relevant to the detachment's mission, but sometimes, something in it might be. He often worked with LT Osborne, but there was no question who was in-charge of intel. Chief Boyle was.

On Lee's first day of work at Bagram, Chief Boyle took him to the planning room.

"Mr. Toliver, we have more crap than we are

able to do anything with. All of it could be useful if we had some system for laying our hands on it when we need it and had a system for knowing when we need it."

The crap he was talking about was intel data and history of past ops that could be turned into useful information for planning if it was organized, including a load of intel left by the detachment they were relieving.

"Yes, sir. Would you like me to work on that?" The Chief, even though enlisted, was an imposing figure, both physically and intellectually. Just his experience was awe inspiring to a new guy.

"Mr. Toliver, listen up. In the real Navy, we don't call Chief Petty Officers sir. Most especially, commissioned officers don't call Chiefs sir. Now let's try that again."

"Right, Chief. Would you like me to work on a system for organizing the files?"

"You are an officer, sir. It would please me if you decided that the files needed organizing and took the initiative to see that it got done."

"Uh, right. Um, I'm sure you have more important things to do than watching me. Why don't you leave me here, and I'll see what needs to be done?"

"Excellent idea, Mr. Toliver."

Chief Boyle turned out to be a skilled mentor. Rather than trying to explain the process to Lee and trying to guide him through files and wasting a day of his own valuable time, he dumped Lee in the middle of it, just like all the other new-guy tasks. Lee had the training from school. He was supposed to be a smart guy. He should be able to figure it out. If he couldn't, he probably shouldn't be there.

Photographs, maps, CIA reports, radio intercepts, satellite pictures, transcripts from interrogations, single source tips, after action reports from the task teams, and reports and photos from recon missions, all had to be organized, prioritized, and annotated in a way that allowed computer files to be linked to hard files and intel relevant to the detachment to emerge, and once a piece of information emerged, it had to support mission planning. An organized system was needed for that. Chief Boyle said he had a rudimentary system set up, but Lee should see what needed to be done to make it functional and effective.

He went through the Chief's file system on a computer workstation and pulled up the database design. Tracing out the tables and relationships gave him a base knowledge of the system. That analysis went quickly. He could see the hand of a Trident data base administrator in the design.

He plotted everything on his own flow chart, first learning what information was there. Then he went through the hard files. He remembered the hierarchy of information he was taught by the Trident Group. The problem was, Trident IAs generally worked at Task Group or Squadron level, sometimes at the Task Unit (TU) Intel or Targeting cell level, but seldom supporting individual platoon planning or small detachments. That was the TU Intel Cell's job, but from the look of Chief

Boyle's files, he went well beyond what a platoon planner is expected to do. But that wasn't unusual for a SEAL. The detachment didn't have a Task Unit intel cell to rely on. Lee decided to tackle the task as though he was setting up the files for an initial Task Unit intel cell.

By midnight he had a handle on what was in the files and how the platoon received the information and where it went in the system. A file of intel SQL queries in the Chief's account helped him to understand how the detachment used the database to build intel folders. From that knowledge, he set out to improve the system's performance and tune the database. By 0200 he understood the system and databases and how to query specific tables and document stores and how to relate them and do related person/topic searches. (SQL- Standard Query Language)

By 0300, he had scrapped every idea he had and sat back and rubbed his eyes. The damn system files were already organized in a manner that made sense, and once you were familiar with the system, it appeared to work well. The on-line files were related in tables and the tables included entries that linked queries to hard files such as satellite photos, map coordinates on specific maps and other resources not stored on-line. The only contribution he made was rewriting a couple of SQL queries to better constrain them, and that was more personal preference than necessity. He finally gave up and called it a night.

The next morning, he was in the planning shack before

the Chief got there. Try as he might, he couldn't come up with any suggestion for improving the file system. He wasn't even sure what the chief wanted improved. He could probably tweak a table or two, but that would just be window dressing. He'd just have to admit defeat to the Chief and ask for help.

Chief Boyle arrived at 0800. The mission was primarily training Afghani commandos and the team was working day hours. Later, when ops started, they would begin keeping vampire hours.

"Well, Mr. Toliver? What magic have you come up with for my planning intel?"

Lee's eyes were red with lack of sleep and he looked like he had a hangover. With his face, that was a sight to see.

"Damn it, Chief. I was up until 0300 trying, and except for some SQL, I couldn't find one thing I would change that wouldn't be window dressing. The system is fine the way it is."

"So, you know all about how my files are organized, do you?"

"Not every single sheet of paper or data entry in them, but yeah, I can probably find anything in there and the system works pretty damn good."

"And you understand the working queries and how we use them to put a folder together?"

"Yes, I rewrote two of them, but the queries are well written."

The Chief watched Lee's face for a moment and then smiled.

"Well, you being a Trident expert and Academy graduate and all, I guess I'll just have to take your word for it. We'll just leave them the way they are. Considering it took me three deployments and the help of a smart Trident guy to refine this system, I'm rather pleased you like it."

Lee was still groggy and his mouth tasted like some bathrooms smell. To say he was a little irritated was putting it mildly, so his slowness can be forgiven.

"Then why in the hell . . .?" And suddenly he understood. With a sheepish grin, he said, "Okay, head up my ass and full steam ahead. When do I get to do some real work?"

"All in good time, Mr. Toliver. All in good time. You've got a lot to learn before you'll be ready to support a Task Unit and although we won't use it all here, we've got the time to do it right. Let's start with the targeting cycle."

Chief Boyle brought in IT1 Bowman, the Trident information systems specialist assigned to the detachment. Between them they gave Lee a quick rundown of the targeting Cycle.

Chief Boyle introduced Lee to planning a bite at a time. He started as a trainee and intel gofer, but even gofers learn important things like where things are, who to see, where to call, what resources are available, and they themselves become known and begin to develop important relationships with experts throughout the battlespace. Tasks tend to go more smoothly when a face in the mind is attached to the voice on the phone. Lee's face had high attachment value.

After two weeks of fifteen-hour days and tedious, mostly boring work, Lee began working real intel and targeting with the chief. Most of what they developed was passed to Army and Marine Corps intel shops, and some to DEVGRU at J-bad. As Lee began to develop insight, Boyle pushed him into more facets of intel gathering, especially where his language expertise would help.

In addition to his other duties, Lee was volunteered to assist in interrogations at the DIF on base. His language and culture skills made him welcome. His twisted face and blazing eyes were a bonus in the interrogation room. Often just his presence in the room was enough to change the whole atmosphere.

Lee hated his scars, but he learned to use them. His fierce appearance coupled with a soft voice became an effective tool. All but the hardest of suspects wanted to keep him happy. The name Igor became known to U.S. intel people and detainees alike.

Two CIA interrogation specialists took him under their wing and broadened his knowledge of technique and psychology. It was a fair trade. He spoke much better Pashto and Dari than they did, and they were much more experienced than he was.

The DIF at Bagram had been in the news while Lee was beginning his training with Trident and fresh out of

Princeton Near East studies. A controversy over water boarding was still raging in the press. Was it torture? Was it effective? Was it necessary? Bagram DIF was run under strict guidelines now, and interrogations were monitored and recorded, at least the ones he participated in.

He knew what water boarding was and how to do it. Part of his training included being water boarded. There was no question in his mind that it was effective, but it could produce false positives. He'd rather use Teddy Roosevelt's method. Speak softly and carry a big stick. His face was his big stick.

Understanding the subject's culture and leaving him some respect and dignity often worked wonders. More important, the soft approach early in the interrogation often helped separate the hardcore from the innocent citizen who just got caught up in something or was the victim of a false report, without stressing or insulting him more than necessary.

New or not, his knowledge of Pashtun culture and the Pashto language made him an effective interrogator. His Pashto got better with every interview and interrogation, taking on the local slurs and gutturals and picking up the idiom that created the dialect. The resident interrogators relied on interpreters, but Lee could work directly with the subjects.

Because he had many intel folders on many subjects open at any given time, his conversation-like interrogations often elicited information without the subjects realizing they were disclosing something important. Sometimes a conversation on one subject revealed information important to a folder concerned with an entirely different subject. At the request of the DIF commander, he began doing as many of the initial interviews as he could fit into his schedule, often as call-outs in the middle of the night.

A new file was added to the intel system: Igor's Sources. Lee kept a running log of his observations and thoughts from interviews and interrogations with cross references to targets on the detachments list augmented by entries from DEVGRU. Secure emails from DEVGRU intel addressed to IGOR began appearing regularly. IGOR became the name of a source file in many Bagram and J-bad intelligence databases.

Since most intel shops depended on interpreters, making their information interpreted second-hand, Lee's sources file was tapped frequently and not only by the detachment. In his first two months with the team, Lee's intel contributed to successful missions for DEVGRU and a Marine detachment and helped the Ranger detachment at J-bad develop two target folders. The little detachment wasn't doing much in the ops arena, but they were becoming known for their intel capabilities.

His life got very busy. Getting called out of his bed in the middle of the night to attend an interrogation became routine, and red, itchy eyes became normal. He didn't mind. The more they used him, the more he learned. Everything about the intel job was still new and exciting, and burnout wasn't even in the picture.

Lee was new, but he was contributing and by the end of his second month in Bagram, the team was glad to have his services. The problem was, his development was slowed because he couldn't get outside of the base. He needed to get out into the culture. He had never been in the mountains or in a Pashtun village. In that respect his experience was like most intel specialists, secondhand. He craved that firsthand knowledge.

Lee's opportunity to get out in the culture came sooner than he expected. A Ranger Captain at J-bad over in Nangarhar Province requested the services of a Terp who could be trusted without question to support a Cav Troop Commander in a meeting with Nuristanis in his AO. A new reconstruction team outpost was being constructed in a remote location, and the CO needed help establishing good relations with the local tribal leaders. His Afghani Terps weren't getting the job done for some reason. DEVGRU at J-bad told him they knew of just the guy he was looking for.

The mountain AOs were dangerous places, so the SEALs made sure he was set up properly for a stay in the hills. LT Osborne wasn't happy about Lee going out in the boonies with operating troops, but he approved the plan in spite of his misgivings. It was like turning your kid loose on a motorcycle the first time. He might get hurt, but you had to do it. Everybody had to start with a first-time.

Rangers would insert Lee by helicopter, and he would be picked up by 10th Mountain Division troops. The SEALs respected the Rangers and 10th Mountain. They often worked together. Still, Lee was a cherry. Bravo platoon had equipped him and drilled him in the use of every piece of gear in his inventory, but LT Osborne told the team to make damn sure he was set up properly for the mountain AO.

His tri-color BDUs were okay, but they would make him stand out from the Army. The SEALs inspected his body armor and set him up with a Rhodesian rig vest. He carried an infrared strobe mounted on his shoulder. He was issued his own MICH helmet (modular integrated communications helmet) and a PRC148 radio in a pouch on his rig. The radio operated from 30 to 512 MHZ and could be set for whatever channel the Army would be using for intra-team communications.

He was given a blowout kit to put in his right front leg cargo pocket, with three Kerlix dressings, Asherman chest seal, two ace bandages, IV, and Clotting medicine. They added a tourniquet in his shoulder pocket. Those additions had a sobering effect on his excitement. They held back when it came to night vision gear. He probably wouldn't need it, and they didn't want to chance it falling into enemy hands.

He would be taking his M4 and Sig P226, so they configure his vest for six 30-round magazines in the front compartments and gave him two extra double magazine pouches to add if he felt the need. He also had hooks for a flashlight and visible strobe, pouches for three 15 round magazines for the pistol, two frag grenades, a smoke grenade, two flash-bangs and a five-quart hydration pack. Finally, they let him choose his own pistol rig. He tried the low-carry holster that placed the pistol on his thigh where his hand hung normally and liked it. It looked cool, probably not the best reason to use it, but there you go. He was a new guy.

The rest of his load brought the weight of his gear up to 70 pounds. That weight would only last until he could unload things like his sleeping bag and personal items in his sleeping tent or hooch at his destination. With it all on, he wondered how the hell he was going to hike up a mountain and still have enough breath left to talk—or make it up a mountain at all.

CHAPTER 4

After a short flight on a C130 to J-bad and a short briefing with the commander of the Ranger company at the JSOC compound, Lee was set up for a helicopter flight out to the Provincial Reconstruction Team at Kamdesh in Nuristan.

The flight to the PRT was at night. After the recent loss of a helicopter, the pilots wouldn't fly into Nuristan in anything but low light. Not only was night their choice, but they only flew up there with little or no moon. They timed their departure so the helicopter would arrive about 0100 with no moon.

The big CH-47 twin rotor helicopter with a load of supplies for the outpost flew them north into Nuristan province just a few miles from the Pakistan border. Those old birds had been hauling Marines and soldiers since the Vietnam war. The flight wasn't long, just 80 miles from J-bad, he was told. They landed in the dark on top of a mountain where the Army had made an LZ that also provided mortar support for the PRT.

The landing was an adventure. Rushing winds howling through the valleys and dispersing up draws and scattering on cliff faces created sudden and unpredictable shifts in the forces acting on the helicopter, turning the pilot's knuckles white and the passenger's stomachs upside down. The pilots and crew were using night vision goggles and the LZ was marked with infrared beacons. Lee was left with nothing but the churning in his stomach.

A work detail waited to offload supplies. As Lee stepped out of the helicopter and moved out of the down draft, all he could do was stare into the dark. Even with limited visibility, he could feel the immensity of the mountains around him. A soldier grabbed his arm and pulled him away from the bird.

"This isn't the time for sightseeing, dude. You can't see anything anyway."

The soldier pulled Lee off to the side behind a Hesco barricade and they both knelt and waited for the bird to lift off. The troops didn't waste any time getting the supplies off the bird, and the helicopter rose into the air as soon as it was unloaded. Lee was led across the LZ and hurried to the CP, a hole in the ground surrounded by big fabric lined, wire baskets called Hescos filled with rock and dirt. Troops were curled up in sleeping bags inside and two men manned radios with a Lieutenant.

"Are you Toliver?" the Lieutenant said.

"Lee Toliver."

"Welcome to LZ Warheit, Lieutenant," the officer said and then got a good look at Lee in the dim light. "Whoa! Damn, Lieutenant. I'm sorry. What happened to you?"

The first-time people got a good look at his face, even soldiers, the surprise or shock usually overcame their sense of decency. But military guys usually recovered quickly. He tried not to let it bother him, but it still did. As soon as they were used to him, they stopped seeing his face, and he became just one of the team.

"Got caught up in a suicide bombing. Is this home sweet home?"

"It isn't much, but it's all we have for now. I'm Andy Clark and this is the new home of First Platoon, Able Troop. First Platoon, Cherokee Company is manning the perimeter and spread out around the site. Two squads from Cherokee will be taking you down the mountain in the morning. Lieutenant Tommy Chan will introduce you to Cherokee after you get some sleep."

"This isn't PRT Kamdesh?" Lee asked.

"No, the LZ down there isn't ready to take the big helicopters yet. You've got a long hike down the mountain in the morning. Better than humping up it though. The PRT is north of us at the bottom of the mountain. You can bag out in here. Try to find a soft piece of dirt and get a few hours of sleep."

"Thanks. Have you had much action up here?"

"Just harassment mostly. We had about ten minutes of small arms incoming earlier this evening. We're new here, and the hajj are just feeling us out. You'll find out on the way down. They mess with every patrol we send down to the PRT."

He found a vacant patch of dirt next to the dirt wall and dropped his pack. It was mid-May, but he couldn't tell it from the temperature. It was cold on that mountain top. He put an insulating pad down on the dirt and spread his sleeping bag on it.

Clark's hajj remark surprised Lee. Hajji only applied to those who had made the Hajj at Mecca and was insulting when applied to locals who hadn't. But he guessed the slang slipped in on everyone when they've been in-country a while. The troops regularly referred to the locals as Hajj or Haji. Well, it was nips or krauts in WWII, slopes in Korea, gooks in Vietnam. There was always some tag to keep them from seeming too human.

A new round of incoming came with the light. Lee woke up to shouts and loud explosions. Someone yelled, "RPGs! where the hell are they coming from?" An RPG round hit the Hescos above him and dumped a load of dirt down the side of the pit onto his sleeping bag. Lee pulled his boots on and just quick-laced them enough to keep them on his feet. Then he pulled his body armor on and the vest over that. With his helmet in one hand and his rifle in the other, he asked Clark where he wanted him.

"Relax," Clark said. "This is getting to be routine. We'll get a few rounds of AK next and then they'll hightail it over the ridge before we can get the mortars dialed in. Have a meal and get your gear ready. You'll be heading out in a couple of hours."

Waking up like that from a sound sleep shoots the adrenalin into the blood like a fire hose, and he still hadn't settled down. His hands were shaking slightly when he opened an MRE and set up his FRH to heat his beef ravioli. Damn if this wasn't a long way from the wardroom on a ship where he'd be sitting down at a table with china and silverware. (FRH-Flameless Ration Heater, a water activated reaction heater included in the Meal Ready to Eat [MRE] packet)

Beef Ravioli was a strange pick for breakfast, but he had been exposed to MREs at Camp Lejeune during his five weeks of combat fundamentals with the Marines when he first came to Trident. There they served Totems, or TOTMs (Tailored Operational Training Meals). They were lower calorie than the combat MREs and came in a clear package, but the menus were close. He learned to avoid the Veggie omelet with cheese, the only actual breakfast on the list. It was horrible, like eating sawdust with glue, tasting vaguely like cheese.

Clark had a pot of hot water on a small camping stove, so Lee fixed his freeze-dried coffee with that in a plastic pouch. It was the best part of the MRE. The beef ravioli wasn't bad, but not something you'd normally pick to eat at 0500.

After cleaning his rifle and checking the rest of

IGOR

his gear, he topped off his hydration pack from a water skin in the CP and laced is boots.

Lieutenant Chan came to the CP after first light after he took care of his platoon. He grabbed an MRE and found Lee after talking to Clark for a few minutes. He sat in the dirt and leaned his back against the dirt wall. He was about Lee's height and had slightly oriental features. He was also covered with dust and fatigue showed on his face. He held out his hand.

"Tommy Chan," he said. "I understand that you're a Terp and can speak the local lingo."

Chan didn't seem fazed by Lee's scars. He laid out the contents of his MRE while he talked.

"It's been awhile," Lee said. "I need time with some locals to see how much I retained."

"Anything at all is better than we have now. Our Afghani Terps are great guys, but they can't speak a word of it. Most of the elders we've met speak some Pashto or Dari and that's how our terps communicate with them, but when the elders talk to each other, they speak the local language and no one knows what they are saying. Hell, they could be plotting an ambush right in front of us and no one would know. It's frustrating as hell. Who are you attached to?"

"I believe you guys call us Task Force Blue," Lee said.

"SEALs? Okay, now I get the handle."

"How's that?"

"Igor, your code name. It was part of the

message we got when we received word you were on your way. Man, that's cold, even for those bastards. What do you want us to call you?"

"Hell, Igor is good. I'm used to it, and it's hard to confuse with something else. So, you don't like the SEALs?"

"Hey, man, I don't want to insult your home team. SEAL or not, we're glad to have your help."

"I'm not a SEAL, just a linguist and intel geek from Trident in a support role. I'm working with SEAL Team Two at Bagram. So, what have you got against the SEALs? Don't worry. You won't insult me."

"Not sure what Trident is, but it seems like we're always cleaning up or living with messes left by Task Force Blue. They come into our AO, fuck up a few people, and then they're gone. We live with the fallout, literally. The fallout ends up being RPGs falling on our heads because the locals are pissed off about what the SEALs did in the middle of the night and we're the closest Americans to take it out on. Well, I guess we all have our job to do. If you're not a Seal and you're just here to get some experience, what kind of combat experience do you have?"

"None, other than training," Lee said. "All my time here has been spent at Bagram or J-bad."

"What happened to your face?"

"I got caught in a suicide bombing."

"Damn, where?"

Lee found it easy to talk with Tommy. He looked right at Lee's face when he asked a question and didn't look away quickly like most people did. Being stuck in a hostile place helped too. Suddenly, it was nice to have a friend—especially one who seemed to know what he was doing. Lee had never felt so much like a novice in his life.

"In London," he said. "Maybe my handle ought to be Lucky instead of Igor. There I was tooling along in a Jag with a pretty, female British Lieutenant on my way to a fine British hotel in the middle of London. We tried to get around one of those big, red two decker busses, and boom, the whole rear end of it exploded. One minute either way and we would have missed it. Only damn suicide bombings they ever had, and I got caught up in it just arriving in London. They had four bombings in one attack that day, all coordinated to go off about the same time. Three of them were on trains in the underground. My escort managed to find the only damn one of them above ground. No criticism of her though. She got a broken back out of it. Just lousy luck for both of us."

Lee was surprised with himself. This was the first time he had ever talked about the actual incident. Maybe it was the shared danger on this remote outpost or maybe enough time had passed so he could deal with it. Whatever it was, he felt strangely relieved at having faced it again.

"Damn!" Chan said. "Not even in the war zone, so you didn't even get that pretty purple heart ribbon to impress the ladies with. That is a bitch. Well, enough about you, let's talk about my problems."

Lee didn't get to reply before Chan barked a laugh and slapped him on the back.

"Come on, Igor, time to earn the big bucks they're paying us."

CHAPTER 5

Chan checked Lee's radio and set it for the channel used by his platoon and did a radio check. He formed his patrol up and they started down the mountain. He kept Lee next to him in the center of the column.

Looking around, Lee thought he was in one of the most beautiful places in the world. The mountains were spectacular and the valleys were dizzying. Tall mountains rising to ten, twelve, and even eighteen thousand feet in the distance were stacked close together forming impossibly steep sided valleys. Undulation after undulation until they disappeared into the glowing misty distance. Except for the fact that there might be killers with RPGs and automatic weapons out there, he would have liked to just stand there and marvel at the view.

"Time to pay attention, Igor," Chan said. "It's Indian country from here to the PRT. The opposition isn't expecting us, but they can adjust quickly. If the word spreads ahead of us, we'll have a surprise waiting for us somewhere down the trail. They're lousy shots, but everybody gets lucky sometime. Stay close to me and do exactly as I say."

"You have my undivided attention," Lee said.

Chan checked Lee's ruck, body armor, vest and hydration pack and then checked his weapon. "I like the EOTech holographic sight," he said. "How's that Aimpoint CCO?" (CCO-close combat optic)

"It's what I trained on and used to. I'm willing to learn though. Why an EOTech?"

"It's a holographic sight and you can get on target quick from all sorts of positions with both eyes open. Good situational awareness."

"Same with the red dot sight. So far, I like it."

Chan nodded and turned to his sergeant.

"String them out, Sergeant. Let's take it easy and safe. We got a four hour walk ahead of us."

Chan's patrol had to hike down a series of steep mountain faces. But that was still to come. The terrain off the ridge where LZ Warheit sat was steep, but a trail gave some relief. Still, Lee's thighs and calves were beginning to cramp before they reached what Chan said was the mid-point, two hours into the hike. Squats and running back at Bagram helped his conditioning, but nothing really prepared you for carrying heavy loads in the mountains, except doing it.

Chan listened on his radio for a moment and

suddenly grabbed Lee's arm and pulled him into a stand of trees cluttered with boulders. The rest of the patrol had scattered for cover as hand signals moved back up the line. Chan pulled out a set of small binoculars and scanned downhill. His sightline stopped on one point.

"Take a look, and tell me what you think," he said.

Lee took the binoculars and looked where Chan pointed. Three boys, maybe eleven or twelve years old were tending six or seven goats and chasing each other in some sort of tag game.

"Just three kids," Lee said.

"You're the expert. Look normal to you?"

"Hell, Lieutenant, I don't know. I guess they do. Not much different than kids anywhere. Horsing around while they do their chores. They have a bunch of goats with them."

"Sergeant, give me two scouts on the flanks of those kids. Let's see what's around them."

When the scouts were out, Chan turned to Lee and said, "Do you feel up to hiking down there and see if you can talk to them?"

"Do you think it's safe?"

"We'll know in a few minutes.

The kids continued to play while the goats grazed on the shrubs and sparse vegetation. The slope was probably thirty degrees, but it didn't seem to matter to them. They were unaware of two squads of American soldiers just a couple hundred yards up the mountain. The scouts returned in fifteen minutes and said the area looked clear. The patrol redeployed, setting up an over-watch, and Lee started down the trail.

Lee had written an honors research paper on the K'om language in Princeton. His Nuristani was learned from CD's that were copies of tapes made by a British linguist and an English written phonetic lexicon. The K'om language didn't have a written tradition. The tapes were well done, extensive, and a mini-language course in themselves. Later, he had reinforced his understanding through a rare and welcome meeting with a Nuristani at a conference. Few K'om ever left their mountains.

The distance between Lee and the kids dwindled to just a few yards before the they noticed him. He was a major shock for them. They froze and stared at him not sure what he was. Nuristan was so remote and with so few roads, outsiders were mostly insurgents crossing the mountains into the valley or people from nearby valleys. Lee, in full battle rattle, looked nothing like an insurgent.

He needed the flow, inflection, and tone of the local dialect and wanted them to keep talking, but that was a lost cause now. They caught sight of his face and their eyes widened. The sight of a man in full battle dress was shocking enough, but the scarred and twisted face under the helmet was almost too much. They started backing up, completely forgetting about their goats.

"Wait," Lee said in Nuristani. "Don't go. I only

want to talk with you."

The oldest boy stopped and his eyes got big. He had never seen an American, nor had he ever experienced an outsider who could speak his language.

"You the language speak," he said. (as close a literal interpretation as English would allow.)

Morphology, syntax, and semantics were coming back, but Lee had to stop and think. Pronunciation wasn't easy and opportunities to use Nuristani were rare. But that's what made him the wiz he was. He retained everything he had learned. He could understand, but speaking was hard. This dialect had too many slurred consonants for his tongue to easily handle and the word order took time to get used to again. Rather than a verb second word order westerners are used to, Kamkara-viri (the K'om language) had a subject-object-verb order, which was mentally awkward for him.

"I the language do not well speak," he said. He wanted to engage the boy in conversation, but he had to stick to simple phrases when he spoke. "Your name is?"

"Yasin."

"Yasin an interesting name is." Lee said. "You with me will speak, Yasin?"

"You a cigarette have?"

"No. I gum have."

Yasin squatted next to Lee in the Afghani way and held his hand out. Lee pulled a stick of gum from one of his pockets and handed it over. The other boys moved back with the goats and watched.

"You of what wish to speak?" Yasin said.

The conversation helped to make the small twist in Lee's comprehension and his natural talent took over making the order seem natural if he went slow.

"Will you . . ." Lee lost the word for describe. "Will you tell me about your mountains?"

"There they are," Yasin said and pointed. "What is there to speak about?"

Already, the boy's short answers were pushing the linguistic fog back. "Then speak about your village," Lee said. "What work does your family do?"

"I will speak about your fire wound," Yasin said. "Are you a great warrior? You speak like a child."

Lee missed most of the first statement and ignored the warrior question. He just wanted to keep the boy talking.

"It has been a long time since I spoke your language last. Have you seen many fire Wounds?"

"Yes," the boy said. Then he scratched his head. "No, not many. What caused yours?"

"A bomb."

The conversation went on for almost a half hour before Chan brought the patrol up. Lee used the time to refresh his understanding, questioning the boy about meaning and asking him to repeat words that were unfamiliar. The boy was fascinated with Lee's burns and kept returning to that topic. Lee expanded the conversation by describing London. He kept it up until he noticed a soldier standing off about ten feet watching him and the boy.

"Time?" Lee said.

"Yes, sir. Way past time. The patrol is forming up."

Lee turned to the boy and gave him a head bow. It seemed that gesture was common to all cultures. "Thank you for your hospitality," he said.

"Wait," The boy said. "Where do you go?"

"To the bottom of the mountain where the road leaves the valley."

"If you would like, I will guide you to the snake road that will take you directly to the road in the valley."

"I will ask my Chief," Lee said. He turned and looked for Chan and waved for him to come over.

"The boy wants to guide us to something called the snake road. He says it will take us directly down to the road in the valley."

Chan looked reluctant while he thought it over.

"He must be talking about the switchbacks. We know the way, but if you want him along, I guess it's okay. He probably knows more about the insurgents than we do, and he's not going to put himself in danger."

Lee turned to Yasin. "My Chief says he would be honored to have an important guide like you. Will you talk with me as we go?"

"Yes. You walk with me. I will go slow. I can see you are not of the mountains."

CHAPTER 6

Chan spread the column out behind Lee and Yasin, and they followed until they reached the top of the switchbacks. The march gave Lee a full hour more of talking and listening to the language. As the patrol came up, Lee bowed his head to Yasin.

"Thank you, Yasin. Peace be upon you."

"And upon you, peace," Yasin said and began jogging back up the mountain. Lee's legs were beginning to tremble.

"You're known now," Chan said. "That kid will tell everybody he knows about you. Did your talk do you any good?"

"I can't tell you how much. I haven't spoken their language in three years and then it wasn't much. This is the only place in the world they speak it, except for a rare few who left the mountains. Is that the PRT down there?"

"That's it. Doesn't look like much from here, does it?"

"No."

Chan laughed. "Doesn't look like much when you get down there either. How are you holding up? It's all down-hill from here and the switchback is easier walking, but it's still a pretty good hump with the load you're carrying."

"Is it safe to take ten?" Lee said. "My legs are beginning to shake."

"Ten minutes I can do, but no longer. Don't sit still too long though. You'll stiffen up. Stay in cover and keep you weapon ready. I'm not thrilled with that kid running off."

"Yasin seemed like a decent kid. What are you worried about?"

"Write this down, Igor. Paranoia is the sign of a healthy mind in this place. Don't trust anyone. The three distinguishing characteristics of these people are greed, vengeance, and murder. The deeper you get in the mountains the worse it gets. They'll smile in your face and feed you to keep you occupied while their buddies set you up for an ambush. It wouldn't surprise me if those kids are hightailing it to the local Taliban right now."

The Pashtuns and Nuristanis of that region were honorable people with their own code of honor and traditions developed over centuries, ten times longer than the U.S. has been in existence, but Lee was too tired to get into it with Chan right then. Cultural morality is relative and one culture's honor killing is another culture's murder. But the working rule here was, when you are receiving the incoming, the guy shooting is the bad guy, no matter which side you are on. The ten-minute break wasn't enough for anything but getting stiff. All too soon, Chan was forming the patrol again and starting down the switchback. Lee had to be helped up.

Chan was spacing the column at fifteen-yard intervals and the point man was already 150 yards down the switchback when the first incoming rounds began smacking into the trail near the point. Lee and Chan with the second squad hadn't left the ridge yet, waiting for the interval to get right before they set out. Everyone took cover against the side of the hill and searched for the source of the incoming. With echoes bouncing from hill to hill and back again, finding the shooters was almost all visual, and finding a few muzzle flashes in that overwhelming landscape was difficult.

Return fire began down near the point and moved back up the column as the tracers from the point-man were picked out by those behind him. The incoming was small arms so far, and as the lower squad found the source area above them they began popping 40mm grenades from M203s on their rifles at a ridgeline above them while the M249 SAWs began saturating the area with automatic fire.

From the cover of large rocks, Lee flicked his safety off. His hands were shaking as he tried to find a target on the ridge. Being higher up the switchbacks, he had a better angle on the small ridge than the point squad did. He wasn't sure if he should fire without an order from Chan or not.

Chan had his map out and was on his radio talking to the LZ giving coordinates for some HE from the 120mm mortars to suppress fire and talking to the PRT troops letting them know what was going on. He didn't seem all that concerned and his calm helped settle Lee's nerves.

He set his rifle for single fire and watched for a grenade burst on the ridge. When it came, he began firing into the same area. This was his first firefight and when he began participating, exhilaration took over. Even in the bright sunlight, he could see his tracer rounds dimly. He got caught up in the moment and lost track of time.

Suddenly, a large explosion raised dust and smoke a hundred yards to the left of target area. Chan corrected fire. A round hit closer but to the right. The next round hit near the target. Then another and another, and then all incoming ceased.

"Cease fire," Chan yelled and passed the command on the radio. A silence set in that jarred on Lee's nerves. He was shaking, but with excitement, not fear. On the ground, next to his feet were three empty magazines. He didn't know how many rounds were left in the one in his rifle, so he dropped the magazine and loaded with a fresh one and put the empties in his empty vest pouches. He wondered if any of his rounds had done any damage to the enemy. He wasn't sure he had seen any of them.

Chan had his squad provide over-watch coverage while the point squad began to move again

"Move it out," Chan spoke into his mike and reinforced his command with a hand signal. His leading fire team started down the trail and spread out. Soon it was time for Lee, Chan, and Chan's RTO to move out.

"Suck it up, Igor," Chan said.

"I could probably sprint if you wanted to."

The RTO laughed and Chan grinned. Mostly it was adrenalin, but the levity was welcome.

"Got your cherry busted, did you? First firefight?"

"Yep. Check with me before we do that again, okay?"

"Sorry, we don't usually get a vote. That was just a little teaser to get our attention, but you never know how serious they are until you're into it. Save your breath. We're not stopping again until we're in the PRT."

CHAPTER 7

The Kamdesh district had a population of about 25,000, but you couldn't have guessed that by looking around. As the patrol made its way down the switchback road, Lee got a better look at the area from elevation and a different angle. Nothing but steep mountains and deep valleys. Most of it was timbered, but there were also large barren ridges, mountain sides dotted with scrub bush and boulders, and cliffs that shot up a thousand feet from the valley bottom. Off in the distance were rugged snow-capped peaks shrouded in mist. It would be easy for an outsider to get lost out there and impossible to find his way out.

The valley they were descending into was more like a bowl formed by the steep sides of three mountains. A river ran along a steep, wooded valley and past the PRT. A narrow bridge crossed the river in front of the PRT but didn't seem to connect to any roads.

Army troops were working on an area near the bridge, digging and leveling.

The deeper he got into the bowl-like valley the stronger his sense of foreboding became. The primitive compound being used as the PRT site was at the bottom of the bowl. Everything else was above it with a clear view right into the site, and as he just found out, there were people up high with rifles.

As firefights go, it wasn't much, but his first firefight had excited him. The sight of this vulnerable outpost scared the hell out of him. This dirty and scary place was going to be his home for an undetermined amount of time. How did a sailor get this far from a ship at sea?

Lee was of two minds as the descent from the LZ ended. On the one hand, his intellectual side was anxious to get some time immersed in the language and culture of a people he had only studied from afar. On the other hand, the embryo of hate he had nurtured since a Muslim suicide bomber had destroyed his face was reemerging. Half formed thoughts of getting some revenge were trying to rise to his conscious mind, and consciously he fought them back. A feeling of something left undone haunted him. He needed somebody to blame and somebody to punish. The son of a bitch who did it had killed himself leaving Lee with nothing but his own dumb luck to blame. It just wasn't enough. How can you ever accept that your life was ruined by nothing but random chance and dumb luck?

Those feelings were never far from the surface,

but the short firefight had caused them to rise again. He was a middle-east linguist and culture scholar. He had learned to be objective, but it was getting harder to separate Islam from Muslim nutcases who blew people up for the hell of it when they did it as a religious act and screamed "God is Greater" as they activated the detonator. They were Muslims, and they were killing because they were Muslims. Case fucking closed.

The patrol left the switchback and followed the road along the river to the gate and into the compound. Four up-armored Humvees were placed strategically inside to cover the mountainous terrain surrounding the compound. They each had turrets with heavy machine guns or Mk19 automatic 40mm grenade launchers pointed at their area of coverage. Soldiers were setting up Hescos in a square and more soldiers were digging a pit between the Hescos and filling them with the dirt and rocks from the hole.

More Hescos were being erected and filled forming part of the compound perimeter. A few old Afghani mud-brick buildings stood on one side and were being used already. Several smaller huts made with Hescos for walls and wood-beam roofs covered with sandbags stood in a line. The tops were covered with tarps to make them waterproof, and other tarps served as doors.

Everything was the color of dirt, even the men, and the whole camp was primitive. It matched its surroundings. Lee was taken to one of the mud brick buildings and introduced to the current CO, Captain Blevins.

"Have a seat, Lieutenant. You had a little excitement on the way down, I see. Did Lieutenant Chan take care of you?"

"Yes, sir. It didn't last long, but it got my blood pressure up."

"It does do that. I want to brief you on the area and mission and then we'll be taking a hike back up the mountain for a Shura with the elders of Lower Kamdesh. When we're done here, get a meal in you and get hydrated. How are you holding up?" (Shura- gathering of elders for negotiations, mediation, or discussion of important matters)

"Right now, I'm having trouble keeping my legs from trembling. I thought I was in pretty good shape, but these hills are something else."

"Trust me. Conditioning will come fast. I'd give you a rest, but the Shura is at their invitation and I can't put it off without insulting them. What do you know about Nuristan and the K'om?"

The briefing lasted an hour and when he was dismissed, Lee knew more about COIN strategy and provincial reconstruction teams than he had any desire to know. What he really wanted was to get this job over and get back to Bagram and the detachment. He was assigned a Hesco sleeping hut with another Lieutenant and turned loose for two hours to get his weapon cleaned and his gear stowed. Rest was also included if he could manage it.

Chan introduced him to his new hut-mate and gave Lee a handful of salt chews when he complained about cramping in his legs.

"They have sodium and potassium to replenish your electrolytes. When your legs start cramping, chew one and drink some water. They'll relieve the cramps."

LT Walker from 2nd Platoon, Cherokee Company shook Lee's hand and helped him get situated in the hut. They talked while Lee cleaned his rifle.

"We'll be finishing up here when this place is built and the LZ across the bridge is finished," Walker said. "The Barbarians will be relieving us."

"Barbarians?"

"Bravo Troop," Walker said. "I forgot you're Navy. Three-Seventy-one Cav is Third Squadron, Seventy-First Cavalry Regiment. A squadron is the same as a battalion in an infantry regiment. Three-seventy-one Cav is made up of Alpha Troop, same as a company, Bravo Troop, and Cherokee Company, a Tenth Mountain Infantry Company, plus the headquarters troop. We are all part of the Third Infantry Brigade Combat Team based at Fort Drum New York. Cherokee's job is to set this place up. I understand you're our new Terp. What are you attached to?"

Lee started to say Task Force Blue, but remembered the negative reaction from Chan. "I'm a linguist and intel geek from Jay-Soc (JSOC) in Bagram. My commander got a request for a Terp, so here I am."

"Do you speak the local language? None of our

terps can understand it."

"I can understand it better than I can speak it, but yeah, I can get by in a conversation."

"Damn, that will help. The CO is going crazy trying to communicate with them. They all speak some Pashto, but they're not Pashtuns. Maybe you can help us reach them. They don't like our terps."

I'll give it a try."

A small but heavily armed group of Cherokees with the CO, left the gate at 1100. Lee's legs hadn't recovered yet and probably wouldn't that day, but he was carrying about 40 pounds less now, after leaving gear in the hut. He popped a salt chew in his mouth and sucked down some water. They did seem to help.

They moved past Urmul, a small village west of the PRT that was just a dozen or so flat roofed houses on a flat spot at a bend in the river. The mountain rose behind Urmul and Lee groaned at just the anticipation of going up there.

Silent children watched them pass from doorways, sometimes with an old man next to them, sometimes alone. Near the end of the village several old men in man-jams stood in a group and watched them pass. (Man-jams- local garb that looked like pajamas with a long top and baggy bottoms properly termed Shalwar Kameez).

This primitive village and people brought back a memory of his introduction to the Qur'an and Hadith in Arabic studies at the Academy. His first reaction to the

Islamic Scripture was one of incredulity.

He could see how the teachings could be considered sublime in the seventh and eighth centuries. Much of what Muhammad taught about the rights of women, widows, and orphans, and the responsibilities of Muslims to each other was radical stuff back then. But it was written for those times and applied to the primitive conditions and cultures of those times. How in the world did people still consider it relevant today? His answer was right there in Urmul and the mud-brick villages up the mountain. Much of the Middle East and other parts of the world were still in the 7th century.

Those thoughts begged the question. Were they Muslim because Islam was relevant to their primitive culture, or was their culture primitive in a modern world because it was Muslim?

Captain Blevins dropped back to talk with Lee.

"Notice anything missing?" he said.

"Women,"

"Yes, that too. It's called Purdah. You won't see women often and when you do they won't look at you. If a woman comes near, look at the ground until she passes. Anything else missing?"

"No young men," Lee said.

"Good. They may be out with the herds, but then again, they may be out with the Taliban. Keep your eyes open and your head in the game."

Hamlets they passed on the way up the mountain were built on steps carved into the sides of steep slopes.

Blevins said the Nuristanis built their villages on these useless slopes so they could save every square inch of land that could be planted and cultivated on the better slopes. The houses were simple, square, one room structures built of Cedar posts and mud bricks.

The whole village clung to the side of the mountain in what appeared to be a precarious accordion like scar on the landscape with buildings stacked one above the other, and all dirt colored. The silent children and old men gave Lee the creeps. He was glad to get by each one. When the patrol took a ten-minute break, Blevins sat with Lee and gave him a history lesson.

"This place used to be called Kafiristan, or land of the infidels, but most of the people were converted to Islam early in the last century. The Pashtuns are Sunni Muslims and it was the Sunnis who converted this region, but the Nuristanis did them one better and became ultra conservative and now consider most Pashtuns to be liberal-minded and wrong-headed, sort of like a southern Baptist might consider an Episcopalian, except Muslims are willing to kill wrong-headed people. Radical Wahhabism took hold here. The K'om practice a brand of Islam that expects the local Mullah to interpret the Qur'an for them, so he holds a power position in the community. Remember that."

Blevins took his helmet off and wiped the sweat from inside. The temperature was moderating from the cold of March and April, but it was still cool. Cool didn't help a lot when you were carrying forty or fifty pounds up a mountain.

"Nuristanis seem to be a practical people and willing to do business, but culturally they have more in common with the Taliban than they do with us or even the rest of Afghanistan. The elders will talk to us and even horse trade, but they always have their own agenda and sometimes that agenda includes horse trading they did the other way with the HIG or Taliban. Keep that in mind. (HIG-Hezb-e-Islami Gulbuddin, one of the three major insurgent groups in the area)

"Can we ever win here?" Lee asked.

"Win what? Their hearts and minds? That's the basis of the counter insurgency program, but I have my doubts. Militarily? The greatest armies in the world have been trying to win in these mountains since before Christ, and none of them have. The Taliban know these mountains and pick their fights carefully. They bleed you one drop at a time. They give you a couple casualties and then disappear before you can hurt them. Then tomorrow, they bleed you again. One brigade for an area the size of New England won't do it, but that's all the administration wants to commit."

"What the hell are we doing here then?" Lee asked as he stood up.

"Obeying orders," Blevins said. "Beyond that? Jerking off."

Lee laughed. "I've heard this war called a lot of things, but military masturbation is a new one."

Blevins grinned and stood up too. "You've only been here a day. Give it time."

CHAPTER 8

The rest of the hike was accomplished with a lot of sweat and groans, but no contact. That was expected. When you came at the invitation of the elders, you were seldom messed with, at least on the way there. In the distance, Lee could see a group of village elders waiting near the beginning of Lower Kamdesh.

"Stay right next to me," Blevins said. "Do you understand Pashtunwali?"

"About as well as any western infidel, I guess. Hospitality, generosity, and vengeance about sums it up. Add in a fierce allegiance to Islam and a whole lot of courage and you got most of it."

"Close enough for government work. We're infidels and outsiders. The fine details only apply to the locals. These folks aren't Pashtuns, but they follow similar traditions. If you behave as you would with Pashtuns, you'll do okay. They all pretty much drink from the same well."

Blevins gave the village, what he could see, a once over with his eyes before going on.

"Getting here wasn't a problem," he said. "We are under the protection of the elder's hospitality. If anything happens, it will be on the exfil, but keep your eyes open. The hajj know we're here, and they'll have plenty of time to get set while we're inside. We'll have to go through a lot of chit chat out here and then some more inside. They will probably serve us tea and some snacks. The senior elder will place us deep in the room away from the door. You know about the right hand, don't you?"

"Sure. Serve, eat, and shake hands only with the right hand."

"Good. Right foot?"

"Enter a Muslim house with the right foot. It has to do with the traditions. Muhammad was big on starting things on the right side."

"Okay, if you say so. Here we go. They like to embrace and then shake hands."

Only Lee and Blevins would enter the Shura house with the elders. The escort troop split and formed blocking forces on both ends of the village after leaving four men to find cover near the Shura house.

Lee was comfortable with and fluent in Pashto, so the greetings and chit chat went well. The senior elder was introduced as Duc'ik Muhammed. Blevins said he was a mix of mayor, tribal chief, and clan negotiator and mediator. Blevins and the elders traded questions about health, business, and family, and Lee was asked how he liked the valley. They openly examined his scars but didn't comment on them. It shouldn't have, but the greeting and warmth left him with confused emotions. Were they the enemy, or were they just people caught up in a war they didn't want? Or maybe both? Then an incident occurred to further confuse his feelings.

As Lee was telling one of the elders about the Navy, a little girl ran from the home and grabbed the elder's leg and just stood there staring at Lee. Her head was covered, but not her face, and across her forehead he could see red hair and big, beautiful, pale blue eyes. What really caught Lee's attention though, were her scars. She had scars like his on the side of her face and down the outside of her arm. She seemed fascinated with Lee's face. The elder kicked his leg sideways and almost knocked the child over. She darted back inside of the building. He continued to talk without interruption.

After about five minutes of pleasantries, the elder invited them inside. As Blevins had predicted, they were led to the far end of the room away from the door. Also, as predicted, another five minutes of pleasantries ensued. Plates and bowls of raisins, dates, nuts, and different balls of pastry with crushed nuts and sugar were spread on the low table. Scalding hot tea was served so sweet he could hardly drink it. The village elder asked Lee about his excellent Pashto. How had he come to speak Pashto so well if he had been in

Afghanistan only such a short time?

As Lee was trying to find just the right words in reply, the scarred little girl slipped into the room between two beaded curtains. A female adult started after her but stopped quickly and quietly moved back behind the curtains.

The child was just a little thing, and dirty. Lee's eyes locked on her face and right arm. As small as she was, she had already been through worse than he had endured. The right side of her face and the outside of her right arm were horribly scarred from fire, worse than Lee's own scars.

She walked hesitantly toward Lee, her eyes fastened on Lee's face, on his scars. She seemed to have the run of the place and was ignored outside, but now everyone seemed to be waiting to see what she would do. The elders recognized the connection between Lee and the child and honored it. The room had gone silent. When she was next to his knee, she folded her legs and sat facing him. She motioned for him to lean closer and when he did, she touched the scarred side of his face.

"Does It hurt?" she asked in child-like Nuristani.

"No, little sister," Lee answered. "Not now."

"Does it hurt inside?"

"Yes, when I let it."

"Don't be sad," she said, and stood up. She turned and looked at Lee once more before she went back between the curtains. Never a smile.

Buc'ik ignored, or appeared to ignore, the interruption.

It wasn't until he spoke to Lee in Nuristani and Lee answered without thinking that he realized he had screwed up. The little girl had spoken Nuristani and he had answered her in her own language. Blevins had asked him to hold back on his Nuristani to see what was passing between the elders, but there would be no clandestine observations of Nuristani conversation made that day.

Crap, Lee thought. And he thought it in Nuristani.

"You speak the language with a strange sound," the elder said. "Like a child."

"It has been a long time," Lee said. "I learned your language far away, and I never had many words. About as many as a child."

"You have never been in Kamdesh (place of the K'om)? How is it you learned to speak our language?"

Lee had to concentrate, but the elder spoke slowly and kept his words simple as to a child.

"I study languages," Lee said. "Your language is one I studied at school."

"That amazes me," Buc'ik said. "The Pashtuns cannot speak our language. Nuristanis from other valleys cannot speak our language. You come from beyond the mountains and you can. It is a strange thing you tell me."

The other elders, or junior elders, as Lee had come to think of them, were watching and listening with wide eyes.

"Why did you not greet us in our tongue?"

"Your own greeting was in Pashto," Lee said. "I did not want to be impolite, and my Pashto is much better than my Nuristani. I pray I did not cause offense."

"I am not offended, just amazed. It is good you speak our tongue. May we continue this way?"

"Thank you. I hoped you would. It will advance my understanding."

Blevins nudged Lee with his elbow.

"Hope you're having a good time, Mr. Toliver," he said from the side of his mouth. Do you think you could find it in your heart to include me in this discussion?"

"Sorry, Captain. We were just discussing how I came to learn Nuristani."

Blevins's eyebrows rose, but he covered his surprise quickly. "Carry on, Lieutenant."

When Lee turned to continue his discussion with Buc'ik, he was surprised to see a young boy whispering to the elder. Buc'ik listened intently for a moment and Lee kept silent. The boy finished what he had to say and moved quickly back through the curtain. Buc'ik looked at Blevins but spoke Nuristani.

"You must leave now."

Blevins looked at Lee.

"He says we have to leave now. That's damn unusual, almost an insult. What just happened?"

Blevins had turned his team radio off for the meeting, so he looked at the door at the other end of the room and spotted a Sergeant pumping his fist up and down in the air.

"Say something polite and thank him, we have trouble."

Lee bowed his head to Buc'ik and the elders and said, "Thank you for your hospitality and patience."

"Go quickly. Peace be upon you."

"And upon you, peace," Lee said while rising. He was confused and wary. He had never experienced anything like this and it went against everything he thought he had learned about the Nuristanis. The elder's behavior was such a breach of hospitality it took Lee's breath away. If it had taken place between Nuristani clans, a blood feud might have resulted.

Blevins wasn't wasting any time or energy on misgivings or etiquette. He was moving quickly to the door. Lee followed in his wake.

"What have you got, Sergeant."

"Hajis are moving into the Ville, sir. The scouts saw weapons. I deployed the men into defensive positions."

"This is not a place we want to have a battle. We can't call in air support or artillery on this Village. Get the men moving back down the trail. Do it quick and quiet. Take Lieutenant Toliver with you and assign two men to get him down the trail."

"What about the village below us, sir?"

"If they are waiting for us there, they've already cleared the village. I'll blow that son of a bitch up. Scouts out. Move them out, Sergeant."

The patrol didn't get far. As the patrol moved out of the village and around a bend in the trail, RPGs were launched from the ridge above them.

CHAPTER 9

Lee was knocked to the ground by the force of an RPG hitting in the rocks down the hill from his position. A few seconds later another explosion rocked his senses. He crawled over the side of the trail into some brush and rocks on the downhill side but couldn't see to shoot and quickly crawled back out. He stood and ran bent over into a cluster of boulders below the trail to find a safe position to return fire.

The volume of fire from both sides was deafening. The patrol's M249s were firing at a rocky flat place on the hillside above them and grenadiers were firing their M203 grenade launchers as fast as they could load. The attackers appeared to be three or four hundred yards above them and spread out along a false ridge.

Lee tried to settle down and understand what was happening, but the noise, dust, and concussions from incoming RPGs exploding close to the unit overwhelmed his senses and left him just staring and shaking. This was worse than the fight coming down from the LZ. That had been just harassment. This sounded like the real thing.

The exploding RPGs rocked his senses and left him confused about what to do next. Everyone in the patrol was focused on the false ridge and trying to suppress incoming. Someone should have saved at least a little attention for the rocks behind them on the downhill side. But even that was a hopeless task at that point. The fog of battle was in command and the Taliban never attacked from lower ground. The soldiers had their training and experience to fall back on, but Lee had only a little training and no experience.

He kept backing down into the boulders below the trail for cover and hoping to find a place to recover his senses and start shooting. When it happened, he didn't have time to even resist. In gaining cover, he had separated himself from the rest of the patrol.

His senses were already stunned and his brain was overloaded. He failed to comprehend what was happening as his helmet was ripped off and failed to resist or even call out when it might have helped. His rattled brain could only comprehend one more shock was happening he had no control over. The next thing he felt was a severe shock on the back of his head, and his sight went blurry. The ground rushed up and hit him right in the face.

Someone was lifting him by the shoulders. He

had to do something. He couldn't make his body respond the way it was supposed to act, and he just twisted his shoulders. Somewhere in the back of his mind he knew he had to resist but couldn't quite figure out why. Then he heard gunfire from close by.

Fortunately, the Cherokee troops weren't as shook as Lee. His escorts had watched him backing into the rocks on the down-slope, and as soon as they could break contact, they moved in to protect him. They came around the boulder just as two Taliban fighters were trying to lift him. Each of Lee's escorts took out one Taliban and then one of them finished the one bending over Lee. They didn't wait for more to show up. Lee's neck and the top of his shoulders were covered in blood, but they didn't have time to check him out. They each hooked a hand under his shoulders and one grabbed his helmet and weapon and dragged him back around the boulder and up to the trail. He struggled to help, but his legs felt like cooked noodles.

Lee's senses began coming back as he stumbled through dirt and rocks. The bouncing jarred his head and shot bright lightning flashes of pain through his brain. The soldiers helping him were struggling and moving fast. They weren't worried about their load.

SFC Towers leading the patrol saw the troops come out from behind the boulder dragging Lee with them and smacked the captain's shoulder. "Trouble," he said.

"They're behind us down the slope," one of the

troops holding Lee said and let Lee drop to the ground. Lee held his head in his hands and tried to shake off the dizziness.

"Is he wounded?" Blevins yelled.

"There's blood. Three of them were trying to drag him away."

"Medic! Medic!"

When the Medic arrived ducking and weaving, Blevins pointed at Lee and said," Check him out." Towers was already leading men to clear the rocks behind them. Blevins had his hands full trying to direct the mortars onto the hillside and correcting fire, and that was an intricate job in this terrain. The maps weren't that good and directing indirect fire onto steep hillsides from over another hill is always difficult.

The medic checked all of Lee's limbs and his torso. He didn't have any obvious wounds. He then checked Lee's head and found the gash in his scalp still seeping blood. Scalp wounds are messy and bloody. The back of Lee's BDU shirt was soaked in his own blood.

"Head wound," he yelled. "Just a grazing hit and I don't see any skull damage. He's coming around."

"Patch him up and get ready to move when I get mortars on that ridge," Blevins yelled back.

Blevins considered the whole situation. The incoming was coming from above them, but it was coming from a small section of rock and trees. Maybe a dozen shooters with rifles and RPGs. The hillside was too steep to assault up. He couldn't wait for more insurgents to come up or spread around and bring fire from more angles. He had to move and either get to a better positon or get to the Compound.

The 60mm mortar down in the PRT dropped the first rounds and that suppressed incoming for a moment. Blevins corrected fire and told Sergeant Towers how he wanted to break contact. Then the 120mm mortars from the LZ began hitting and the hillside began coming apart. Blevins corrected fire until he could order fire for effect. The sixties and one-twenties took the false ridge apart.

"Now!" Blevins commanded.

The small patrol began moving quickly down the trail toward the PRT with two men helping Lee. His head cleared after a hundred yards and he could move his legs and support his weight with his escorts holding him up and moving him forward. They picked up the pace.

Blevins leapfrogged his small patrol down the trail with one squad and an M249 keeping the hillside under fire the whole time. With the firepower of a squad focused on the hill while the other squad moved, and the 120mm and 60mm mortars dropping, incoming from the false ridge was suppressed. The patrol was soon out of effective range and covered by the shape of the terrain—and leapfrogged right into a second ambush, this one an L shaped bastard. A machine gun in cover in front of the patrol enfiladed the lead squad, and a line of seven or eight rifles fired on them from boulder cover a hundred yards up the mountain. A sweet little ambush. While the patrol had been fighting through a teaser ambush, a second group had prepared their trap.

Lee's escorts helped him into cover and left him behind a tree in the rocks with his rifle. There was fighting to be done. Lee was still dizzy, but he was recovering his senses. He checked his weapon and rolled over to get his sights on the hillside. He heard and felt the rounds screaming through the squad from the machine gun up ahead, but he couldn't see it and couldn't return fire.

He had a good fighting position, but the squad had moved ahead to assault the machine gun and he was alone again. He took three magazines out of his pouches and put them close to his chest. All the outgoing was happening fifty feet down the trail and that's where all the incoming was being directed, leaving Lee to sight his rifle in relative peace. He watched for a target.

The muzzle flashes were close this time, just a hundred yards away and he could see flashes of movement as shooters raised up to shoot. His rifle was zeroed in at a hundred yards. He continued to look for a target. In a few seconds, the Hajj obliged him. One brave soul stood up in full view with an RPG rocket launcher on his shoulder and sighted down on the squad ahead of Lee. He had to stand to fire the thing, else the back blast would have cooked him and his buddies.

Lee was suffering from a light case of shock, but he was strangely calm. The hajj calmly took aim with his rocket. Lee got his sight picture, center of mass, held his breath, let half of it out. The figure he was seeing divided into two figures. He blinked his eyes. A drop of sweat dripped off the point of his nose. He got his sight picture again, let half a breath out, steadied, and compressed the trigger smoothly. As luck would have it, a tracer was in the chamber. He watched it through his sights all the way to the target.

Just like on the range, his round hit dead center of mass on the guy's torso. Lee immediately fired again. No tracer this time, but he saw the guy jerk and drop his RPG. Then the guy collapsed. First kill, he thought, but didn't have time to consider it. He looked for another target. The Hajj were still willing. Another man stepped up and shouldered the RPG. Lee relaxed, let out half a breath, and compressed the trigger. The Marines at Camp Lejeune had trained him well and Lee stayed in the fight. The guy jerked. Lee hit him again. He dropped the RPG as he fell backwards out of sight.

Lee waited. Would another one try it? Instead he saw flashes of movement in the rocks and trees moving higher on the ridge. Then he noticed the silence. The shooting had stopped. He stayed where he was. He wasn't going to move again until someone gave him an order. A few minutes later Blevins moved cautiously back toward him.

"You okay, Lieutenant?"

"Better than I was," Lee said.

"The RPG up there. Was that you?"

"Yes, sir. They just stood up and stayed still.

Easy shots. No one was shooting at me."

"I wondered who the hell was back here. What the hell were you doing back there when you got hit?"

"Trying to find some cover I could fire from. Was I shot?"

"You don't know?"

"All I remember was the lights going out. Next thing I knew, I was being helped down the trail."

"Doc says you got a grazing round to the head. He'll get a better look when we get inside the compound."

They made it back to the PRT without any more attacks. That was the way it was on almost every patrol. The hajj picked their place to suit them. They did what they could until it got too hot, always from higher ground. This one was a little more sophisticated than most, but when the machine gun was put out of action with M203s, the rest took off. They were still feeling out the Americans and learning how they responded to attacks. Each time they learned a little more and got a little better. As Blevins said, one drop of blood at a time, they were bleeding the Americans. The patrol had two wounded from the L-shaped ambush.

Lee was taken to the dispensary in the back of the old mud brick building and the Medic made him strip off his gear. He made sure there weren't any other wounds and then cleaned the gash on the back of Lee's head.

"Do you know what caused this, Lieutenant?"

"I have no idea. I was trying to climb up between two boulders to find a firing position and the lights went out."

"This doesn't look like it was done by a bullet. Maybe a rifle butt. Well, I'd say you almost ended up on the internet losing your head in spectacular technicolor. Talk to Specialist Mike Brown and Private Johnny Kane. They're the ones you can thank. They caught the hajis trying to drag you away and killed all three of them."

"Damn! I didn't even know."

"Looks like you just got a cluster for your purple heart."

"I don't have a purple heart."

The medic turned Lee's head with his hands.

"What are these burn-scars on your head from?"

"I got caught up in a suicide bombing in London," Lee said.

"Well, you have a Purple Heart now, sir. That split in your scalp was caused by enemy action. I'll note it in your paperwork." The medic went to a box in the corner and dug through the contents for a few moments until he found what he wanted.

"I'm going to give you a super Motrin to help with the pain. With a head wound, I can't give you anything stronger. It might upset your stomach, so eat something before you take it."

After the sutures were in, Lee met with Captain Blevins and then found his rescuers to get the full story of his near-capture. After that he was too tired and hurting to worry about anything else and wrapped up in his sleeping bag in the hut.

CHAPTER 10

Lee woke up hurting in his head and itching everywhere else. Fleas had made a feast out of him. The hut was infested. He stripped and shook-out his BDUs. It helped, but the bites started as soon as he dressed again. There was no help for it though, so he put his armor and helmet on and went out to find something to eat.

The damn place stank. At the back of the compound, two troops had the half-drums from the head out and were burning the contents with diesel fuel. He corrected himself. Not head. It's a latrine in the Army. The latrine was just a wooden shelf with holes cut in it over some 50-gallon drums cut in half. One of the soldiers was stirring the drums with a big stick and the other was pouring diesel fuel in the drums and lighting them. A shift in the wind brought the smoke across the compound and the odor made Lee gag.

There weren't any showers, so that wasn't an

option. The closest he would get to a shower while here was baby wipes for the armpits and crotch and some water to wash his face and shave. Water was hauled from the river by hand, so there was none to spare. He felt cruddy with dried sweat and dirt covering his body, and blood, dirt and sweat caking his hair where the medic missed with his cleaning swabs. He wanted to rub his eyes but didn't dare.

He looked around the camp and tried to quell the nausea he was feeling. Looking up at the towering slopes around him made him want to crawl into a hole and not come out. Both times he had been up in those hills someone had tried to kill him. He stared at the mountains. He had to admit, the place was beautiful in a grim sort of way.

Contract workers from the local area were already at work building more huts and mounting piss-tubes back by the latrines. The piss-tubes were just big six-inch-wide tubes sunk in the ground to provide quick relief without having to strip off your gear.

Cherokee Company troops were manning the gun trucks, gate, and bunkers on the perimeter, and those not on duty were working with the contract workers filling Hescos. A team was setting up claymores in the wire at the back perimeter. A large group of soldiers were across the bridge working on leveling the new LZ. A guard tower was being erected at the gate. He had to hand it to the Army. A firefight yesterday with two of their buddies wounded, and today was just another work day.

Lee stopped and looked up and turned 360 degrees. That wasn't smart. The mountains rose above him so steep he got a pain in his neck just looking at their tops. The entire outpost was only about an acre and a half in area and every square inch of it was visible from ridges above the post. The view caused him to shiver. I could be in some Taliban's sights right now, he thought. Worse, any helicopter trying to get in there would have to do an almost vertical hovering descent, leaving them vulnerable to almost any weapon the hajj high in the mountains wanted to use.

After using the head and shaving, he ate an MRE and thought about the two men he killed, or assumed he killed the previous day. It didn't seem real. He wasn't bothered by it. It was just something that happened. He thought it would be different. He got some revenge. He should feel something about that, but he didn't, nothing. The itching, hurting, and fatigue were more important right then. He took care of his trash and headed for the CP. Captain Blevins was having a cup of coffee and looked like he had time to talk.

"Morning, Captain. Can I ask you about the location of this camp?"

"Sure. Coffee?"

"That would be good. Seems like I've been limited to a cup a day since I left Bagram."

Blevins pointed at a pot on his camp stove. "It's just four packs of freeze dried in hot water, but it's not bad. Use that mug and be careful with it. These are the only two I brought in with us."

The soldiers all brought some small token of comfort and civilization with them. For the troops it might be video games, or snacks, or books. For Blevins, it was his coffee mugs. Lee was glad for the offer. Since he used a hydration pack, he didn't carry a canteen and therefore didn't have the advantage of a canteen cup. He filled the mug and sat down.

"So, what's bothering you?" Blevins said.

"Well, the location I guess. I don't mean this as a criticism. I know there must be a good reason, but why in the world did the Army locate this camp here in the bottom of a valley? From the top of the switchback I could see everything in the camp. Give me a Remington 700 deer rifle halfway up there, and it would be like shooting fish in a barrel. Why not up at the LZ? It looks down on everything."

"That's the first question everyone who comes out here asks. Took you a little longer than most."

"I'll admit I'd be more comfortable on the bridge of a ship at sea," Lee said. "I had five weeks with the Marines for combat training, but that's about it. Even with my limited knowledge of military tactics, I remember one principle. Go for the high ground."

Blevins stretched and picked his coffee mug up. He took a sip before answering.

"Usually, but not always," he said. "Sometimes the mission dictates the terrain. We've got two missions here. One, you are a part of, and that's the counter insurgency mission; make nice with the locals, build things, try to organize them against the Taliban. The other is our military mission, and that's to disrupt the flow of men and materials from Pakistan though the Kamdesh valley and then up the road you see outside the camp. The LZ on top the mountain would be ideal for our COIN mission and much easier to defend, but it's nowhere near the road. This location is hard to defend and a bitch for logistics, but it's right next to the road giving us a controlling position, and its close enough to Kamdesh Village to be useful for the COIN mission. It's not ideal, hardly even acceptable, but it's the only choice that allows us to pursue both missions with some expectation of success. Answer your question?"

Lee thought for a few moments. "Yes, sir. I'm glad I didn't have to make that decision."

"Not sure I would have, but it's the decision Cherokee has to live with, so we have to get on with it," Blevins said. "I was going to send for you anyway, so I'm glad you showed up. Twelve-hundred. Be here. I just got word from the Kamdesh district administrator that your friend wants a pow-wow. He's coming down here.

"Buc'ik?"

"The very same. Any idea what he wants?"

Lee thought for a moment.

"Just guessing, but I'd say it has to do with what happened yesterday. I've been expecting some gesture."

"The ambush?"

"No," Lee said. "Before that most likely. The way he broke off the meeting was an insult by their way of thinking. He may be wanting to make amends."

Blevins thought for a moment while he sipped his coffee.

"That could work to our advantage. Keep me involved this time. I might want to do some bargaining."

"Yes, sir."

"Okay, get the hell out of here. I've got work to do."

When Lee stood up, Blevins leaned back and put his feet on his field table. Lee smiled as he left the office. Blevins probably didn't get a lot of time for just thinking and enjoying his coffee. It was nice of him to share a few minutes of it.

Lee went to the sickbay (Navy speak for dispensary) to get some salve for his flea bites and to get something for the pain in his head. The corpsman (Navy speak for medic) checked and cleaned his head wound and replaced the bandage. He gave Lee an ointment for the flea bites and a handful of Motrin for the pain. Then he gave Lee one other item that made him laugh. A flea collar. Honest to God. A dog flea collar. The Medic told him to hang it from his belt when he slept and roll it up in his sleeping bag during the day.

Walker was finishing up an MRE in the hut. Lee sat down to put slave on his legs and asked him what was so important about the road. Walker wrapped up his trash before he answered.

"First, it isn't much of a road, but it's the only one that exists out here. A few convoys of Toyota Hilux pickups and jingle trucks managed to make the supply run from FOB Naray on it, and the up-armored Humvees made it here, but the road is deteriorating so fast, I don't have much hope of using it as a supply route for long. We'll probably have to fly the Hummers out eventually. A lot of that road has at least a hundred-foot drop-off into the river, and coming in, the outside wheels on the Hummers were right on the edge of the cliff. Scary as hell." (Jingle trucks – Civilian cargo trucks named for the jingle sounds made by decorations the owners hung on them)

Walker scratched at some flea bites on his leg while he thought for a moment.

"An even bigger problem is the frequency of ambushes on any vehicle attempting to make it to the PRT on the Naray Road," he said. "Running the Naray Road is like running a gauntlet. You can get hit by multiple ambushes between Naray and Kamdesh. The insurgents are aware we're determined to establish a permanent base in Nuristan, and they are just as determined to stop it. I sure as hell don't want to take a convoy up that road again."

Lee scratched a few bites of his own.

"So, the primary reason for putting the PRT here, the road, isn't of any use anyway," Lee said.

"I wouldn't say not any use. It's certainly useful to the insurgents. They don't have to move big trucks and ten-thousand pound up-armored vehicles down it, and it's the only route out of here that even resembles a road. Our being here denies them use of the road."

"Do you think it's worth it?"

"The answer to that is way above my paygrade. My platoon is here, so I'm here, and we'll be here until someone with more authority than I have says to go somewhere else. This is the infantry, LT."

Chapter 11

When Buc'ik arrived with three elders at the PRT for the Shura, he brought a surprise for Lee. Next to him and clinging to his leg was a small child in a black dress with a head cover, but no veil over her face. Even though the Nuristanis were Sunni, they didn't go for the face cover. The red hair and blue eyes still surprised him. He knew red and even blonde hair wasn't unusual in Nuristan, but in Afghanistan in general it was strange. His scarred little friend smiled.

"Hello, little sister," Lee said in Nuristani and smiled at her.

"You are not sad," she said.

"No, I am not sad today."

"She will not obey," Buc'ik said. "No one will correct her. How she will ever marry, I do not know."

As guests of honor, Buc'ik and the little girl were escorted to the far end of the room away from the door in the CP. The long list of ritual questions began. How is your health? Is your family well? What does your father do in America? Strong tea was served with sweet treats Blevins brought in for just such occasions. Little Sister, a title she seemed to like, sat next to Lee and was on her best behavior. She waited to be offered a sweet date and a lady finger cookie with her tea. Having her there was highly unusual, unheard of, and Lee wondered why Buc'ik allowed it.

The polite conversation continued, as was custom, and translating helped clear some of Lee's cognitive confusion. He had to think in both languages and consider each word. Many words used by Buc'ik and the elders had confused him earlier because they simply didn't follow Nuristani phonetic patterns. Finally, his Dari and Pashto came to the rescue. The local dialect of Kamkara-viri included a lot of loan-words from Persian, Arabic, and Pashto. The difficulty came because they were often Persianized-Arabic or Pashtoized-English, sort of a Nuristani pidgin English and Arabic, but adopted and mixed liberally with the Nuristani. When he realized what the bastard words were, his understanding increased and his conversational Nuristani took a big leap forward. Already, his amazing talent for languages was building his Nuristani vocabulary.

When Blevins estimated enough time and pleasantries had elapsed, he asked Lee to offer the floor to Buc'ik in an appropriate manner. Lee looked at Buc'ik. He knew he had to be cautious with his words.

Pashtuns and Nuristanis tended not to differentiate between will and maybe or might. A vague statement like "We might be able do that" would be accepted as a promise to do that.

"I sense something is troubling your spirit," Lee said. "May I ask how we can serve you?"

Buc'ik sipped his tea slowly and then placed the mug on the table carefully. He folded his hands in his lap.

"Yes, I feel a sadness. I fear I am guilty of a grave breach of hospitality and have insulted you and your clan. The last time you visited my home with my invitation, I was forced to rudely end our meeting in a most insulting way. I wish to make amends so there will be no feud between us. Tell me. How can we erase the insult and restore our friendship?"

Lee translated for Blevins and his Executive officer.

Blevins looked at Buc'ik and said, "Were any of your people hurt in the attack?"

Lee had taught the staff that eye contact was very important, even when talking through an interpreter. He translated even though he was sure Buc'ik could understand some English.

"A young man died," Buc'ik said. "Whether he died of the attack or of your response we do not know, but he is dead. We suffered also. So, you see, my insulting behavior was meant to get your people to safety as quickly as possible. The attack was a surprise to us."

And move the fighting away from the village, Lee thought.

He translated and waited for Blevins's response.

"Ask him if he knows of any outsiders in the valley planning attacks on the PRT?"

Buc'ik said he knew many Taliban had come over the mountains from Pakistan, but he didn't know where they were or when they would attack the PRT. Lee translated for Blevins and then held up his hand to silence him before he could speak again. Lee needed to think.

Something in the way Buc'ik had phrased his response had caught his attention.

"Sorry Captain, I had to think about Buc'ik's words. We need to debrief this conversation later. You had another question for Buc'ik?"

"Ask him to warn us if he becomes aware of any fighters planning an attack. Make it a request for a favor or repayment of a debt if you can phrase it that way without insulting him."

"Do not be sad," Lee said to Buc'ik. "Any insult on our previous visit is minor and easily made good. May I ask a favor of you? If it comes to your attention that any large groups of fighters move into this area to threaten this camp, will you send a warning to the camp?"

Lee would like to have asked for more but knew he shouldn't. They didn't have a close relationship yet, and they were negotiating a matter of honor. Buc'ik sat silently with his hands in his lap for a few moments.

Little sister had moved back against the wall of the building when the business of the meeting started and was quiet. A subtle negotiation had been conducted, terms had been offered, and now Buc'ik had to decide if the price was right. If he did, he would not go back on his word. Finally, he looked at Lee.

"It is right that one who enjoys your hospitality should feel safe. That is a principle both the Pashtuns and the Nuristanis understand. While you are here in our valley, I will try to provide what is needed so you will be safe."

He used the personal pronoun referring to Lee himself. It wasn't exactly what Blevins wanted. Buc'ik had countered with a promise only to the extent of Lee's presence in the valley. It wasn't the alliance Blevins wanted, just a temporary expedient. At least it covered the immediate future and the insurgents already here. By the set of Buc'ik's mouth, Lee also understood what Buc'ik offered was the best he was going to get and any further bargaining would be insulting. Even the small concession he offered endangered Buc'ik and his family. Lee smiled and translated for Blevins. The meeting ended on a good note.

Little sister sat next to Lee as the meeting wrapped up with more tea and pleasantries. He slipped her a handful of lady fingers and a stick of gum. After giving him a big smile she hurried down the room and out the door. Buc'ik had a pained look on his face.

"That is what she should have done at the

beginning. She will never bring a bride's price to my home. What is a father to do?"

"She is a special one," Lee said. "One day she will bless you in many ways."

Buc'ik smiled.

"Possibly," he said, "but probably not with grandsons to tend the herds."

Chapter 12

Blevins gathered his officers and senior NCOs for a debriefing with Lee in the Command Post. The ambushes outside of camp were becoming more frequent and brazen. Everyone in the COP, especially the Afghan Terp and the Afghan National Police (ANP), had been hearing rumors of Taliban moving into the area in numbers, so everyone in camp was waiting to hear what had come out of the meeting just held with local elders. Blevins got everyone quiet.

"Lieutenant, why don't you start the briefing. Give us your impressions and tell us what you think you learned. Except for your translations, I'm not sure what went on there."

Lee took a big swig of coffee and set his mug on the table.

"Yes, sir. Let's start with the general and then get more specific. First, the meeting was called to make good what he considers a breach of honor when he abruptly ended our meeting in his village and told us to leave. That's plausible."

"Why?" the First Sergeant said. "I thought he saved your asses by getting you out of there."

"Hospitality is an important principle in Pashtunwali and in the honor code of the Nuristanis. It's an important principle in Islam in general. When they say hospitality, they mean a lot more than making you welcome and making you happy while you're there. Hospitality means protecting you as well. By their code, they are obligated to fight for you if necessary while you are their guest. An attack on you is an attack on their honor. Believe me, ending that meeting and telling us to leave was a huge breach of honor. Buc'ik had to make it right, even to an outsider. We were there by his invitation."

"Okay, if you say so," Top said. "What did he want from us though?"

"Actually, nothing. At least he didn't ask for anything yet. Let me move on. He admitted the breach of honor and wanted to know what the price was for making it good. They're very practical people. Even blood feuds can be settled for a price, usually in cattle or goats or land. This is the place the term "blood money" comes from. Anyway, that was the basis of the meeting."

"Why did he bring the little girl with him?" Blevins said. "I can't ever remember having a child present in a shura. That's men's business."

"Two things, both guesses." Lee said. "Buc'ik is an experienced negotiator. He mediates disputes for his village. He probably understands meeting dynamics as well or better than we do. First, a child present reduces the formality of the occasion, and second, he knows I formed a connection with the child at our first meeting. She is scarred worse than me. I call her Little Sister. I'm sure he saw the sympathy factor there and didn't hesitate to use it."

"Okay," Blevins said. "Go on."

"That sets the general tone and purpose of the meeting. I think he was serious about the honor thing. We can't understand how important it is in their culture. He could lose face and lose his place as the Elder and mediator for the village if his honor or courage comes into question. That led to your suggestion to ask for a favor."

"I don't make suggestions," Blevins said with a smile.

"Yes, sir," Lee said with his own smile. "I framed the request for a favor in a way that suggested it was the price for completely removing the breach of honor. His response to that request and our question about his knowledge of Taliban moving into the area were the most interesting parts of the whole meeting. Now stay with me.

"First we asked if he was aware of any groups of fighters in the area. His response was there were large numbers of outsiders in the area, but he didn't know where they were or when they would attack the PRT.

Are you listening?"

"Okay," the executive officer said. "Sounds about like the rumors we've been hearing."

"Maybe," Lee said. "But I think this was more than a rumor. It was the way he said it. Nuristani has a subtle structure. There are many ways of saying the same thing. There are a lot of nuances that are hard to catch, but I think I caught one here. The way he phrased his answer could also be interpreted as, I don't know when, but they are going to attack the PRT. I think he tossed us a bone. He didn't have to say it that way."

Blevins made a note on his pad and thought for a minute.

"So, we have two pieces of intelligence. One, they are here in unusual numbers, and two, they plan to attack the PRT, but we don't know when. Under the circumstances, I think we can take that as better than a rumor. What else?"

"Only one more thing," Lee said. "The favor I asked for was that he send us a warning if he becomes aware of when the attack will take place. I'm afraid I didn't get all I wanted out of that. He bargained the favor down and I didn't think it was smart to go for more. He promised to warn us if I am here, maybe because I speak the language and he feels more responsible for me, or maybe it is the attachment his daughter has formed for me, I don't know. In any case, it was obvious he wasn't going to get locked into an open-ended alliance. The risk is huge for him."

"Still," Blevins said, "that's a valuable

concession. We're still vulnerable and the mortars at the LZ are at risk too. Gentlemen, we have a lot of work to do in a short time. Good job, Lieutenant."

The following two weeks went by slowly, with a lot of stress and little rest. The PRT was on high alert at night and working harder than ever during the day. Bunkers had to be covered and reinforced. The Hesco wall had to be completed. More wire had to be spread on the back perimeter. The combat CP bunker had to be completed, wired and manned. A thousand tasks had to get completed much sooner than anyone expected. The PRT's defenses had to be hardened quickly. On top of the work, patrols had to be maintained. The sense of urgency was palpable in the compound.

Lee went out with a squad sized patrol during the morning hours each day to talk with locals just to get a feel for the mood of the people living close to the PRT. They only went as far as Urmul and stayed near the river. The Cav troops took it as a challenge to teach the sailor with them how to patrol properly. Lee learned how the Army does wedge formations, horseshoe formations, and split team assaults on a hill. They taught him how to withdraw under fire, how to move and fire as a team and how to respond to an ambush by gaining fire superiority. They taught him to always turn his plates toward the incoming, speaking of his armor. Lee ate it up. They were great guys and knew their business. The all-volunteer Army was about as professional an outfit as Lee had ever experienced.

Normally Blevins would have patrols going up in the hills and villages, but his resources were limited, and he had to keep most of his company working on the PRT and hardening his defenses.

Lee's Nuristani improved with every conversation. Each day he looked for changes in behavior, changes in the way he was greeted, anything that might indicate fear or anticipation of attack.

It was harder on your nerves when you knew it was coming. No one at the PRT really expected Buc'ik to keep his word, so twenty-four hours a day, the command looked for the coming attack, looked and prepared.

The problem was, when you are surrounded by mountains higher than your location and your opposition was sitting on those mountains higher than you, they can see everything you do, but you can't see them at all. No matter how Blevins prepared his command, the enemy knew everything he did, every change to the perimeter, every change in the deployment of his assets, every change of the guard, everything. When patrols left the gate, the enemy knew. When supplies arrived, the enemy knew. When villagers visited the COP, the enemy knew.

The first sign that something was up was when the contract workers didn't show up Tuesday morning of the third week after the meeting with Buc'ik. By now, Lee had almost a month at the outpost and was getting comfortable with the Army's routine. He was getting stronger from the patrols and the work. In his spare time, he filled Hescos just like the Army privates. All the officers did. Then, on Tuesday morning, the contract workers were no-shows. Everyone in camp doubled-down and worked harder.

The next day the District Administrator refused to answer a summons to the PRT by Captain Blevins and made some half-assed excuse. Cherokee continued their work. On Friday, Blevins received a report from one of his sources that villagers from Urmul and the hamlet at the top of the switchback road were leaving. He immediately made a request for reinforcements to FOB Naray and put the PRT on 75% alert with a rotating 25% getting a two-hour rest throughout the night and 100% alert for dawn when the Taliban liked to attack. Blevins sent for Lee on Friday afternoon.

"I can't risk getting you up the switchback to get you out of here from the LZ and nothing can get into our little LZ across the creek yet. The only thing coming or going will be medevac or close air support if we need them. Looks like you're here for the duration of this one."

"Where do you want me?" Lee said.

"In the CP with me. When it comes, your languages might help."

Blevins moved his CP to the Hesco reinforced bunker for the duration of the crisis. His Communications specialists spent the day moving furniture, radios, sat phones, and laptops with tac-chat capability to the new bunker. That evening they tested everything and brought the new CP on-line. Lee moved his gear to the CP and spent the night there with Hescos for walls and heavy beams covered in three layers of sandbags for a roof. The generator was loud, but he couldn't sleep anyway. The atmosphere had the feel it gets just before a thunderstorm. Or maybe not. Lee's imagination did.

Chapter 13

When it came, the start of the attack didn't seem to be much more than harassment. Just after first light Saturday morning, two RPGs hit inside the Hescos near the front of the PRT but didn't do any damage. Not much short of 120mm mortar could damage the Hescos, and then they would only scatter dirt.

Blevins yelled, "Lieutenant, get on the scanner and make yourself useful. See if there's any chatter on the hajj hand-held channels."

He pointed at a commercial frequency scanner with a transmitter. Lee had used a similar one during his training at Trident and knew what it was. It was designed to scan across all the frequencies used with the commercial hand-held walkie-talkie radios in that part of the world, sort of like a sophisticated police scanner with transmission capabilities. When it found a signal, it locked on and set the transmitter to the crystal for that channel. It was limited to eight of the most commonly used channels, but it was still a valuable piece of equipment since probably 90% of commercial radios used one of those eight channels. Lee moved in that direction and listened while the Army communications specialist gave him a quick lesson on the one they had.

He plugged the headphones in and heard chatter on the scanner. It was scratchy and full of static, but he could tell the language was Urdu. The hand-held radios used by the Taliban produced line-of-sight radio signals. They had to be on a mountain side in sight of the PRT. Pakistani Taliban were either making or participating In the attack.

"Captain, I've got Pakistanis on this one."

"Can you understand them?"

"Hold on," Lee said. "It's mostly noise with voices in the static."

He pressed the headphones tight on his ears and tried to make sense of what he was hearing. Someone was ordering someone else to move forward. The static eased slightly and he could make out more. Numbered units of some kind were being maneuvered by their unit number.

"Captain, someone is moving numbered units forward. I'm up to four different units so far. Hold on . . ."

The scanner resumed scanning and stopped again where it had been. Lee noted the channel on a note pad. More Urdu. The speaker was asking for permission to move his unit to the next point. The scanner picked up the reply. That pegged the channel as some kind of command channel.

Then the scanner began hopping around with voices on multiple frequencies, groups of men coordinating their approach on different channels. Lee didn't have to think too hard to figure out what they were approaching.

"Captain, we've got multiple groups approaching the camp, and it's all being coordinated by one guy. This looks like what you've been waiting for."

"Thanks. Keep listening and don't be afraid to interrupt if you hear anything interesting."

Captain Blevins had shifted into high gear suddenly. The radio watch was contacting each of the defense points to let them know what was coming. Another man was working the TAC-Chat channel with text. Blevins used the Sat-phone to notify the 3/71 Cav commander at FOB Naray.

In minutes the volume of RPGs hitting inside the camp increased, and the first RPG hit the CP. It was followed with several more. The CP was well constructed and nothing short of a concentrated artillery strike could damage it, but dirt was flying inside, the air was full of dust, and the noise was unbelievable. An RPG hit at the seam between the roof and the Hescos and blew dirt and over-pressure into the bunker. Lee was splattered with high velocity dirt and his ears popped, correcting for the pressure. Blevins was off his chair and squatting near his table and the radio operators had also dropped to the ground.

Everyone got back into position quickly. Lee sat on the dirt with earphones over his ears and pressed the phones with his hands to block out the sound. That helped, but he couldn't block the concussions from explosions on the CP and nearby.

The rest of the PRT was suffering under a coordinated and sustained RPG attack. The attacks kept coming one after another in twos and threes. Within minutes no one could move in the 60mm mortar pit and the gun positions were isolated and cut-off.

Blevins was receiving a constant set of status updates and was in contact with the LZ on the hill. The LZ was receiving the same treatment the PRT was suffering. The Taliban had launched a coordinated attack on both camps and no one in either place could leave cover long enough to find a target and get the mortars into action. The communications specialists worried about the antennas and staying in communications. Blevins worried about the generator.

When the RPG attack reached a crescendo, Lee heard the Taliban commander order something on the radio. Immediately the PRT came under fire by multiple machine guns shooting straight down into the compound. Now, 7.62mm machine gun rounds were hitting in the compound and ricocheting through the explosions. No one reported any 12mm incoming though, and that was a relief. The big 12.7mm (.50 caliber) guns could do some real damage to the gun trucks. Still, nowhere above ground was safe.

The TOC walls were thick, but Lee could hear the constant roar of incoming and feel the concussions as the air inside compacted and expanded with each close strike. He wondered how in the hell they could defend the compound.

"Captain," the Commo-man said, "the mark nineteens are using a lot of ammo. They're pounding that shit out like they have their own factory. They're taking a whole lot of incoming too. We can't get them resupplied."

"Tell the Hummers to go easy for a while until we see how this develops. Don't fire unless they have a target."

The commo-man made his call and reported.

"The gunners had to drop down out of the turrets. Too much shit flying around. None of them has taken an RPG yet, though."

Lee heard a call on the scanner and listened in. The Taliban were apparently in the village at the top of the switch-back and bringing men to the village in groups of ten or more. The COP would be subject to plunging fire from the village and it would be concentrated fire from cover, very hard to suppress. If they got a mortar over there, they could watch the strikes and correct fire immediately. Bad news.

"Captain, they are in the village at the top of the switch-back. They're moving a lot of people in there."

"Can you talk that shit too?"

"Yes, sir."

"Remember C-cubed, Lieutenant. Command,

control, communications. Take any one of the three away from them and the attack falls apart. You got a transmitter on that thing. See if you can mess them up. Screw around with their commo. Mess with their communications. Mess with their minds. Take control of the attack away from them."

"Aye, aye, sir."

The commo-man laughed and Captain Blevins grinned. That eased Lee's tension some. If they could still laugh in the middle of that crap, it wasn't the end of the world.

"Maybe the Navy can order us up a battleship," Blevins said.

"I'll process your request," Lee said, but didn't feel any urge to laugh along. Then he listened for the guy who seemed to be in-charge of the attackers. It didn't take long. The guy ordered unit two to move down the hill toward the PRT.

He didn't get to listen long. He hardly got the earphones on his ears when an RPG hit smack in the middle of the roof blowing sandbags apart and dumping dirt between the cracks in the roof beams. He had to spit dirt after that one. He listened on the channel and then clicked the transmit mike.

"No, no, no," Lee yelled into the radio. "Move back. Move back. Hold your position."

The Taliban radios went silent and the incoming slacked up for a moment. The scanner cycled and cycled trying to find a signal. The pause was long enough for the 60mm in get in action. Blevins gave the village coordinates for the target. Then the scanner began stopping on multiple channels again.

On the command channel. "Who countermands my orders?"

The scanner landed on another channel. Lee yelled into the mike, "Unit two, move back.

As the scanner continued and stopped on different channels he yelled, "American aircraft. All units, cease fire, cease fire, conceal your positions," on each channel. He spoke in the language being used most on that channel. Some Dari was being used, Pashto on one, and Urdu on most.

A new, excited voice came over the command channel. "No radios. No radios. Messengers are dispatched." The scanner picked up the same command on several other channels.

Then the channels went silent. Just that quick Lee's Urdu became useless. The units attacking the PRT were well trained and knew something about radio discipline. They weren't local-yokels out for a thrill. The break was a game changer for the PRT and, apparently, for the LZ too. The groups attacking the LZ went silent and lost coordination. Blevins took coordinates from the FOs on the perimeter and passed them to the mortars at the LZ and the big 120mm mortars began slamming into targets on the hills around the PRT. Even better, Blevins said he had gunships on the way.

Forward observers in the bunkers began calling in coordinates to the tubes, and ordnance was in the air as fast as the loaders could dial in the numbers and drop the rounds. With the armored Humvee units in the PRT back in service, their Mark Nineteen 40mm grenade launchers and Ma Deuce fifties were added to the fray. Incoming had slacked enough for men to run resupply of ammo to the trucks. The Taliban was going to have a tough time getting everything back under control before the close air support arrived.

Lee continued to issue confusing commands on different channels. Occasionally he got a response and replied causing even more confusion. He keyed his transmit to block valid Taliban calls and then gave contrary orders. Some of the sub-commanders were getting so confused they forgot the order to stay off the radios. Lee's calls encouraged more Taliban to get back on the radio. Confusion created more confusion.

A few RPGs kept coming, but they weren't coordinated. Soldiers on the line were spotting enemy machine gun positions and calling them in to the mortars. Two Carl Gustav recoilless rifles got in the game on the perimeter and the troops began laying down some serious fire from their personal weapons on the closer enemy positions.

Blevins had the momentum and he didn't intend to give it back. The Army burnt through their ammo supply and saturated the hills explosive rounds. Taliban messengers couldn't move quickly or often.

Thirty minutes later two Apache gunships arrived and called for targets. Blevins told them to concentrate on the village. Later an AC130 gunship arrived and began sweeping the slopes with their mini-guns. Then two A-10 Warthogs arrived on station and began saturating the ridge-tops with their 30mm, seven-barrel Gatling guns. Lee could hear all the coordination on the radios in the CP, but he wished he could see it. All hell was breaking lose outside and he was stuck in a hole. Through all of it, the Taliban held on and tried to reorganize. They tried, but finally had to accept defeat and began to withdraw over the ridges and down the rat-lines along the mountain ridges.

It was just one battle, and of a rare kind, and it could have been much more serious than it turned out to be. From the number of languages used on the radios, Lee deduced that Afghani Pashtuns, Pakistani fighters, some Arabs, and even a few Uzbeks participated in a coordinated attack. Blevins estimated 50 or more fighters had participated from the positions identified by his troops. No one knew how many were in positions not identified. For Lee, the battle was huge, but it wasn't a big battle and it didn't last long. The enemy didn't achieve much, but they learned some valuable lessons about how the PRT could respond and how long it took them to respond. They would be back. He couldn't tell if Blevins was disappointed or relieved.

Lee didn't realize it, but in the last month he had earned his Combat Action Ribbon, the Navy's equivalent to the Army's Combat Infantryman's Badge. Besides his been-there-done-that ribbons he would get for being in-country, he now was entitled to a purple heart, and the Navy CAR. His low Kinetic training tour was turning out to be something far more serious. He was still an intel geek, but Kamdesh had turned him into a combat veteran.

Chapter 14

The PRT had been hit hard and Lee wanted to see the damage up close and personal. He pulled on his body armor and Rhodesian rig and picked up his rifle. The COP was so exposed to the surrounding mountains, he swore he wouldn't leave a hut or bunker without wearing body armor.

He was used to the body armor and the stink of constant sweat with raw armpits and crotch, but the flea bites still bothered him. The flea collar helped, but it didn't eliminate the bites. The fleas were breeding so fast in the sleeping quarters nothing helped. He offered a moment of silence in thanks that he was Navy and would be able to leave Kamdesh when his current assignment was done. He offered another for the soldiers that had to remain in those brutal mountains for fifteen months.

He watched crews inspect the armored Humvees. This place was a disaster waiting to happen. What if the Taliban had come with 200 insurgents? The PRT was lucky this time, but the Taliban wouldn't give up. Each time they attacked, it got a little worse. The Army's response was static, the same every time. They were stuck in one place with the same number of troops and weapons. The U.S. was focused on Iraq, and Afghanistan was just an annoyance for the military planners at the Pentagon. The resources just weren't sufficient to do the job.

The roof on one of the old buildings, the alternate CP, was burning and smoke was rising from the mortar pit. A detail was trying to salvage the contents from the building. The small, unfinished tower at the gate had taken a direct hit and was burning. He stayed close to the CP, not wanting to get in the way of man or bullet. Blevins came out of the CP and stood next to him.

"You did a good job on the radios. You have my thanks for that. A platoon is flying in from Naray and we're going to do a RIF (recon in force) up the switchback and through the village. Could get hot if any of them are still around, but you're welcome to go along and see what you can learn."

Lee had to think about that. Big, sustained battles were rare in Afghanistan, but a whole lot of firepower had been brought to bear on the PRT in this one. Even inside the CP he had been shaken and scared. He couldn't let it show. He had a job to do, and he still wasn't sure he had done anything useful or learned anything that would justify the resources spent on getting him out to the valley. The SEALs would ride his ass about his holiday in the mountains if he didn't take something worthwhile back.

"Are we going to check out Kamdesh? I'd like to find out why Buc'ik didn't keep his word."

"Igor, the first thing you need to learn is we are outsiders and infidels. Muslims have a flexible sense of honor when it comes to infidels. Read that as they lie like hell."

"Still," Lee said, "we ought to find out."

"It's on the agenda."

"Yes, sir, I'd like to go."

A reaction platoon came in by Blackhawks the following morning. The Blackhawks were all the new LZ could handle. The QRF platoon plus one squad from the PRT left the gate and started up the switchback at 0900. Forty-seven men was an unusual show of force for patrols in this area, but the previous day's attack had not been normal and might be a portent of things to come.

Lee stayed with the platoon leader and tried to watch everything at once. RPGs were his biggest fear. The Cav troops taught him to keep his head swiveling. An RPG launcher can't be used everywhere, and the guy using it almost always had to expose himself. He needed plenty of open space behind him because of the back-blast and that generally meant he would be exposed to view for the few seconds it took him to sight the rocket on his target.

Lee was learning, but still new to patrolling, and the effort took his attention away from where it belonged—where he was placing his feet. He was limping from two falls by the time they reached the switchback. The Cav troops were used to him now, and they just helped him up and continued without comment.

The trip up the switchback was slow and cautious. That was okay with Lee. He was getting stronger and his legs could handle a lot more than when he arrived, but anything could happen. Scouts were out and every foot of terrain was examined before the troop moved forward. The enemy had occupied this area just the day before and were sure to have left some surprises.

Or maybe not. The PRT, LZ, and close air support had dumped an amazing amount of ordnance on those hills. The slopes on both sides of the road were pockmarked with craters. The path wasn't much to begin with, and now it would need some serious repair.

First Lieutenant Axel, the patrol leader, stood next to Lee when the patrol was held up by a signal from one of the scouts.

"It will be like this on the way up," Axel said. "You have to check everything, but the real danger is on the exfil. They aren't sure what we're doing right now, or how far we're going, but they know the route and there aren't many alternative routes for getting back.

They have time to plan, move people, and get set up. What's the Navy doing in Kamdesh?"

"Trying to stay alive,"

"That's always a good thing," Axel said with a grin. "You're obviously not a SEAL. What's your connection to them?"

That "obviously" stung a little, but Lee let it go.

"With them, but not of them," he said. "I'm a linguist and intel geek for Team Two."

Axel just nodded as he scanned the road ahead and made a quick visual check of his platoon's positions. He was talking, probably to steady Lee, but his mind was on business. Lee was doing well. He was hyped and ready, but he wasn't shaky at all.

"We don't work with special ops much," Axel said. "Captain Blevins said you handled yourself well while you've been here. You were out here with him not long ago, weren't you?"

Lee felt a little embarrassment. They don't forget, he thought.

"You don't have to beat around the bush, Lieutenant," Lee said. "Yeah, I screwed-up by the numbers and got my head split. But I'm still here, and I don't plan to screw-up again."

Axel scanned his troops with his eyes again.

"It happens, Toliver. Training makes it easier. Experience helps. Even then, we still fuck-up. Can you use that M4?"

"I hit what I aim at."

"Okay. Stick close to me and do what I tell you.

Time to move."

Axel caught the signal from the scouts and put his patrol in motion again. They made it to the top of the switchback without contact and entered the village in a skirmish line, or as close to a line as the terrain would allow. It was a formidable line with eight M249 SAWs, two anchoring each of four squads. Each of the gunners had a 200 round, linked belt magazine loaded and carried two more. Each member of the fire teams carried one also. Together, they could lay down covering fire of over 5000 rounds a minute. Add to that the firepower of the individual riflemen and gaining firepower superiority over a force of rag-tag insurgents wasn't difficult. The mountain troops were trained-up, experienced, and impressed the hell out of Lee.

The village didn't look a whole lot different from the last time he had seen it. Several mud-brick houses were damaged and falling down the first time he came through here. A few more walls were damaged by the pounding the village took the previous day, but it was hard to tell how much additional damage had occurred. Those mud and rock buildings could absorb an amazing amount of punishment without showing much effect.

The local people had not returned to the village yet and the Taliban seemed to have moved out and took what bodies there might have been with them. When the patrol reached the communal bathroom (a field) on the other end of the village, Lee was hyped and his nerves were tight as guitar strings.

Axel stopped the command group at the end of the village and sent a scout squad up the trail leading to Buc'ik's village outside of Lower Kamdesh. When the scouts had the lead Axel wanted, he stretched the column out and moved forward with the remainder of the patrol.

IGOR

Chapter 15

Moving up the trail through these mountains almost overwhelmed the senses. They weren't high enough to make breathing difficult yet, and wouldn't be on this hike, but the view was spectacular. Lee was marveling at the massive snow-capped peaks in the distance and the 3D impact of the valleys close in when the column suddenly stopped ahead.

The explosion was muffled at first but followed by a clap of sound that assaulted his ears. Lee wasn't sure what he had heard, but Axel knew right away. A cloud of smoke rose in the distance as Axel moved the remainder of his patrol forward on the double. He was on the radio trying to contact the scout leader. What he heard was a call for medevac.

When the command group arrived with three squads, the site of the IED explosion was chaos. The trail wasn't much more than a goat path to begin with, and now there was a gaping hole where fifteen feet of the trail had been. Several troops were providing security and five more were tending to the wounded and dead. One wounded soldier was still on the trail just short of the crater and two men were tying compression bandages around multiple wounds on his torso and legs. Two men were down the hillside kneeling near what appeared to be another wounded soldier.

As Lee watched, one of the two men below raised his arm and made a thumbs-down motion. Another man was struggling to climb down a steep section of hillside to get to another fallen comrade. His movements were desperate and risked catastrophe at each rock and ledge he struggled across. Finally, he reached the crevasse that held his friend. He leaned in and then immediately jerked his body back and fell to his knees. Lee could hear his retching from a hundred feet away.

"Sergeant, get a man down there to help," Axel said. "Sparks, what have you got on the medevac bird?"

"It's in the air, sir. Twenty-five minutes. We'll have air support overhead in five."

"Where's my scout leader?"

"Here, sir."

"What was it?"

The scout leader was visibly shaking. He had lacerations on his face and hands, and his BDUs were shredded on one leg. He was so covered with dirt and dust, he looked like he had just been dug up from a grave.

"All I can figure," he said, "is command detonated. It was in the side of the hill, not on the trail. We were being super careful, Lieutenant. There weren't any wires or detonators on the trail. It was probably there for a while. Probably radio activated."

"They're watching us then," Axel said. "If they haven't bugged out. Sparks, warn the medevac there might be hostiles in the area, but make sure he knows the site is not hot now."

These troops were easy to like and easier to respect. They had just lost four friends, friends close in a way no civilian could ever understand, but they moved forward professionally. Teams worked together to recover bodies and body parts while other teams provided overwatch and security. Everyone knew his job and no one shirked. One man risked life and limb to climb down a truly scary rock face to recover a foot. A foot. One piece of his friend.

Two Apache helicopter gunships arrived overhead five minutes before the casevac bird and began a slow orbit. The casevac bird came in and hovered over the site. They took the wounded trooper out first and then lowered a basket with body-bags for the bodies and body parts.

Axel ordered the scout leader out also. His wounds weren't life threatening, yet, but his experience was sanity threatening. The last thing Axel needed right then was a team leader bent on revenge or feeling he needed to redeem himself. He'd be back, and he would lead his team again, but for now Axel wouldn't take the chance. He had a good excuse to get the guy out of there without loss of face, so he used it. A good leader.

Lee was amazed at how quickly it went. Within an hour of first contact, the patrol was moving toward their objective again. Because of the terrain, getting above the village and coming down on it from high ground was more effort than Axel wanted to expend for the slight tactical advantage it provided. He had limited time, and the more time he spent here, the longer the opposition had to set up something for the exfil. The patrol remained on the trail and slightly above and below it.

Axel moved to the head of the column as they approached the village and kept Lee with him. He pulled his scouts back and brought the platoon up at a point where they had some cover and could observe the village. Lee was handed a pair of 7X50s to look the scene over after Axel had a good look.

Lee focused on the house where he had met with Buc'ik before, and then scanned the rest of the village. No welcoming committee this time. No committee of any kind. The village looked deserted. He pointed out the shura house to Axel and explained what it represented. Then he resumed a slow scan of all the village that could be seen. Nothing. Not a single person in sight and no sign of movement. The village had become a ghost town. He wondered if upper Kamdesh would be the same. If you have to evacuate from a place as remote as this, where the hell do you go?

"They would have heard the explosion," Axel said. "May have known it was going to happen anyway. We'll target your buddy's house and clear everything around it. If we find him, you lead the interrogation."

"Okay. There's a little girl living in that house. Let's be careful."

"Always. Sergeant, by squad. Here's how I want to do it..."

They went in by squad. First squad led in and found cover and set up the over-watch. Second squad followed and enlarged the perimeter. Axel and Lee went in with third squad, and fourth squad came in last and set up a blocking force and rear guard near the entrance to the village. Neither sound nor movement came from any building in the village, but Lee could feel a presence. He knew it was just a superstitious reaction in his mind, but he couldn't shake the feeling of being watched.

"We're not alone," SFC Polk, the platoon sergeant said as if reading Lee's mind.

Axel looked at his perimeter and then scanned the village. "I want a fire team on that door right there. Lieutenant, you're about to earn your door buster badge. You up to it?"

"Tell me what to do," Lee said.

"You are the last man in the stack. When we are ready, I want you to call your friend, more as a distraction than anything else. We're going to hit the door while you are talking. Sergeant Polk, get your team over here."

Lee had one man assigned to do nothing but hold his hand, literally. He kept hold of Lee's arm and physically moved him to his position and held him there. The troops knew how to stack on a door and how to enter a building. Lee didn't. He wouldn't be allowed to enter until the building was cleared.

He was moved up close to the door, his escort still holding on. When the team leader indicated, Lee yelled, "Buc'ik Muhammed. It is I, Lee Toliver. Open . . ."

He was jerked back and pulled against the wall of the building. The door had been kicked in and the fire team rushed in while he was still talking. Lee listened for shots, but all he could hear was men yelling, "Clear right. Clear left."

Finally, the team leader came to the door and yelled, "All clear."

Axel came on the run and waved Lee in with him.

The house was empty. Lee walked through the room where he had talked with Buc'ik and Little Sister. The room hadn't been changed. Everything was in place. He walked through the bead curtains separating the meeting room from the private quarters where the women had remained. A different story here.

The room was tossed. Furniture was smashed and sleeping mats were pushed into a corner.

"Did we do this?" Lee asked.

"No," Axel said. "Your friend must have pissed someone off."

Lee saw a dark stain on the floor near one wall. It was a big stain and the air in the room had a disgusting smell. He knelt and touched the stain. It was sticky and easy to see what it was.

"Blood," Lee said.

"Yeah," Axel said. "There's more over there. I doubt you'll be talking with your friend again. The Taliban are not forgiving people. Let's get on with it, Sergeant. We need to see what else happened in this village."

Chapter 16

They found Buc'ik, his wives, and Little Sister, at the far end of the village next to the communal latrine. They were laid out next to each other. Each body was pale in death and each throat was cut. Lee knelt next to Little Sister and forced himself to look at her.

The sight was vulgar. He felt a grief and anger that rattled him. All the hate came back. In her short life, the kid had already been horribly burned and suffered through an existence that could be called primitive at best. Who knows how much pain she endured in her few years? And now this. Who the hell could do a thing like this? A desire for revenge grew until he wanted to shout.

Tears came and he tried to hide them. He hadn't felt this kind of sorrow when the soldiers, his own kind, had been blown apart. But the kid was innocent and special. She knew. She knew his pain. Christ, this was a cruel, fucked-up country. He knew now how he would handle the first one he could get his hands on. Cut his fucking throat. He felt like he was going to scream if he didn't get his emotions under control. He found the strength to submerge the hate and anger. He didn't dare let it show. It was something to be hidden and nurtured. One day, he would get his chance.

"Did you know them?" Axel asked.

"Yes. This is Buc'ik, and his family. The little girl is his daughter. The women must be his wives. What kind of animals would do this to a little kid?"

"Jihad animals. I suspect Blevins won't get any cooperation out of this village again. Have you seen what you need to see?"

"No," Lee said quietly.

"Okay. What else are we looking for?"

"The scum that did this."

"Get yourself under control, Lieutenant. They're long gone. Are you going to be okay?"

Lee took a deep breath and savored the hate.

"Yeah," he said. "Should we bury them?"

"You're the expert." Axel said.

"Sorry," Lee said. "I'm not thinking well right now. Leave them. They have their own ways. The village will do it properly. Let's get the hell out of here."

The enemy knew where they were, knew the way they

had to come back, and had time to set up in the place most favorable to them—if they were waiting. There wasn't any good way to do it. They had to get from point A to point B. They were at A and the PRT, safety, was at point B. The Cav hadn't been in the area long and hadn't run enough patrols to find alternate routes down the mountain. Trying to do so now in this steep, unforgiving terrain would be more dangerous than returning the way they came. Axel stretched his patrol out in a long column so there wouldn't be any concentration of targets to make it easy for the enemy, for snipers or hidden IEDs.

The M249s were spaced evenly along the column and ready to bring concentrated fire on a shooter or engage multiple targets in multiple directions. But if a battle came before they reached the village at the top of the switchback, it would be a bitch. As Lee had learned the last time he was up here, the trail was exposed and offered very little cover from above for the troops. The mountainside above them offered the opposition plenty of cover and high ground. If they were waiting, that's where they would be.

It was a stress filled exfil, but as it turned out, the Taliban had tired of their game or were licking their wounds in one of their holes.

They made it to the gate without taking any further incoming or running into any more IEDs. Lee went straight to the CP and grabbed the first bottle of water he found. He drank half and poured the rest over his head. May temperatures had set in and the grind in the hills was worse than ever.

Blevins was sitting with his boots on the radio table and reading an intel report.

"Learn anything useful?"

"Buc'ik and the little girl are dead. Throats cut. Maybe he would have kept his word if he was alive."

"More than likely. Well, your little adventure is coming to an end, LT. Your boss isn't happy with you. Got a call on my sat-phone while you were gone. He wants to know what part of stay inside the wire don't you understand."

"What did you tell him?"

"Relax. You're covered. A bird will be in sometime after midnight, so pack your gear. You'll be in J-bad before light. Find a hole and chill out for now."

"Back up the switchback to the LZ?"

"No. A Blackhawk can get into our LZ now. One will be in shortly after midnight."

Back in his hut, he thought about his five weeks at the PRT. His life had changed. He learned just how fragile life is. He'd never thought of life that way before. It had always seemed more substantial. He learned how hard it is to hold on to it, and how easy it is lost. A simple pressure with just one finger, something even an idiot can learn, and a life standing a football field away ends. One slash of a sharp blade, and another life ends. It shouldn't be that simple.

And he was surprised at how quickly remorse

passes.

He'd like to do more for these soldiers he had come to respect and care for, but he couldn't say he was sorry to be leaving. He was surprised he had been allowed to stay for five weeks. The experience had been valuable personally, but it wasn't a good one. This was a totally screwed up war. He had studied military history at the Academy and nothing he read had prepared him for the reality of war in the mountains or the brutality of the primitive people they fought. Life was hard here, and cheap. Every idea he had about what was and wasn't sacred had been smashed.

He wondered if the war all over Afghanistan was as different as it seemed to be here. Mostly it was about grinding up and down hills, fatigue, filth, bugs, and boredom. There didn't seem to be an achievable goal. The few TICs (troops in contact) that broke the boredom tended to be brief and violent, and seldom involved more than a few enemy, often single digits, but then the grind and boredom set back in. The troops bled a little every day and fought boredom and stress the rest of the time.

He guessed the uncertainty was the hard part. It might be only one or two shots, or an RPG or IED, but it could happen at any time, and it was always at the time the enemy chose. Compared to Vietnam or Korea, or even Iraq, casualties were low, but low only means something to the planners and desk people who keep those records. To the guy who took the shrapnel or bullet or was deranged for life by the explosive force of an IED, it was 100% casualty.

Chapter 17

Mallory passed through the outer reception room to Commander Faulk's office. He didn't bother stopping at the reception desk. He simply tapped on the door frame and walked in unannounced.

"Jake, one day you're going to walk in on something, and I will, reluctantly, have to disappear your ass."

"You wish. Let's talk about Toliver."

"What about Toliver? The paperwork is done and the orders are gone."

"He surprised the hell out of a lot of people. Are you still worried about him?"

"No. He's proved he can take the heat. That does beg the question though. Why Iraq?" He's already with the SEALs in Afghanistan."

"Higher Kinetic ops, different languages, and different culture," Mallory said. "Team Three is rampaging across western Iraq, and Ramadi is back on the radar for a major urban operation."

"You are a manipulative son of a bitch. You know that, don't you?" Faulks said.

"Thank you. All compliments are sincerely appreciated. With his Arabic, he can make a big contribution in Iraq, Commander, but mainly, we don't want him to get too attached to any particular team, place, or culture. He's going to be moving around. He has to learn to adapt quickly and operate alone."

Faulks knew it was time to shut up. Toliver had the basic training and had done well under fire so far. All the services sent men to the war without much more training than he had. Now he had experience under fire. But the Navy had a big investment in him, four years at the Academy and two years at Princeton. It just seemed foolish to risk all of that.

"I made my objection clear, so I'll shut up about it. Tell me more about Iraq."

Mallory looked over Faulk's head thinking for a moment.

"Different environment, different kind of war," he said. "We know he can operate in the primitive areas of Afghanistan. Iraq will be a step up for him. The insurgents there are a different breed, more fanatical, ready to die for the cause, tougher to crack. And Ramadi is an urban environment. Ultimately, that's where his real value will be."

"You are throwing a lot at him in a short time."

"Part of the training. Toliver is a smart guy and he's obviously tougher than he looks. Hell, he's tougher than he thinks he is, but he's beginning to find his strength. This isn't a short-term project, Commander. The war on terror won't go away any time soon, and we expect to benefit from Toliver's unique talents for a long time."

Faulks sat back and thought for a while. Mallory was thinking three moves ahead and Faulks wasn't sure he liked the game he was playing. He realized he didn't like the CIA and he didn't like this split role he was playing. He didn't like anyone who tried to manipulate people like Toliver.

"Toliver may object to all this," Faulks said. "The last time I talked with him, his biggest fear was getting too far from his chosen career as a Naval officer. If he objects, I'll back him."

"Christ, Commander. We're on the same team here. Give the guy a medal or something."

"If you had done your homework, you'd know he was wounded over there and received a Purple Heart. He earned that. He also qualified for the Navy Combat Action Ribbon. He earned that too."

"I have done my homework," Mallory said. "This isn't a hobby for me. You have the authority. Give him a Bronze Star for his work when the PRT was attacked. My understanding is his contribution helped bust up the attack and he functioned well in two other firefights. The star with a nice ceremony will help him to feel like he's doing something important for the Navy."

More manipulation, Faulks thought. It's the way this guy thinks. But the star isn't a bad idea. It's something he can bring back to normal duty when this is over and will help with his fitness report.

"I'll think about it. Are we about done here? I've got work to do."

"That's it. I just wanted to be sure the orders were issued. I'll get out of your way."

Chapter 18

Harris was waiting for Lee with the rest of his gear when the helicopter landed at J-bad. Lee was packed into a Humvee and transported to the loading ramp at J-bad main-side and put on a C130 that was already warming up when they got there. He was back in Bagram two hours later and an hour after that he was sitting in LT Osborne's office.

"I was going to ream your ass unmercifully, but Captain Blevins gave you such a glowing review, it's difficult to find the words. Just tell me this. Were the chances you took worth the risk?"

"I think so," Lee said. "Besides giving me actual face time with locals and improving my understanding of the local languages, I think my contribution helped when the PRT was attacked."

"Blevins said as much. So, do you think your stay with us was worth the trouble to you and the Navy?"

"Yes. No question in my mind. I appreciate the opportunity to work with the detachment. You sort of referred to my stay in the past tense. Am I going somewhere?"

"Which brings us to the next order of business. Yes, you leave tonight. Frankly, I'd like to keep you for the rest of our deployment, but you don't belong to me. Spend the day getting cleaned up and get some decent food in you. Turn in any worn gear or uniforms you have and get a reissue. I've laid on a Hummer and driver for you. You will fly out to the Task Unit in Ramadi tonight."

"Iraq?"

"Yes. Don't ask me why. We can use you right here.

"But I'm just getting my feet on the ground. I was supposed to have another month to six weeks here."

"Sorry, Lee, I'd like to have your services, and maybe I will down the road, but your orders for Iraq are in."

Crap, he was just starting to feel like he was part of something useful. There wasn't any use in arguing though. If Trident had issued orders for him, he was on his way to Iraq. Getting used to Team Two and the detachment had been hard enough. Now he had to do it all over again with a new team. Crap! A new guy again. At least he wasn't a total cherry now.

"I better get my uniforms ready."

"I have one more thing for you."

Osborne handed Lee a blue oblong snap case. "Your forgot-to-duck medal. I always feel uneasy congratulating someone for earning this award, so I'll congratulate you for earning it and walking away. Did you know you also qualify for the Navy Combat Action Ribbon, the Afghanistan Service Medal, and the War on Terror Medal?"

"No, I hadn't thought about it."

"DoD will get the medals to you sometime, but you can pick the ribbons up at the Exchange. Good luck."

Osborne held out his hand. Lee took it.

"Take care of yourself and keep your head down, Igor. If you're ever looking for an intel home, tell your boss you're welcome in any team I command."

Getting back to Bagram was almost like coming home. Almost. Incoming was rare and the base was built out like a stateside base. All the amenities of home. The driver took him to the PX where he purchased his new ribbons and picked up a sheath knife to strap on his arm. He bought the knife the Chief recommended, a SOG Pentagon with a five-inch blade. It wasn't just a killing blade. A fixed blade knife had a thousand everyday uses and he was constantly borrowing someone else's out in the mountains. Besides, carrying one upside down on your arm looked cool as hell.

While he was at it, he stocked up on snacks.

Next, he stopped at the officer's uniform shop and turned in his damaged BDUs for two new sets. He packed, and then got a real meal at a sit-down table with plates and everything. Finally, he soaked in a shower until his skin got wrinkles. His body looked like he had chicken pocks, so he put salve on every flea-bite and then hit the rack. The flight wasn't until 2300. He had some time to catch up on sleep.

The C-130 left on time and Lee was on-board minus his radio. He was going straight into hostile territory, so arrangements were made with Squadron Three to take care of property transfers to account for his gear and weapons.

Chief Boyle checked him out and made sure he would be ready for anything when he hit the ground. Boyle had talked to the Senior Chief in the Task Unit in Iraq and put a good word in for Lee. He also got the word on what Lee needed to be prepared for when he got off the aircraft. The answer was, "Be prepared to fight. No place was safe in the AO. A gun truck would pick him up at the plane and take him to Shark Base at Ramadi.

He had six loaded magazines attached to his vest and the latest body armor. His M4 was clean and sighted-in and his Hydration pack was full. Chief Boyle convinced him to mount his knife on his vest with the handle up and forget about all the handle down stuff from the movies. The only thing he didn't get was night optical devices (NODs) and a radio. If he needed night vision gear, the Ramadi TU would issue it in Ramadi. It was tightly controlled.

Chapter 19

Most SEAL Teams arrived in Iraq with their gear and weapons packed away in shipping crates, cruise boxes, roller boxes, and Pelican cases after a long flight across the Atlantic. They arrived on secure bases and had time to sort things out. Lee arrived at Habbaniyah armed and fully outfitted, ready to go with his personal gear in two cruise boxes.

He slid a cruise box across the ramp to the tarmac at 0230 and went back up the ramp for the second box. By the time he had the boxes stacked and ready to go, he was drenched in sweat. The temperature had to be in the high 90s with humidity to match. The air was moist with the smell of swampy water—and other things less pleasant. If it was that hot in the middle of the night, he dreaded what the day would bring. He sucked down some water.

No one was waiting for him so he sat on his cruise boxes. The base was still active. A jet took off every few minutes and helicopters buzzed round. Off in the distance he could hear occasional gunfire, and muffled explosions. Christ, he thought, it's two in the morning. Who the hell is fighting in the middle of the night? In Afghanistan, night attacks were rare, unless it was special forces on a raid. Americans had night vision and the opposition didn't. The Taliban chose to sleep at night. He couldn't see much, but what he could see was flat, and that was encouraging. He had had enough of mountain warfare.

Lee had to admit though, he was in the best shape of his life. Slowly over the last six months, the best way, his conditioning had improved. First came the conditioning program led by physical therapists back in Texas. Then daily PT with Detachment Bravo in Little Creek, followed by his daily workouts with the detachment in Bagram. His SEAL friends in the detachment had taken special delight in pushing him until he collapsed. Finally, he had almost five weeks in the mountains with the Army, climbing up and down mountains with sixty or seventy pounds on his back where collapsing wasn't an option. His thighs and calves had ballooned out and were ripped.

He sat with sweat running down the inside of his body armor and watched Air Force cargo handlers unload the plane until he spotted two up-armored Humvees with turrets racing across the field. They were heading right toward him. Hopefully his ride. Sitting alone on an airfield waiting for armored vehicles to pick him up didn't seem strange now, and that was a little scary. What the hell was happening to his life?

Both Humvees stopped near him. Gunners were in the turrets of both trucks. The front door opened on the lead vehicle and a man in full gear climbed out with an M4 in one hand. Helmet with NODs, body armor with MOLLE gear with ammo pouches and assorted other gear on the waist, gloves on his hands and knee pads on his legs. He approached Lee.

"Igor?"

"That's me."

"Chief Taylor, Task Unit Ramadi. If you're not already locked and cocked, lock and load now and safe your weapon. Let's get your gear in the vehicle."

With his gear loaded, Lee got in the rear seat of the lead vehicle. Above him the gunner was manning a Mark 19 40mm grenade launcher. It could fire those exploding rounds at a rate of 300 rounds a minute if needed. The vehicle behind them had twin M240 machine guns in the turret. Three SEALs plus the gunner were in Lee's vehicle, five seals were in the rear vehicle. His convoy was only two vehicles, but it had teeth.

With everything loaded, Chief Taylor made sure the radio signal jammers were on and told the driver to move out.

"Up top," the Chief said, "is SO2 Mark Lazinski. Next to you is EN1 Chuck Jones, LPO of Charlie Platoon.

Driving is Hospitalman second class Larry Snyder, our corpsman. I understand you've been out in the hills playing games with the Tenth Mountain Division. Good guys."

"Part of Mountain, yes. I was with Three-Seventy-One Cav, Alpha Troop mostly and embedded with Cherokee Company at an outpost near Kamdesh in Nuristan. Believe me, we weren't playing games."

"Yeah, I heard about your forgot-to-duck medal. Chief Boyle speaks well of you. I think the Task Unit can put you to work and broaden your horizons. What languages are you fluent in?"

"Lately I've been focused on Pashto, Dari, and Nuristani, but my primary fluency is in Arabic."

"Baghdadi dialect?"

"Baghdadi, Oman, and Jordanian. I can handle any of the gulf dialects."

"That's damn good news. We have them all. Trident knows what they're doing. I've got plenty of work for you Mr. Toliver. Gentleman, our new guy's handle is Igor."

"That's fucking cruel," Jones said. "What do you want us to call you, Mr. Toliver?"

"Igor is good," Lee said. "I'm used to it, and it's easy to understand on the radio."

"Igor is a Trident IA," Chief Taylor said. "But he's making the rounds for experience, so make nice and help him acclimate to his new environment."

"To clear the air of unasked questions," Lee said. "I got this face from a suicide bomber in London. It doesn't hurt except when I smile, and you don't want to see that."

The SEALs were listening and laughed, but not one of them had taken his eyes off the road ahead during the conversation. It was like holding a conversation with someone running a dangerous machine. You know they are hearing you with one part of their mind, but most of their attention is focused on not losing a finger. Lee took the hint and shut up.

Later, he asked where they were going.

"You'll be working at Shark Base near Ramadi. We'll be there soon."

Shark Base was a walled SEAL compound sharing a wedge of land with a Ranger compound just outside of and sharing a wall with Camp Ramadi, a larger U.S. and Iraqi Army Base, near the Euphrates River outside of the city. The Ramadi TU was located at Shark base. Lee thought the SEALs had come up with a cool name for a SEAL camp, but Chief Taylor told him it was a bunch of Army Special Forces guys that named it long before the SEALs took it over. Go figure.

The two Humvees rolled through the gates around 0400, so Lee didn't get to see much of his new home, but he could see the team house, a large building with a front portico supported with large columns. It was impressive.

He was taken to a large air-conditioned tent with plywood partitioned rooms inside and shown a place to stow his cruise boxes and assigned a room. Chief Taylor told him to catch a couple of hours sleep and then he would be shown the rest of the compound. The place was almost empty. The platoons worked vampire hours in this neck of the woods.

Once again, as he relaxed with his hands behind his head, he was serenaded with the sound of distant small arms fire and muted explosions. He tried to remember what his life had been like before the exploding bus had changed it but couldn't. Time and life was measured in BE and AE now. Before the explosion and After the explosion. Somehow only AE seemed to matter. New place, another war. The sounds of war, distant war, were lulling, and he drifted off to sleep.

Chapter 20

Lee woke up to the sound of a machine gun that seemed right outside the tent. At first, he thought he was back in Nuristan. He rolled off his cot and hit the floor. The tent was air conditioned, but not very well. He was suddenly soaked in sweat.

Two SEALs entered the tent and began stripping off their gear and hanging it over cruise boxes in the stowage area. Lee sat up and looked around. The gunfire had stopped. The SEALs stopped outside his cube with towels around their waists.

"Hey, new guy, we have cots here and everything. What are you doing on the floor?"

Lee rubbed the sleep from his eyes and awareness of his present location woke him up.

"What was the shooting about?"

"Probably a guard tower probing some real estate. Happens all the time. Are you the new intel geek? Oh shit, yeah, you are. Welcome aboard, Igor."

"Thanks. This place got showers?"

"Showers, shitters, all the comforts of home thanks to our Seabees."

His handle was out already and obviously, his description was also. The shower station had hot water and plenty of room and privacy, something he hadn't had much of lately. The shower stations were enclosed by plastic curtains. Lee remembered Captain Blevins's remark about C-cubed (command, control, communications) and dubbed his morning routine S-cubed (shit, shower, shave).

He dressed in summer weight BDU's with clean, brushed boots. The Chief warned him that the TU commander expected his staff to live up to the same standards the Army and Marine units followed. He went looking for something to eat, someone to brief him in, and something useful to do, in that order. He was directed to the TOC in the Team House.

The morning was already hot. Not many people were working, but the TOC was busy. Chief Taylor and a Lieutenant were there with the Coms people.

"Morning, Chief. Where can I get some chow?"

"Morning, Igor. LT this is Lieutenant Toliver from Trident, handle Igor. Igor, this is Charlie Platoon OIC, LT Wayne, or The Duke, to those of us who know and love him."

Lee and Wayne shook hands. "Screw you,

Chief," Wayne said. "Charlie Platoon is standing down today so the Commander assigned me to show you around this morning and introduce you to the right people. I need some chow too. Let's go over to Camp Ramadi and get a hot meal with the Army."

Shark base sat on a small wedge of land against a northeast wall of Camp Ramadi with the camp wall on the west side of the compound and the Euphrates river on the east side. He wasn't sure about the river though. Wayne called it the Euphrates or the Habbaniyah canal alternately. Somewhere south of Shark base the Euphrates doglegged to the east and the canal continued south.

They entered Camp Ramadi through a break in the camp protective wall. Hydration was going to be a problem. Lee was sucking water down before they got to the officer's mess. The mess wasn't much, but the air conditioning inside was welcome. They were on their way again before he could recover fully. He wondered if he would ever get acclimated to that kind of heat.

LT Wayne took him for a short ride around the base so he could get a feel for the locations of important sites. He stopped at a guard tower on the north side of the base so Lee could see some of the surrounding terrain.

A mist of dust hung over a village in the distance and dust covered everything he saw. Most of the buildings in the distance were small one or two-story houses, tan in color like everything else he saw.

No people were evident in his view. Rubble of destroyed buildings and even some wrecked vehicles dotted the landscape. Dirt, rubble, dirt and more dirt. There was some green close to the river, but everything else was wasteland.

Wayne pointed out the interesting things to see and moved back to Shark Base quickly. Shark Base had been built out by the Seabees with all sort of tents and building, but a prewar building that was said to have housed Saddam's personal guard was still used. The Team house, the original guard's residence, was an impressive building from the outside, but everything had been looted on the inside after the fall of Saddam. It had space behind concrete walls though, and the TU made good use of it.

One road ran up the center of the camp with berthing tents, laundry, and other buildings on one side and working buildings on the other. The compound was small, but the TU packed a lot into it. Most of the buildings and tents were working spaces. Twenty berthing tents surrounded with Hesco walls provided berthing. The Hescos provided some protection from Mortar incoming, at least if you didn't take a direct hit.

A multi-stall shower and laundry building with water supplied from Camp Ramadi served the TU. There was a small mess-hall built by the Seabees that also served as kind of a community center. The camp didn't have its own food service. The food was supplied by Army food services at Camp Ramadi and hauled to Shark Base in insulated containers.

The Iraqi interpreters had their own quarters. Lee met them and was welcomed. They were good guys. They worked for the U.S. Navy, but they made it clear they fought for Iraq. All of them were putting their lives on the line just associating with the Americans. They were easy to like and respect.

There was a small mission planning building for the platoons. On the working side stood a huge shed for parking and servicing the vehicles belonging to the TU. A row of porta-potties served the camps need for bathroom facilities. Electric was supplied by redundant diesel generators, so the camp was never quiet.

When Lee had seen the camp, Wayne took him back to the team house to meet the TU commander. Senior Chief Taylor was there also.

"Frankly, Lieutenant, I'm not sure what to do with you," LCDR Wallings said. "We were informed of this assignment a week ago, but all they said was we were getting a Trident intel and language IA and to put you to work. What experience do you have working with SEALs?"

Lee gave them a run-down on his Trident training and what he had been doing for the Bagram SEAL detachment and his work in Nuristan with the 3/71 Cav.

"I'm not sure why I'm here either," he said. "I thought I was going to be in Bagram for another month and then go back to the states. I do speak Arabic fluently though, and I have some intel experience with the detachment. I'm a Chief Boyle disciple. I've also done some interpreter and interrogation work at the detention facility. This tour was to get some experience in the intel shack supporting Teams on the ground before I moved back to train for DEVGRU Intel."

"Well, a Boyle disciple is always welcome here," Taylor aid. "Your experience with the Army will help. We're closely integrated with the Army and Marines here. We sure as hell can use another Terp, especially an American. You say you've done interrogation work?"

"Some in Bagram, but it was with Pashto speakers. I don't have a problem working in Arabic though. Arabic is my primary language."

"Okay, I'm starting to understand your boss's thinking," Commander Wallings said. I think we'll make use of your Arabic as an interpreter with the platoon training Iraqi scouts and get you started at the Army DIF. Are you ready for direct action Ops in the city?

"I'll be happy to start wherever you need me, sir," Lee said.

Chapter 21

The SEAL Platoons had a twofold task in Ramadi. One was supporting the Marines and Army in Ramadi. The other was training Iraqi Army scouts. The SEAL trainers welcomed Lee's Arabic language ability to assist them in training when he had the time. There were never enough interpreters go around. Direct action had first priority for interpreters, but training required more of them. Those training sessions added to his work load, but they also allowed him to get closer to the SEALs and Jundi scouts. (Jundi-Arabic for soldier)

Lee enjoyed the hours with the scouts and probably got more out of the training than they did. He had to interpret and explain every training evolution to the Jundi scouts and therefore, gained a solid knowledge of the training for himself. The SEALs focused on range shooting, close quarters battle in the kill house, urban combat training, and basic fire and maneuver drills.

They weren't training rocket scientists and the skills were learned quickly. After three training sessions in each evolution he got good at it himself and began helping with the training, especially the range training--except for the kill house close quarters work. He, like anyone new to kill house drills, needed a lot more work and practical experience. He was enjoying the experience—dehydration, heat exhaustion and all. At the end of the first three weeks, he was as dark as the Iraqis, he had lost five pounds, mostly fluids, and looked more like the Iraqis he was training than an American.

After three weeks of training with the Iraqi Scouts, Lee was invited to go to the range with two SEALs for one-on-one live fire training. SEALs never stopped training. The more you do it, the more instinctive it becomes. Everything was important, trigger pull, grip, position of the stock on your cheek, sight picture. Even in the middle of an intense campaign, they got range time in when they could.

Live fire weapons training is a lot like golf training on the driving range. You practiced the right stance, grip, swing, posture, follow-through over and over. You will never achieve perfection, but you work toward that instinctive pulling together of all the sub-skills to make the perfect swing or shot. The practice built both mental and muscle memory. He put his gear on and grabbed his weapon.

The gun truck was waiting. They drove over to Ramadi Base and out to the range. Even here, the risk of incoming was high, so the danger added a little reality to the exercises. You had to practice the exercises, but you had to maintain situational awareness also. The SEALs began training and testing Lee. They had Aimpoint red-dot sights on their weapons like Lee. No magnification and it offered a wide field of view. Lee liked it because he could get on target fast with both eyes open and still be aware of what was going on outside of the sight picture.

His SEAL trainers were preparing Lee for ops outside the wire. Both had lasers and lights on their rails and set Lee up with AN/PVS-15 Night vision and an AN/PEQ-15 ATPIAL Infrared laser/illuminator and adjusted the Aimpoint so he could use either one. The SEALs worked mostly at night, and the IR laser could only be seen through NODs. One side had an aiming laser and the other had an IR illuminator, like an infrared flashlight. It was great for lighting up a target at night without him even knowing he was lit up. It added weight to the muzzle end of the rifle, but training with it compensated for that change also.

They started on the known distance range working on trigger pull, position, and accuracy. The range wasn't much, just a stretch of desert with silhouette targets set at 100, 300, and 500 yards in the sand. Each of them burned though several mags of single shot, letting Lee get used to red dot shooting at different ranges, dot sizes, and intensity. Then they moved to a crude moving set-up for some run and gun. More silhouette targets and metal pop-up targets. All their targets were human figures. It got you in the mood.

One of the SEALs moved through the course first to show Lee the idea. Next Lee took a turn with a SEAL behind him timing his run and counting his hits. He wasn't allowed to stop or set up for a shot. He had to carry his weapon at the ready, using the Aimpoint to scan the target area ahead as he moved and take the target as soon as it came into view or popped up. It was a lot like practical shooting, but with a rifle.

They made the run over and over, burning through seven 30-round magazines each. By the time they were finished, Lee was worn out and ready to get back to base. The SEALs were pleased with his shooting and let him know. It was one of the few combat skills he had that allowed him to at least keep up with the SEALs.

Prior to his first patrol, Lee went through the process of mission planning with Wayne, getting area clearances, and setting up backup and QRF response. Two nights later, fourteen Charlie Platoon SEALs, eight Jundi Scouts, an EOD Tech, an Iraqi interpreter, and Lee crossed Camp Ramadi in three-gun trucks and a sandbagged flatbed for a patrol in the Ta'Meem district across Route Michigan from the Camp Ramadi gate.

The area was known for insurgent activity, but nothing like the areas on the eastern side of the city or downtown. Ta'meem was an insurgent favorite place for setting up mortar tubes to fire on Camp Ramadi. They left the vehicles at the edge of the city and entered on foot to reduce the odds of being seen before they reached the streets.

The Jundis had just finished the training and were being exposed to their first night patrol. Lee too. He was assigned to a column of four Jundis, seven Seals including LT Wayne, and the EOD Tech. A second column of Seven SEALs, four Jundis, and the interpreter would patrol opposite them on the streets. Wayne's column would patrol the left side of the street and the other column would patrol the right side, both columns covering the roof tops on the opposite side. The patrol was planned to cover a four-block square near the edge of the city, returning to the vehicles at the close of the square.

It was unusual to leave the vehicles behind, but this patrol didn't have a target to secure and Wayne felt moving fast and quiet was the safest way to get the inexperienced Jundis through the exercise without bringing down a hoard of insurgents on them. The vehicles would be short minutes away.

They went out light, just body armor, weapons, ammo, and water, but light is relative. Lee had on a two-and-a-half-pound Kevlar helmet with NODs, thirty-five pounds of body armor, a five-quart hydration pack, blow-out kit in his cargo pocket, reinforced knee-pads, a radio, four frag grenades, two stun grenades, nine loaded magazines, a Sig 9mm pistol with three magazines, his SOG knife, and his rifle with attachments. Going light still meant carrying over fifty pounds of gear in ninety-degree heat with his BDUs bloused and sleeves down and sealed and gloves on his hands.

Some of the SEALs liked the drop rig that had the pistol at mid-thigh, right where your hand hung, so he stuck with that. In Afghanistan, he learned the thing moved around too much there, but it looked cool as hell. It takes a while to get over being a new guy.

The night was cooler than the day, but not by much. It was in the low nineties rather than high nineties. By July, the temperature would be ten or more degrees hotter day and night.

LT Wayne stayed near Lee and coached him.

"This field used to be a city block. We'll be coming up on a massive pile of rubble soon where an old building was dozed. There's an old culvert nearby. We sometimes take fire from there. Pay attention to me. I'll be ordering the Jundis up to clear that area before we pass. Do your terp stuff."

"Do I move up with them?"

"You got it. Let's see how much you got out of the training."

The patrol moved quietly through the demolished block of what once had been Iraqi dwelling and business buildings on the edge of the city. Wayne halted them and spread the SEALs out to provide security. He sent Lee and the Jundis forward toward the rubble pile which was just visible as a dark shape in the night to the Jundis. Lee led them in a column half the distance and then squatted while the Jundis came up to him. He spoke in his shoulder mike and said, "Ready."

"Tell Sergeant Abbas to move forward and secure the area around the rubble hill. Let him run the show."

"Roger," Lee said.

In Arabic, "Sergeant Abbas, form your men and clear the rubble pile area. If it is clear, set security and bring the SEALs up."

Abbas looked around slowly from a squatting position for a few moments before answering.

"I think we should watch and listen for now," he said. "Why are the SEALs not here?"

"The Duke said Sergeant Abbas is a good leader. He should secure the rubble pile for us."

That put Abbas in a spot that didn't leave much wiggle room. His men were listening.

"He is correct," Abbas said. "We will observe for now and then we will secure the pile of bricks and concrete. It appears to have many places where a Jundi could hide."

The Jundis were happy enough with that decision and all stretched out on their stomachs to observe the rubble. Hell, Lee thought, when in Rome. He stretched out and watched the rubble pile too, except he had his NODs down and could see better than the Jundis. There wasn't any cover out there, just a few rocks on churned up dirt and a few scrub bushes. He had the ATPAIL mode switch set on illuminate so he scanned the ground around them and illuminated the rubble pile. It was about thirty feet high and Abbas was right, there were a lot of potential hides in that thing. It was a weird green view. He could make out a lot of detail, but no people or movement.

Five minutes later they were still observing and two of the Jundis began opening one of the power bars the SEALs had given them. Lee heard a double click from the radio.

"I think the Duke wants us to move up," he said.

"Insha Allah," Abbas said. If Allah wills it, or when Allah wills it, a response that seemed to cover a lot of sins. What it usually meant was, I don't think I want to do that right now.

Lee keyed his radio and said, "Insha Allah."

"Cover the rubble," Wayne said. "We're moving up."

"Cover the rubble pile," Lee said in Arabic. "The Duke is bringing the SEALs up."

The Jundis seemed happy enough with that too, especially Sergeant Abbas.

When Wayne got there, he didn't even mention the delay. He just assigned SEALs to the Jundis and then moved the patrol forward and cleared the rubble. When they were formed in column again, Wayne fell in with Lee.

"They don't have the best initiative in the world," he said. "Remember that. They are poorly paid and have lousy leadership and this is not their home.

They are Shia and as much outsiders as us in this Sunni town. Not much motivation to stick their necks out."

Chapter 22

When they reached the edge of the city, the effects of the war became more apparent. The outer buildings were just burned out shells and rubble. The streets were covered with trash and chunks of concrete and brick. Broken bottles and empty cans covered the street between the rubble and broken furniture. He was walking on a sea of trash. The IR laser made it all look eerie in his NODs. The darks were very dark and the lit areas were unnaturally light.

Even at night there was a fine mist of dust in the air that reflected the IR beam. There were a lot of squat, two-story dwellings and a few larger buildings. All the buildings were damaged in this sector. Everything was a tan color in daylight and just gray or black at night and shades of green in his NODs.

Navigating wasn't difficult because the streets were laid out in a grid. They moved down the first street in two columns close to the walls with seven SEALs and four Jundis in each column. Wayne, the interpreter, Lee, and the EOD Tech formed the command group in the left side column and both columns stayed in contact via their intra-team radios. The patrol moved quietly and quickly, leapfrogging from cover to cover and covering the roof tops over their sister column. LT Wayne didn't want any serious contact and they didn't have a target objective. His only goal was to build the Jundi Scout's confidence and not lose any of them on their first patrol.

An experienced SEAL was leading each column and always locating his next cover before he moved, teaching the Jundis by example. It was stop and go, but Lee and the Jundis were all winded before they got to the end of the first block. It was the short sprints that did you in, and probably the excitement also.

Lee was huffing short shallow breaths that come more from anxiety than effort. He was feeling that itch between his shoulders that felt like watching eyes, like when the QRF platoon had entered Lower Kamdesh. He kept telling himself it was just nerves then, and it was probably just nerves now.

His labored breathing introduced another unpleasant sensation. The city stank. Exerting yourself in clean mountain air was one thing but breathing Ramadi air was like breathing in a sewer. The city smelled of trash, sewage, decay, and death. The river scented the air unpleasantly to begin with, but open sewers, decaying animals, rotting trash, and probably, human bodies combined to form an exquisite olfactory torture.

Small piles of trash were everywhere and large piles of trash were on every corner. IR laser beams danced over the street looking for command detonator wires and examined each trash pile. More beams danced over every window and opening in every building and into every alley opening. The city's infrastructure, never very good to begin with, was destroyed and electricity was long gone. The streets were dark except for the dim light from the sky. It was enough to make the NODs effective.

Every pile of trash could hide an IED. IEDs were often cemented into the walls of buildings or buried in the roadway. Insurgent trigger men could be standing night watch to detonate an IED as the patrol passed by. Even here in the safer part of the district, the patrol wasn't just a moonlight walk. Each dark alley and each trash pile tightened Lee's nerves until he was hyper-alert and hyperventilating. The SEALs had done a good job of preparing him for this patrol, maybe too good of a job.

LT Wayne passed the few remaining undamaged buildings by. This wasn't a clearing operation and he wasn't interested in residences or over-watches. He wanted to expose Lee and the Jundis to nighttime urban ops and maybe poke the insurgents in the eye by patrolling the city streets under their noses.

Traveling at night was generally the safest time on foot. Americans had night vision devices and the insurgents didn't or didn't have many. The patrol moved to the end of the second block and turned left. That street looked the same as the first, but it had a few walled residences still occupied and some interior lights were on, supplied by private generators that buzzed in the background.

Lee had his NODs down and scanned the roof tops with IR. His laser illuminator didn't provide a lot of IR illumination at that distance, but it did catch edges and flat surfaces that made recognizable images in the NODs and gave some depth.

Midway down the first block he saw movement on a roof top, spoke in his mike, and gave the stop signal. Quickly the whole patrol moved against the walls and disappeared into cover.

"What?" Wayne said.

"Up there," Lee said. "Movement."

Wayne spoke into his mike and then watched the roof Lee pointed out. Soon Lee saw it again. Five lasers lit it up. A man stood at the edge of the flat roof and urinated over the low roof-wall into the alley. When he was done, he disappeared.

"Iraqis often sleep outside and on their roofs in the summer," Wayne said. "Probably some sleeping on the ground in the courtyard behind that wall too."

Wayne spoke into his mike again and the patrol resumed movement. They cleared the street for two blocks and turned left again. Another trash and rubble-filled street. Looking straight down the street Lee could see the glow of lights in the sky from Camp Ramadi's wall off in the distance. That sight produced a good feeling. They weren't far from help if they needed it.

Wayne held up the patrol and put them in cover while he took a radio message from base. Having gained line of sight back to Camp Ramadi, he could communicate with Shark base and the Army Com Center. He could hear them a lot better than they could hear him, but he had communications. He acknowledged the message and paused to look around.

"Trouble?" Lee asked.

"Shark base has been trying to reach us. An intel report came in from the DIF. The Muj are setting up something in this district for tonight. The Army is sending two Bradleys to pick us up near the water tower. Pay attention. We're going to be moving fast." (Muj – Mujahideen)

Lee felt the tension and excitement, almost anticipation, of a potential fight. He also felt a sense of strangeness in his excitement. If it happened, this fight wouldn't be like the firefights in Kamdesh. Everything was closer here. Fighting on this urban street would be like fighting in a tunnel.

They started down the street, back toward the edge of the city. There was enough light from the night sky to make the NODs effective, but the street was full of shadows. The scene he saw through his NODs was like a scene from Star Wars. IR lasers, green in his NODs, like death-rays from futuristic weapons danced over the street and buildings and probed into every opening and shadow.

Lee began seeing furtive movement along the roof-tops almost immediately. Wayne leapfrogged the columns down the street at a run, two men moving, one on each side of the street, the rest in cover. As soon as the called "set," the next two on opposite sides moved and leapfrogged the first pair and immediately looked for their next cover and scanned alleys, windows, and rooftops.

The radio contact from shark base had been timely. They were half way down the street when an incoming round hit the wall next to Wayne's head and chipped a piece of concrete into Lee's face. He heard the report of the AK rifle from above them immediately. That was the signal round for the ambush.

Suddenly, his NODs lit up with streaks of light from tracers and his ears were filled with the sound of small-arms from above.

Another AK opened-up on automatic from their rear and a third began firing fast single shots from in front of the patrol. As nice a little ambush as they could hope for. Fortunately, only a few insurgents were close enough to answer the call, but the call went out. Whistles could be heard coming from several directions. The patrol had stumbled into an insurgent operation launched for some other unknown reason, but the Muj were willing to adapt and tackle this unexpected opportunity.

Wayne immediately had the patrol begin maneuvering and firing. The SEALs knew what to do. Don't get pinned down, cover to cover, always locating your next cover before you ran. Two columns kept up an astonishing amount of firing while moving further down the street to set up to cover the next movement. All of them kept firing while they were moving. The Jundis remembered their training and fought like demons, but their fire discipline was lacking. Tracers were flying everywhere. Lee lost his fear while moving, firing, and watching the SEALs maneuver. They were magnificent. They operated like a machine and didn't even need to communicate. Not so much Lee and the Jundis.

"Igor! Pay attention! There's an alley opening on the left about two hundred feet. Do you see it?"

"Got it," Lee said.

"Cover that son of a bitch. If you see anything at all go cyclic on it."

"I'm on it."

The column leapfrogged again, and Lee kept his shouldered weapon pointed at the alley opening as he moved. The IR illuminated the opening as they got closer. Sure enough, he spotted movement. It probably didn't register in his conscious mind, but he was hyper-alert and caught the movement in the dim light. He didn't hesitate. He began patting the trigger and kept moving toward the alley entrance spraying bursts of 5.56 into the alley at an angle that sent ricocheting rounds screaming off the wall and back into the dark. The volume of tracers in the air began to degrade the view in his NODs.

The rest of the patrol was engaged and small arms hit around him as Lee moved forward. He was caught up in the fear and excitement. He emptied one magazine and took a knee near a large piece of rubble, dropped the magazine, and loaded a fresh one without taking his eyes off the alley. As he began emptying that magazine into the alley, Wayne and the EOD guy leapfrogged past him to take cover. Wayne and the EOD guy covered above and Lee blasted the alley entrance.

"You ready?" Wayne said. "We're going to take that alley."

Lee was so hyped-up he just said, "Go!"

They ran forward and slammed against the wall at the mouth of the alley. Wayne was first and stood against the wall with his M4 held up and down in front of his chest. Lee hit the wall next to him and the EOD guy stacked behind him.

Wayne took a deep breath and then nodded. He spun around the edge of the wall and moved sideways with his weapon on full automatic. Lee followed him and dropped his rifle level as he cleared the wall. He pulled the trigger—and nothing happened. His bolt was locked back. He had emptied another magazine and forgot the state of his weapon in the excitement. He grabbed for another magazine, but the firing had stopped. In front of him, his IR illuminated three bodies in the alley against the wall.

Wayne grabbed him and pulled him past the alley as the EOD guy joined them.

"What the fuck were you doing just standing there?"

"Sorry, I lost it for a moment."

"Keep moving or find cover. Lock and load."

Lee still had a full magazine in his hand. He dropped the empty and loaded the fresh one. This time he put the empty back in his pouch. The platoon was still moving and consolidating. All incoming had ceased. As the columns moved forward, Wayne held his group near the alley so the patrol could come together and consolidate their firepower.

"All set?" Wayne said.

"Ready."

"You are now a meat eater, Igor. Those Muj were down before I got there."

"Me? You sure?"

"Yeah I'm sure. Now pay attention. We're getting down to the water tower before they bring more help up."

Chapter 23

The Muj had other ideas. The first RPG came in before they could move, and an RPG volley started driving the patrol back up the street to a partially destroyed building that offered more cover. Rockets flew over their heads while they ran and some fell short. A squad of Muj carrying nothing but RPGs had managed to get ahead of the patrol on their retreat and drove them back into the city. These weren't local yokels. They were trained and disciplined soldiers practiced and drilled in their tactics.

    They came in a skirmish line and fired their rockets in volleys keeping the patrol under a constant barrage. Their haste was a blessing though. They were trying to get their rockets off so quickly none of them were sighting properly. RPGs are not very accurate launchers to begin with, and when fired with haste, are just shoot and pray weapons. Still, with that many rockets coming at the patrol, one of those prayers was going to get answered if they didn't start suppressing fire.

Lee rolled behind a large piece of wall that had fallen into the street and waited for a chance to return fire. The explosions kept coming. After one group of Muj rocketeers launched their rockets, they knelt and reloaded, and another group launched their rockets, volley after volley. They kept up the volley and pinned the patrol down in the rubble.

Had the insurgents coordinated their attack better it would have been over right then, but the patrol was close to help and their movement toward the edge of the city forced the enemy's hand. They committed their RPGs before enough supporting arms could get to the scene, and now the SEALs in the patrol got into action. They saturated the street with withering fire.

"Igor, the Terp is down. Get those Jundis in the fight. Have them cover the other end of the block."

The Jundis were hunkered down as deep in the rubble as they could get and weren't even trying to return fire.

"Get up. Get up," Lee yelled in Arabic. "Fight or you will die." Get up!"

Sergeant Abbas started to respond, but another RPG hit the building above him and showered the Jundis with dust and rubble. They tried to dig even deeper.

"Get up and fight!" Lee yelled. "We are leaving, and if you don't fight we will leave you here."

That was all Lee had time for. He had to get in the fight himself. Every gun counted. He didn't want to stick his head up any more than the Jundis did, but he had to do it. He raised up enough to see the street. There was scurrying about a hundred yards away. He fired two bursts in that direction and ducked back down. The SEALs kept the street under constant fire. A small-arms round hit the rubble near Lee. From behind him.

He rolled over and searched the street behind them. He saw muzzle flashes from a block away. He fired a burst in that direction and looked for better targets. He didn't have enough ammunition to waste it on suppression. He turned on his targeting laser. Sergeant Abbas crawled up next to him and began firing at the Muj moving in from that direction.

Soon, with Abbas's encouragement, the other Jundis came out of their holes and found firing positions. The volume of RPGs had petered out to just single uncoordinated rockets, but with the patrol pinned down, the Muj were taking their time and getting more accurate. With the Jundis covering the rear, Lee turned and looked for targets down the street toward the edge of the city. He laid the rifle on the edge chunk of wall providing him cover and sighted down the street. He used his Laser to search out every shadow looking for something to light up. Sweat stung his eyes, but he didn't dare wipe them.

A shadow figure stepped out of cover with a launcher on his shoulder. Lee put the laser on the center of the shadow and began popping single rounds at it. Two other lasers tracked in on the Muj. He saw one of his tracers smack dead center into the Muj, and then watched two other tracers hit him from a different direction. Two SEALs had the same target. The son of a bitch got his rocket off though and it hit the rubble in front of the patrol driving them down into cover. Seeing the sucker coming almost caused him to lose control of his bladder.

No one stayed in cover long. Lee raised back up and looked for another target. He left his rifle on single fire. He had already burnt through four magazines. Five left. Nine magazines had seemed like a lot when he set out that night, but right then, he wished he had a ruck full of them.

Suddenly, all the Jundis opened-up at once. Lee spun and laid across the rubble behind him, a little behind and next to Abbas. A dozen figures were moving toward them up the street, moving close to the walls and firing while they moved. Scurrying through alleys and back streets, the Muj were moving in. He moved his laser along the wall looking for a sure target and suddenly he heard a hollow smacking sound alongside him that sounded like a something hitting a ripe melon. Something wet splashed the side of his face. Sergeant Abbas dropped his rifle and his lifeless body slid down the rubble. The back of his head was missing.

Two of the Jundis started to move toward

Abbas's body, and Lee snarled at them. "Stay where you are! Fight! Keep shooting! He used his sleeve to wipe the gore from his face but only managed to smear it. His stomach started to heave. He swallowed hard and forced the gorge back down. He looked for a target.

Things were getting hairy. While the patrol was burning through their ammunition, the Muj were moving more attackers in. For every one the patrol put down, three more replaced him. They were under fire from two directions and from above. Wayne worked his way over to Lee

"Keep them in the fight, Igor. You're doing good."

"Hope you know some secret SEAL shit to get us out of here," Lee said. "I'm about to piss myself."

"Hang in there for a few more minutes. The cavalry is on the way."

Wayne turned and began taking measured shots down the street. He hadn't even noticed Abbas at the base of the rubble pile. Two new sounds occurred then. They started taking more fire from the roof tops, and the sound of diesels and tracks punched through the sound of battle. The first was bad news and the other was salvation.

Suddenly the tops of the buildings began disintegrating and a line of explosions walked up the street and into the Muj moving toward the patrol. Lee turned to see what was coming from the edge of town. First came an up-armored Humvee with its Mark 19 spewing death. Behind the lead hummer two Bradleys were firing their 25mm chain guns and clearing roof tops. Behind the Bradleys came another Humvee with a Ma-Deuce .50 chewing up every window and opening it could reach.

"Get the Jundis ready," Wayne said. "You load with them on the first Bradley. Assign two Jundis to take the Terp with you. He needs help."

"Abbas is dead,"

"Aww shit! Well, you know what to do.

The first gun truck drove by the patrol's position and continued firing its Mark 19. The first Bradley stopped and dropped his ramp while the rest of the convoy provided cover. Lee had the Jundis drag Abbas to the Bradley and he helped the Terp. It began lumbering forward as soon as they were aboard. The second Bradley picked up the SEALs and EOD guy. They turned to reverse their direction one at a time, coordinating to always have three vehicles providing covering fire. Three-sixty fire saturation. They were taking the street apart and not leaving any time or space for a Muj with an RPG to set up.

Finally, they moved back toward the edge of the city, firing continuously. Lee looked at his watch and blinked sweat out of his eyes. His BDUs were soaked and his hydration pack was empty. Abbas's dead eyes stared at the roof of the vehicle. His forehead puckered in and had a neat hole in the center. It had only been forty minutes since the start of the firefight. That seemed impossible.

Chapter 24

He was hardly given time to catch his breath. Traumatic experiences were as common in Ramadi as death, and compassion was as rare as mercy. There was no time to mourn or time outs to get over things. Lee cleaned up and hit the rack. Reaction and fatigue combined to drop him into a coma-like sleep. He was working SEAL Team hours now, and their pace was insane. Lee hit the rack at 0400 and was back up at 1000. Chief Taylor wanted him at the team house.

The battle had gained Lee a measure of respect and acceptance with the SEALs. In Ramadi, they were required to take Jundis on DA Ops for political reasons, so their ops weren't exclusively SEAL affairs anyway, and he had done well in their eyes. Lee had worked hard, listened well, and learned his lessons. Just as important, he didn't become a wannabe and knew his limitations. He had the makings of a warrior.

It doesn't take long to establish your rep with a SEAL Team, good or bad. Lee had functioned well under fire and hung in there with them. The TU commander and Chief Taylor were willing to see what else he had to offer the Task Unit. Lee had established himself as a reliable interpreter who could handle direct action, but what the TU really needed was actionable intelligence. Chief Taylor had his next assignment ready by the time Lee finished breakfast.

Lee didn't have time to deal with the previous night's trauma, so he pushed it back inside for another time. His first visit to the DIF at Camp Ramadi came that afternoon. He was used to the pace of the big detention facilities in Bagram where intel collection and targeting might take weeks. The demands were different here. The facility at Ramadi had seven interrogation rooms and the interrogators had an air of desperation about them. The conflict goes kinetic more often and to a larger extent in Iraq and time was limited for getting actionable intelligence. Interrogations were often the best hope for useful HUMINT. Several prisoners came through those forbidding doors every night.

The first thing he noticed was the stink. Human waste and dirt—and fear, something that seemed common to all DIFs. Chief Taylor got Lee an invite from Army intelligence to sit in on an interrogation to see how it was done in Iraq. When the DIF Army interrogator found out Lee was fluent in Baghdadi Arabic, he asked him to keep quiet and find out not only what the suspect was saying, but also what the Terps were saying. Distrust, or at least a lack of full trust in the local terps seemed to be a problem at the DIF.

Before they went in the interrogation room, the Army intel guy stopped Lee and told him to wait. He was gone for a few minutes and when he returned he handed Lee a large square piece of red checked cloth.

"You can keep that," he said. "We took it from a Jordanian detainee. A Keffiyeh is nice to have in the area. It can protect your face from dust and sunburn better than that camo dust scarf you have. The red checked one is Jordanian and might help to confuse the detainees about just who and what you are."

Lee wrapped the scarf around his neck, tucked it under his collar, and entered the room with the interrogator. He remained quiet and observed. He was still tired and strung out from night ops and welcomed the opportunity to let someone else do the work.

The Army interrogator worked through his terp even though he understood some Arabic. The problem for most American Arabic speakers, unless they were naturalized from Arabian countries, was the dialect they spoke. In school, you learn classic or formal Arabic. No one speaks that. Natives speak a dialect, and Arab dialects can be as distinct as different languages. Lee had the advantage of perfecting his dialects through full summers of immersion living with Arab families and studying in Arab universities coupled with the unique gift he possessed.

As he listened, he determined the terps were translating accurately and giving accurate translations back. He watched silently for a time. The detainee was a suspected insurgent and was belligerent. Lee listened closely for a while. He had caught what the Iraqi terps were missing right away. Still, he waited to see if the terps would give away why they hadn't caught it too. They were local and should have noticed as soon as the suspect opened his mouth.

Then Lee knew why. They were probably trustworthy, but they didn't take initiative. They only asked the questions the American's told them to ask, and they only translated back what the suspect said. They didn't add anything or skip anything. While giving a faithful and accurate translation, they failed to mention the most important piece of information about the suspect—because nobody asked.

Lee signaled the American interrogator and pointed at the door. They went out of the room and closed the door.

"He's not an Iraqi," Lee said.

"How do you know?"

"That's not Baghdadi. He's speaking in an Oman dialect. Bring your terp out and ask him."

When asked a direct question, the terp agreed quickly.

"No. He is not Iraqi. I thought you knew. You arrested him."

"Okay, thanks. Go back and just watch him."

The terp went back in and closed the door.

"Want to take a shot at it?"

"What did he do?" Lee asked.

"We think he builds IEDs. I want to know where his cache is."

"Yeah, I'd like a shot at it," Lee said and felt the burning in his gut. "Give me another room though. You have faux blood, don't you?"

"Sure. It's there with the supplies. That room is empty. Go ahead and get set up. I'll hood him and bring him over."

Faux blood was a mixture of fluids that resembled real blood and could be used to set the stage. Lee found the jar and took it into the interrogation room. He splattered the faux blood on the floor around the interrogation chair, just enough to be noticed.

He signaled he was ready. He was settling down. He had to control his anger, his desire for revenge. This wasn't the guy that destroyed his face. The best revenge with this one was breaking and turning him, using him as a weapon to destroy his friends. He watched the Army interrogator lead his hooded subject into the new room and then went in and shut the door.

He knew how to handle this interview from his experience at the detention facility in Bagram and decided to take a page out of the CIA's book. The Army interpreter took the hood off the insurgent. Lee took out a length of nylon cord he kept in one pocket and put it on the table. He asked the army interrogator for his lighter.

At this point, it didn't matter what the object was if it got the detainee wondering what was coming and what you might do with the object. The suspect watched him silently, stealing quick glances at the faux blood on the floor. He seemed especially interested in Lee's face. Lee turned so his scars could be seen easily and smiled. The suspects eyes opened wide. Lee's smile was not a comforting sight.

He took his SOG knife out and laid it next to the cord and lighter. Lee clicked the lighter and let the subject see the flame. He turned his back toward the detainee and pulled his Keffiyeh up over his ears. The Keffiyeh didn't matter. Any movement or activity that looked like it was part of the process got the detainee thinking about the process and helped to shake his confidence. Each movement was a subtle mental nudge that said, I am in control. I can do what I please. You are helpless. He began speaking in Oman dialect, fluently, quietly like to a brother.

"If you are strong, you will suffer. Some of us are strong. Some of us not as strong as others. It is not our fault. God made us just the way he chose. We can only live with what God gave us. We can only bear what God has given us the strength to bear. It is given to me to find out what your limit is."

Lee's Oman dialect got through to the suspect immediately and he began squirming. His hood was on the table. Lee took the hood and put it over the suspect's head. The guy had seen enough to worry him. Lee turned to the interrogator and put his finger to his lips. They watched the suspect silently for one full minute by Lee's watch.

"Why do you not ask questions?" The sound through the hood was muffled, but understandable. Lee went to the door and opened it and then closed it again and returned to watch the suspect.

"Who has come in?" There was a little fear in the voice now. "Did someone leave? Who is there?"

Fear and confusion. This was going more quickly than he expected. You can never tell though. Every detainee was different. Some were so deranged they couldn't be influenced at all, but you had to start soft to find their limits.

Lee took the knife from the table and scraped the top of the blade across the stone floor and then put it back on the table. Just random sounds to feed the Detainee's imagination. He was helpless and in the dark. Every sound was threatening.

"What was that? What are you doing? You are Americans. You cannot torture me."

Lee walked behind the suspect and with one hand on the suspect's forehead pulled his head back to expose his throat and ran his finger across the guy's neck from ear to ear.

"What are you doing?" The voice was panicked now. "Why do you not ask questions?"

Lee leaned down close to his ear and spoke

softly. "We already know what you are. You know nothing we want to hear."

He took the knife and pulled the flat of the blade across the guy's neck. The cold steel made his neck quiver. In the quiet, Lee's soft voice was evil. "You are in a very dangerous place. No one knows what I do here. No one can hear. How much does your god ask you to suffer? My God would not ask this much of me."

Suddenly Lee could smell urine. The guy had pissed himself.

"You cannot do this. You must ask your questions."

Crisis point. Sometimes, and for certain kinds of personalities, psychological pain is worse than physical pain. His imagination was torturing him, and it was reinforced with memories of what he himself had done to others and what he had witnessed being done to others. For one without a conscience, the imagination can be a cruel interrogator.

If Lee had chosen the right time, the interrogation would be productive. If he was too soon, he could botch the whole thing and delay or kill any cooperation. Sometimes it was quick and easy. Sometimes it took longer.

Lee pointed to the interrogator and raised his eyebrows.

"Highest priority is his base. Where is his cell? Where does he cache his supplies?"

That was part of technique also. Assume what you suspect. Don't ask him if he builds bombs. Assume it and proceed from there. Lee translated. With the memory of cold steel on his neck, the Muj answered quickly, but without much detail. It was all Lee expected, just a start, a hole in the dam to work at. The interrogator wrote down Lee's answer.

"I need a better location, land marks, a description."

Lee reinforced the fear and then became the good guy. He spoke soothingly and then became the bad guy again. Then he began asking for details. The insurgent, and he was one, slowly told his tale, sometimes encouraged and sometimes ridiculed, often with dissimulation, but multiple questions on the same topic, asked in different ways, sometimes as sudden changes in topic, revealed inconsistencies. Repetition, fatigue, fear, and a reinforced desire to please his inquisitor all worked to break down resistance.

As one fact built on another, Lee's narrative began to sound as though he knew the whole story anyway. The barrage of questions laced with Lee's narrative and reinforced with fatigue and fear increased the subject's confusion and left him unable to distinguish between what he had revealed and what Lee already knew. His resistance collapsed slowly, but it did collapse, one disclosure, one revelation, one fact at a time.

One facet of interrogation most people don't understand is, the process is emotionally charged and draining for the interrogator as well as for the subject. Although he had not lifted a hand against the subject and had hardly moved more than a step or two during the questioning, Lee was feeling the effects of serious fatigue. He felt drained and wanted the interrogation to end as much as the subject did.

"How is the place defended?" the Army interrogator asked.

Lee pulled himself together and asked the question. He marveled out loud at the insurgent's ingenuity, using ego to keep him talking. He used trick questions to go back over previously asked questions, ridiculing when he found flaws and praising when the information checked out. Finally, he wiped sweat from his face and sat down, unwilling to go any further.

"Damn, that's good intel," the Army interrogator said. "We need confirmations. Take his hood off. I need to get pictures to prove we didn't abuse him."

The prisoner was allowed to clean up, and after he was photographed with witnesses, he was returned to his cell. The Interrogator said they would have another session with him later that day using the transcript of Lee's interrogation to keep the intel coming. He was talking now and had given up something important. The flow would continue until he was empty.

"That was a bitch of an interview, Igor. These are some damn desperate people. Your method stuck to standard practice mostly. Why'd it work so well?"

"I gave him an out," Lee said. "You have to understand. This guy is Al-Qaeda. These people believe.

I mean really believe. The closest I can come to an example you might understand is snake handlers. Are you familiar with the Appalachian churches in America that handle rattlesnakes as part of their worship?"

"Yeah, sure. Crazy fuckers."

"Some would say they have an amazing faith. Well, these guys are probably even more convinced in their faith. They'll die for their belief. They came here to die, but, and this is the key, not in an interrogation facility. Interrogation is not battle. For the idea of martyrdom to work, it needs some glamour and drama and glory. That's step one. Take away the glamour. For the guy with visions of going down in a blaze of glory for Allah, sitting in a chair smelling his own piss is not a glamourous way to die."

"Yeah, I got that from the set-up. What's step two?"

"A CIA interrogator in Bagram took me to school one day after a botched interrogation. The best lesson he taught me was to give them an out with their God, every time. You see, they believe they must resist to the extent of their ability. In other words, bear all they can, but no more. Allah doesn't expect them to bear more. Reinforce that. You must give them enough threat or pain so they can give in without fear that Allah will punish them, every single one of them.

"It's a balance. If you give them more than they can handle, they believe Allah will punish you, and that may give them the courage to hold out more. If you don't give them enough, they can't give in or they will burn in hell for all eternity. They believe that. It's got to be a credible threat or actual pain. They have to believe they can't take anymore. I didn't figure a bomb maker would have a high tolerance for pain. It turns out he wasn't too good with threat either. Always find that out first. Always set up the threat, and always give them an out with their God."

The interrogator just shook his head. "I never thought something like that would work with these sons of bitches. Learn something new every day in this business. Look, you're welcome here any time you want to help out."

"Thanks. I plan to. I better get back. I think the SEALs will want a look at this. You going to pass it through channels?"

"Sure. If we're going to do a DA on this, it'll probably be the SEALs."

Chapter 25

The intel had already been passed to the intel cell at Shark Base by the time the Army got Lee back to the compound. A target folder was opened and Targeting and Intel were working on different source confirmations for the information. Planning was already underway for a DA (direct action raid) on the location provided by the insurgent. Lee ran to the TOC to find Chief Taylor. He was there talking to the Duke.

"Chief, I want to go on the DA." Lee said.

"Whoa, whoa, whoa," Duke said. "This isn't a training patrol. My boys won't take you on something like this. You'd be a danger to yourself and them too."

"I can do it. Come on, you're taking Jundis. What's the problem?"

"No!" Chief Taylor said. "End of fucking

discussion!"

Well, that didn't leave any wiggle room, and Taylor wasn't someone you argued with, so Lee backed off. Taylor, noting the disappointment, changed his tone. He was used to dealing with disappointed new guys and bringing them along until they were operators. Lee would never be an operator, but the principle was the same. Winners always wanted to play, and Taylor wanted winners.

"Igor, every man going out on this DA has done it a hundred times. You did a good job your first time out, but this is different, and you weren't sent here to be an operator. Find them for us. Find their Caches. Find their commanders. Find the bomb makers. Find their financiers. Find the holes those fuckers are hiding in. Find me a sniper cell I can take out, damn it. That's your war, and you can kill more of them with your intel than any SEAL in the platoon can with a rifle. We need actionable intel we can depend on."

It was interesting how a name he once hated had become a handle of inclusion. When the Chief switched from LT and Lieutenant to Igor, suddenly Lee felt included and part of the team. A term of endearment, for crap's sake. Even the SEALs used it to treat him the same way they treated any new guy SEAL. It took the desire to argue right out of him. He was part of the team, and they were depending on him to do his part.

Over the next three days the address was viewed from a

UAV, and a separate interrogation added credence to the information developed in Lee's interrogation. One of the Iraqi interpreters provided another confirmation from a locally developed source. Electronic intercepts were combed to find cell phone and radio traffic that mentioned the site. By the afternoon of the third day, the Intel and Targeting people were satisfied they had a valid target and the TU had the capability to take it down. The TU commander briefed the Army, and they gave the necessary clearance for the DA.

The DA went off without a hitch and the DA team, ten SEALs and a dozen Iraqi scouts with an interpreter and an EOD tech, took the door and found a cache of explosives including American 155mm rounds, plastic explosives, tools and bomb components including radio and wire-controlled detonators, RPG rounds, and sixteen AKMs (modern version of the AK47) in the basement. They also found another prize, a Russian Dragunov sniper rifle with a 32X scope. That one gave them all chills. They didn't find any insurgents on this one, but that just meant no one was shooting at them. The value of Lee's stock went way up with the team.

His interrogation duties weren't relaxed and his intel duties at Shark Base were increased. His work days often spanned 20 hours. He was getting a rep in the TU and in other less desirable places too.

One day in July, the intel cell OIC stopped Chief Taylor to talk.

"Chief, I think Igor is becoming known to the opposition. Word has gotten out of the DIF about a devil interrogator with a burned face who puts people in a spell and gets the truth out of them in ways they can't resist. That's somebody covering his ass, but the same tale was repeated by others. Just wanted you to know. He'd be hard to miss if any of them saw him."

"Thanks. He's not going any place they can get to him, but we'll take extra precautions.

The Humvees had armored doors, impact resistant glass, run flat tires, and armor reinforced under-carriages that gave the occupants a chance with all but the largest explosives. As time went on and Lee's services grew in demand, he was only allowed outside the compound in a gun truck or one of the better armored vehicles. Chief Taylor knew something Lee didn't know. The insurgents had their own name for him. For Lee, at least in this case, ignorance was bliss.

The area of al-Anbar Province they were in was called the Sunni Triangle and was bordered by Baghdad, Ramadi, and Baqubah. It was the wild, wild west, especially around Ramadi. All the insurgents and local radicals were bad-ass and armed to the teeth. When Saddam was defeated, dozens of well stocked armories had fallen into the hands of loyal Baathists and local radicals and ended up arming insurgents. When Fallujah was cleared of insurgents in 2004, the baddest of the bad just move down the road to Ramadi.

Even with his command of Baghdadi Arabic,

something no other American serving the TU had, Lee wasn't even allowed to go on the day-time patrols and raids into the safer areas close to the base. The one thing you could depend on if you went out was, you were going to run into trouble, every single time. There were no low or non-kinetic patrols or DAs.

Lee spent his time with the intel cell and at the DIF, but he still harbored a desire to get out on patrol. Just a DA occasionally is all he wanted. He had a taste of it and wanted more. He had never felt so alive as when he was in the middle of a firefight. Adrenalin produced a high he liked. Then there was the opportunity for revenge. He still had the desire. Just one more bomb maker, that's all he wanted, one son of a bitch that made bombs—in a free-fire zone, with a unit whose job was to take them out, not just talk to them.

He was welcome at the DIF, so much so, they began calling him out during the night to do the initial interviews when suspects were brought in. He was good at it and knew the culture. He'd get a call, and whoever was available at the compound would roll a gun truck through the wall and over the short ride to Ramadi Base DIF. His initial interviews were especially valuable to the Army, because he cleared several innocent Iraqis that just got caught up in a bad situation. Those cases made him feel good, but he still wanted another shot at an insurgent. He was the only non-qual IA in the unit with confirmed kills and he wanted more.

Lee had been working with the Army interrogators for a

month and knew all of them by then. He must have assisted in a hundred interrogations, sometimes four in a single night. Some nights it was like being an emergency room doctor during a disaster. The patients just kept coming in. He was called out to the DIF at 0200 one night early in July, his second month at Shark Base, to assist with a particularly difficult and dangerous prisoner. He strapped on his gear and checked his weapon, once again hoping for a firefight, but the short trip, as usual, was peaceful. The interrogation turned out to be short, strange, and troubling.

Inside, he was briefed by the Army Interrogator. The suspect they had might be a big-wig in the insurgent hierarchy. Fearing for their lives and families, the Iraqi interpreters refused to enter the room unless they had hoods over their heads. That was the first hint the guy was more than your average insurgent. The Army didn't want to boost the guy's ego by interrogating him with Terps who were afraid to reveal their identities in his presence, so they called Lee.

Lee was becoming known for innovations in his methods, so his first request didn't surprise anyone at the DIF.

"Before I go in, do you have anything I can cover myself with so no uniform shows?" Lee asked.

"I've got a whole box of robes and stuff we've taken from insurgents. You're welcome to look through it."

Lee went through the box and found a black cotton, full length robe with a hood. Perfect he thought.

He donned the robe and went back to the interrogation room.

"Okay, let's get a look at this guy."

"You look like Darth Vader's boss in that get-up," The interrogator said. "Pull the hood over and cover the good side of your face."

Lee did as he was requested. The guy hadn't even hesitated in making that kind of request—the good side of your face. But Lee knew them all and just smiled to himself. It was just another sign of inclusion. His face no longer bothered them, so they assumed it no longer bothered him. He was just Igor, and the face went with the handle.

"Damn! You look absolutely evil. Dude, you ought to keep this set-up."

They entered the room and Lee looked at the guy strapped in the chair. He was about six feet tall, hard to tell with them sitting down, but he was big. He had a swarthy complexion with pock marks on his face and a three-day beard shadow. He had a fat roll over his belt, and he was dressed in a dirty suit and shirt with no tie. He watched Lee for a few moments and then smiled.

"I know who you are," he said. "Ad-Dajjal," and then he laughed.

His dialect was a mixture of Baghdadi and Coastal Emirates, very guttural. Lee just stared at him with half of his face hidden. Silence was often his best tool. He wasn't sure if he was being taunted or insulted. Ad-Dajjal is the Deceiver, the Islamic version of the Anti-

Christ. In the Hadith, he is said to have an ugly, deformed face with one eye budging like a grape and the word "Kafir" between his eyes. The guy couldn't take the silence and spoke again.

"Some of us thought you were a myth."

That was a bit unsettling. Some of us? They know me, Lee thought.

"I am real and here," Lee said. "Ad-Dajjal may take your soul and probably will, but you are my guest right now." He spoke in a Jordanian dialect to keep it confusing and spoke softly. "What is your name?"

The insurgent slob regarded Lee for a few moments.

"Some have said you are from Oman," he said. "I think not. You will know my name soon enough, apostate. You should ask what I know about you."

Apostate? The prisoner thought Lee was a Muslim who had abandoned Islam. That was interesting, but this interview was getting away from him. The subject was taking control, but at least the guy was talking. Lee decided to play along to keep it going, but he was losing confidence in his ability to handle this interrogation.

"And what is that?" he asked.

"There is a reward for your head. Five thousand American dollars. How does that make you feel, ad-Dajjal? Someone will always be watching for you, apostate. Much money and much honor."

The shock was difficult to cover, but Lee had lots of practice covering his emotions, and his scars hid most reactions. He wanted to ask how he could be known and what was so important about him to justify a bounty on his head, but he had to regain control of the interrogation. He had to turn the shock back on the subject. So, he smiled, knowing its effect.

"It is a pleasing thing you tell me," he said. "So few come here to this chair. I sometimes get lonely and bored. Perhaps your reward will tempt more to come and make my acquaintance. I look forward to my conversations with your Jundis. How long have you been away from the Emirates?" Lee hid two little tricks in that speech, "your Jundis" and "from the Emirates." If he could be goaded into an acknowledgement, one would confirm he was a commander, and the other would confirm his origin.

He was good. He didn't react in any way. This one was a tougher nut than Lee could handle with his limited experience. The guy had taken control away from him. This guy was more than a simple Muj and needed to be moved to a higher level facility where experts could take over. Lee pointed to the door and stepped outside with the Army interrogator.

"You need to refer him up to Baghdad. This guy is an insurgent and he's probably a commander. We don't want to screw this up, and you probably don't want him in the cell block with the other prisoners. Keep him isolated until he's moved."

"I'll handle it. What did he call you? I caught a little of it, but my Arabic isn't good enough to follow as quick as you guys were talking."

"Ad-Dajjal. Sort of an Islamic boogeyman."

"He said something about a bounty. On you?"

"Yeah. That surprised me."

"Well, you're getting a rep. We turned loose as many of your subjects as we kept. It had to get out, and you're not exactly a forgettable figure. Don't let it worry you."

"Fat chance. Sorry I couldn't do more for you on this one, but I think the experts better handle this. I better get back and get my report filed."

Chapter 26

An operation had begun in early June before Lee got there to clear Ramadi of insurgents and take the city back for the Iraqis. In Ramadi, Iraqis meant the Sunni Anbari tribes led by Sheikhs who resembled Mafia Dons more than Arabian Knights. There were twenty-one of them in the city and surrounding areas. They didn't like the insurgents, but they liked the Americans and the Shia Iraqi Army even less. They could be an important part of the strategy to take the city back if they could be won to the American side, but like the opportunists they were, they waited to see which side would come out on top. Standing up to the insurgents was a short path to the grave unless you were sure of your position.

The U.S. military strategy for taking the city back was to move in from the outskirts of the city and begin setting up combat outposts (COPs) as strong points and launching raids and clearing operations from them. This was urban warfare in its essence and designed to avoid the massive destruction that occurred when the U.S. cleared Fallujah with armor, bombs and artillery.

As each COP got control of its immediate area, the Army and Marines would move deeper into the city and set up a new COP and repeat the process. This was a difficult process because not only did they have to move out to subdue a new area, but they had to maintain control of the area just pacified and keep it from being reoccupied by the insurgents.

The SEALs were working with the Army and Marines providing sniper over-watch, busting doors, and pulling DAs based on intel developed by the TU intel and targeting cells. The city was out of control, and the pace of operations was crazy.

There was no police or government presence in Ramadi. The insurgents controlled most of it, and al-Qaeda in Iraq controlled most of the insurgents. Ramadi insurgents were a different breed than those in Afghanistan, more violent, better trained, better armed, and seemingly more determined. They came here to die in Jihad as martyrs. Many were foreign Jihadists and true believers come to claim their place in paradise, but they recruited large numbers of locals from the tribes. In many places in the city, the insurgency was the only source of income.

When Lee arrived, the COP building strategy

had just begun. American and Iraqi forces had a presence at places on the fringes of the city, but even there the attacks were relentless and unpredictable. Lee developed dark smudges under his eyes from little sleep and a lot of work. In that regard he looked like everyone else in the Task Unit. The SEALs worked harder than anyone.

The only break Lee got from Shark Base compound was when he was called out to assist at Camp Ramadi. Even with the work load, he got a little stir crazy being stuck inside the compound and mostly indoors. A mortar could drop into the compound at any time. The uncertainty kept him indoors when he wanted to get out and just walk around to get some exercise. He was young and in the best shape of his life and push-ups in the tent just didn't cut it. He grabbed every chance he got to work with weights in the veranda gym and work out with the SEALs when they ran or worked one of their insane circuit training routines.

In early August, an incident happened that temporarily quieted his desire to get outside with the SEALs. A SEAL was killed in action and one was wounded severely, costing him his eyesight. The entire TU was in shock. SEALs came in from the entire Anbar Province to pay their respects at a memorial service held at Shark Base.

SEAL Teams are a tight group of warriors, true brother warriors. The grief in the TU was palpable, but the work went on. The SEALs accepted their grief, paid their respects, and went back to work. Shark Base was renamed Camp Mark Lee in their brother's honor.

As the heat of August built up, the action in Ramadi was heating up with it. Local Iraqi Sunnis were becoming disillusioned with the oppression and murderous tactics of the insurgents. Their lives and families were in constant danger and the insurgents often didn't distinguish between local Muslims and the Iraqi government or seem to care. So many versions of Islam were being mixed in the insurgency, internal conflicts were bound to arise.

It seemed the different sects of Islam often hated each other more than they hated the Great Satan, America. A true religion of peace. They couldn't even get along with each other. A difference of opinion about who should have been the Prophet's successor created a violent rift between Shia and Sunni that lasts to this day. Sufi and Salafi schools of Islam are considered little more than infidels by Sunni and Shia alike.

Lee ignored the threat of incoming and worked-out in the compound to keep improving his conditioning and better acclimate to the heat, and sometimes just to get the hell out of the building. There were always two or three SEALs around the compound and sometimes a few trusted Iraqi terps. His legs were still strong from his mountain time and he didn't want to lose that strength. He began jogging around the interior of the compound and down past the guard tower and the

Ranger compound with his ruck weighing in at eighty pounds to work his legs.

SEALs, being SEALs, couldn't let that pass. They had to turn it into a contest. Soon, one of the SEALs joined him with an equal pack and egged Lee on to see who could go the longest. The SEAL did, of course, but Lee wasn't far enough behind to feel any shame.

This went on every day for a week with the SEALs taking turns and adding more and more calisthenics before the weight carrying competition. They tried to burn him out before he strapped on the eighty-pound pack, but being fair, they pushed out the push-ups along with him. He couldn't beat them, but he made them work for the victory.

Word of the challenge worked its way through the platoon. No matter which of the SEALs was in the compound on any day, he found Lee and challenged him to a race. The SEALs needed the workout anyway, and Lee made it more interesting than just pumping weights on the veranda. After two weeks of that training, one of the SEALs decided a little variety was in order and challenged Lee to a race with terps on their shoulders. The terps loved it. Even Taylor and the Duke came outside to watch.

Taylor put one terp at two corners out near the guard tower where the competitors would turn to complete a square of about two hundred yards. He then picked the two lightest terps and assigned one each to Lee and the SEAL. The rest of the terps served as the cheering section. Lee figured the loads were about equal and about 130 pounds each. He squatted down and his Jundi climbed on. Oh God, he was heavy. Thank God for all the squats he had been doing.

He began to push up and had to put his hands on his thighs to get leverage to straighten his back. The SEAL struggled too. When they were both upright and the terps were cheering, Taylor, hardly able to talk for laughing, yelled Go! Lee stepped out. He was already covered in sweat. One step, then another. He got a pace going and just focused on holding on to the terp's legs to keep him still and putting one foot in front of the other.

They made it around the square once and Lee wanted to quit. He was so hot he was getting dizzy. His shoulders were aching and his face was beet red, but he kept going. The SEAL was in front of him, not far, but Lee could see his back. His neck was as red as Lee's face. On they went and completed another lap around the compound.

By now, sweat was running down Lee's face and his heart was pounding. The sweat wouldn't last long. He was close to heat exhaustion, but he wasn't going to quit. The Seal was struggling too. Lee forced himself to pick up the pace. He caught the SEAL and took a step to get ahead, but the SEAL just dug deeper and increased his pace until he was in front again. Second place is the first loser. Lee cursed himself for his stupidity. Now he had to keep up a faster pace. He wanted to throw-up.

On the next lap, Taylor and the Duke added a touch to increase the challenge. They each threw a handful of dust onto the competitor's heads so that it covered their faces, got in their eyes and noses and on their lips. That was almost too much for Lee, but he spat and blinked and blew snot from his nose and kept on going. The SEAL didn't even seem to notice. He'd suffered far worse during hell week at BUD/S.

As they made the turn to the finish on their fourth lap, Taylor stepped in front of them and stopped them.

"Okay, enough," he said. "You guys are going to get heat stroke. I declare a draw. You got a problem with that, Baker?"

They bent over and dumped their loads, then remained bent over catching their breath.

"Hell no," the SEAL said, huffing air like a winded horse. "Good job, Igor . . . Keep up the good work . . . and I might even let you clean my weapon."

"Up yours," Lee said. "You damn near killed me."

The terps landed on their feet and ran over to their buddies laughing and joking about their "horses." Lee's thighs immediately cramped forcing him to sit down and try to rub out the Charlie-horse forming in his left leg.

"You're okay, Igor," Baker said and slapped Lee on the back. He could still walk, but he was struggling too. They were fitness nuts, but the pace of operations hadn't given any of them much time for conditioning in the past two months. What they did have was an unbeatable determination to win. The only way that

211

SEAL would have stopped is if he passed out. Those three words, you're okay, Igor, gave Lee a better feeling than getting a medal.

He was sore and exhausted, but the workouts and friendly competition of the past two weeks had busted up the routine, and he tackled the intel incoming that evening with renewed energy and interest. The Chief had more variety to perk him up though. Taylor was a good and experienced leader and knew the signs of burn-out and knew how to treat it. Lee had been doing one thing too long and too hard. It was time for some variety in his life, variety that would add value to the TU's mission.

Chapter 27

The next morning, Chief Taylor told Lee to pack. He was being moved to COP Corregidor to enhance the Corregidor SEAL detachment's support package by providing them an on-site intel cell.

Corregidor was an Army COP on the eastern fringe of the city and right smack in the center of the hottest insurgent activity happening outside of center-city. It was located on Route Michigan, the MSR for Anbar. Ramadi SEAL TU's Delta Platoon supported the Army's First Battalion, 506th Infantry regiment in an AO that included Mu'laab, Sufia, and Julaybah districts. (MSR-Main Supply Route)

Corregidor SEALs provided sniper over-watch for the army patrols in the AO and conducted DA operations of their own. The COP had made some progress in its local Mu'laab area but the COP itself still came under attack daily. Army patrols were expanding their outreach and pushing into the Sufia and Julaybah districts. The AO was hot and was expected to remain that way for quite some time.

Lee was taken by gun truck over to Camp Ramadi to meet up with an Army convoy taking supplies to Corregidor. Two SEAL gun trucks joined the convoy. Lee's truck had a MK19 in the turret and the other had a Ma Deuce .50 caliber heavy barrel machine gun. Three Bradley fighting vehicles were spaced along the line, each sporting 25mm chain guns with coaxial 7.62mm machine guns. The lead vehicle was a buffalo, a big, heavily armored IED buster with a hydraulic arm for handling the things. Four Cougars rigged for cargo were also in the line. These were lightly armed, but heavily armored trucks.

This was a daytime convoy and the commander was glad to have the SEAL Humvees with him. He expected trouble and welcomed all the firepower he could get. They left the main gate at 1000. Unless a vehicle was disabled, the convoy would keep moving, even under attack.

Road names didn't mean much by this point in the Ramadi Battle. There weren't any dependable street signs and the Anbari tribes, insurgents, and Americans each had their own names for the main roads in the city. They crossed Camp Ramadi on the southeast line road to the main gate to pick up the Route Michigan dog leg that would take them back northeast over the

Habbaniyah Canal to Hurricane point and then east to Camp Corregidor on the portion of Route Michigan SEALs called the shooting gallery.

Lee squinted as he viewed the destruction on the way along Route Michigan. It was hard to find a building that wasn't damaged. Some were just rubble piles. Others were rubble piles at the base of one wall still standing. A few were still standing, intact and occupied, but their walls were pock-marked from incoming rounds.

Darwin's evolutionary selection was in high gear in this city. Only the toughest and smartest survived, and that wasn't a good thing for the coalition. After months of conflict, the insurgents remaining in the city were tough, battle-hardened, crazies. There were no easy targets left. The SEALs had a saying that covered it. The only easy day was yesterday.

Suddenly, the convoy speeded up.

"Third vehicle took a round of small arms," the driver said. "Come on assholes, keep it moving. This isn't the time for sightseeing."

A gunner in one of the Bradleys fired a burst with his chain gun, but the convoy kept moving.

The convoy finally took two turns at Hurricane Point on Route Michigan, one to the east and one for the worse. The roadway was littered with rubble and trash, and literally glinted with spent shell casings. Potholes were everywhere, some filled with trash and sewage, and some, very possibly, hiding an IED.

The gun truck with its heavy armor was

relatively safe, but Lee slid down to keep as much of his body and head below the window as possible. Small arms weren't a problem, but he worried something bigger, big enough to puncture the windows, would come at them. Then there were the IEDs. Humvees like the one he was riding in had been blown into the air or rolled completely over by some of the more powerful bombs. Before long, the thought of RPGs elevated his stress to the banjo string level.

The environment remained quiet as the convoy made the turn east. The big Buffalo truck out front was going slow and checking out each trash pile, each pothole, each suspicious looking place on the road surface. So far, they weren't finding anything, and the convoy stretched out, increasing the space between vehicles, each gun turret covering sectors of the rooftops and alley openings.

This was a bleak part of the city, even worse than the bombed-out area along Baseline Road. No one was on the street or visible in the buildings and that wasn't a good sign. Lee watched and waited. The SEALs were hyper-alert and silent. The gunner in the turret was in constant motion. And then it happened at the Sunset Road intersection just before they reached the government center Marine compound.

"God damn!" the driver yelled and swerved to the right. The front end of the Cougar with a trailer two positions in front of their gun truck lifted in the air and disappeared in smoke and a flash of light. Lee felt the force of the explosion inside the SEAL gun truck. The entire convoy immediately lit up with three-sixty outgoing. Alternating vehicles immediately angled left and right with vehicles at the rear covering the six. With that initial blast of outgoing, if an ambush was planned following the explosion, the ambushers were heading for the deepest hole they could find.

The initial defensive burst only lasted a few seconds, but a little less of the surrounding buildings were still standing. The MK19s and chain-guns do an amazing amount of damage when they go cyclic.

The smoke cleared ahead and the Cougar became visible again. It was the smaller four-wheel model and was upright and back on four, run flat, wheels. The tough truck had an armored V bottom that directed the force of the blast out away from the interior. Black smoke puffed out from the exhaust that ran along the top of the vehicle. The front of the Cougar was scorched and black, but the tough truck was ready to go again. Lee wondered how ready the guys inside were. What they just went through had to be like going over the falls in a barrel and hitting a rock.

The radio command to form the convoy came and they moved east once more. Lee held his hands up. They weren't shaking. Shit was getting routine. He had worked with all the Camp Lee Charlie Platoon SEALs either in training with the scouts or developing intel for mission planning. He was getting a rep as a go-to guy who was always willing. Therefore, the SEALs did everything they could to develop his kinetic skills. He felt close to them and part of the team.

"You okay up there, Chuck?" he called up to the gunner in the turret.

"Just peachy," Chuck said. "Can you operate a nineteen?"

"Qualified on one in training. Never used one in the real world."

"Want to sit up here for a while? We'll be at Corregidor, soon."

"Hell, yeah!" Lee said.

"Put your goggles on and wrap you mouth with your scarf. The dust is a bitch up here."

It wasn't much but having a SEAL trust him in the turret with the big gun meant a lot. He didn't get to use it, but he got to ride into Camp Corregidor and pull up in front of the Team House in the turret. That would be a good introduction to his new team.

He looked around the compound from the turret. A dust devil swirled a funnel of Iraqi grit across an open space where Abrams tanks, gun truck, buffalos, Cougars, Bradleys, and flatbed trucks with turrets were parked. The camp was packed and busy. The resident Ramadi stink was infused with diesel fumes. An involuntary sigh escaped his mouth. New place. Same war.

Chapter 28

The SEALs were quartered on the third floor of a gutted brick and concrete building at the front of the COP near Route Michigan with some motor pool people, EOD folks, and a specialized Marine unit. The SEAL floor had been partitioned off with scrap lumber and sandbags to form cubicles for sleeping and gear stowage. The few windows in the building were closed off with double rows of sandbags. Lee was assigned an empty sleeping cube to dump his gear in. Camp Lee had been the height of civilization compared to this place.

Corregidor was home to the Army's 1/506. The compound wall was about a hundred yards from the city. The defenses consisted of a wall topped with concertina, a zigzag entrance lane formed with concrete barriers, a gate with a five-ton truck parked across the entrance, and the hundred-yard clear field of fire between the COP and the city. All that was a decent defense against an attack by troops but didn't do anything against indirect fire. The camp took mortar incoming daily.

The COP was located just south of the Sufia district and north of the Mala'ab and Zeraa agricultural districts all of which were hotly contested areas with the insurgents in control. The great thing about Corregidor for the SEALs was the commute. When they left the gate, they were at work. There was more than enough work close to the COP, but the Army was pushing into the Mala'ab and had plans to push into Sufia. Where the Army wanted to cordon and search, the SEALs went first to set up sniper over-watch for Army patrols.

LTJG Dan Parsons got Lee set up with a cubicle and took him to the TOC to introduce him around.

"Are you okay with Igor, Toliver? You're getting an intel rep and that's how our Army partners know you."

"Sure," Lee said. "I wasn't happy with the handle you fuckers gave me, but hell, I wouldn't know who you were talking to if you used my real name now."

Parsons slapped Lee on the back. "And it is so you. You're a brother now, Igor. If you weren't, my boys would call you Mr. Toliver . . . or maybe, hey you."

That made Lee laugh. Parsons was right. Early in Lee's tour a SEAL had actually yelled at him, "Hey you, new guy, move your ass out of the way."

"Let's stop at the TOC," Parsons said. "You have a few fans there."

"Do they really know who I am? That's kind of scary."

"They know about Igor. You're not famous, but your work is. Enjoy your fifteen minutes of fame. Tomorrow you start working with the platoon."

"Interrogation?"

"Won't know until we get there. Pat yourself on the back. We're going to take a door that one of your interviews identified. We've had a target folder on it for three weeks and it's starting to look good."

"So, you're bringing a detainee back here and want me to interrogate him?"

"Nope. You're going with us. Ever stacked on a door?"

"Once, in Afghanistan."

"Good. Tomorrow night you can put another notch on your door buster badge. The Duke says you're ready. We'll do some drills in the afternoon with the scouts."

"Outstanding," Lee said.

"That's what I wanted to hear. Come on, they're waiting for us at the TOC.

The TOC watch standers were glad to meet Lee. It was obvious that Parsons had a close working relationship with the Army troops. Lee saw a lot of respect there, both ways. Their IT network specialist got him on the camp secure WIFI and added his Laptop to the network management log. When they left the TOC, Parsons took him to the S2 and S3. They knew who Igor was also. The intel people set him up for access to the intel files and made a point of getting him on their schedule while he was there. They wanted to discuss interrogation techniques and intelligence data modeling.

When he and Parsons left S3, Lee was a bit overwhelmed. He had been isolated at Camp Lee for so long everything outside was new and exciting, and yet, he wasn't new to the troops outside.

"I've been in the Middle East for not quite six months. I've only been here eleven weeks. For most of eleven weeks I've been stuck at Camp Lee and the DIF. I'm amazed that anyone outside of Camp Lee even knows who I am."

"When you do good work, word gets around, Parsons said. "Don't let it go to your head. They know some mythical creature called Igor who casts magic spells and gets insurgents to spill their guts. They only see these great summaries. That's who they think Igor is. They don't see all the interrogations that came up with nothing or the hours of intel research that produced nothing. Which would you say is the majority of your work?"

"The latter, of course. The Eureka moments are few and far between."

"To you, but the hits are the only summaries that get distributed, and you've had your share. Enjoy it. They're good guys, and you and them will learn something from each other if you pay attention."

Corregidor was never quiet. Multiple diesel engines maintained a constant roar and the camp was awake twenty-four hours a day. Something noisy was always happening. Along with the noise came the dust. Lee kept his Keffiyeh covering his nose and mouth all day and his goggles on as much as possible and still had to wash his eyes out several times.

Late that night a mortar hit in the armor parking lot and a few rounds of small arms pinged off the SEAL building. The guys on duty on the roof returned fire. Off in the distance a firefight was in progress. Sometime during the night an IED exploded off in the distance. He woke up briefly, but fatigue helped him to submerge the sounds of war and he managed to get back to sleep.

Lee's alarm clock the next morning was two incoming RPGs and an automatic weapon spraying the wall and the SEAL building. Response from the camp was immediate and loud, but only lasted for a few minutes. He remained prone and let his mind clear before getting up.

The camp had secure WIFI, so the first thing he did was download the morning intel summary from the intel cell at Camp Lee to see if anything had come in that might be of interest to Delta Platoon or the planned op that night. Next, he opened his folders. Nothing had been added.

After S-cubed, he got some chow at the Army

mess hall, then picked up his laptop and went to the TOC. Parsons was there with his Chief completing the planning and clearances for the coming night op.

"Chief, meet the infamous Igor. Igor, Chief Good. Why don't you do a final intel check and make sure we have the latest."

"Good to meet you, Chief," Lee said. "I'm ahead of you. I downloaded this morning's summary earlier. Nothing new from targeting. I'll check again when the evening summary is ready."

"Good. Chief, why don't you introduce Igor to the terps and the team. I'll finish up with the clearances. I still haven't got air cover lined up."

"Come on, Igor. I'll take you across the street to meet the Iraqi scouts going out with you tonight. The terps and the team won't be up until around noon."

Before they left the camp, Chief Good took Lee back to his quarters and checked out his equipment. He made one change to Lee's load out.

"Add a grenade pouch," he said. "Since you're working security with the Jundis, take the M68 impact frags with you."

The M68 is an M67 frag grenade with the M217 impact fuse. It has a safety clip, pull ring and spoon. Once the ring is pulled and the spoon released, it arms in one to two seconds and explodes on impact. It weighs almost a pound and has 6.5 ounces of Composition B explosive in it, a powerful and handy little bomb, but once armed, you don't want to drop it. Lee made a note and they moved on.

They had to leave the camp and cross Route Michigan to visit the scouts. They had their own compound on the other side. The Iraqi Army compound was a little better than the compounds occupied by the ANA in Afghanistan. The Iraqis seemed to take a little more pride in their unit and living quarters, and their leadership was better and demanded more of them, but their standards were still low. The officers lived good, but the enlisted made do with what they could get.

Lee's excellent Baghdadi dialect made him welcome quickly. His head was covered with his red checked Keffiyeh in the Arabian tribal way with a rope ring holding it on. Americans who could speak their brand of Arabic were rare. More and more Jundis began gathering around Lee, shaking his hand and smiling. The questions came too fast for him to answer. Finally, Chief Good interrupted the love fest and pointed at the door.

"Let's get back and get some chow. You've got a busy afternoon."

The drill that afternoon was more of a rehearsal for the coming op and gave Lee a good feel for his place in the team. The SEALs were setting up a sniper over-watch in an Iraqi house in the Mala'ab district. Intelligence Lee had gathered on the whole block allowed the SEALs to choose the house they wanted. Lee's job was to stay with the scouts on the first floor and guard/protect the residents. Of course, intelligence gathering was always on his agenda. They rehearsed loading the gun trucks, exiting the gun trucks, approaching the gate and entering the residence, and setting up security. The SEALs would be working in the upper level of the building, leaving Lee to oversee security and manage the Iraqi residents.

The scouts knew their job and worked with Lee until he knew his job. They seemed to be a cut above the Jundis Charlie Platoon worked with back at Camp Ramadi. These guys were combat vets and knew their business. He didn't hold the Iraqi officers in much esteem, but the enlisted scouts were open and friendly, and seemed to be good soldiers. He enjoyed working with them and getting to use his Arabic exclusively.

After the drills, Parsons, Chief Good, and Lee reviewed the plan and checked for the latest intel. Clearances were in and an F18 would be circling above with electronic observation capabilities. Above him, a C130 command and control bird would be orbiting all night.

They wrapped up the planning in a meeting with the Army company commander they were supporting. Everybody was on the same page, so Lee was turned loose to have chow with the SEALs from Delta and get his gear ready.

Chapter 29

The trucks left the gate at 0130. The night was dark with no moon. Lee was too excited to sit still. The Jundis had picked up on the Igor handle and they loved it. They used it every chance they got.

Normally, the vehicles would drop the assault team off at the end of a block and the assault team would patrol quietly to the target house while the vehicles set-up security with a blocking force. Tonight, the insert method chosen was drive-by site exploitation, a fancy name for jumping out of moving vehicles and taking the house they wanted quietly and on the run while the convoy drove on, hopefully leaving no indication that a sniper team was left behind. The convoy was six vehicles. Two were SEAL gun trucks carrying two sniper teams and one was the big flatbed with the sandbag reinforced bed carrying the Jundis. The rest were 1/506th Bradleys with an Abrams tank as backup.

Two sniper teams were being inserted. The sites were preselected to be mutually supporting and gave solid coverage of the streets the Army would search and clear the next day. It might seem counter-intuitive, but going in as a large, loud convoy was probably the safest way to enter the tightly packed streets of the neighborhood they had to clear.

Insurgents tended to stay in cover and sleep at night. They didn't want to tangle up close and personal with Americans ready for battle in the dark. The sound of military vehicles at night was common. Iraqis and insurgents heard the trucks go by, but unless they stopped, they weren't a cause of concern. From the insurgent's point of view, they were someone else's problem if they kept on going.

IEDs were the real concern. Command detonated bombs buried in the roadway or cemented into walls along the street might have a trigger man assigned to a night watch. Those bombs tended to be massive and could do real damage to any vehicle in the convoy.

The convoy moved slowly down the first target street and the turret gunner in Lee's vehicle gave the Seals inside a warning. Site coming up. The turret gunner on the flatbed carrying the Jundis did the same. As Lee's Hummer came abreast the target house, the gunner said go.

Lee and one sniper bailed out one side and a second sniper and another SEAL bailed out the other side as the truck kept moving. They moved against walls on both sides of the street and covered for the Jundi truck.

The Jundi truck came by and six Jundis and one more SEAL bailed out and pressed against the walls until the last vehicle in the convoy passed. The whole team joined together against the wall that surrounded the target house. The same process would happen again farther down the street at the second site and the convoy would continue, make a turn, and proceed back to the camp, never stopping until inside the wire. The planners hoped the convoy's passing would be noted and the teams would get in place undetected.

A Jundi was boosted to the top of the wall to open the gate. The gate was opened without excessive noise or damage and the team moved through the courtyard to the front of the house. The breeching team stacked on the door while the remainder provided security. This time they knocked on the door. Sometimes it was just that easy. Other times it took a shaped charge to blow out the lock.

Soon, someone inside called out something. The terp answered and told them to open the door. The door opened slowly and a man's head pushed through the opening. The assault team pushed in and cleared the house. Lee and the Jundis followed, gathered the family in the main living room, and secured the first floor. As perfect a site exploitation anyone could hope for.

While the SEALs set up their shooting positions upstairs and the Jundis secured the grounds and set up security, Lee sat with the family. The intel geek in him took over.

"It is with sorrow we make use of your home," he said to the woman. "If any damage occurs you will be well compensated."

"Insha Allah. Better you than the Saudi dogs. I must go to the kitchen. Am I to be watched in everything I do?"

"No, this is your home." That was a judgement he wasn't sure he had the authority to make, but he didn't sense any hostility in these people. The less they were antagonized the easier the task would be.

The man and woman had one male child and he and his father remained silent. The woman returned with tea and a bowl of pastry balls covered in nuts.

"You speak very well for an American," she said. "Your manners are good manners too. How is it you know our ways so well?"

"I have many Iraqi friends. I studied at university in Oman and Jordan. May I ask about your community?"

"Ask what you wish."

"This street you live on. The homes are well kept and seem to have little damage. How is that when the city has suffered so much war?

"We all are related on this street. Our sheikh is

strong and not many would wish to anger him. But it appears the war is coming to us also. You are here. The Saudi dogs are here also. There will be a fight."

"You do not like the Saudis?"

"I like them fine when they stay in their own land. I like them fine when they concern themselves with their own souls and leave us to work out our own fate. I do not like them when they tell us how to live, what we can drink and eat, threaten our men when they smoke, and recruit our young men to their deaths. I do not like them when they threaten our Sheikh."

"Enough woman," the man said. "Our tribal business is our own business."

"Our own, is it? Have you returned the Sheikh's son to him? Have you?"

"The Sheikh's son is missing? Lee asked.

"Kidnapped," she said. "And now the Saudi dogs tell us how to live."

"Do the Saudis occupy any of the houses on this street?"

"Who can tell," she said. "We hardly leave our home now. But I will tell you something." She looked intently at Lee to make sure he was listening. "The third house down the street," she pointed, "on the other side. That is my cousin's house. Something funny is going on there. She is being very unsociable, even with family. She hardly leaves the house and when she does, she never has time to talk. It is like she has an unwanted guest she can't get away from."

"Woman, I said be silent," the husband said.

Lee excused himself for a moment and went up the steps to make some notes.

He returned to sit with the family, and the conversation went on until light with Lee leaving the room occasionally to make notes of things he didn't want to forget. He had picked up several more pieces of information that tickled his memory and knew there was one or more of his folders that would be enhanced with the new information. Other than the unwelcome guest, he didn't get anything earth shattering, but intel folders grew into target folders by the accumulation of information, often one tid-bit at a time.

They had a small basement and Lee moved the family there as the sun came up. Things were about to go kinetic any time now. SO2 Kelly was the designated team lead and Lee informed him of the family's status.

"Good move," Kelly said. "How are they dealing with the situation?"

"Pragmatically," Lee said. "I didn't see any real hostility, which amazes me."

"Shoot, pragmatic is all the feelings they have left. If it isn't us, it's the insurgents. Did you get anything out of them?"

"No Eureka moments, but I did get some solid intel about the community. It will help."

"All right. See what you can do to keep them out of harm's way."

"Talk to you later," Lee said.

Chapter 30

The house was solid concrete and stucco surrounded by a nine-foot wall and a gate now locked. Second story windows provided good positions for the snipers and the roof had a low wall around it, providing a second shooting position. Even inside, Lee heard the diesel engines at the end of the block. The Army had arrived with the light. He didn't know it yet, but so had the insurgents. Fact is, they were already there.

The piercing sound of a .300 Win Mag sniper rifle cut through the growing sound of diesel engines. Since the view from on top the residence might reveal targets out to seven or eight hundred meters, both snipers brought .300 Win Mags and one of them opted to forego the suppressor. They were powerful weapons with a flat trajectory. The SEALs said for the kind of work they would be doing that day, they just dialed in the 500-meter data and eyeballed the corrections. They were good to go from 100 meters out to 800 meters without having to recalculate their shots. The rifles were bolt action, but they were also magazine fed and could keep up a decent rate of fire in the hands of an expert. The SEALs were experts.

Suddenly the house vibrated with the shock of something impacting one of the walls. The sniper rifle fired again. Then the second rifle fired. They were finding targets. Lee was shaking with frustration. A battle was going on and he was stuck in the basement. The house shook again and a jar fell from a shelf in the basement. One of the Jundis came down the steps two at a time.

Lee spoke in Iraqi. "Stay here and guard the family."

The Jundi smiled and shook his head yes vigorously. He figured Lee would chase him back up to the fighting. Lee took the stairs two at a time and emerged on the first floor just as another explosion shook the house. Plaster from the ceiling fell and hit his rifle. Where to go?

He checked to make sure his magazine was seated and a round was in the chamber. Good to go. He went for the door. Another explosion made the door wobble on its hinges and he heard something hit the wood like a bucket of rocks. He processed that and waited next to the door.

He tested the door and jerked it open. The

scene in the courtyard was chaos. Blowing dust obscured a clear view, but he saw two Jundis down halfway between the house and the wall. Two more were huddled against the front wall. He couldn't locate the sixth Jundi. The wall was good cover, but the entire courtyard was just a flat dirt patch with no cover at all. As he tried to decide what to do, a grenade came across the side wall. He pushed back inside the house but didn't get the door closed. The explosion took most of his hearing. He was back up immediately.

"Coming out!" he yelled in Arabic and went through the door. The Jundis were huddled behind the front wall next to the gate. At least the gate was closed and locked. He ran to the two fallen Jundis. Both were unconscious and bleeding from several shrapnel wounds.

Body armor provided a place for a grip and he dragged one Jundi through the dust cloud back to the house. The second one seemed lighter, or maybe it was adrenalin. As soon as he dropped the second Jundi inside the door, he ran bent over to Jundis near the gate.

"Grenades," he yelled and pointed at the side wall where the incoming grenades were coming from. "Toss a grenade over the wall." Lee removed the safety clip and pulled the pin on his grenade. He let the spoon fly and tossed it over the wall so it would hit just on the other side.

The two Jundis seemed to know what they were doing and understood what was needed right away. The battle outside of the wall had intensified and they couldn't hear a word Lee said, but they saw what he did. They moved down the wall, pulling pins and tossing grenades. The explosions rippled along the length of the wall. The Jundis immediately ran back and pressed against the wall on both of Lee's sides.

"Inside," he yelled. They heard that.

They ran across the yard and through the door. Two of them assumed a prone position on each side of the door and covered the gate. Without thinking of his intra-team radio, Lee ran up the stairs to find the SEAL who was also a corpsman. He should have used the Jundis blowout kits to work on the bleeding, but his inexperience can be forgiven considering the level of violence outside.

He found Kelly lying on a long dresser sans mirror in the middle of a bedroom concentrating on his scope. Lee waited a moment, but Kelly didn't shoot.

"I've got two Jundis down," Lee yelled.

Another SO2, Sammy Clark was working a second window with what looked like an M4 with a heavy barrel. "I'll go," he yelled and followed Lee down the stairs.

The sixth Jundi had shown up and was working on his buddies. Clark did a quick inspection of the wounds and spoke in his radio.

"We need a medevac ASAP."

A few moments later, "On the way," was the reply.

"Take two Jundis and wait at the gate," Clark

said.

Lee tapped each of the Jundis guarding the door and they ran out to the gate. Soon he heard the distinctive sound of the Bradley's diesel. The fighting vehicle didn't draw any fire so Lee opened the gate. He leaned out and looked up and down the street. Nothing was happening. An Abrams tank sat in the middle of the street at the army end and nothing but rubble was in the street at the other end. He sent the Jundis back to help move their friends.

They got the wounded in the Bradley without any new incoming and it was gone as soon as the vehicle was closed. Lee returned to the house and reported to Kelly.

"Stay with the family," Kelly said. "The Army is wrapping this op up. Be ready to move out fast."

"Got it."

Twenty minutes later Kelly stopped on the basement stairs and waved Lee out. They loaded in gun trucks and returned to Corregidor.

Chapter 31

Back at Corregidor, Lee opened his laptop and began building a new target folder with the information obtained from the wife at the sniper site. It was a minimal folder, but he sent it to the targeting cell at Camp Lee and to the S2 at Corregidor. As soon as that job was done he attended the SEALs debriefing. He was moving on adrenalin and couldn't slow down.

During the debriefing, he found out the rest of the story about the op he had been part of and got an atta-boy. Unknown to Lee when he left the basement to get into the fight, a small group of insurgents had managed to maneuver through the snipers' blind spots and made it to the wall just below Kelly and Clark. The wall provided another blind spot the SEALs couldn't cover without leaning out the window and that was not an option with the volume of incoming at that time. Lee's grenade attack had busted that attack up and deterred an unknown amount of havoc that could have resulted.

He asked why the op had been aborted.

"Politics and destruction, Igor," Parsons said. "The Colonel has managed to establish a half-assed relationship with the Sheikh in that area and made a commitment to limit destruction in his bailiwick. He didn't want chain guns, mark nineteens, and Abram's main guns blowing the neighborhood away. Fortunately, the insurgents decided they didn't want to continue the fight. It would have taken the Abrams to clear those blocks and the Abrams would have cleared everything including the buildings and homes. The colonel is not a big fan of destroying the city to save it. He decided we had poked them in the eye and that was enough for today. A cordon and search ops is being planned as a follow-up. Now tell us more about the target folder you opened."

Lee went through his intel and discussed his suspicions.

"I need cross-confirmations and some time to work with the targeting cell at Camp Lee. I'll schedule a detailed AC130 observation for tonight and see if we can task a drone for a closer look. ASO (Advanced Special Operations) at Camp Lee is running an electronic intel scan for the folder, phones, radios, everything. If it is real, this could come together pretty quick."

"Okay, sounds like you have it under control,"

Parsons said. "Keep me informed. "Chief, keep Igor plugged in and stay on top of this one. It sounds good. Everybody got what they need?"

Everyone nodded.

"Okay, let's get back to work."

Over the next two weeks the target folder filled out and the ASO at Camp Lee agreed Lee had an important target. Phone intercepts and one interrogation provided confirmation that something unusual was going on in the target house. A name came up from two sources. Ahmed ibin Saad, an important al-Qaeda-in-Iraq sub-commander. Lee notified LT Parsons of the new information and Parsons discussed the folder with the Colonel. Game on.

The Army would cordon off the neighborhood and the SEALs and Jundis would take down the house. If Saad wasn't found in the target house, the ARMY would do a house-to-house search.

Lee had done excellent interrogation work. He followed through and built the target folder like a pro. The platoon had a solid mission with actionable intelligence because of him. It was his baby, damn it. But Parsons wasn't listening to Lee and he wasn't being included in the op to take the house down. His success was turning on him. He had become an asset for the TU and the 1/506th. The TU Commander and the Colonel didn't want to risk him outside the wire. Parsons was sympathetic, but adamant.

"I'm sorry, Igor. I have orders. We need you too

much to risk it. Keep working this thing. It's your brothers going out there. Keep them safe."

"But I'm the best terp you have, Dan. We have to get his guy. The Iraqi terps might miss him. He's not just going to stand up and introduce himself."

"I hear ya, but you're not going out on this one. Give it time. I'll work on the bosses. You'll get out there again."

"Well, hell! There's no way at all?"

"Sorry, Lee. No wiggle room at all."

The order was disappointing, but Lee doubled down on the intel work. If he couldn't go out, he had to give the team the best intel he could find. He worked with the ASO at Camp Lee to comb through OGA data bases for pictures of Ahmed Saad. Again, through ASO, he worked to develop a profile and came up with a big identifying-marks confirmation. The CIA confirmed information that Ahmed had been punished in Saudi Arabia with a public whipping of fifteen lashes that scarred his back for life. With that final piece of intel, he felt like his folder was complete and could brief the assault team with sufficient information for them to make a positive identification.

Both teams, Army and Seals, were assembled and briefed. The raid was schedule for the following night. Parsons asked Lee to stay in the TOC during the operation to be available by radio if he was needed. He was still sulking a bit about being left behind, but he felt a little better being assigned where he could follow the action through the entire operation. He even got some sleep the night before the target date.

His sleepy mind cleared quickly with the morning incoming. At 0500, the local Muj let fly with an RPG that landed in the armor parking and maintenance lot. The SEALs even had a name for him, Five O'clock Ali. Almost like clockwork, Five O'clock Ali would launch an RPG or fire a magazine of AK into Corregidor. Lee figured it was more than one guy, but putting a name on it made it less threatening

He grabbed a towel and prepared to perform S-cubed but didn't get out of his cube. He heard someone hurrying across the quarters toward his cube. Parsons leaned around the opening with a big smile on his face.

"Get your ass in gear, Igor. Our Terp doesn't want this one. I cleared it with the Commander back at Camp Lee. You're in the stack."

"He just quit?"

"No, but he probably will if we try to force him. No time to bring another one out from Camp Lee and get him up to speed."

"That's not a good sign," Lee said. "Something's up he doesn't want to be part of."

"Yeah, but you da man!"

"Hot damn! What's on the schedule for today?"

"The assault team is rehearsing on the range at 1000. Be there. You are in the terp position."

Chapter 32

They loaded the vehicles at 0300. The plan was to arrive while a sleeper's body was at its lowest ebb and take the door while the occupants were confused with sleep muddled minds. This raid wouldn't be a gentle entry like the last one. It would be balls against the wall from the moment the vehicles stopped. A climber would open the gate from inside and the assault team would flow in only stopping to breach the door. Today, a shaped charge would punch through the lock. With the door open, the team would clear the house and roof and collect all the residents in one place for Lee to interrogate.

They were going back to Mala'ab and their presence would be challenged. Parsons hoped the presence of Army vehicles cordoning off the neighborhood would help keep the Muj unaware of their exact target until they arrived.

The assault team moved through the dark streets fast in four gun-trucks and the flatbed. Ahead and behind them, two Bradleys, each with a squad of infantry accompanied the convoy. They would provide a blocking force above and below the house. Having those 25mm chain guns with HE rounds out there to reinforce the gun truck's 40mm mark-nineteens and Ma Deuce 50s eased some of Lee's growing apprehension. He had asked for this, had argued for it, but now that it was here, the reality of what was coming up sobered him. This was the real deal. Breaching a door knowing bad guys were inside was a first for him.

The convoy turned down the street for the target house and didn't slow or hesitate. Nothing subtle about this stop. Everything depended on speed. The first Bradley moved past the house and took up station a couple hundred feet past the gate. The gun trucks screeched to a halt and the assault team poured out. The second Bradley stopped a couple hundred feet back.

Lee was at the back of the stack with the Jundis and EOD guy. The breaching team would go in first and the assault team would begin clearing the house. Lee would follow and examine each occupant, handing off each insurgent or suspicious occupant to the Jundis to escort back to the vehicles. Parsons wanted to be done and gone before the insurgents in the neighborhood could get their act together and attack. This was a snatch and grab and once they had the guy they wanted, there was no reason to invite more trouble by hanging around.

The street was quiet and the house was dark. He ran to the wall and took his place in line ready to push inside as soon as the gate was opened. He knew what would happen next. His own intel had provided information about the gate. There was a heavy bar inside locking the gate. It had to be lifted out of its brackets.

Two SEALs made a saddle with their hands. Two other SEALs were boosted up and held there to cover a third SEAL who went over the wall. The locking bar was removed from inside and the gates opened. So far, so good.

They didn't have time for finesse. Lee ran with the assault team to the door and took his place in the stack.

The breacher set a strip charge on the door.

That's when things went to shit.

"Fire in the hole!" he yelled but had to dive sideways as chunks of door began blasting outward as bullet holes stitched across the door about waist high from inside. Whatever it was inside blasting the door was big. At the same time, plunging fire started from the roof and more accurate incoming with a better angle began striking the ground and house around the team. One of the Jundis went down with a leg wound. Muj were on the roofs of the houses surrounding the target house and poured small arms fire down on the team and engaged the Bradleys and gun trucks.

The battle outside the gate grew quickly as more and more Muj moved in on the house in what appeared to be a well-coordinated ambush.

"Igor, take the Jundis back to the wall and get an angle on the roof. Shut that fucker down!" Parsons ordered.

Lee told the Jundis what he wanted to do. They knew how to do it. All of them turned around facing the house. Firing bursts on full automatic above them, they laid a wall of covering fire on the edge of the roof. As they fired, they backed up getting a better angle.

Lee was caught by surprise at their initiative. He stayed with them and emptied two magazines in four and five round bursts as they moved back to the wall. Two, three or four weapons were firing constantly as the whole group staggered the changing of magazines. Finally, they had a good angle on the roof and cover from behind by the wall. The volume of incoming fire decreased as the Jundis went to single fire at any movement in sight.

The Bradleys and gun trucks were engaged with roof-top Muj and those moving through alleys and side streets. The noise and flashes of light were enough to take your senses away, but the vehicles took enough pressure off the assault team so they could blow the door and toss several crash-bangs inside. The team went in behind the stun grenades.

"Igor, move up!"

Lee left the Jundis to engage the roof tops and

moved to the door. Not a single RPG had been fired at them yet. No IEDs had been detonated. Maybe an indication the house held something important to the insurgents they didn't want to risk harming with the heavy stuff.

He went through the open doorway behind Parsons. The air was filled with smoke. The large room they entered had a smaller room off each side. At the far end was a machine gun behind a row of sandbags. The barrel was pointing at the ceiling and two dead Muj were sprawled behind the gun. They wore American Kevlar helmets and body armor. Each had blood coming out of his ears, and one hole in his face.

Both rooms off the main room had glow sticks stuck to the door frame, the assault team's way of marking a cleared room. Lee checked out the room on the left. Empty. Parsons called him to the room on the right. A woman and a young child sat on the floor.

A firefight broke out on the floor above while Lee questioned the woman.

"Who is Abeer?"

"Abeer, my cousin?"

"Yes, thank you. Please stay low on the floor so you will be safe. This will be over soon. You will be compensated for the damage to your home."

She pointed at the middle of the floor. "Remove that rug. Go to the basement," she said. "There is a man and a child. Kill the man."

Lee patted his heart and thanked her.

"Dan! Right here. The basement. She says

there's a man and a child. She wants us to kill the man."

Lee pulled back the rug and found a trap door.

He looked at the Iraqi lady. "What are the steps like?"

"Steep. Up and down like a ladder."

"Take your child to the other room and lay on the floor, please."

She grabbed the child and ran to the other room.

"Come on. It's got to be me and you," Parsons said. "The rest of the team is engaged. Here's how we'll do it. Lift the trap door. Carefully, Igor."

Chapter 33

The firefight upstairs wasn't slacking up. Outside, the big guns were still pouring out fire. It was hard to hear and hard to concentrate. It was hard to keep from climbing into a hole until it was over. Lee looked at the trap door.

"There's a kid down there," he said.

"No help for it. He's dead if we don't get him out of there anyway. Crash-bangs are the only way we're getting down there. Tie this to the handle."

Parsons handed Lee a length of nylon cord. The door had a rope loop for a handle. He tied the cord to it.

"Stretch out away from the opening on this side. When I tell you, pull the door up enough for me to drop in a crash-bang, then drop it closed."

He got in position on one side with Parsons and

a crash-bang lying prone close to the opening on the other side.

"Now!"

Lee yanked the door open and held it. Parsons had a crash-bang prepared and dropped it in the hole as a burst of AK fire lit up the opening with green tracers. Lee dropped the lid and the stun grenade blew. Parsons had the lid open again and was over the edge and on the ladder before Lee could react. His hesitation only lasted seconds until he regained his senses. He felt for the rungs with his boot and then went down the ladder.

They were in a small concrete walled room. Parsons rifle light was the only light shining. He scanned it around the room through the smoke and stopped on two figures just beginning to move.

"Get the kid," Parsons said as he flipped the Muj over and put his knee in the middle of his back. He pulled flex cuffs out of his vest and cuffed the Muj. The guy was bleeding from his ears.

The boy was small and still unconscious, but he was showing signs of reviving. Lee grabbed him and tossed him across his shoulder in a fireman's carry and climbed back up the ladder. Up top he laid the boy on his back and felt for a pulse. His Carotid artery had a strong pulse. His ears seemed to be okay. No blood.

The kid suddenly took a deep breath and opened his eyes.

"Lay still," Lee said. "You are safe now."

He didn't seem to understand. Lee realized the child couldn't hear yet. He put his hands together like in prayer, smiled and then patted his heart. The child responded with a smile.

"Igor, get the hell down here and help me get this guy up the ladder."

"Hold on."

Lee leaned back and called the Iraqi woman. She came right away.

"He probably can't hear yet," he said. "Please take care of him until we are done."

She put her hands together and smiled. "Oh, little Sheikh, you are safe." Lee wasn't sure what that was about, but he didn't have time to worry about it. He suspected they had the target in the basement. The description matched. He had to get him up from the basement and do an ID check.

Between them, with Lee pushing the guy's butt from below and Parsons pulling from above, they got him up the ladder. He was conscious now and getting feisty. Lee was kicked in the face twice. He took his knife out and pressed the point into the guy's butt cheeks. The kicking stopped.

Up top, Parsons put the guy on his face and bound his legs.

"Why the hell didn't you do that down there?"

"I was just a bit busy, Igor. Who is this guy? Is he important?"

"Let's see." Lee used his knife to slit the back of the guy's shirt.

Scars crisscrossed his back.

"Meet Ahmed ibin Saad," Lee said. "We got

him."

"You're sure?"

"Everything fits the intel. This is our guy."

Parsons sat back on his butt and wiped his mouth with his hand.

"All we have to do now is get him and ourselves out of here," he said.

The battle outside was still raging. The battle upstairs had changed, shots were more deliberate. It sounded farther away. Parsons talked on his radio for a moment.

"The house is cleared and my boys are on the roof. The Army is coming, but we may be here for a while. They're having problems of their own."

The Iraqi Lady crawled across the floor with the two children behind her.

"You should kill this pig," she said.

"He is more valuable alive," Lee said. "He will tell us where more like him are hiding."

She leaned over and spat in Saad's face. "Pig!" she yelled.

"Will you take me to my father?" The child said.

"As soon as it is safe," Lee said. "Who is your father?"

"Why, the Sheikh, of course," the woman said. "They kidnapped the child and kept him here in my home to stop the Sheikh from sending the young men to join the police."

Lee translated for Parsons. "Son of a bitch!" Parsons said. "Igor, you are going to make the Colonel very happy. I've got to get on the radio. The Colonel has to make this delivery. This has got to be the best damn coup we've ever had. Two big hits on one raid. Take care of these people.

The battle raged for two more hours and didn't seem to be letting up. 1/506th troops were bogged down in house-to-house clearing and the Bradleys had been relieved once already. The SEAL gun trucks were conserving their ammunition as best they could, waiting for a resupply. The assault team was running low on ammunition.

The Iraqi lady identified her husband among the bodies. The Muj had killed him before the assault team got to him. Each time she passed Saad, she spat in his face. Got to give the guy credit. He took it stoically. The stoic lasted only until she told him she would castrate him as soon as she could get her hands on a knife. He had taken her man from her. She would take his manhood from him. Lee kept his eyes on her. He figured she was serious.

Parsons was notified that the Colonel had informed the Sheikh that his son was safe and they would bring him home as soon as the insurgents could be pushed back and a vehicle could get in to pick the kid up.

Shortly after the Sheikh was notified, odd things began to happen. Muj began attacking Muj positions. The Sheikh had mobilized his tribe, some of whom were fighting with the Muj. That action turned the battle.

By 0900 the battle had fizzled into individual firefights, with some Muj retreating into the city and local Muj standing watch over the target house. The gun trucks got a resupply of water and ammunition and the Bradleys were relieved with fresh vehicles.

"You escort the boy, Igor." Parsons said as a Bradley backed up to the gate. "This one is yours."

Lee loaded on the Bradley and the Sheikh's son sat next to him and held his hand. He was still shaky, but he had never seen the inside of a Bradley and like most kid's in a situation like that, was excited and fascinated. He recovered from his ordeal quickly. He asked questions about the vehicle, guns, and soldiers all the way to the Colonel's command post. Kids were kids regardless of nationality or religion. On the way to be reunited with his father, the little future Sheikh was just a little boy in awe of his heroes.

The Colonel was waiting with a tall Arab in white robes and a white Keffiyeh with a golden rope that circled his head. He had a thin, severe face with a black goatee. A real Arabian knight. Lee held the boy's hand as he led him across the ramp and up to his father. The Sheikh squatted down and opened his arms. He had tears in his eyes. Well, Lee thought, I guess fathers are fathers no matter, too.

The Sheikh didn't speak, was probably afraid his voice would break, and hugged his son to him for a few moments. Finally, he held the child at arms-length and smiled. He stood up and turned to Lee.

"You are the one who rescued my son?" he said and waited for the terp to translate.

Lee answered in flawless Arabic as guttural as the sheikh's own.

He held out his arms and said, "Not just me. We all took him back from the people who held him. It was an honor. He is a brave child."

The terp, with nothing else to do, translated Lee's words into English.

The Colonel smiled. "I'm really going to be sorry to lose you, Igor. Good job."

Lee didn't have time to think about what the Colonel said, because the boy spoke up.

"It is he who came into my prison and carried me out, father. And then he kept me safe while all of the guns were shooting."

The Sheikh came forward and embraced Lee. He kissed Lee on both cheeks twice. "You are of my family now and welcome in my home. You have my eternal gratitude."

The terp translated for the Colonel.

"Now I'm really sorry to lose you. Make nice, Igor, and say goodbye. I've got to get you back to the Camp."

Lee was confused about that statement, but he made his manners and thanked the Sheikh for his graciousness. The boy offered his hand, and Lee shook it and patted his heart. Five minutes later he was back in the Bradley and on his way to Corregidor.

Chapter 34

Jake Mallory tapped on Commander Faulks's door and walked in without looking to see if he was busy. Faulks was used to it.

"You've got two minutes. What can I do for you, Jake?"

"Everything is set up in London. Are the orders cut?"

"Cut and gone. Toliver should be arriving in London in two to three days depending on how long it takes him to get out of Baghdad."

"Good. That takes care of the paperwork. You should be proud of our boy. The SEALs and Army both are bitching about losing him."

"Our boy?" Faulks said.

"Come on, Commander. Let's not get back into

that. He's got talents that will take him beyond either of us. I'm not managing this project for us. You know where I'm getting my orders from."

"Yeah. I'm not bitching at you. Just bitching. Well, he's been over there seven months. That's a normal deployment for a SEAL Team. He should be coming back to Trident for further training and be preparing for another deployment. I agree with you though. He did a hell of a job in Iraq. The TU commander put him in for a bronze star with a combat V. An Army colonel submitted a citation to go with the medal. I didn't have to do it myself. Jake, Toliver is not your typical Trident analyst. The SEALs turned him into a warrior."

"Now it's our job to turn him into a covert warrior. The work he will do for Black Wolf will help us all."

Why Toliver? He's a linguist and a damn fine intel analyst. You can have any SEAL or Delta Operator you want."

"That's the reason. We don't need another special operations operator. SQT or green team training makes great operators. We need a guy with good enough combat skills, but with outstanding intel savvy, somebody who can infiltrate a population, remain undetected, observe and know what to look for, and then get out with the intel.

"Okay, I understand what you're doing. I just hate to lose him. What's next for him?"

"Training with the British SAS to shape him up

and give him some important martial skills and then RUT training being developed by Special Activities Division. London is made to order for what we have in mind. He can do some work for MI6 while we train him up to Black Wolf standards."

"I don't speak Acronym," Faulks said. "What the hell is RUT training?"

"Real Urban Training," Mallory said. "First we train him up with covert skills and then drop him in a real urban setting to conduct a training op without the civilian population knowing the op is going on. It's the best test of his skills before he goes operational."

"Why London? Why not bring him back here and let the experts train him?"

"London is the perfect environment. They're starting to call it Londonstan. They've got over 600,000 Muslims in the city with whole neighborhoods solidly Muslim. Lots of unrest and problems with radicals. What better place to test his covert abilities with Muslim populations? The city is a low risk environment for testing how well he can fit into the culture."

"It would be lower risk right here. I'm sure we can find Muslim communities suitable for his training."

"London also has an asset you don't have. A young British Lieutenant named Abilene Dundee."

"Dundee? Wasn't that the name of the woman involved in the bombing with him?"

"You got it. She's excited about working with Toliver. You couldn't ask for anything better for a control agent. Should be interesting."

Faulks sat back and smiled.

"Jake, you are a manipulative son of a bitch. You know that, don't you?"

"Thank you. Your faith in me is deeply appreciated. She will be good for him."

Faulks shook his head.

"Only in the CIA would that be considered a compliment. I suspect he's changed. How do you know those arrangements will work with him now?"

"What? A pretty lady in a wheel chair? He ain't changed that much."

"Maybe you're right. Well, the orders are cut and he'll be on his way probably today."

Chapter 35

By the time he entered customs at Heathrow, Lee was disoriented and confused. It had been a good flight from Germany and the flight attendants had been female, good looking, and kind, and that just added to the confusion in his mind. He hadn't thought much about his face after a few weeks in Iraq. He was Igor and the face went with the rep. It wasn't long before no one even noticed his face.

Coming back to civilization changed all that. Suddenly he was an object of pity or macabre interest again. The kindness of the flight attendants helped, but the change from combat to civilization in just 48 hours was a hard adjustment and becoming conscious of the discomfort his face caused civilians again made the transition more difficult.

IGOR

Fact is, he missed the team. He missed the Task Unit. He even missed combat. Once again, just as he was settling in with a team, he was yanked out and moved on without an explanation.

He looked around for the exit, and a sight he wasn't expecting added to the dissonance his mind was suffering. It was like landing back in time two years before. Abilene Dundee in a wheelchair held a little sign with his name on it. He knew her right away.

"Hello, Lee. Care to take a chance with me again?"

"Abilene. . .I'm surprised you remember me."

As though my face was something you could miss, he thought.

"Of course, I do. We were blown up together. One doesn't forget that sort of thing. What about you? You knew me right off—or am I wrong?"

"No, you're right. I recognized you even before I saw the name sign. I've thought about you many times over the last year. I guess those things do stick in your mind."

"Would a ride into London be welcome?"

"Sure. You won't blow me up again, will you?"

Abilene smiled her crooked little smile. "I'll see if we can avoid that this time. You'll have to deal with your bags alone I'm afraid. I can stand for a few moments, but I have no strength for anything more."

He watched her face for a reaction to his changed looks, but she covered well. Before Afghanistan, his reaction to meeting anyone was to automatically look for the reaction but being with the troops had dulled that pain and habit. He was surprised at how quickly it returned in the real world.

"Are we going to the embassy?"

"No. That comes later. We've booked lodging for you at a hotel on Hallam street. The Astor Court. I think you will like it. It was a gentlemen's club at one time and now converted to a hotel. I thought you could use a couple of days to settle in.

"You thought right," he said. "Can I help you with anything?"

"Seeing you here and looking somewhat pleased with yourself is already helping me. It was a good flight, was it?"

They talked on the way to the baggage carousel.

"In a lot of ways, yes. You're a Lieutenant. Do you ever wear a uniform?"

"Yes, of course. I'm only seconded to MI6. Leftenant Abilene Dundee at your service."

"If this is something you don't want to talk about just say so and I'll shut up," Lee said. "But do you find that people look at your injuries differently when you're in uniform?"

Abilene cocked her head to the side and thought for a moment.

"Why do you ask?"

"Coming here on the plane, I just felt like people looked at me differently in uniform. Like my . . . this," Lee said waving at his face, "was different, not repuls . . . you know what I mean, like it was okay because I was military. I wondered if you experienced the same thing."

"Hadn't thought about it, but. . .yes, maybe they do. It's as though it's okay to be disabled if you are a soldier, even, perhaps, a point of pride. That's not a feeling I get in civilian attire. Stop here for just a moment"

They moved to the side of the hallway and Abilene motioned for Lee to lean down closer.

"Let me see what they did to you."

Lee leaned down and Abilene put her fingers gently on his face. She traced the outline of his ear and down the side of his face.

"I hate it when they look away," she said.

"Yeah, I'm sure." Lee said. "Sorry. I shouldn't have brought it up."

"Forget it. You did get a singe, didn't you? You are not repulsive, Lee."

Abilene pointed to a new Audi at the curb with a soldier standing guard at the rear bumper. He saw Abilene, touched a finger to his hat, and walked away.

"Can you manage it on your own?" Lee asked.

"Oh, yes. My arms have become quite strong, and I have become adept at transferring from the chair to all sorts of places. Go ahead and load your bags while I get in."

Lee watched her as he loaded the bags. The Audi was a two-door model. Abilene opened the driver's door and maneuvered the chair close to the seat. She might not have the use of her legs, but she was still a beautiful woman and obviously a strong one.

Once in, Abilene loaded her chair with one hand and got her legs positioned the way she wanted them and grasped a lever-like handle with a motorcycle-like gas control. The car started and she maneuvered out into the traffic with one hand on the wheel and the other on the lever contraption.

"Thank you for suppressing your masculine urges to be overly helpful."

"You were doing just fine. Nothing to have urges over. Will we be working together?"

"Yes. For a time, anyway."

"Do you know what this is all about? There I was fighting for God and country in beautiful and scenic Iraq, and zap, I had orders to London. No explanations. No warning. It was like they couldn't wait to get me out of there. It's really screwing with my head."

"Well, it was not quite zap. You were in the Middle East for seven months. You will be going back at some point, but perhaps in a different role. We'll give you a few days to settle in and then get right to it. May I ask you a personal question?"

"Sure."

"How is your sex life?"

Lee almost choked on his own spit.

"Abilene! Jesus. What has that got to do with the assignment?"

"More than you might expect. Now that I have

your attention, let me rephrase it. How are you adjusting to, well, to what happened to you? That kind of trauma can have unexpected consequences. Are you getting laid?"

"Is this official? Unless you're making an offer, we better change the course of this conversation."

"Answer the question!"

Suddenly, Abilene's voice had the snap of authority in it. After seven months with the SEALs, Lee's response was Pavlovian.

"Hell, no, I'm not getting laid. When the hell would I have had time in the last year? And with who? Whom? Jesus, that's a hell of a question to ask someone you hardly know."

"I'll tell you why I ask. You have been taking unnecessary risks. You were wounded in Afghanistan, weren't you? You didn't have to go out into the populace in Iraq, but you did. Repeatedly. At great risk. Something is going on. Are you compensating?"

"Nothing is going on, damn it. I'm just trying to do my job and salvage a career. I can't believe this. How about you? You're as beautiful as ever. Are you getting laid?

Abilene's arms went rigid for a moment. But then she relaxed as quickly as the anger had come on her.

"Perhaps I deserve that," she said. "And thank you for the compliment. No, I am not getting laid. Men don't generally look at a woman in a wheelchair that way."

"Are you able to. . .you know. . .to. . ."

"This is getting a little too personal and I'm not quite sure where it is going, but yes, quite able. All the parts still function just like they are supposed to except for the legs. I still have some control of my legs, just no strength in them. Now we've reached the limit for me. I think we better change the course of this conversation."

"You started it," Lee said.

"Yes, and I apologize. I don't know why I felt I could delve into your, well, personal life like that. I've only known you for a few hours and that ended badly for both of us. The shared disaster might be it."

"Yeah, maybe you're right," Lee said. "You don't seem like a stranger at all, but you are."

"Let me explain where I was going. Lee, you are not taking care of yourself. It is your lax, rumpled appearance. It isn't what I was expecting and that coupled with our reports of your behavior in Iraq . . . well, it worries me. What happened?"

"May I call you Abi?"

"If you like."

Lee took a moment to get his thoughts together. He was getting a little pissed.

"Okay, Abi. Three days ago, I delivered a little boy to his father in Iraq after a five-hour battle. The kid had been kidnapped. We got him back. Then without so much as a beer bust to celebrate my departure, and without a shower or change of clothes, I was put in a gun truck, taken to Baghdad, and put on a plane to Germany. If it hadn't been for a kindly Air Force

Sergeant in Germany, I'd look a lot worse than I do. I did manage to get an S-cubed in Germany and some time to get the oddball six-month storage creases out of my dress blues and some regulation creases put in. What the hell do you mean I'm looking shabby? Of course, I am. I haven't even got the Iraqi dust out of my nose yet."

This wasn't turning out to be a great start for a new assignment and relationship. People back here obviously had no idea what the hell was going on in Iraq and Afghanistan. Did they expect him to look like he just stepped off the parade deck at the Academy? Did they even know a fucking war was going on? They were both quiet for several miles and then Abi spoke.

"What in the world is an S-cubed?" she said. "You said you got one in Germany."

"Shit, shower, and shave," Lee said absently. Then he realized what he said. "Oh hell, I'm sorry, I'm not fit to be around civilized people yet."

Abi snorted and then laughed outright and the ice that was setting in melted.

"You Americans do have a way with the Queen's English. Don't apologize. My chaps in the SAS are just as bad.

Lee let his tiff evaporate. Meeting up with Abi was as strange as suddenly finding himself in civilization again. Their relationship was as strange as it was brief. But what the hell, not many people got blown up together. They both had survived something incredible, and they were both damaged. They had a connection.

"You've said several things about my deployment," he said. "Has someone talked to you about me?" he said.

"I've talked about you with several people. It's my job."

"I'd like to know what this is all about."

"You'll be briefed soon."

An uncomfortable silence descended again and lasted until they were looking for things to say. Lee noticed he was also suffering from another kind of discomfort. Abi might be crippled, but she was still a beautiful woman, right there next to him, and he hadn't been close to woman in a long time, and she said everything still works, and she said he wasn't repulsive, and . . .

"It hasn't been easy for you either, has it?" Lee said.

"Do you think?" she said.

"You haven't let down at all. You are still a gorgeous lady."

"Thank you."

"Are you angry with me?"

"Perhaps a little disappointed."

"Would a back-rub help?"

"That will be enough of that!" she said and blushed.

Chapter 36

He took two days to settle in, and looking in the mirror, agreed with Abi. The desk attendant gave Lee the names and locations of two men's stores with tailors. He decided to report-in in uniform and wear it as much as possible. The uniform gave him a feeling of comfort and a sense of the familiar. He had the tailor take in his dress blues leaving enough material to let them out again as he gained weight. The tailor promised to have one set of blues ready the following day and the rest done in three days.

He hadn't realized how much he let his standards slide during his time with the SEALs. It wasn't the SEALs. It was the place. Lee found a barber and got his hair trimmed to Academy standards. When he got back to the hotel he pulled all his shoes out of his closet and shined them. The hotel provided laundry service and he had all his shirts starched and pressed. It felt good to return to the Academy routine of spit and polish again.

With a freshly-pressed service dress-blue uniform on, loose but presentable, spit-shined shoes, and white combination cap, he set out to explore the underground and learn something about London. He grabbed his tailored Reefer on the way out. Compared to where he had been, London was cold in October.

The Astor Court is located just north of Oxford Street in the area called Fitzrovia in Westminster, allowing an easy walk to just about any kind of shopping and dining he might want. Like all big cities in the world, London had places you could move about without fear and it had places you didn't go unless you lived there. The problem for Lee was discovering which were which. With eleven lines serving 270 stations, the underground had a lot to offer. Too much for a newcomer. He had a choice of several tube stops nearby, all within a half mile of the hotel. He chose Great Portland Street stop about a quarter mile away to begin his adventure, and his trial.

Civilization. He had to face it.

Lee spent the first two hours discovering the interchanges that allowed him to change tube lines. Late morning travel was only moderately crowded and allowed him to explore and move around without many delays.

During the afternoon, he found his way to the Central Line and took the tube to Marble Arch and walked down to the U.S. Embassy security checkpoint. Okay, he now knew how to get to work in inclement weather. How about nice days? Walk. He needed the exercise.

Lee opened his tourist map provided by the hotel and started up Grosvenor Street. The walk was a little over a mile and let Lee get up close and personal with a small part of London.

Straight crosswalks were easy. You naturally looked both ways. But the roundabouts could be hazardous to an American's health. Lee found out that walking in the U.K. could be as dangerous as driving for a right-hand-thinking person. As he crossed the lobby the deskman signaled him. He had a message from Abi and returned it immediately.

"Lee, I have some materials I want to give you. Would it bother you if I came over to your room?"

"Sure, come on over."

"On my way," she said.

He stripped and took an Academy lower classman shower. Wet, wash, rinse, dry, all in two minutes. He was dressed and ready when the knock came at the door.

"It's open," he yelled.

Nothing happened. Lee waited for the door to open and then kicked himself mentally. He jumped up and pulled the door open. Abilene watched him with a small smile on her lips.

"I wondered how long it would take to sink in," she said. "I can open doors like this one, but it takes a lot of maneuvering."

"Christ, I'm sorry. Do you need help getting through the door?"

"Yes. It is rather narrow. I don't like scraped knuckles."

"Okay. Back up a little so I can get out."

Lee maneuvered her through the door and closed it behind them. Abilene rolled the chair close to his desk and put a stack of folders on his chair.

"I've collected summaries from several daily journals kept by British nationals who have lived and worked in southwestern Pakistan. All of them are Pashto speakers and have lived with the Pashtun and in Pashtun areas for extended periods of time. There's a lot of solid cultural information in them that might help you."

Lee wasn't successful in controlling his hormones. For whatever reason, they were starting to rage again. He found Abilene in a wheelchair to be—to be, well, exotic. He was more successful at controlling his behavior though and restricted his erotic thoughts to mental pictures.

"Thanks," he said. "Is the Pashtun material a hint?"

"We can talk about that if you like. How about over dinner?"

"Great. Do you. . ." Lee was interrupted by a

knock on the door.

"Who could that be?" he said.

Abilene smiled and said, "Easy to find out."

"Yes, sorry."

Lee opened the door and was greeted by a gorgeous and smiling face.

"Yes?" he said.

She didn't wait for an invitation. She looked up and down the hallway and walked into the room with a sexy swing of the hips.

"A surprise, Mr. Toliver," she said and stopped in the middle of the floor and stared at Abilene.

"Oops," she said. "Did I get the wrong room? Are you Mr. Toliver?"

"Yes," Lee said. "I'm Toliver."

"Sorry, Mr. Toliver. No one said anything about a three-way. But I'm game if you are."

Abilene with a millimeter smile on her lips started rolling toward the door.

"I have incredibly bad timing," she said. "Help me through the door, Lee."

"Abi, I . . ."

"Hush. No explanations now. We'll have our dinner tomorrow. You obviously have more pressing matters this evening."

"Abi, damn it. I don't. . ."

"Lee. Stop. It's not necessary. We'll meet tomorrow."

Abi didn't wait for Lee, got a good roll, and lifted her hands to coast through the door. "Shut the door, Mr. Toliver," she said.

Lee closed the door and turned slowly. His guest was standing by the bed with one hand on her hip.

"Did I interrupt something?" she said. "Sorry, do you want me to leave?"

Lee watched her for a moment. She was obviously a prostitute. A high class one. Sexy and gorgeous. He didn't know why she was there or how she had his name, but Abi had started the hormones raging and it had been over a year and Abi had deserted him and wouldn't let him explain that he didn't know what was going on. Screw it.

"Would you like to sit down?" he said. "What's your name?"

Chapter 37

Lee's adjusted blues fit well, his hair was trimmed, and he looked as sharp as he had on graduation day at the Academy, with the exception that he didn't have a lot of hair on one side, and the scars on his chin, cheek, and temple were grotesque. He felt good though. There was nothing he could do about the scars or hair, but the sex fairy had visited him, and right then he had that old satisfied stud feeling.

    Feeling a woman moving in those special ways under him again, and over him, and next to him, and—gee-wiz she had been creative—had done wonders for his outlook. He ignored Abi's instruction to stop shaving. He could do that anytime. Right now, he wanted to look as good as he could, and whiskers were not on his agenda. He was a Naval officer again, and by

God he was going to look like one.

The tube ride to Marble Arch was brutal. New York City had nothing on London when it came to congestion. He decided to walk the next time. He showed his ID at the security check-point and was allowed to proceed to the embassy.

When he found Mallory's office, Abi had her chair pulled in next to an empty chair in Mallory's commandeered office. She patted the chair for Lee when he walked in.

"The mystery is solved," Abi whispered with a wry grin. "It seems your CIA boss felt a little meddling in your sex life was in order. I apologize for my behavior."

Lee just shook his head in feigned bewilderment.

"Why is everyone obsessed with my sex life? Is nothing sacred anymore? You left me in a very awkward position."

"I can imagine. How did you . . ."

Mallory walked in with his glasses on the end of his nose, glancing through a stack of papers. Saved by the bell, Lee thought. And you can just go on wondering, Abi. It's none of your damn business.

"Abi, I have your itinerary for Toliver," Mallory said. "It's too heavy on the military side. I'd like to suggest a little more emphasis on covert skills and a little less on physical and martial training. We want a spy, not a commando."

"He still has to be able to defend himself if he is caught."

"His best defense is not getting caught. A week with your boys in Wales for the training I specified is enough. Add a week of Islamic studies and let him get on with the covert training."

"I'll mention it to Commander Domville."

"Do that now while I brief Toliver in."

Abi left and had red rising on her neck. Mallory's charm factor was low and his prick factor was high. He sat back and got serious.

"I see you received your medal. You should be proud."

Lee had his new bronze star ribbon with combat V sitting above his Purple Heart, Combat Action Ribbon, and been-there-done-that ribbons. At least the TU commander had time for that little ceremony before Lee was put in a gun truck and taken to Baghdad.

"Well, I appreciate the honor, but I honestly don't think I did anything to deserve it."

"Commander Task Unit Ramadi thought so," Jake said. "Igor, do you mind if I ask you something personal?"

"First tell me about the little gift I had last night."

"Don't look a gift horse in the mouth. Anybody ever tell you that?"

"I'd prefer that people stop meddling in my sex-life."

"I noticed you didn't kick her out. I wanted your head clear. I'd say it worked. Now, can we get back to business? Can I ask you something personal?

"Depends," Lee said. "I wondered how long it would take that handle to catch up to me."

"Get used to it. You have a rep. Do you mind if I ask you about your religious beliefs?"

Lee considered that for a moment. Mallory had paid for and sent a hooker to his room and he hesitated to ask about his religious beliefs. Unbelievable. He didn't mind, but he wasn't sure he had an answer.

"In what regard?" he said.

"Do you think you can impersonate a devout believer?"

It was Lee's turn to think. Mallory was getting to the point.

"I'm not even sure what that would entail," he said.

"Lee, are you willing to volunteer for a hazardous assignment?"

"I'm not sure. What's the assignment?"

Mallory watched Lee for a moment before replying.

"Good answer. I wouldn't volunteer blindly either. You're a cautious guy."

"I like to think I have some common sense," Lee said.

"I think your performance in Kamdesh and Ramadi showed that. Okay, here's the deal. Delta needs a man on the ground who can impersonate a Muslim with conviction. A man who can blend in with the population and whose word they can rely on one hundred percent. That kind of Afghani native doesn't exit. We need an American. I think you can be that man."

"Jake, get serious. No westerner can do that. Family, clan, tribe, religion. That's what life is there. You can't invent an identity like that. You have to be born into it."

"Are you sure of that? Let me just throw this out for discussion. Take Kabul. Kabul is full of refugees and immigrants. There are people from Pakistan, and all the other 'Stans. There are refugees from all Afghani provinces. The cities are huge Islamic melting pots, Sunni, Shia, Sufi, and various shades of each. Men without families or ties are common. More important, faces like yours wouldn't cause a second look. They've been at war a long time. You are about the right height. Maybe a little more muscle than would be expected, but that can be hidden with clothes. Some time in the sun will take care of the complexion, and the scars obscure your face anyway. It could work."

Lee wasn't sure if Mallory was dreaming or smoking funny weed. Culture wasn't something you could learn in a classroom. He found that out in Kamdesh. And It wasn't something you could shed like a skin.

"I'm an American," Lee said. "You can't change that in weeks or months. Religion is the culture there. I have an outsider's understanding of Islam, but you can't turn me into a born and bred Muslim. It just can't be done. It effects everything, how you think, what answer you give to questions, what you like, what you are repulsed by, everything, and you can't fake it, not the way it is when you are born into it. It's something a Muslim doesn't even think about."

"How about if you only have to get by for a couple of weeks or maybe for even shorter periods of time? Days, or even a single day? A stranger who keeps to himself isn't unusual. Most people would avoid you if they suspect you are an insurgent. Would it be possible for that long?"

Passing as a refugee or itinerant worker for a couple of weeks might be possible if he didn't get too friendly with anyone, Lee thought. The language wouldn't be a problem. Enough of the culture and religion could be internalized so major faux pas could be avoided. He already had academic knowledge of the culture.

"Maybe," he said. "But what could I do worthwhile in two weeks, especially if I'm spending all of my time trying to remain undetected?"

"You could learn to become invisible and you could listen, observe. Lee, the battlespace for the War on Terror is the whole world. London, New York, Berlin, Paris, Baghdad, Kabul, Mogadishu, Manila, every damn place. For now, and for Delta, it's Pakistan and Afghanistan.

"Pakistan?"

"Yes. The mountains on the border in the FATA region. A lot of hiding places and a lot of smuggling trails. Sit back and let me tell you a story."

Chapter 38

Lee didn't remember actually volunteering, but within days of Mallory's interview he found himself in Wales. He had to admit though, he had bought in on Mallory's vision. It sounded exciting and interesting, and he was one of the few who had a chance of being successful in the role needed. He also knew he could never go back to regular Navy duties; days, weeks, months on a ship as a very junior officer with a dozen collateral duties, all boring and tedious. The task unit in Ramadi had ruined that for him forever.

He wasn't being asked to become a spy. That was CIA's job, and he would have refused an offer to join the CIA. He was a Naval officer and he intended to remain a Naval officer. He didn't need agent recruiting skills or spy network control or any of the clandestine skills civilian intelligence officers required. His would be a clandestine military role.

His only job would be to go behind enemy lines and locate high value targets, sort of a covert forward observer. With the target located and communicated to higher command, Special Operations Command would decide how to take the target out. They might decide to launch a drone attack, a SEAL or Delta team operation, or any one of the alternatives in their inventory. Once the target was designated, it was Lee's job to get free and exfil to a pick-up point.

British Soldier Development Wing training at Army Field Training Center Sennybridge in Wales gave Lee the workout his body had been craving since he left Iraq. The SEALs had started it and addicted him to the insane body punishing workouts they performed even in the war zone. The hills of Kamdesh had developed his legs and contributed to his urge to test them. Ramadi had shown just how important it was.

He was placed with a class of British Army boots from training regiments in their ninth and tenth weeks of training. The course was called adventure training, a prime example of British understatement. It was an adventure all right. He completed it at the front with the eighteen-year-olds. They had a few years of youth on him, but they hadn't had three months carrying sixty pounds of gear up and down Nuristani mountains.

Adventure training was just a warm up, a favor arranged by Abi to loosen him up and prepare him for the testing and training with the SAS that was to come.

Next on the agenda, he was turned over to the SAS for seven weeks of weapons training, self-defense, and the Combat Survival Course with Survival, Escape, Resistance and Evasion (SERE) training. Abi and her boss had overruled Mallory, went over his head, and stuck to their original itinerary for Lee. His SAS DS (directing staff) began with an assessment of Lee's fitness. First came the BCFT, Basic Combat Fitness Test, fundamentally a mile and a half run in under eleven minutes with trunk and upper body tests. That wasn't a problem.

Having passed the BCFT, Lee was placed with a class of SAS candidates in their sixth day of testing for the High Walk, a 23 KM escorted march in the Brecon Beacons (read big hills and rough terrain) in, what was to him, horrible weather. This test was a major bitch. He was put in with a group of mostly British Paras testing for the SAS. They called the hike Tabbing. In the U.S., it was called a forced march. 23KM across a big, long hill, round trip, with a full ruck and rifle at a fast pace. Only the hills in Nuristan had been as tough as that ordeal.

The "hill" was a small mountain. The pace was insane. The weather was horrible. The weather forecasters said you can't have four seasons of weather in one day. The Brecon Beacons said, Really? Hold my beer.

He didn't excel, but he completed the tab at the back of the pack. He limped for two days, but he gained a small measure of respect. His ability to keep his mouth shut and listen gained him more. Lee didn't get cocky about completing the tab. The SAS candidates who tested with him, and led the way, had already completed a week of daily beasting, and faced worse in the coming days.

Next on the agenda was the Combat Fitness Course with SERE; three weeks of survival training capped by a week of survival, escape, evasion testing that culminated in capture and 36 hours of interrogation. A cute little twist over the SERE training he completed in California as a senior at the Academy was being dressed in a great coat and boots for the escape and evasion phase of the test. Trying to maneuver through the woods in a great coat was nothing like doing it in BDUs and kit.

    The interrogation was a reasonably good simulation of actual interrogation techniques, but not nearly as comprehensive as what he had performed in actual interrogations—and he was forearmed with the knowledge his interrogators couldn't harm him. The subjects of his own interrogations hadn't had that benefit. Uncomfortable positions for long hours, cold rooms, little rest, badgering, humiliation, all on top of the fatigue from the escape and evasion, were effective. The greatest value of the course for Lee, was experiencing once again the effects on the mind of those techniques. The interrogator seldom gets to experience first-hand, the effects of his techniques on others.

After the CFC, it was back to Sennybridge for the final phase of his training.

Fortunately for Lee, weapons training came next on the training agenda. Although the SEALs and Cav had trained him up on small unit maneuvers, his primary military skill was weapons. He could shoot.

The SAS troops he trained with were a cut above the regular army. They were a lot like Navy SEALs, full of confidence and in your face. They expected one hundred percent all the time and didn't have a lot of respect for outsiders, especially Yanks. They liked SEALs even less, but for some reason they seemed to get on with the American Delta Force guys. Lee didn't talk much about his connection to the SEALs.

His first day on the range reduced the level of sarcasm from the DS considerably. There's not a whole lot of difference in weapons training anywhere in the world. He tried some new weapons, but the L85 the Brits used was an excellent weapon, especially with the SUSAT optical sight, and the M4 and M16 were in the SAS inventory. The SIG P226 was an old friend and the HKs were good weapons. The ranges were like those the SEALs trained on and involved a lot of pop-up targets and practical shooting. Before the week was over, he and the instructors were discussing weapons like equals and they were sufficiently confident in his shooting ability to take him on to the last phase.

Every training phase was also a testing phase

for his readiness to go on to the next phase. Lee was getting spot training, something the SAS DS weren't comfortable with. Normally, they ran their candidates through a rigorous and set testing and training program designed to reveal the candidates' skill, knowledge and fitness as each training element evolved. Lee was getting custom treatment that didn't give the DS a lot of time to evaluate him.

Lee was taken to a range with multiple-target set-ups in several configurations. One was just a table with ten circular metal knock-down targets in a row. Another was six torso profile, knock-down targets in a circle. There was a running course with multiple pop-up targets he had to engage at various distances. The instructors focused on the arrangements for close-up multiple targets. This was hostile disengagement training, last-ditch effort, where the only choice is get away or die while taking as many as you can with you.

This phase was normally reserved for MI6 officers. Since this was a custom covert ops training evolution drawing on SAS expertise, but not normally taught as part of the SAS qualification training, pistols were the only choice for this phase. The object was to break an engagement with a group of people at close range by suddenly drawing his pistol and taking as many targets as possible while he backed out of danger. Sudden, fast, accurate shooting was required. Shock and awe. Even trained troops ready for trouble could be shocked into inaction for a split second by audacious, sudden, devastating violence, possibly providing enough time to kill them and hopefully disengage while the rest sought cover. It would take balls of steel in a real situation. The skill had to be instinctive. As the man said, last-ditch effort.

Lee's pistol of choice was the 9mm Sig P226, TACOPS Extreme with a twenty-round magazine. They started with the table set-up and timed his shooting with a beeper on his shoulder. Ten small, knock-down targets on the table. Ten head-shots. Hit as many as he could put down in the shortest time from seven meters. Practical shooting at the national match level.

Next came the circular arrangement. He was in the center. When the beeper went off, he had to draw and fire while spinning around the circle. Then they folded down the targets on the circle with Lee in the middle. He had to draw when the targets popped up and drop them while backing out of the circle. Not exactly real-world stuff, but definitely shock and awe, and it built confidence.

Lee's assessment and conditioning training had been more of an opportunity for Lee and his hosts to adjust to each other and assess his skills than to teach him anything new militarily. He was already in good shape and he had actual experience in the Middle East. The real work was adding to his basic skills to make him a better close combat fighter.

Hand to hand self-defense and edged weapon training was the primary reason Mallory had arranged for Lee's training with the SAS, especially edged weapon training. For whatever reason, none of the American forces spent a lot of time developing knife fighting techniques and skills. The Brits, on the other hand, had a long tradition of using edged weapons in war and had made a science of it.

From behind the scenes like a puppet master, Mallory chose to make Lee a skilled knife fighter. A knife was one of the few deadly weapons a covert operator could carry without raising undue suspicions. The rest of the training was useful, but it was window dressing in Mallory's mind. Killing efficiently and silently was the key to self-defense and extraction for a covert operator working alone. It took fitness, knowledge, practiced proficiency, and a certain lack of squeamishness not all people had or could develop. For those who had the potential, the SAS knew how to teach it.

Prior to Afghanistan, Lee would have been repulsed by the thought of fighting with a knife. Now—he remembered a little girl with scars like his and an open throat. Doing the same to those who could do that kind of thing just seemed like justice.

Lee was a total novice when he stepped on to the padded mat in the gym with his SAS edged weapons trainer the first time. During the fundamentals phase he was a clumsy but willing student, and he found that he liked the feel of the knife in his hand. There was something primitive and reassuring about the weight and balance of the steel. It wouldn't jam in an emergency, it wouldn't give away his location, and it never had to be reloaded.

In the technique phase, he found he had a knack for handling the blade and a bent toward innovation. The innovation got him slapped down a few times. The instructors liked Lee for his interest in their specialty, but an apprentice's job is to learn the trade, not invent new ways to do it.

Since he showed interest in their specialty and displayed a talent for it, his instructors brought him in after-hours and gave him the long course that included Ju-jitsu moves to improve the dance, and a dance it was, a fast-paced, deadly, face-to-face dance that ended with one combatant dead in a most gruesome way—when it was real. Preferably, if done right, a short dance. The odds of getting hurt or disabled in a knife fight grew exponentially with each second the fight lasted.

The SAS folks had one final phase that included bleeding, anatomically correct mannequins that moved side to side and back and forth on tracks, controlled by the instructors. Strikes to the vital organ strike-points produced a flow of red fluid that looked and felt identical to blood. Besides becoming intimately familiar with all the strike points, Lee got dirty and learned to grip a slippery knife and finish his attack. After a few days with the dummies, squeamishness was diminished considerably. The Brits used the same target principle the SEALs used. Human shaped targets got you in the mood.

As a favor, he was shown a wicked, locking, serrated razor edge folding knife he could carry and told where he could get one. The hate he still carried was a quiet hate now, more mature, more of a determination. Besides seeing a compact weapon, he saw vengeance in that blade. He didn't know where or when, but he would find the opportunity someday.

His hand-to-hand instructors literally beat him up, but he took it and gave back as best he could. Lee was no longer the quiet, academic he was before his tour in the war zone. His puppet master had brought him along nicely. He thought it was the toughest training he had ever experienced, not physically, but mentally. He gave 100 percent and didn't complain.

He completed the training, albeit with multiple bruises and stress injuries. But he held up. The training was good for Lee. His confidence soared. He was tougher than he had ever been and in the best shape of his life. During the nine weeks he spent with them, the SAS instructors loosened up some and by the last day, he was Igor to them. Somehow that awful handle was the instrument of inclusion again. The minute he put on his rank the camaraderie would all change, but for a few hours, they treated him as part of the team.

Finally, the day came to leave his Brit hosts. The unit commander presented Lee a mug with the SAS Saber Badge on it and turned him over to Abi.

The nine weeks he spent in Sennybridge left Lee heavier

than he was when he got there. Besides the constant physical and mental demands of training, the SAS fed him well. He couldn't remember ever having been in the physical condition he was in when Abi wheeled across the room with a smile on her face that day. He also felt a confidence he hadn't felt since before he and she had encountered a suicide bomber. Maybe not a SEAL or SAS Commando, but Lee felt like he could kick about any other ass that walked the earth. He would get over that.

Abi was in uniform. She smiled at his eyes and held out her hand.

"I have good reports on you, Leftenant. You made an impression on my chaps."

Lee took her hand and held it a little too long. She blushed and pulled her hand back.

"Your boys are good. Thanks for setting that up, Abi. I'll have to admit, though. I wasn't thanking you when they were slamming me into the mats. It was a good experience. What happens now?"

Abi's smile returned and she turned her chair.

"Come along. You get the night off. It's too late to start back to London. We'll start with some decent food and a drink if you want it. We have rooms at the Railway Inn in the park."

"Can I help you through the door."

"If you like."

Abi was avoiding eye contact. He wondered what that was all about. He hoped he hadn't embarrassed her with the hand holding. On the way to the Inn, Lee gave Abi a slip of paper with an address on it.

"Can you find this place?"

"No problem," she said. "What is it?"

"Just a shop your boys told me about. They sell a particular kind of knife and I want to get one."

Chapter 39

The Railway Inn was a comfortable looking little inn, not one of your plastic and stainless-steel chain hotels. The barroom was warm, shiny, and full of wood. Abi and Lee decided to have dinner there instead of the dining room.

"Lee, if you will steady this wheelchair, I think I'd like to sit in a regular chair for a change."

"Sure, do you need help?"

"Just steady the chair. That will be enough."

Abi used her arms to lift her body to where she could pull her legs under her and then stood up straight. She stood there for a moment and then took a tentative step away from the wheelchair.

"All right. Pull the wheelchair back and then, if you would, pull my chair out like a gentleman."

"At your service, Madame."

Lee pulled the chair out and bowed."

"Your table awaits, Madame."

Abi took a step forward and then another. She put one hand on the back of the chair and turned so she could sit. She must have been exercising because she had a very round and pert little bottom. She lowered herself to the seat and then swung her legs around and in front of the chair.

"If you will?" she said.

She lifted her bottom slightly and Lee moved the chair forward. She relaxed and turned her head to look at Lee, smiling.

"Very good," he said. "Is that new?"

"Yes, I took a chance. The nerves in my spine are recovering. The doctors are very pleased."

"That's wonderful," he said. "What exactly happened to your spine?"

He rounded the table and sat across from her.

"At first, we were afraid that irreparable nerve damage had occurred, but gradually sensation and control began to return. They fused my spine and healing took place more quickly. I had one treatment with stem cells, but we are not sure they contributed to the improvement. Whatever it was, I'm grateful. I still have a long way to go before I can walk any distance, but the future is looking much brighter than it was just a few months ago."

"Abi, that's wonderful news. I can't describe how happy that makes me."

"What about you?" she asked. "You said you have more surgeries scheduled."

The server interrupted and took their orders and Lee had to pay attention to the menu for a moment. He picked the conversation back up when the server was gone.

"I'm not sure what's going on," he said. "I thought I was going to be in Texas three months ago for more surgery to release these scar constrictions on my cheek. I was running around shooting bad guys instead."

"Does it bother you a lot?"

"The constrictions? Some. They pull my face into this . . . well, you can see for yourself. I'd like to get it taken care of and over. Maybe there will be some improvement this time."

"You sound like you're keeping your expectations under control. I know that feeling well."

"Yes. After every surgery, I look for the improvement, but so far, it's hard to see. The Docs rave about how much better it looks, but I just don't see it. Can't help hoping though."

"I'm glad you can talk about it," Abi said. "I wasn't very good with that."

"With you it's easy. Not so much with others."

Abi blushed, but she didn't look away this time.

"I'm glad. You're like my brother in crime, so to speak."

Lee took a sip of water and held her eyes.

"I'd rather you didn't think of me in a brotherly

fashion," he said a little too seriously.

Abi blushed even deeper, but she held his eyes. "Then a hillbilly cousin?"

Lee laughed out loud. "What do you know about hillbilly cousins? That's an American joke."

"We have TV and everything," Abi said and laughed along with Lee until they noticed the looks from the other diners. Then Abi put her hands in her lap and looked down at the table, but she was smiling. "So, are you going to pour that wine, or should I?" she said.

They finished a glass of wine before the meal came and finished the bottle with the meal. That was a lot of wine for Lee. He turned his glass over and asked for mineral water. Abi kept the conversation going almost as if she were afraid to let a pause turn into a silence. When the remainder of the meal was taken away and Abi received a sniffer of brandy they relaxed and talked some more.

"What has Mr. Mallory told you about your mission, Lee?"

"Just that it involves inserting me into a situation in Pakistan, and it involved locating a high value target."

"That's a possibility, of course. It could be a different crisis in a different place. These things are fluid."

Lee lowered his voice and leaned forward. "Are we supposed to be talking about this?"

"It is as much our mission as his. Don't worry. I selected this table for privacy. Yes, I'm authorized to talk with you about the mission."

"Okay, no he didn't get into specifics."

"Good. He has priorities, of course, but missions are fluid. Today's high value target can be captured or killed while you are planning. Others may remain on the list for years. Sources of human intelligence have been spectacularly unsuccessful in locating our highest priorities so far. Mallory thinks you can be more successful than our usual sources. Have you given it any thought?"

He had thought about the kind of mission he was facing, but not knowing who or what the target was, he hadn't considered the probability of success.

"Some," Lee said. "I'll tell you what I told Mallory to begin with. Impersonating an Afghani Muslim with other Afghanis is impossible. My language is good, and I have a pretty good handle on the culture, but the key is Islam. No westerner can impersonate a born and bred Muslim living in his own culture. Not for long, anyway."

"What was his response?"

"He said it is possible for a short time and I tend to agree, but it will be risky. There's a thousand ways to slip up."

"Let me tell you a little more," Abi said. "And, by the way, Mallory knows I'm briefing you. Think generally. What if we can build a legend for you that can't be checked on from the bush. Names in Pakistan and others in Afghanistan of people who would be known to the insurgents and provide you with a background and a reason to be in the area. Could you impersonate a smuggler with small groups of locals for no more than a few hours at a time?"

Lee thought for a few moments and twirled his water glass.

"It's possible, I guess. Islam is the problem. I'll have to think about it all the time. They were born to it and behave instinctively. You see the problem?"

"All too well, and I've made that point repeatedly," Abi said. "Let's stay with the smuggler idea and think about any Muslim country. If you were a smuggler, or anyone living on the edge of legality, would you be expected to be a devout Muslim? Wouldn't they expect you to be lax about the finer points of religion?"

Lee thought that over for a few moments.

"Abi, I just don't know. I need time with the target population. Iraq taught me you can't assume anything about a people just because they are Muslims. There are as many shades of Islam as there are of Christianity."

"Which takes us to the next step in your training which we will discuss tomorrow. It's time for you to start letting your hair and beard grow. Now, I am getting tired, and If you would be a gentleman and hold my chair for me, you can escort me to my room and help me negotiate that narrow doorway."

Chapter 40

Lee walked alongside Abi as they moved down the hallway toward her room. She was a difficult woman to understand. Sometimes she was amazingly strong like in the barroom, doing things for herself. Other times she seemed fragile and wasn't afraid to ask for help, like now. Maybe that was part of her strength.

"Here is the key," Abi said. "If you will open the door and go inside, I'll give you my hand and you can pull me through."

Why don't I just push you through, Lee thought. The wine was making him a little slower than usual. He opened the door and went inside and turned and held out his hand. Abi took his hand and she was blushing again. He pulled her into the room.

"You are not making this easy for me," she said.

"Close the door, Lee."

With a look of complete confusion, he turned and closed the door.

Abi said from behind him, "You once offered me a back-rub. Is the offer still good?"

He turned around slowly and looked at her. She looked scared as hell. Suddenly the confusion was gone, and he knew he had to do this right. For the first time in a long time he forgot about his face.

"I hardly dared to hope," he said.

"Oh, you silly bloke. Come here and hold this damn contraption so I can get on the bed."

Lee returned to his own room in the wee hours. They were both starved for affection as well as sex. Just holding each other had occupied most of the night. The new day was going to be a long, tired one.

He was up and ready for the day at 0600, though. Today he'd wear civilian attire for traveling. And it wouldn't start with a close shave. Running shoes, jeans, sweatshirt and ball cap would do nicely. A Jacket too. Late November was cold in England. He was just squaring the ball cap on his head when he heard a tap on his door. Abi was ready for breakfast.

"I like the casual look, Mr. Toliver," Abi said when he opened the door.

"Mr. Toliver? Is that how we're going to handle it?"

"Flaunting it would be worse, Lee. We have to work together."

Lee looked at her and had a very tender feeling that brought a gentle smile to his lips.

"You're right as usual. It will be hard hiding my feelings when I look at you though."

Abi smiled a small, almost mocking smile.

"We had one night together in bed," Abi said. "It was very sweet and very satisfying, but it's been a long time for both of us and our need was intense. Let's be very careful about making it possibly more than it was."

Lee felt a little pang of regret, but he understood. He certainly wasn't anybody's long term prize.

"I was referring to lust," he said, and immediately regretted it. The hurt and embarrassment on Abi's face was quick and intense. He grabbed her hand and pulled it to his cheek. "I'm sorry. I don't know why I said that." He kissed her hand and released it.

"This is getting out of hand," Abi said. "Let's get some breakfast before we make complete fools of ourselves."

They regained their composure in the dining room while Abi explained the schedule for the following week. His room at the Astor Court had been canceled and his belongings were packed for him. He would be staying in the country while his hair and beard grew out. Experts in religious studies, ethnic clothing, and culture would come to him for training and leave materials for his studies. He had one month to become a credible

Pashtun immigrant of Afghani/Pakistani origin.

"Just how urgent is this mission?" he asked. "I've already been training for nine weeks."

"We've been searching for Bin Laden for years already, Lee, and he's just one example. The war on terror won't end soon. CIA, MI6, the military of both countries, and most other intelligence services all have their feelers out for multiple targets. You will be one more feeler, one more tentacle adding to the intelligence. We have time to make you as effective as possible."

Abi said the drive back to London wasn't very long, about three and a half hours via the M4. They left Sennybridge on High street and found A4 and then watched for the signs for the M4. They certainly could have made it back easily the previous night and that thought made him smile. Abi was already planning when she said it was too late to start back to London the previous night. It was a set-up and that pleased him. She caught his smile.

"You have a very ornery smile, Lee. Penny for your thoughts?"

"Do you have that saying in the UK too?"

"Where do you think you Yanks got it? Don't be evasive. You are thinking ornery thoughts."

"Guilty. I was thinking about silky smooth thighs parted by a cute little . . ."

"Leland! Stop that . . .it sounds absolutely pornographic. Were you honestly thinking about my legs and . . .?"

"Yes. I have this image in my mind and, well, it's erotic as hell. Tell me something. How did you keep your legs and bottom in such good shape while you spent a year in a wheelchair?"

"Oh, it wasn't difficult. Physical therapy three times a week with electro-stimulation machines and weighted pulley machines and sadistic little therapists absolutely determined to find every point of pain in my lower torso. I had some control and sensation even at the start just after the incident, and they made me work at it constantly. The thought of losing my career as well as my ability to walk was a strong motivator."

"I know the feeling. Are we going to find a way to get together while you transform me into a smuggler?"

"It would be nice, but we will just have to see. You are going to be busy."

Chapter 41

The flat where he was lodged for the next month was in a little village called Bucklesham off the A12 on Main Road near Ipswich in Suffolk. The flat was a converted upper level in a private home near a large field, plowed and prepared for the winter. The area was rural and pleasant. Abi got him situated and showed him around Bucklesham and the nearby historic parish village of Trimley St. Martin.

The gentleman who owned the home was a retired SAS Sergeant Major and provided Lee with plenty of privacy and a cover from nosey villagers. The pantry was stocked and he had a fully functional kitchen. The spice rack was interesting. Brown cardamom, green cardamom, cinnamon, cloves, nutmeg, mace, black pepper, cumin seeds, chili pepper, turmeric, and bay leaves. There was also a fragrant mix of spices called garam masala. Abi explained they were used in Pakistani and Afghani cooking. He not only had to get his appearance right, but he had to work on his smell also. They weren't leaving much to chance.

His first week in Bucklesham was a busy one. Besides studying the material left for him, he was visited by two tutors who worked with him on Muslim customs and traditions of the mosque. One spoke Urdu so Lee had a whole day to work on his Urdu. He studied the Hadith and the tutors helped him to understand how the traditions translated into modern Muslim life in Afghanistan and Pakistan.

The risk was in knowing too much detail. Most Pashtuns knew the Sunnah (traditions) taught by the mullah at their mosque. Few read or understood Arabic except for the recitations at prayer and most learned them by rote. The last thing Lee wanted to do was get into a debate about the meaning of Sunnah traditions with Sunni Muslims.

The second week, Abi showed up with more reading materials and took him to dinner at a small inn nearby. She stayed with him overnight and complained about his whiskers. His beard was becoming more than just a shadow now.

Week three brought a different tutor each day and each spoke Urdu or Pashto. He began to learn to pray at mosque: call to prayer, ablution, prostration, standing form, and recitation. Since he was fluent in Arabic in several dialects, recitation became a rote exercise and came quickly. The work came in dumbing down his correct pronunciation.

The instructors pointed out he didn't have to memorize all or even many surahs. Al-Fatiha, the opening Surah in the Qur'an is required for prayer, Surat Al-Quaraysh Qur'an 106, Surat Al-Ma'un Qur'an 107, Surat al-Kafiroon Qur'an 109, Surat An-Nasr Qur'an 110, Surat Al-Masad Qur'an 111, were good to know and easy to memorize, and Surat Al-Ikhlas Qur'an 112, Surat Al-falaq Qur'an 113, Surat An-Naas Qur'an 114 had a special significance. He was told to be especially careful to memorize 112, 113, 114 and recite them quietly before going to sleep, because the Prophet did. All told, that amounted to about 250 words, give or take, depending on how you counted the Arabic.

Lee couldn't become the image of a devout Muslim in a month, but the first thing his tutors stressed is that Christianity doesn't have a monopoly on hypocrisy and religious sham. The people of Islam range from the ultra-conservative who pray at mosque five times a day and memorize the Qur'an and Hadith, to those who never attend mosque and observe Ramadan and the traditions only when convenient.

In the mountains, if the mountains of Afghanistan were his target, he wouldn't be attending Mosque, so the list was sufficient. It contained all short Shuras even a weak Muslim might know. Making it even better for Lee, he already knew most of them from language study and could recite them from memory. But his language expertise would be a problem. His pronunciation was too precise.

By week four his beard was coming along nicely, but as expected, was patchy on the left side. Lee was one of those men who had to shave twice a day if he had to go out in the evening. He had a heavy beard and it grew fast. Tutors appeared each day and he was drilled in cultural and social aspects of Islam in Pakistan and Uzbekistan. The team decided his legend would be a Pakistani who had lived most of his life among the Pashtuns but traveled and did business in Afghanistan and Uzbekistan. He learned to dress in Shalwar Kameez or Khet Partug (man-jams) and how to wrap a Parahan wa turban.

The tutors were strict. There are many cultural factors that are second nature to a native and had to become second nature to Lee. In what direction do you wrap a garment? How do you sit in company? With which foot do you start off? In what direction do you serve at meals? Who is deferred to in conversation? Even how you urinate is important. Fortunately for Lee, he had studied Pashtun culture with the language, but understanding it intellectually and living it were two different things. His real-world test wouldn't allow him time to think about the answer.

They spent a half day explaining his real-world test. He was to be turned lose in London as a Pakistani Pashtun immigrant and he had to establish himself in a Muslim community. He had to get comfortable in a Muslim's skin and try to live a normal life amongst Muslims.

He spent most of his study time in the sun, when it was shining, letting his skin darken. It didn't help the scars, which remained white, but the contrast just made his face look rougher and weather-beaten. When Abi and Mallory showed up on the last day, Lee looked more like a native of northeast Afghanistan than a U.S. Naval Officer. Well, at least he didn't look like a Naval officer. Lee was waiting for them in Man-jams and turban.

"*Assalam O Alaikum. Sehat de Kha de?*" Lee said in greeting. (Peace be upon you. Your health is good?)

Mallory replied. "*Assalam O Alaikum. Za teek Yum.* (Peace be upon you. I am fine.) That's enough Mr. Toliver. Abi doesn't speak the language. I like the look. A bit more beard, and I think you will be ready."

Abi was in her wheelchair but stood up and pushed it back. She looked steady.

"Hi Abi," Lee said. "What do you think? Am I ready for the back streets of London?"

Abi stepped back toward her chair and gave Lee a good look. She hadn't seen him in three weeks.

"I'm amazed. I guess the old saying that clothes make the man is true. At least in appearance, I think you'd pass for a Paki immigrant. Do you feel ready to try?"

"If I waited until I felt ready we might not ever get this show on the road. I feel like I'm standing just off stage waiting for the curtain call. What's the plan?"

"Let's load up," Mallory said. "We can talk in

the van."

Mallory brought a van to accommodate Lee's baggage and the study materials. It took a few minutes to get everything loaded. Lee helped Abi get her chair in the sliding door of the van and helped her up into the seat. She turned her head and smiled.

"Sit back here with me, Lee. I'll brief you on London while Jake drives."

Mallory drove and watched Lee in the mirror when he could.

"Lee, don't take this assignment in Londonstan lightly," he said. "The reason you got the SAS training is because you just might need it."

"Really, Mr. Mallory? Londonstan?" Abi said.

"How many Muslims in London, Lieutenant?"

"Well, yes, about six hundred thousand. But Londonstan?"

"Six hundred thousand," Mallory said. "I rest my case. If you Brits keep on the way you're going with immigration, your high court will be adjudicating Sharia law in ten years. Lee there are places in London where gangs of Sharia law enforcers roam the streets without interference. This is training, but it's not a soft assignment. You may have to use your training to protect yourself. Abi give him the rundown."

"Right," Abi said. "Lee, we've chosen for you the East End, one of the more active Muslim hot spots in our dear city. The Boroughs of Newham and Tower Hamlets are about 30% Muslim and there is a lot of tension between Muslims and Non-Muslims, but the area has the attractive feature of being a Muslim melting pot, as you Yanks put it. I'll have to read this, just a moment."

Abi opened a sheet of paper and began to read.

"Newham is home to about 86,000 Muslims. There are Pakistanis, Algerians, Kurds, Nigerians, Afghans, Albanians, Ghanaians, Swahilis, Arabs, Bangladeshis, Indians, Somalis, and Iraqis. The different groups tend to cluster, but we think you will find it easier to blend in this multicultural environment. There is everything from nominal Muslims who were born and raised in London to radical conservatives from the mountains of Pakistan and Africa as well as home-grown radicals. It will be a good test of your cover."

"We'll drop you at Heathrow and you can make your way to town by train. I've got the address of a flat where you will stay at first. Three other young Muslims live there and they have a single bedroom to rent. Finding accommodations in that area is difficult and four or five single people often rent a larger flat and then share out the cost of rent. It is a place to sleep for them and little socialization takes place, but still, it will be your strongest test.

"Find your way there as any immigrant would. It's not the nicest available or the worst, closer to the least expensive we could find, the kind of place an immigrant with some money, but not a lot, would seek. Ask questions, get lost, be confused. Eventually you'll find it. If you are cautious, you will seem genuine.

We've got traveling clothes for you. Watch for signs of suspicion and be prepared to improvise."

"You mean right now? You're going to throw me into the fire today?"

"You got it, and Lee, understand, we can't watch you. The best cover you have is to be as uninformed and confused as any new immigrant. You're supposed to be scared and nervous. You're in a new country and seeing sights you've never seen. You'll have a cheap cell phone. It has one London number in the memory. That's us. That number will always be answered in Urdu. We don't expect it, but if you get in trouble, call. We'll have a car to you in minutes."

Lee was quiet for a few moments. This all was a bit more abrupt than he liked.

"All right, so I find my way to the rooming house. So, what's the objective of this exercise?"

"Rehearsal," Abi said. "Learn how to behave as a Muslim stranger in a Muslim community. Make friends, get along in society, get a job if you can. Find out what is expected of you. Other Muslims can teach you much better than we can, but you must be careful and be prepared to improvise. Face the unexpected and improvise to deal with it. That's the way it will be in the field. Think on your feet. Pick up habit. Let your behavior become habitual. This is the only rehearsal you get before you go operational. There is an element of risk If you are found out and that will be an added incentive to do well. You could get hurt if you are careless. You must live your part twenty-four hours a day. You must *be* a Paki immigrant."

"You are the expert," Mallory said. "Everything you've done in life has brought you to this point. Let's see if all that work has any practical value. If you can do well here, your chances of success in the field are good."

"And one final thing," Abi said. "You have several languages. Act dumb and keep your ears open. Don't intentionally spy. Just keep your ears open. The East End is full of radicals, so there is no telling what you might pick up. And Lee, let's not get morbid with all this. You are to be cautious, but you are in London. There are tube stops everywhere. You are only minutes from the embassy."

Chapter 42

With his faked Pakistani passport and UK visa, battered suitcase, rumpled clothes, and a modest and polite attitude, finding the flat wasn't difficult. A young boy at Whitechapel Station pointed him in the right direction and Lee gawked at the city sights as he made his way to the address on the paper he was given. Acting like an immigrant wasn't hard. He was an immigrant to London. Everything he saw in this part of town was new.

    The name chosen for him was Al Siddiq Hassan. Al Siddiq meaning the truthful, a popular boy's name, and an Arabic heritage last name, Hassan. It was a reasonably neutral name combination from common Muslim names in Urdu Pakistan and didn't tie him to any tribe or lineage. Just the kind of thing you might expect of a person living on the edge of legality.

The apartment building wasn't anything to write home about, but it wasn't a slum either. After he was admitted to the building and met the Bangladeshi who had his name on the lease and who sub-let the small, one-bed room and collected the rent, Lee dumped his suitcase and went out to get used to the East End of London.

His first search was for a Halal restaurant (serving foods permissible for a Muslim to eat) that served Pakistani food. He wanted to sit in a crowd, eat, and let the sounds and sights flow over him. He couldn't deny the nervous tension that was building up inside him—or the anticipation of testing his knowledge and skills. What would happen if someone called him out? What he didn't realize was nervous tension just looked like confusion and fear, just what he ought to look like.

He discovered a tube stop just a two-minute walk from his flat. He noted the Zone two, Mile-End tube station in his memory and continued his search. He had worked out how to get from the Astor Court to Marble Arch, but that was the extent of his confidence in the London tube system. That ignorance would be a help in his cover. He had no more idea of how to get around than any immigrant freshly landed in the city.

Stopping strangers on the street and asking directions was his first test, and it seemed to go well. A Pakistani who spoke Pashto directed him to Brick Street and finding a Pakistani restaurant with a halal sign in front was easy. Going in and taking a seat was hard on the nerves. Sitting and eating with locals involved all the little mannerisms and behaviors that could trip him up. Just before entering he stopped and put things in perspective. I'm in London, he thought. This isn't Ramadi. They don't carry guns here. It didn't rise to the surface, but subconsciously, he also delighted in the secret, the idea of putting one over on everyone else. There's a bit of the little boy in every man.

He ordered rice haleem and mutton karahi. Naan bread and hot, unsweetened tea came with the meal. He used the bread to scoop up food from the dishes as would be common in Pakistan. The food was good and he ate with a good appetite which helped him to settle down and behave naturally without thinking about everything before he did it. Hungry people eating look similar everywhere.

Gulab jamun was available and made a nice desert. It is made by boiling down milk and then kneading the solids into balls, and deep frying the balls. It is then soaked in a light sugary syrup and flavored with green cardamom and saffron. The ones Lee had, were covered with crushed nuts.

He stopped with a jamun halfway to his mouth and smiled. He was thinking in Pashto. The immersion in culture and language had caused that subtle little shift in his mind that brings fluency. Until the mind made that shift, you are just translating.

The restaurant was authentic and seated patrons

randomly at takhts, raised platforms where the patrons sat cross-legged after taking their shoes off. One of Lee's socks had a hole over one toe. He stood out at his takht because he was seated with five young people who were obviously office workers. Through the conversation around him, he determined two of them were from Pakistan.

"Hey, country boy," one of the Pakistanis said in Urdu. "Where is your home?"

Lee stumbled over his Urdu and asked if the other man spoke Pashto. The other guy listened closely and said he did.

"My home is in Parachinar, but I haven't been there in many years," Lee said.

"A mountain man. It would be impolite for me to ask what you do."

A nice neutral statement. Lee could ignore it or answer.

"I trade," Lee said, leaving it ambiguous.

The Pakistani smiled and let it go.

"You are eating those jamun like they won't make any more. How long have you been in London?"

"Today," Lee said. "I arrived today."

"Well, good fortune to you. Peace be upon you."

"And upon you, peace," Lee said.

The Pakistani got up and left. The others ignored him. They were busy with their food and in a hurry to get back to their business. He seemed to have passed his first test. He could eat and converse with the locals without raising suspicion.

The local people were only a small test. London had worked its frantic magic on them. They were enclosed in their gossamer thought cocoons and nothing got through but the sight of their food. The hurried necessities of city-dwelling had overcome custom and culture. Lee took his time with his food and sipped his tea slowly while he listened in on the conversations around him and picked up as much local gossip as the diners were willing to share.

Later, he decided to walk around and see how well he fit in. So far, so good. It felt good to stretch his legs and loosen up. Getting enough exercise was going to be a problem. Immigrants didn't normally go out on five or ten-mile runs through the city. He wandered through Tower Hamlets back streets. Soon he was lost but wasn't worried. Getting lost is the best way to find your way around. He walked slowly with his hands behind his back. As Abi said, he was in London and never far from a tube stop.

After a while, common sense reemerged and it occurred to him that even if it was New York City in America, wandering around a place you didn't know was something less than a good idea. He stopped and tried to figure out his location. Turning back toward what he thought was the way he had come, he took time to observe and take in his surroundings. He was surrounded by high rise apartment buildings and beat-up playgrounds.

He concentrated on finding something familiar as he walked. He passed a group of children but didn't really see them. They were just part of the drab urban scenery.

Suddenly, he felt a sharp pain as something struck him on the back of the shoulder.

He turned quickly and grabbed his shoulder. A stone zipped by his ear and he spotted six or seven small kids laughing. They were trying to pelt him with stones. He started toward them, but they ran away laughing.

The children followed him down the street making fun of him. It was damn awkward. He wanted to catch them and slap the piss out of them but knew he couldn't do something like that. Kids are just naturally cruel. It's not even cruel to them. Maybe that's humanity's natural state. They were calling out, ad-Dajjal, ad-Dajjal. Oh, Christ, not again. Did he really look that bad? The insurgents in Ramadi had given him that name too.

It took him a while to catch the word because they weren't pronouncing the Arabic correctly, but he finally caught on. In the Hadith, Ad-Dajjal is the deceiver and is supposed to have the word Kafir (disbeliever) between his eyes. That shook Lee's confidence to the core. He was a deceiver and disbeliever and the last thing he needed was a bunch of kids calling attention to it.

Fortunately, a shop owner stepped outside to see what the noise was about. He took in Lee's face and what was happening quickly and chased the kid's off. Lee finally found Brick Street again and returned to his little bedroom as quickly as he could. He'd had enough of innocent cruelty for now.

When he unlocked the door, and entered the flat, he didn't need scar constrictions to make his face look dark and angry. He was angry and hurt and discouraged. Nothing was going to change. It was going to be like this for the rest of his life. How in the hell could he have lost all that he had so completely, to become an object to be mocked and made fun of by children?

Three young men, about Lee's age, were sitting in the kitchen. Two of them were drinking beer. Well, Abi said the East End had all kinds of Muslims from devout to nominal.

"Our new mate returns from his secret pursuits. Come and join us. How was your first day in London?" He was speaking English, like an Englishman. That was always disconcerting, hearing someone so obviously middle-eastern with a British accent. His was cockney, almost a separate language. The young men had obviously been briefed by the landlord. They had been looking at Lee from his good side, and when he turned, the room got silent.

"What language do you speak?" Lee asked. "My English is bad."

"Better practice it, mate, unless you plan to spend all of your time on Brick Street."

"I will tell you how my day was," Lee said.

"Children, children of the faith, chased me and stoned me and called me ad-Dajjal. Never have I wanted to hurt someone so much in my life." Lee let out a string of profanity in Pashto that would have made his professors at Princeton blanch.

"That is a bad day. A bloke could be put off by a day like that. Come and sit with us and tell us about yourself."

They didn't seem impressed by his ordeal, or very concerned about his discomfort. Two of the quiet ones seemed amused.

Your hospitality is welcome," Lee said. "But I will be alone for this night. Forgive my bad manners. Peace be upon you."

"Sure, mate. There's a saying the Americans have. Shit Happens. Join us anytime you want to. What do we call you?"

"I am Hassan."

"Hassan, I am Ali. The bloke on this side is Majid, and the one over here is Aarif. We will talk another time."

Lee locked his door and stretched out on the bed. The incident with the kids had affected him more than he wanted to admit. Suddenly he longed to be back with the SEALs. It was one thing to be mocked or insulted by an adult. That was a deliberate attempt to hurt you, and you could pass it off as that, but kids just reacted to what they saw, and what they saw was obviously something repulsive or funny to them.

As he was trying to think of something else to put the incident out of his mind, he heard a soft sound at his door. He looked that way and saw a shadow on the light coming through the crack at the bottom of his door. He began reciting his short bedtime surahs softly but loud enough for anyone listening to hear. Soon the shadow at the bottom of the door disappeared.

The next three days passed much the same as his first day, sans humiliation. He ate at the same Pakistani restaurant and could tell some of the diners recognized him. That was encouraging. He was fitting in. They noted his entrance, but when they saw who it was they went back to their meals. The young men at the flat seemed to accept him as a loner and let it go at that. They left early before he got up each day and didn't return until after he was in his room. They didn't make any further attempt to be sociable.

Chapter 43

On his fifth day, someone sat next to him at the takht in the restaurant.

"Peace be upon you, brother. You have come a long way. Do you have family here?"

"And upon you, peace," Lee said. The stranger had spoken Pashto and Lee answered him in kind. "I have very little family anywhere. Your dialect is familiar. You are from Miran Shah?"

"And you are from Parachinar, but your dialect is mixed. You could almost be Afghani. I am Ghazan Khan."

Regions and even particular cities can be recognized by the way certain words are spoken, much the same as Delaware people can be recognized by the way they say water, or in Delaware, "wooder," or the way Long Island people say "longilan" with a hard G and missing D. In many other countries and languages, the identifiers are even more striking.

That name got Lee's attention. Ghazan would translate as holy war fighter. But names were given by parents and often reflected their wishes rather than reality. Still, sometimes men took on names that reflected what they aspired to be—or were.

Al Siddiq Hassan," Lee said. "It has been a long time since I have been in the FATA. (Federally Administered Tribal Areas in Pakistan bordering Afghanistan)"

"I could have mistaken you for a Nuristani," Ghazan said. "Your features resemble them."

"I have known the K'om," Lee said. He was getting nervous. His last instruction from Mallory was not to get close to anyone or get into any extended conversations where his cover could be taken apart and he was afraid he had already slipped up.

"I thought as much," Ghazan said. "You are a trader. Is that right?"

Trouble was staring him in the face. This guy obviously knew the area and the people—and had been talking to someone. Lee was going to get caught if he let this go on. Besides, Ghazan was being deliberately impolite. It might have been just the influence of living in a foreign country, but Lee didn't think so. You just didn't start a third degree with a Pashtun stranger, if you valued your life. It was time to get righteous. Lee pushed the remainder of his meal away and stood up.

Ghazan was being impolite so Lee wasn't worried about a polite parting.

"I have business to attend. Peace be upon you."

He paid his bill and left. Just before he went through the door, he heard laughter from the takht where he had been sitting.

Ghazan waited for Lee to leave and then said quietly to two men sitting across from him, "Ad Dajjal." All three of them laughed.

"What do you think of Hassan?" Ghazan asked.

"He is hiding something," one said.

"Nuristani, maybe Pashtun, but if so, he has lived in Nuristan," the other said. "His Pashto is too formal."

"I thought the same," Ghazan said. "He didn't get those scars from sleeping too close to the campfire. A fighter, maybe a bomb maker. A careless one."

"Why do you think he is in London?"

Ghazan shrugged expressively. "Why are we in London? Many people, many reasons. There is something strange about him though. The Nuristanis all look western when they are young. I have even seen some with blonde hair and blue eyes, but Hassan, on his good side, looks very western. Have you ever seen a mountain fighter sit the way he does? He isn't comfortable at the Takht and his manners are primitive."

"Why do you think he is trying to pass himself off as a Pashtun?"

"He is cautious," Ghazan said. "It is easier for a Pakistani to get a British visa than a Nuristani from the region where the Americans are fighting. I don't trust him though. Something is not right about him. What does Ali say about him?"

"He was very angry last night. Children threw stones at him while he was exploring the streets around here. Ali invited him to sit with his friends, but Hassan refused. He went straight to his room. Ali said that later he heard Hassan reciting the Qur'an in his room. Nothing else."

"We will keep an eye on him. Perhaps he will be useful for us and perhaps not."

After his meal, Ghazan found a private place and dialed a number he had saved on his cell phone. The man who answered did so in Urdu.

"Allah is the one and has no partners."

"And Muhammad is his apostle," Ghazan replied. "Do we have an agent in the East End I haven't been informed about?"

"Other than you and Ali, no. Why do you ask?"

"Give me a reading on a name. Al Siddiq Hassan. Just arrived in London last week. Claims to be Pashtun from Pakistan but has western features. One side of his face has been burned and is scarred badly. About five-ten, dark hair, brown eyes, about eighty kilograms."

"Call back in one hour."

The call clicked off.

The communications specialist turned and waved for his supervisor.

"Query from Ghazan."

The supervisor glanced over the message quickly and said, "forward it to Leftenant Dundee. A moment later Abi's laptop pinged, signaling an incoming message from the communications center. She clicked on the icon and Ghazan's message came up. She smiled and shook her head. Everything seemed to be working but Lee's cover—or maybe his cover was working better than they had any right to think it would. Ghazan was an experienced agent and trained to be suspicious. Something had raised his suspicions, but he had doubts. She forwarded the message to Mallory.

Mallory read the message and called Abi. "Tell Ghazan everything checks out on Hassan, but to keep an eye on him. Tell him Hassan could be the real deal and dangerous. Lee needs to learn what being hunted feels like."

"You could be throwing him to the wolves,"

"He's in London just minutes away. What do you think it's going to be like in the field? Send the message."

"Lee didn't sign up for this," Abi said.

"Your loyalty is commendable and noted, Abi. Send the message."

Abi didn't like it, but when Ghazan called in, the

message was passed. Lee's status as someone to be watched stepped up a notch. With Ghazan and Ali increasing their surveillance, a radical organization they had infiltrated became aware of Hassan and Ghazan was questioned about him. He let them know Hassan might be a potential recruit.

But Ghazan and Ali had their own problems and didn't know it. When they left the Mosque, they were followed.

Lee's life was about to get more exciting than he expected or wanted.

Chapter 44

When you live a covert life, it is easy to become paranoid. If a stranger passes you on the street and looks at you twice, you panic. If you see the same person twice in the same day, you are being followed. You begin to look over your shoulder a lot.

Lee began changing direction abruptly and going to his destinations along odd routes when he went out, watching to see if anyone followed along. He watched for unusual interest in his presence when he ate or shopped. He stopped at store windows to observe the reflection and see if anyone was watching him. He practiced all the little tradecraft techniques he had been taught. The more you practiced, the more natural you looked when doing them.

He thought he should begin looking for a new

restaurant. His movements were becoming too predictable. Maybe it was time to broaden his activities, but he liked Pakistani food and the restaurant he frequented did a good job of preparing it, and he was comfortable there.

He began stopping a few doors down from the restaurant to observe comings and goings for a few minutes before entering the restaurant. Just a precaution. He was in place before dinner and watching on his seventh night in the East End. Nothing much was happening on the street. It was early yet. An old man was leaning against the wall of the building next to the restaurant. Lee noticed him because you don't see many old men with backpacks. Young guys, yes, but old men not so much. Paranoia, he thought. I've got to get this under control. Still, he continued to watch.

Cars dropped off diners and other diners began showing up on foot. He saw Ghazan and Ali, one of his roommates coming down the street. They entered the restaurant together. A moment later the old man went in too. A busy night for the restaurant, but nothing exciting happening. His stomach growled and his covert observation got boring. He went to the restaurant too.

The restaurant was crowded when he entered. As he had been taught, he did a quick scan of the inside with his eyes. Ghazan and Ali were at a Takht with one place held open. The old man with the backpack was at their Takht. Most other seats were already taken. No one seemed especially interested in him. When they saw Lee walk in, Ghazan and Ali waved and signaled for

Lee to join them.

"Hassan, it is good to see you. What have you been doing with yourself?"

Hot, unsweetened, strong tea was served immediately and Lee ordered a mutton dish for his supper. He spoke Urdu to the server.

"I have been looking for employment," Lee continued in Urdu.

"You are a man of many talents," Ghazan said in Urdu. "Your Urdu is good."

"A trader must be many things," Lee said. "If you cannot haggle with your customers, you do not eat often." He was more comfortable in Urdu or Pasto because he didn't have to fake mispronounced words and accent like he did with English. An English speaker trying to mimic broken English, sounds like someone trying to mimic broken English. Not many can do it well.

Ali said, "Greetings roomie. It is good to see you out of your room. I was beginning to think you were a hermit. Will it offend you if I ask about your family?"

Bad luck, Ali spoke in English.

"We will have to see," Lee said. "What do you want to know?" He spoke slowly and precisely, sounding as though he was picking out his words carefully. His careful English didn't seem to bother anyone.

"Do you have a European in your lineage?"

Lee paused and looked directly at Ali. He clamped down his jaw.

"What you ask is a matter of honor and is

something I do not wish to discuss. Your question is insulting."

Ali held up his hands. "No offense intended. I asked if it would offend you first."

Lee relaxed and smiled his crooked, scar-twisted smile. He offered his hand to Ali.

"And now I cause offense. Pardon me."

Ali took his hand and smiled. "It is nothing," he said.

"You are a touchy one," Ghazan said. "I'm almost afraid to ask you anything. Without any offense intended, I suspect your English is much better than you let on. It is meant as a compliment."

Lee sipped his tea for a moment.

"I am new here," he said. "Many people have been friendly, but many others have been cruel and insulting. It is like anywhere else in the world. A man must be cautious. I prefer to speak Urdu or Pashto, but Dari is comfortable for me also. I also have a few words in Uzbek. Does that answer your questions?"

"I have no problem with caution," Ghazan said. "May I ask where you learned your English?"

"The best way," Lee said, ignoring the "where." He was improvising now and on dangerous ground. "I learned as a child as I learned my own language. My mother was a maid to an English family, and my father was—missing. Ah, my mutton arrives, and this conversation has gone far enough. *Bon Appetit*, my friends."

Lee's server placed his dish and topped off his tea. The ambiance of the restaurant was Pakistani mixed with Anglo touches. Many customers were British and their expectations as to service lent some western touches to the traditional atmosphere. Lee tore his bread apart and used it like a spoon. The food was authentic and very good. He didn't have to pretend to like it. One of the things Pakistan and Afghanistan did right was food. But one thing was putting him off his food and making him nervous.

The whole time he had been questioned by Ali and Ghazan, the old man at the end of the table had been studiously trying not to look interested, so much so it became obvious. He didn't introduce himself, and neither Ali nor Ghazan offered to introduce him or even acted like they knew him. He was an older man, maybe in his sixties, hard to tell with some Middle-Easterners. In any case, he was far senior to Lee, and it would have been impolite for Lee to make the first move. He tried to put the eavesdropper out of his mind.

Ali and Ghazan were hanging out, sipping tea, and sharing a bowl filled with Gulab Jamun. When Lee had completed his meal, the questions continued, but Ali and Ghazan began sharing information about themselves this time. Ghazan was asking Lee about his Mosque when the old man got up and hurried out of the restaurant. The owner ran toward the door shouting something about paying. Lee noticed a backpack on the takht where the old man had been sitting. Why did he leave it? He looked to see if the old guy was coming back, but he was gone.

Chills raised the hair on his arms. Why did the old man run out and leave his backpack? Oh shit, what the hell should I do? He just forgot it, that's all. But why did he run? Panic set in. This couldn't be happening again. Lee stared at the backpack for another instant and then panic won. Memories of the bus exploding pushed everything else out of his mind. He scattered dishes and tea with his hand as he pushed himself up.

"What? What?" Ghazan yelled.

Lee's eyes were wide and wild. Panic seized him and he ran. He crashed into the owner at the door, tripped and rolled, and regained his feet. He turned left to get away from the door. The old man was there ahead of him parting crowds and still running up Brick Street.

The explosion came as Ghazan ran after him at a full run. The force of the blast lifted Ghazan and slammed him into Lee and then tumbled them both for another twenty feet in the street. Ghazan was down and out. His body had shielded Lee from the worst of the blast.

Lee held onto consciousness through shear panic. He let himself roll and came up on his feet and ran as fast as his dazed senses would allow him. He couldn't feel any pain, just panic and an insane need to get away. His hearing was gone, but he could still see since he had been running away from the blast.

He ran headlong for a block and then slowed to a walk as the panic subsided. Lights were flashing up ahead. People were coming out of buildings and running toward him on both sides of the street. Breathing hard, he backed against a building and turned to get a look at the blast scene. Smoke and total chaos at that end of the street. He looked at the crowd, and then he looked up the street in the opposite direction.

Then he saw him again, the old man, now walking calmly with his arms folded in front of him about a block further along, just like he was taking his nightly stroll before prayer. Lee started following. He increased his pace. Maybe it was just an old man out for a stroll, but one thing was wrong about the picture.

While everyone else in the area was running toward the blast site, this guy was walking calmly away against the stream—and his clothes were the same as the old man wore. Lee took his folding knife out of his pocket. He opened it carefully, making sure the blade locked. The hate and anger he felt bordered on insanity. In Lee's mind, the old man took on the aura of all that had haunted Lee's life.

He had to make sure. No mistakes here. He had to see his face, the one who had listened in and tried to hide his interest. The one who left a bomb to kill whoever happened to be there for whatever twisted reason the bastard had. The one who had destroyed Lee's face and life. The one who made him a freak. Can't make a mistake.

Lee increased his pace. The guy was stupid—or very good. He never looked back. He walked calmly and didn't draw attention to himself. Lee began to have doubts. Can't make a mistake. The crowd had thinned out. Soon it was only Lee and the old man and a few scattered people looking down the street. But Lee didn't see the street. Just the old man.

The old man turned a corner and was out of sight for the few moments it took Lee to reach that street. He turned the corner. The old man was running now, but he wasn't fast. Lee pumped his legs into a dead run. The old guy finally turned his head when he heard running footsteps behind him and tried to run harder, but he didn't have the strength or youth Lee had. Lee was ten feet behind him and gaining when the guy found his second or third wind and began opening a lead. Lee dug deep for everything he had and closed the distance again. The guy zigged and Lee gained. He zagged and Lee gained some more.

The old man looked over his shoulder. Lee saw his face clearly. No mistake at all. No further doubt. Lee kept moving forward and caught the guy by the shoulders, pushing him hard, moving him on a diagonal toward an alley opening.

Now Lee didn't look back. If anyone was watching, that was just too bad. He tightened his grip and hustled the guy forward as he resisted and twisted. The old man tried to reach Lee's eyes with his hands, but Lee wrapped his shoulders and lifted him, pulling him close, pinning his arms. He didn't even feel the kicks to his legs. He hustled him into the alley and slammed him against the wall.

The old man was strong, he struggled, but he

didn't have the size and muscle strength to resist a 190-pound American in prime condition. Lee didn't see an old man. He saw everything that was evil to him. Everything that had made his face the way it was and took away the life he had known and crippled Abi.

He pressed his forearm across the guy's throat and pressed until his eyes bugged out and his knees got weak. The old man had guts though. He stared at Lee with hatred so vivid it caused Lee to pull back for a moment.

The hate was tangible and electric. It matched Lee's own.

Lee put his knife hand across the old man's forehead and pushed his head back into the brick. The old guy was so winded he couldn't resist. With the guy's throat exposed, Lee put the razor edge of his knife against the old man's skin. As he pressed the blade, a trickle of blood began to run down the side of his neck. Lee heard running feet getting closer.

Lee spoke in Pashto. "Look at my face."

"It is the ugly face of an infidel," the old man said.

"You insane pig. You did that, you and your insane religion."

The old man didn't flinch. He just stared hate into Lee's eyes.

"Not me," he said. "I would have cut your head off."

Footsteps were louder and closer.

Lee's mind crossed the line then. All his pent-up

fear, humiliation, loss, and despair urged the hate on until it became insane rage. He began pressing the knife hard, but then a light made a silhouette of him.

"Drop the knife and step away from the wall!"

Shit! He wanted to scream. He wanted to draw the blade across the skin letting the old bastard's life gush out onto the street. But he couldn't. A lifetime of obedience and discipline held his hand. At least the law would get the bomb making son of a bitch. The rage began to cool, and disappointment and frustration took the strength out of him.

"Be calm," Lee said without releasing the old man. His voice was trembling. "Let's do this safely. I'm going to lower my knife and drop it."

He held the old man with one arm across his forehead and started lowering his knife hand. The old man smirked. That was too much for Lee.

As his hand reached his waist, he shoved the blade into the guy's gut and ripped it upward, grabbed his shirt with his other hand, spun, and shoved the dying body into the Bobby behind him. The Bobby was the only one there and all he had was a nightstick and flashlight.

As the old man brought the Bobby down, Lee ran as hard as he could.

Chapter 45

The phone was answered on the first ring. The voice on the line spoke Urdu.

"Allah is the one and has no partners,"

"Muhammad is his Apostle. This is Hassan. I need help."

"Are you in immediate danger?"

"Not this minute."

"Hold the line."

The call went silent for a moment and then a click.

"Where are you, Lee?" It was Abi.

"I'm at the Mile End tube station. I need to be picked up."

"Were you involved in the explosion on Brick Street?"

"Yes. I'm okay."

"A car has been dispatched. Is it safe for you to go out to the street?"

"Yes, briefly."

"What time does your watch have?"

"Nineteen-ten."

"All right. At Nineteen twenty-five go up and stand at the curb. A yellow mini will stop in front of you. Get in quickly."

"Nineteen twenty-five. Yellow Mini. Got it."

The yellow Mini was exactly on time. It swooped in just as Lee stepped up to the curb. The driver was a pro and took Lee along the scenic route, and some routes not so scenic, before pulling into an underground garage. Abi was waiting with the door to the lift open. She waited until he was inside and punched a button for the sixth floor.

"Mallory is here. Care to give me a quick briefing?"

"Had dinner in a Pakistani restaurant on Brick street where I usually eat. Met up with two locals. One is a resident of the flat you put me in. Name, Ali. The other, named Ghazan, met me in the restaurant last week. Old Middle-Eastern guy at the table, left in a hurry and left a backpack on the table where he had been sitting. I panicked and ran. Ghazan followed me out and the blast happened just as he came up behind me. I had got past the door and was out of the worst of the blast. Ghazan shielded me from the rest. I don't know what happened to Ali or the rest of the people in the place. I stayed conscious and ran. Found my way to Mile End and called. I don't know if my cover was blown or what.

"That's good for now. We'll get into details later. Are you sure you are all right?"

"Some aches and pains, but nothing serious. My hearing is coming back.

"Here we are. Help me with a push. Come along."

Mallory was sitting inside, and Lee stopped in the doorway and stared. Ghazan sat on a desk looking like the angel of death while a medic worked on his back. He looked at Lee and grimaced. "I should have known." he said. "Appreciate all of your support and help back there. You could have given a bloke a hand."

"What the hell is he doing here?" Lee said.

"Sit down, Lee," Mallory said. "Are you all right? Need anything?"

"An explanation would be helpful. What the hell is going on?"

"Is that blood on your hands?" Abi said.

Lee held his hands up and turned them over. He had kept them in his pockets while waiting at the tube stop.

Must be someone else's," he said. "I'm not wounded."

"You didn't notice it before?"

"Hell, I guess I did. I just didn't think about it.

Honestly, Abi, I haven't noticed much of anything since the blast. I panicked and all I could think about was getting to a safe place and making the call. I just wanted the hell out of there."

"There's enough blood back there to go around," Ghazan said. "I looked for you, but you were gone by the time I came-to."

"How about Ali?"

"He wasn't fast enough, but he missed the worst of it."

"Okay. Will someone please tell me what the hell is going on?"

"Lee, meet agent Amin Danyal, MI6," Abi said. "Amin, well, you've figured it out, I assume."

"As soon as he walked in," Amin said. "Why was I misled?"

"It's complicated," Mallory said.

"I'll deal with my agent's questions, thank you very much," Abi said. "We felt it necessary to fully test Lee's cover, Amin. It is important, even critical, for another mission. If Lee could pass as a Pakistani Pashtun, even for a short while here, he may be ready. How you, a trained agent, reacted to him is an important test. We couldn't reveal his identity."

Amin's miff seemed mollified with Abi's explanation.

"He raised suspicion, not about his authenticity, but about what kind of secret he was hiding. I suspected him of being a radical. He acted too suspicious, like he was hiding something. His cover is pretty damn good, at least with people you will find in the east end."

"Do you think he could pass for a Pakistani Pashtun in Afghanistan, at least for short periods of time?"

"With natives? Maybe, if he kept his contact informal and short, like he did with us. The face helps. No offense, Hassan. People are reluctant to look too closely. It worked with me. His language is good, and his manners single him out as a country boy. I don't know what you have going on, and I don't want to know, but listen. I *am* a Pakistani Pashtun and I doubt my survival odds would be more than fifty-fifty if I tried to infiltrate an actual in-country insurgent group.

Mallory coughed. "Thank you, Amin. I'm sure you are anxious to find out about your mates. Abi, thank your excellent team for us. They did an outstanding job getting Lee to safety. Now I think it's time to get Lee to the embassy for a full debrief. I'll send you a full transcript."

"No need," Abi said. "I'm coming with you."

Chapter 46

The debrief included a CIA interrogator who took Lee over and over the same ground. Each inconsistency was pointed out and Lee was questioned some more. Around 2100 the session was interrupted and Mallory was handed a message. He read it and waved for the session to go on. The interrogator finally wrapped the session up near 2200.

"Abi, you can take off," Mallory said. "I'm going to keep Lee at the embassy tonight. We'll need a safe house for him for the rest of the time he's here. Can you handle that?"

"Yes, of course. I could take him there tonight, if you would like."

"No, I want to get his thoughts on a mission tonight. Tomorrow will be fine."

Abi looked disappointed. Lee was just beginning to come to grips with what he had done and missed Abi's look.

"Well," Abi said, "I'll get started on that right away. Noon, Lee?"

"I'll be ready," he said absently.

Mallory waited for Abi to leave before he spoke.

"Do you two have something going on?"

"Who?" Lee said.

Mallory just stared at him.

"Me and Abi?"

"Knock it off, Igor. Coy doesn't work with a guy who just gutted another guy."

Lee's shock gave it away.

"Yeah, we know," Mallory said. "Want to tell me about it? Who was he?"

There wasn't any sense in denying it, and Mallory didn't seem upset about it.

"The bomber," Lee said. "As I told you in the debrief, I ran out not far behind him. After the blast, I panicked and just started running, in the right direction, as it turned out. He was just strolling up the street like he was taking his evening constitutional. Never even looked back. I got close, saw an alley, and well, I lost it. It all happened so fast I'm having trouble putting it back together."

"You don't seem torn up about doing it. As far as we can tell, you got the right guy. The police think so too. He's known."

"I'm just confused right now. I'd do it again if I could, but I'd make it last this time. He got off too easy. By the way, you don't seem overly concerned about it either."

"Tickles the shit out me," Mallory said and grinned. "Here I was wondering how I was going to introduce you to wet-work without throwing you to the wolves, and all along you were the big bad wolf yourself."

Lee wiped some grime off his forehead and flexed his hand. He still had some blood on it.

"Don't go overboard on the big bad wolf thing. He wasn't that big and he wasn't a fighter and I don't know how I'm going to feel about this crap in the morning. Right now, I'm so full of adrenalin I'm not feeling anything."

"Don't dwell on it. He needed killing. If you hadn't done it, I would have sent someone else. Got to admit though, I had my doubts about you becoming a knife man."

"Can we talk about something else? Did the cop make me?"

"You are an unknown assailant, but they are investigating leads the nature of which they are not at liberty to disclose. That means no. They haven't got the foggiest. That won't last. Standing around in a tube stop with bloody hands wasn't the smartest thing you ever did."

"Yeah, well, it's probably not the only dumb thing I did. Things were kind of hectic right then. So,

345

how did the people who did this make me?"

"What makes you think they did?"

"Isn't that obvious? He damn near blew me up again."

"I doubt it was you," Mallory said. "You were sitting with Ghazan and Ali and you said he was already there when you got there. They have been working that area for a long time. If anyone got made, it was them."

Lee thought about that. The old man did follow Ali and Ghazan into the restaurant.

"Okay, I hadn't thought about them being the target. Hell, I didn't know they were good guys until just now. Look, I'm going to need some time to unwind and work this out."

"Way ahead of you. We have a month to get you in shape for the mountains. I think you're ready. We can spare a week. I'm sure you and Abi can figure out something to do with the time."

"Mallory, damn it, if you . . ."

Mallory held up his hands and grinned.

"Just saying, just saying. Believe me, I have no objections at all. When you get done with her just roll her into a closet or somewhere and we'll . . ."

Mallory didn't get to finish his vulgarity. Lee was on him without waiting for the sentence to end. And then, before he knew it, Lee was on his back trying to get his breath back with Mallory standing over him.

"You're pretty good, Igor. Much better than I thought. The Brits did a good job with you. But you ain't that good, sunny boy. Keep it in mind. You can probably handle anything you'll find in the Middle East, but you are not a Delta operator. Now sit down."

After Lee regained his seat and had time to rub the arm Mallory used to put him on his ass, Mallory grinned and said, "I apologize for the crude remark. Abi is a nice lady, and more important to me, she's not a security risk. I deliberately provoked you to see how you would come at me."

"Why?"

Mallory pointed at Lee's pocket. Blood had formed the shape of his knife on the material.

"I wanted to see if you would use your hands or your knife. There are men who will use a knife if they have too and some who prefer it. Among those who prefer it, there are those who like it, and there are a few who like it too much. They are a risk. I needed to know how you fit. The way you took out the bomber really surprised us. Where would you say you fit?"

"I can handle it, but I can't say I like it."

"Yeah, that's how I see it too.

Chapter 47

Lee had one week with Abi and she helped him deal with the memories. He had killed in Afghanistan and again in Iraq, but they were all long-range kills. It was different when you ripped the life out of a man up close. The smell was the worst part. It was sudden and almost overwhelming. Abi listened to his tale and then loved him. Then she listened some more. She was one hell of a woman. By the end of the week he was able shut the memory off and get on with the mission.

He started a three-week course of conditioning with SAS trainers. He needed his legs and lungs strengthened and conditioned for higher altitudes. He had to master the AK47 rifle and Czech Semtex plastic explosives with detonators. They would be his stock in-trade as a smuggler. A few rifles, a couple of mines, and a lot of Semtex would make a credible cargo, even on one donkey. The value was great enough to tempt a smuggler into the mountains in the winter.

The first thing he learned to detest was the damn donkey. It was a gentle creature, but it had a mind of its own when it came to starting and quitting times. Abi's boys took Lee back to the hills of Wales and introduced him to his beast of burden.

The next week consisted of Lee in man-jams and turban pulling the donkey in harness with cargo up and down mountains and along ridges while the SAS troops harassed and laughed at him. He asked them to just load all the cargo on him and leave the donkey home. It would be easier than dragging the stubborn thing up and down hills.

They had their fun with him, but they also taught him a lot about living in the mountains and concealing his presence. He was already in good physical condition from his previous training with the SAS. Each day his legs got stronger, and by the third week he could travel most of the day at altitude without undue fatigue. But when he pulled his sleeping bag around him at night, he crashed.

For his last week of conditioning he was flown to Spain for hiking in the Pyrenees mountains on the French border. For this torture, two French Legion mountain specialists took him up on the Maladeta Massif in Argon, Spain. The Massif contained the highest peak in the Pyrenees, Pico de Aneto. The peak stood at 3400 meters, or 11,000 feet. At least he didn't have to climb the entire mountain. His trainers were more interested in conditioning his lungs for high altitude effort.

They made their base camp at the Renclusa Refuge at 2140 meters. Still, the ascent to the peak was a twelve-hour climb that thoroughly tested his conditioning and prepared his lungs for high altitude aerobics and cold weather mountain survival.

A side benefit was getting Lee used to heights and moving along trails with precipitous drop-offs. On the way to the peak of Aneto, he had to cross a narrow ridge called Mohammad's Bridge, a knife-edge ridge with exposed drop-offs on both sides. It was safe enough. Tourists crossed it several times a day in the summer. But even with time in the Kamdesh Valley, Lee found the experience unsettling.

The high-altitude sun was also important where his appearance was concerned. His face was burnt the first day and got ruddier every day for the rest of the week. By the time he was flown back to Wales, Lee looked the part of a mountain smuggler. He spent three more days in Sennybridge being tested by the SAS.

At the end of his time in the hills, Abi again picked him up at Sennybridge and they had a night together at the Railway Inn. There was no coyness between them now. Lee held the door and Abi shot through with one spin of the wheels.

"You may lift me and carry me in your arms to

the bed," Abi said.

"And may I undress you as well?"

"If it pleases you, but not yet. We need to talk while I can still think clearly."

"Can't it wait? That's not a penknife in my pocket."

"I believe I heard that one before. And, in fact, it is so a folding knife in your pocket. No, we need to talk. Before, not after. After, I'll be much too mellow to say what I need to tell you."

Lee set her on the bed and let her stretch out. She turned on her side to see him better and he stretched out next to her.

"Okay, so what's more important than satisfying your favorite lover?"

"Favorite and only. Lee, what do you know about Mallory and his organization?"

"He's CIA, and he heads up a special unit in the Special Activities Division."

"You rolled that off your tongue rather smoothly. Do you know what they are? What they do?"

"I'm not sure I'm supposed to be talking about this, even with you."

Abi smiled and patted his face.

"One of the things I respect about you is caution, even with me, as you say. Let me tell you then. I know exactly what I can discuss with you. Mallory started in your Delta Force. He is a special warfare operator and heads up a ground warfare unit in the Special Activities Division. He was recruited directly out of Delta Force. He is management now, but still formidable as an operator. He has a reputation of always putting the mission first."

"I can attest to his skills. He put me on my ass and I still don't know how he did it. One second I was coming at him and the next I was looking up at him."

"Yes, I should have warned you of that. Lee, he is not a bad person, just totally focused on his mission. He is the consummate intelligence professional. And that is what I wanted to talk about. Don't ever think that you are anything more than an asset to Mallory, an asset much less valuable than the mission, or his unit's cover. In some ways, I admire him a great deal. In other ways, he is everything I detest about Americans."

"I don't work for Mallory or the CIA. Unless something has happened I haven't been informed of, I'm still a Naval officer and I'm still attached to Trident and seconded to Navy Special Warfare Command."

"When is the last you spoke to your commanding officer?"

"A long time. Before I deployed to Afghanistan."

"You wouldn't be here if your command hadn't signed off. For now, you work for Mallory. Has Black Wolf been mentioned to you?"

"No. What is it?"

"I'm not going to say any more. Just cover your back. I have a wide degree of freedom on this project. I can go where and when I please. I'll do everything I can to see that you are covered no matter what happens, but always cover your own back. That's the first lesson every new intelligence officer should learn. End of talk . . . Now, where were we when I so rudely interrupted?"

Chapter 48

Mallory didn't waste any time preparing for Lee's deployment when he returned to London. Lee was moved to a safe house and told to dress as his alter-ego, the Pashtun smuggler.

"I have some people coming in from Afghanistan tomorrow. You'll spend today with our Pashto speakers. Total immersion, Lee. Speak it, think it, live it. From this moment forward you are Al Siddiq Hassan. By the way, I like the dark and dangerous look."

"I'll accept dark. I'm not sure how dangerous. Who are the people?"

"Don't worry about it. I want to see how your act holds up. You'll be briefed when it's time. Just remember, these folks will be told you are a recent immigrant who is willing to go back and work with them for a price. If you can fool them, you stand a good chance of pulling this off. Each of them is fluent in Pashto."

Lee spent the day with the CIA Pashto experts. They had lived among the Pashtun people of Northeast Afghanistan and knew the food, dress, and customs. The whole day was an intense immersion experience and class. They kept him speaking and gave him advice, always in Pashto, cooked meals, corrected his manners and posture. He was already well versed in Pashtun culture and customs and was more than fluent in the language, but the experts helped him pick up inflections and slurs that gave his diction more of a street flavor and helped him relax around a meal. By evening he was thinking exclusively in Pashto again.

When Mallory introduced him to three men in the morning, Lee immediately thought, spooks. They had long hair and beards, had weather beaten faces and hands, and their eyes never stopped moving. These guys had been in deep shit often and for extended periods. He wondered if they were SEALs or Delta Force. They had the look and attitude.

The interview went on until lunch. It was more of an interrogation than an interview. It was obvious these guys had worked together for a long time. They handed off the lead seamlessly and switched the good guy – bad guy role without blinking an eye. Lee's interrogation skills were as good as they came, and none of the visitors could trip him up. After lunch, Lee was sent away with one of the CIA language exerts so Mallory could meet with his visitors privately.

Mallory sat back in his chair and looked at each of his visitors one at a time.

"Well, what do you think? Is he worth anything? You first, Blount."

"I don't trust the ugly son of a bitch," Blount said. "He didn't get those scars by sitting next to his fireplace. Probably one of our mortars, or one of his own damn IEDs blew up on him."

"Okay," Mallory said. "How about you, Jackson?"

"I don't know. You can't trust these Pakis that ran supplies for the Taliban and then suddenly find a love for the west. Notice how fuzzy he was about his tribe? There's something in his dialect too. That's one mixed-up Hajj. He's been playing both sides."

"How about you, Polaski? Anything?"

"Hell, you said he's a smuggler. Yeah, he's suspicious. We're suspicious of him and he's suspicious of us. I don't know. He probably has contacts, knows the rat-lines, and can probably get in and out again. The question is, can we trust anything he says when he gets back? One other thing that bothers me. He's in pretty damn good shape for Hajj."

"Okay, good input. Is he authentic?"

"In what way?" Blount said.

"Is he what he says he is?"

Jackson looked around the group and leaned forward. "Hard to tell. I'd say he's done some smuggling across the border. If he did that, he'd be in pretty good shape. Shit, the old men in those mountains can walk your ass off. Whether he's a Paki Pashtun is questionable, but he's certainly lived with them. From his looks, he could be Nuristani, Pashtun, or any of the mountain tribes. It's the scars. You can't tell what the hell he is by his looks."

"He's been in the shit," Polaski said.

"All right, let's bring him back in and you can ask him anything else that comes to mind."

Lee was brought back to the room.

"Hassan, introduce yourself."

Lee looked confused and started to say, "Al Siddiq . . ."

"No," Mallory said. "Tell them who you really are, Lee."

Mallory sat back with a big shit eating grin on his face. Lee was still confused and wasn't sure what to do.

"Gentlemen, let me introduce you to U. S. Navy Lieutenant Junior Grade, Lee Toliver, better known in Task Force Blue as Igor."

That got Lee off the dime and pissed him off.

"Knock off the Igor shit, Mallory. These people don't know me."

The shocked look on three faces, the owners of which were all Delta operators attached to a select group called Advanced Force Operations (AFO), made Mallory laugh. There were only 45 of them in Afghanistan. They were the Creme de la creme of Delta and specialized in high-risk recon missions, including infiltrating enemy territory and impersonating locals in civilian garb, and high value target snatches and snuffs.

Master Sergeant Blount was the first to recover. "He don't cuss enough to be a SEAL."

Lee promptly cussed them out in Pashto, Dari, and Urdu and that got a laugh from all three Delta operators.

"I'm not a SEAL," he said. "My parents were married."

That got another laugh and a cat call.

"You said he's TF Blue," Jackson said.

"Lee's an intelligence analyst and linguist from Trident and seconded to SAD," Mallory said. "The question is, will he do?"

That question started a new discussion and included questions about Lee's training. The Delta guys would have been happier if Lee had had special operations training, but they agreed he could pass as a smuggler with the proper preparation. In the end, they agreed he could add real value to their operation if he survived. And having made clear that last "if" part about surviving, Mallory dismissed Lee.

Chapter 49

The flight to Bagram was noisy and cold. London to Germany was great, but the C17, configured for Medevac and empty except for crew, was anything but comfortable. The medical crew spent the entire flight setting up stations and equipment for the patients they would be bringing back. They already had the list of casualties and the special needs of each patient. The turn-around would be quick for them and the return flight full of stress. There would be no turn-around for Lee. This new deployment to Afghanistan was open ended.

    His departure and farewell with Abi left him wondering what their relationship was about. She always seemed ready to hop in bed with him, well, be lifted onto the bed with him, and that was great, but when it was over, she reverted to the professional intelligence officer. He didn't doubt the friendship, and loved the sex, but wondered if the relationship would ever be anything more. When they parted, it was with a handshake and wish for good luck. Perhaps he just didn't understand British reserve.

Lee was in BDUs when he arrived at Bagram, but his escorts, two bearded, long hairs from AFO north, made him change into his Pashtun garb before they left the base. By now, Lee was a bearded, long hair himself and looked ridiculous in BDUs. Leaving the base was another surprise. He was to be prepped for his mission at an AFO safe house on the outskirts of Kabul rather than be housed at the JSOC compound in J-bad.

The move from Bagram to Kabul, about 30 miles, was in a white Toyota pickup truck. While Lee could easily be mistaken for a local Afghani, the size of the Delta guys escorting him screamed American, and the small pickup cab didn't leave much room for him between the operators. It was a crammed and uncomfortable ride with men and weapons vying for space.

The streets they moved through once they reached the outskirts of Kabul were almost vacant of traffic and pedestrians. Everything was dirt colored, either because it was made from dirt or because it was covered with blowing dirt. And it was cold. Damn cold. The sights, sounds, and smells were too familiar.

They stopped at a walled compound. The

wooden gate was about twelve feet high and wide enough to pass a large truck. The walls surrounding the compound were a couple of feet shorter than the gate, maybe ten feet high and appeared to have jagged glass embedded along the top under concertina wire. A guard station was mounted on the wall on each side of the gate. Lee could see the muzzles of heavy machine guns pointed at the truck from each guard station. The gate opened slowly, and as soon as the opening was wide enough, the truck shot forward, and the gate closed behind them.

They stopped in a courtyard next to two other white Toyota pickups. Looking around, Lee could see guard stations at two other corners of the wall and assumed the remaining corners he couldn't see also held defensive positions.

The house was large by Afghan standards and was probably some kind of commercial establishment before the AFO took it over. It was two stories with several windows to a side indicating a lot of rooms inside. Most of the windows on the second floor were bricked in, but one in the center on the front was left open with glass in it. Probably the same on the other sides.

"Checked you out with some guys from DEVGRU," the driver said. He and his partner hadn't said much other than to give Lee curt orders until they were inside the gate. "They checked you out with Team Two and reported back that you hit what you aim at and did okay under fire. Said your handle is Igor. I'm

361

Buster and that criminal next to you is Lester. You okay with Igor?"

"Yeah, Igor is good." Lee said. He was back and might as well get used to it again.

Come on inside and we'll introduce you around. Your clearances have been verified and updated. This place is home until we get things set up for your insert and exfil. It's not as bad as it looks."

The safe house was better than not bad. Lee had a private room with a twin bed and a thick mattress. Booze was available in the team room, but he wasn't interested in that. They had their own Afghani cook, and he was interested in that. He had developed a taste for Afghani food.

After giving Lee enough time to dump his gear, Buster brought him to the briefing room. Inside sat Blount, Polaski, and another bearded gentleman who was obviously not a SEAL or Delta operator. He was about five foot four inches, with a slight hunchback, slim, and he twitched. Buster introduced him simply as Twitch. All the names were operating handles, so Lee was addressed as Igor.

"We'll get into your mission in detail later," Buster said. "Until then, you have the option of stopping the train and getting off. If you hear anything you can't live with, just say stop. Understood?"

"I'll listen."

"Okay. Fair enough," Buster said. "You've already met Blount and Polaski. I'm sure you have formed some idea about what Lester and I are. Twitch is a signals intelligence analyst and our resident technical genius. Here's the deal. The mission we need you for differs from the one you thought it was only in the target and area. Most of the rest of it is the same. We have a high value target we need to find and can't get any reliable HUMINT on his location. I should say their location. There's two of them, but they run together. Both are Arab, originally Al Qaeda, but now fighting with the Taliban. Lester, take over."

"We are interested in a particularly brutal and intelligent Arab Taliban commander and his personal bomb maker," Lester said. "The name of the commander, Abdal Amit, is obviously an assumed one, and assumed for effect. The name of Abdal's personal bomber is Esmail. No last name."

"Cute," Lee said.

"You caught it?"

"Sure. Abdal Amit in Arabic means Servant of Death. Esmail means God will hear, a metaphor for a huge noise. Just what I need, a comedian who blows things up for laughs. I would love to get my hands on that sick bastard's throat."

"You speak Arabic too?" Shank asked.

"Fluent," Lee said. "Read and write."

"Baghdadi dialect?" Twitch said after jerking his head up.

"Yes, all of the gulf dialects."

"I'd like to get together with you later, if that would be okay."

"Sure," Lee said.

"Let's save that for later," Lester said. "Maybe God heard or not, but JSOC heard, and Special Activities Division along with Delta's AFO were tasked with finding the pair and putting them out of business. That's where you come in, but first, will you explain that little comment you made?"

"What?"

"The one about getting your hands on his throat."

Lee pointed at the left side of his face. "Did Mallory tell you where I got this? Did he tell you what turned me into Igor?"

"No. Is it important?"

Very quietly and calmly, Lee said, "A suicide bomber blew my ass up in London. I would gladly cut your bomber's throat and watch the fucking light go out in his eyes."

The three AFO men watched Lee quietly for a few moments.

"So, you got a big vendetta going against the Hajj?" Buster asked. "That's why you volunteered for this?"

"First, I wasn't asked to volunteer, until you said I could get off the train if I want. Second, no I haven't got a vendetta going against anyone. But when it comes to bombs and people who blow-up innocent people, I'll gladly stand in line to . . . well, I've already expressed my opinion on that."

"Well," Lester said, "I guess I can skip the

motivation part of this briefing."

Chapter 50

A nice feature of the safe house was the men housed there. They all spoke Pashto and some of them were close to fluent. Lee's presence was a double bonus. The Delta guys got to practice their language with an expert and Lee could speak Pashto exclusively. Even more importantly for Lee was the expertise in mountain topography located in the house. The operators were intimately familiar with the AO in which he would operate. They had worked the ratlines throughout the mountains along the Pakistan border.

Ratlines were the escape and infiltration trails through the mountains and passes between Pakistan and Afghanistan. Often, they were an intricate labyrinth of creek beds and goat paths that provided overhead cover and access to shelter. Lee would have to become intimately familiar with those in the area he would infiltrate.

Twitch's place in the scheme was explained later that day. He was a strange little guy. Kind of likable too. In addition to being brilliant and tenacious, he was the team's puppy. Twitch wasn't a Delta operator, obviously at five-four and probably 120 pounds soaking wet with a full belly, but just as Lee served DEVGRU as an expert in languages, Twitch supported Delta AFO with world class computer, communications, and signals intelligence. He was an electronics and programming whiz.

Twitch was a Sergeant Major with degrees in mathematics and computer science. His computer science degree was from MIT. He had refused a commission fearing it would keep him away from his toys and had to receive a weight and height waver before he could enlist. But the Army wanted his skills and found a way to bring him in.

He was a strange little guy who cared nothing for money. In civilian life, he might have made millions in Silicon Valley, but for reasons of his own, he wanted to be a soldier, and being accepted by the special operators in Delta was the greatest thrill in his life.

Special Operations Command gave him all the toys he wanted and saw to it he was promoted every time at the earliest opportunity. Early on as a specialist, Twitch was too easy a target for assholes with three stripes, so he was made a sergeant as soon as he had time in grade and he was promoted up the line all the way to Sergeant Major in the same way. As a Sergeant Major, he caused eyebrows to raise, but no one screwed with him.

Twitch was from a secretive special ops organization that has been known by several names and will be known by several others in the future. It has been around for almost 25 years and almost no one has ever heard of it, except in Special Ops. The largest it has ever been is about 250 members in the late 90s. They specialized in human and signals intelligence in the riskiest environments, often behind enemy lines, but they kept a few like Twitch out of harm's way and mined their brains. In its latest incarnation, it is known as Black Wolf and works closely with DEVGRU and Delta often embedding operators with the teams and sometimes using the teams to insert Black Wolf operators in place behind enemy lines.

Lee met with Twitch in the com shack that evening. Twitch was working on a flashlight.

"You fix flashlights too?" Lee said and smiled.

"I'm putting something special together for you. You'll see later. The reason I wanted to see you is I need some help. I can decipher some Arabic, but I'm not a linguist. I've got a tape of an intercept and was told by one of the terps it sounded like Arabic, and he thought it was Baghdadi dialect, but he couldn't do much with it. Could you take a listen and see if you can decipher it?"

"Sure. Can you start it for me?"

Twitch set up the recorder, plugged in noise

canceling headphones, and showed Lee how to run, rewind, and restart the tape and gave him a pad and pen. Lee spent about an hour translating the scratchy recording and then shut the machine off.

"Here's the best I could make of it. There's several places I just couldn't understand the words through the noise, but it's definitely Baghdadi Arabic. Where'd you get it?"

"It was a pick-up from the mountains by a Navy Aries electronic warfare aircraft. Thanks for the help. Are you really a Navy officer?"

"Sure," Lee said. Naval Academy."

"How'd you get hooked up with the CIA?"

"Long story. I'll tell you about it sometime if we have time."

"I'd like that. You don't seem like an officer . . . I mean, you know, you're not a tight ass like most junior officers."

Lee grinned, a sight that would have been hideous to most people, but Twitch just smiled back. "I guess I've had my ass kicked enough so my rank doesn't seem like anything special."

Twitch put the wire cutters he was holding on the work bench and wiped his hands.

"I think I'll like working with you. We're . . . you know, me and you, we're different." Twitch blushed.

"Yeah," Lee said, "we'll make a good team. You should meet my team back in London. One's a female British lieutenant in a wheelchair."

"The British lady is Lieutenant Dundee, isn't

she?"

Lee snapped his head up. "Yes, Abi, how'd you know?"

Twitch blushed again. "Everything that came in about you came through me. Delta was organized and trained on the SAS model and still have a special relationship with them, did you know that?"

"Never heard that before? How'd you know she's in a wheelchair?"

"We work with SAS and MI6 on missions in Pakistan and in the southern part of Afghanistan and know most of their regular operators. Before Abi had her accident, we worked with her in Iraq."

Lee boosted his butt up on the workbench.

"It wasn't an accident," he said. "I was with her when a suicide bomber blew us up. That's where I got this," he said waving at his face.

"I know. Sorry. I didn't want to bring it up."

"That's okay. So, what do you think about this mission, Twitch? Why me? I'm not even close to being a special operator."

"That why," Twitch said. "You're trained well enough to succeed, but you're not special ops. A special ops guy would do a lot of things instinctively from his training and experience. If he was observed for a while, that skill would stand out, and his observers would become suspicious. Nothing is for sure in this place, but if you're careful, I think we have a good chance of pulling this off. You'll have a lot of support waiting just over the horizon, and I can launch it as soon as things look bad."

Lee thought about that for a few moments. He felt a little better about his chances with Twitch's explanation, but he still had a lot of concerns.

"Still, I'm not much of a spy either. It seems like somebody has been hiding in the background and pulling strings like I'm a puppet. Every time I started to settle in with a team, I was pulled out and sent somewhere else to something new. I can't believe I just happened to be available when this mission came up. Strange that, just as I finished my mountain training, my original mission is called off and bingo, another mission pops up."

"We don't do one-offs, Lee. If it hadn't been this mission, another would have been found. You've been brought along since Mallory saw you the day you reported back to Trident after you got out of the hospital. How many Americans do you think we have who can impersonate someone from this part of the world effectively? Hold up five fingers and then close four of them. You're it. I hope you like us, because this is where you belong."

Lee turned on the work bench next to Twitch and thought for a few moments. Twitch as much as said he was being manipulated. He was surprised at how little he cared.

"You seem to have found a home," he said to Twitch.

Twitch rooted through a drawer looking for something, but he was listening.

"Out in the civilian world I'd just be another hunchback midget, even with two degrees. Anywhere else in the military I'd be a freak. Thing is, the rest of the military wouldn't have me, or at least wouldn't have kept me. Here, I'm just as important as an operator. I am an operator. Through my gadgets, I go with them on every mission, and a lot of times it's me who gets them home safe. These are my guys."

Lee was silent for a few moments. A lot was coming at him he needed to think about, but Twitch was sincere and it was good to finally talk to someone who seemed to know what was going on and wasn't being cagey about it.

"Yeah, I can see that," he said. "So, they left it to you to recruit me? One freak to another?"

"Lee, you and I have something most of the special ops guys can never hope to have. With you it's languages and the ability to assume an identity. I have a gift for mathematics and technology. The thing is, here they want us, and we can do more for the mission than the guys who can run up mountains all day and shoot an eye out of a Hajj from another zip code. We're not freaks here. We're part of the team and just as important as the shooters. Think about it."

Lee put his hand on Twitch's shoulder and stood up.

"Well, thanks for the talk. I've got a lot of things to think about. Let's talk again later."

"I'd like that," Twitch said.

Chapter 51

The second morning at the safe house Lee was called to the briefing room after morning chow. Twitch, Buster, Lester, Jackson and Polaski were in the room when he got there.

"All right, let's get the show on the road. Let's go over the schedule first. A Recce (recon) is laid on for tomorrow. Launch time is 0400. Igor will come along for familiarization. The area is considered low risk for contact in winter and it should be a walk in the sun, if the sun comes out. We will be observing a high mountain pass at 2500 meters. Figure on snow and temperatures below freezing. Equip accordingly. Lester, see that Igor is equipped properly.

"Twitch, rig your locators and commo in Igor's gear. We'll be there long enough for you to get some good data and test everything."

"It's all ready," Twitch said.

"Igor, suit up in your winter man-jams and don't shower. You'll need all the body oil your skin can produce. Don't wash it off. It's good insulation. You get some range time with the AK47 today and then a nice warm-up hike in the foot hills. Twitch, can you hook him up today? It's a good opportunity for a preliminary commo check and the GPS chip test."

"Sure," Twitch said. "Soon as you're dressed, come down to the Com Center, Lee. I won't call you Igor except on the radio."

"Thank you," Lee said. "I'll be there."

"Twitch is your eyes, ears, and big daddy in the sky," Buster said. "He will track you, give you guidance, and launch your rescue if you get into trouble. He'll even hold your hand electronically if you get lonely at night. He doesn't sleep and hardly ever eats anything besides Red Bull and candy bars, so he's always available."

"If Twitch is going to be my partner, I'm feeling better about this operation already." Lee said. Twitch smiled shyly and gave Lee a thumbs-up.

"Okay then," Buster said. "Any questions? If not, Lester can lay on transportation to the range and Jackson can confirm the lift out to the hills. Got it?"

Jackson and Polaski who hadn't said anything in the meeting just nodded and everyone else stood up.

The hike in the foot hills turned out to be a contest for

the Delta guys to see how soon they could trash Lee's legs. But there was a reason for their intensity. In Afghanistan, terrain is your first and worst opponent. Lee fooled the hell out of them.

After a short helicopter ride to the mountains, he was strapped into Molle web-gear with ten loaded magazines and two canteens hooked on and given an empty rucksack that was promptly loaded with ammunition, rations, and other gear by the Delta guys. His turban had a GPS chip embedded in the wrappings and his belt had an experimental Satellite phone hidden in a four-cell flashlight. The top battery was the phone circuitry connected through the off/on switch to a copper band on the case that acted as an antenna.

The light provided white light in one position, but if it was pushed-in in that position it became a powerful infrared beacon. Both the phone and the GPS chip had been developed by Twitch. The GPS chip had its own power source in the form of a flexible sheet battery that molded with the fabric of the turban. A thin copper wire woven into the fabric acted as antenna wire and the turban formed a shallow dish antenna.

The chip was small and unlikely to be discovered. The flashlight/sat-phone was pretty slick. On the outside, the light was of a common type found in markets in Pakistan and Afghanistan and shouldn't raise suspicions. The batteries were something else. Although they looked identical to a popular brand of commercial flashlight battery including the markings, they were an experimental battery that had a useful life almost ten times that of commercial batteries and available only to certain secretive organizations within the Special Warfare Community. Twitch was from one of those organizations. The top battery holding the sat-phone circuitry looked just like the others.

Under his Kameez he wore two layers of insulated clothes and he wore heavy wool socks under Uzbek boots made from animal skin that still had hair on the outside. All told, he estimated he was carrying about 70 pounds.

The Delta guys took him into the hills and set an aggressive pace. Lee hung with them for five kilometers, and then stepped up the pace. The hills got steeper and the temperature dropped. He was grateful for his training in Wales and Spain.

The patrol leader called a break and made sure Lee hydrated. He accepted a hand to get up to resume the march with seventy pounds on his back. His conditioned legs hadn't stiffened up yet. He set out at his former pace.

The Delta Guys kept him out until just before dark, found a safe LZ, and had Lee use his radio to have Twitch dispatch their ride. The sat-phone worked fine, and the GPS chip nailed their location so the helicopter found them with minimum trouble.

Back at the safe house, Lee warmed up and ate a high carb meal. The layered wool clothing he wore under the Shalwar Kameez had worked well for the cold but didn't provide protection from moisture. Jackson provided Lee baggy civilian Gore-Tex pants and shirt that would provide a water proofing layer and wick away sweat moisture. He added an Afghan scarf for warmth at high altitudes. The next morning would be the real test.

At 0500, Lee and two Delta operators would be inserted about a kilometer up the mountain and climb to about 7500 feet to set up an observation post where they would remain overnight before climbing back down to the LZ to be extracted by helicopter the following day. This outing would be the final check-out for Lee and his gear. Lee turned in at 2000 and was asleep almost before his head hit the bed.

Chapter 52

The high pass observation went off without a problem and all of Twitch's gear checked out. His hike in the mountains and his climb to 7500 feet the previous day taught Lee a lot about mountain operations. The terrain was the first and biggest enemy. The weather was the second. His conditioning got him through the exercises, and the Delta guys taught him about surviving a night at altitude.

The day before he was to move to Pakistan, Buster woke him up and told him to get dressed and report to the briefing room. They had a guest who would participate in the final briefing.

"What kind of guest?" Lee asked.

"Just get dressed. You'll find out soon enough."

Lee dressed in his Shalwar Kameez as he had

every day since he arrived at the safe house. He was surprised at how easy it was to adapt to and feel comfortable in a mode of dress completely foreign to him just a couple of months before.

The door was closed on the briefing room so he tapped twice to warn the people inside to cover anything he wasn't supposed to see, and then started to walk in. Only one person was in the room. Abi. Lee stopped dead in the door.

"Jesus Christ! You could have given a guy some warning,"

"I arrived in Kabul in the middle of the night and just now arrived here," Abi said.

Abi was sitting at the conference table and her wheelchair was not in sight. What he wanted to do was pick her up and squeeze her, but what he did was shake her hand.

When he sat down, he tried to keep it formal and business-like, but he couldn't help holding Abi's eyes for a few moments. She smiled her little smile and then smoothed her trousers and tugged her field jacket in place.

"Yes, well, it's good that everyone is happy to see one another," she said. "Shall we get started?" We have a lot to cover and not much time. Your boys have plans for you today, and they're not happy about my intrusion. We wish to add another face to your target list. Please look at these pictures."

Lee sat next to Abi and took the 8X10s she handed him. One was a head shot of a British Soldier in an officer's uniform and one was a full length shot of the same man.

"Okay. He's a target?"

"Not in the same sense as your other targets. We want to find this one if possible and mount a rescue."

"Who is he?"

"Leftenant Ian MacRae," Abi said. "Kidnapped in Pakistan two years ago, during a clandestine operation. We thought he was dead, but he turned up in a video on the internet recently. CIA also has recent reports of a European being held by insurgents in Northeast Afghanistan where your mission will take place."

Lee heard a knock on the door and turned. The door opened and Twitch came in looking even more twitchy than usual.

"Am I late? Hi Abi. I checked out your phone-light, Igor. You're good to go."

"Igor?" Abi said.

"My radio handle," Lee said. "SEAL humor."

"Sorry, Lee," Twitch said. "I have to start using it all the time so I won't forget when you're in the field."

"That's awful," Abi said. "Does everyone get a nasty name?"

"Sure, even you," Twitch said, and then he blushed big time.

"Already? But I just got here. Okay, I'll bite. What is my handle?"

Now Twitch turned beet red and twitched while he looked to Lee for help.

"I didn't even know she was here," Lee said. "Go ahead. It can't be as bad as mine."

Poor Twitch looked absolutely horrified. He said something so low no one could hear."

"What?" Abi said. "It's okay, Twitch. I'm a good sport."

Finally, Twitch took a deep breath and blurted, "Meals on wheels," and then looked like he was having a stroke.

Abi had a sudden coughing fit. Lee lowered his head and snorted.

When she caught her breath, Abi said, "Oh my, this is going to hell fast, isn't it? Your Delta boys are as bad as my SAS chaps. May we please get back on task here? By the way, where did you put my, uh, wheels?"

"I have your chair in my lab. I can get it if you want it."

"No, no, I'm quite well for now. Shall we get on with it? As I was saying, word of a European prisoner has turned up in several Recce reports and has been mentioned by other sources. It could be MacRae. MI6 gives it a low probability, but SAS never leaves a man behind and we must try to confirm or discredit the intelligence. It may be that his captors feeling the heat in Pakistan moved MacRae into Afghanistan for safe keeping. Why? No one has come up with a good reason. They tend to keep them if they feel some value might be obtained later. So, in addition to seeking intelligence on the location of your primary targets, we would like you to keep your ears open for word of a British soldier being held by the insurgents."

"Do you want me to do anything if I do find him?"

"No, absolutely not. Pass your intelligence along to Twitch and a mission will be planned."

Lee considered the pictures for a few moments.

"I don't see a problem," he said. "Three isn't a big list. Look, not that I'm in any way against it, but why did this change need to be delivered personally by you."

"I told you I have wide latitude on this project. Mr. Mallory thought it was a good idea to see to it you got the message without interference. Not everyone was happy about adding this task on your first mission. This is an interagency effort, Lee. In exchange for your cooperation, we will be flying UAVs in support of your mission which will free up CIA drones for, well, for what they normally do. And frankly? I've never been to Afghanistan."

"Hey, I'm all for it," Lee said. "Uh, look, can we have a few minutes in private?"

Abi was housed at the safe house for her five-day stay in Afghanistan. Lee and Abi managed a few hours in his room before he was packed up and flown to Pakistan. No one on the AFO team or from Black Wolf cared much if Lee got his ashes hauled before his first mission. As far as they were concerned, it ought to be SOP.

Chapter 53

Lee was flown to a small LZ in the foothills of the Hindu Kush on the Pakistan side of the border, but beyond the Pakistan military checkpoints. Delta operators had everything ready for him at a camp concealed in a draw near where his trail began. Lee's only objection to their preparations was the beasts of burden, as in plural. They provided two donkeys with harness that kept them together in single file.

    Water wasn't a problem for the first part of his trek with plentiful snow around, but he would have to carry water once out of the snow. Hence the two donkeys. He had to present a credible picture, and if he didn't take enough goods with him, the people he wished to find would wonder what was important enough to motivate him to risk the high passes in winter.

Early in the planning phase for this mission, Black Wolf covert operatives working Western Pakistan had determined that a well-known smuggler was planning a try at the winter passes with a load of arms and munitions, especially Semtex-H for IEDs. That intelligence was the motivation and basic idea that spawned Lee's mission. Black Wolf and AFO arranged for an untimely, for the Taliban, exit of the smuggler, and brought Lee in to replace him.

A winter passage through the mountains was difficult and sometimes impossible, but a few smugglers risked it when the conditions were right. The Americans would not be watching the passes closely during the winter months. On the insurgent side, the typical insurgent was not equipped for the frigid and windy conditions in the mountains in winter and mostly hunkered down in a friendly village or cave until spring. The spring insurgency was their time. Except for the weather, winter was the ideal time for smuggling because no one was watching, or almost so—if you could handle the frigid conditions and predict the weather.

Lee was well prepared with boots from Uzbekistan, gloves from Russia, wool shirts and trousers from Pakistan, heavy Shalwar Kameez from Afghanistan, and various accessories such as Afghan scarves, heavy socks, insulated long underwear, a wool ski mask, and a Gore-Tex jacket and trouser combination, all purchased in the

Kabul open market along with a stack of home-made, chemical-infused fire logs made from compressed newspapers Afghanis used in lieu of wood. Wood was too heavy to carry, and there wasn't much of it above the snow line.

Another happy find at the market was MREs. They were a popular item with the FATA Pakistanis and probably a source of side income for some Pakistani quartermaster. All this plus Lee's AK47 and his shelter and food and the donkey's food would be carried by the first donkey.

The second donkey carried the Semtex-H, some of which, about five kilos, was real, the daily water cooked down from snow, and a few extra items like Arabian, Pakistani, and Uzbek spices, which, to the insurgents wintering in a land not their own, would be almost as valuable as the Semtex. On his person, he carried a commercially available Sig TacOps 9mm with three 20 round magazines, his knife, and one frag grenade.

The trail Lee was on began in the Bajaur Agency in the FATA in Pakistan and was called the Sheik Babu trail network. Lee would transit a pass north of the Goradary Pass into the Sirkanay District in Afghanistan.

The Delta people kept Lee at the camp for two days waiting for the weather to clear and going over his route through the mountains and the pass he would use to enter his target valley. He had been drilled on land marks along his entire route by the AFO Delta guys every day since his arrival at the safe house. Satellite, drone, and Recce photos were used to show prominent landmarks from several angles. A sandbox model of the valley was used to go over and over the route until Lee could visualize the entire route in his head. He was coached in evade and cover maneuvers to use while on the trail, not to evade the Taliban, but to evade American drones, aircraft, and patrols. And he had Twitch's flashlight/phone and GPS chip if he got lost.

Finally, the weather report was right and Lee rigged his donkeys up and set out toward the high pass. He had trouble with the donkeys right away. They had to be the horniest creatures in the world. The rear donkey continually tried to mount the front donkey. When he switched them in order, the other one tried to mount the one that had attempted to mount him. He didn't seem to care either. It just seemed logical to either one, that if there was a donkey shaped creature in front of him, he should be humping it. Lee considered gelding both damn things, but he didn't have the time and didn't know how anyway.

His AFO guys gave him a final briefing.

"Look Igor, this isn't a hundred-yard dash. Remember your training. Take your time getting up to the pass. Let your heart and lungs adjust to the altitude gradually. Follow the wind-sweeps though the pass wherever you can. It's why we picked this pass. Close to the peak-slope side of the pass there's always a stretch of ground, sometimes just an eddy, swept by the prevailing wind where you can find bare ground or shallower snow.

"Once you're through the high pass, you'll be descending into a high valley. Take it slow and give yourself plenty of rest and water. To leave the valley, you've got to pass along a high ridge at 9000 feet for more than two klicks before you have a safe descending trail. Look for the wind sweeps. Deep snow and altitude can kill you. Don't get caught on the ridge at night. Take plenty of rests for yourself and don't forget the donkeys. Even if you must stop every hundred feet, do it. If they get too tired, they'll rebel. You good to go?"

"About as ready as I'm going to get," Lee said. "Thanks."

The trail started at 1800 feet and he had to climb to 11,000 feet to pass between two 14,000-foot peaks, each being the end peaks of a high and steep ridgeline. The trail to the pass had multiple natural switchbacks that reduced the grade in most places, but it was a trying climb for man and beast.

"Come on, dumbasses," Lee said to the donkeys in Pashto. "I'm not going to pull you up the damn mountain." The lead donkey snorted and followed Lee, leaving slack in the line. They had lost their insane horniness, and once they were moving, the donkeys didn't need any further encouragement. That was a relief.

The trail was the narrow bottom of a zigzag draw between two finger spurs off the main mountain ridge he had to cross. Up to the 5000-foot level it had a pebble and rock bottom giving decent footing for him and the donkeys if they took it slow. Taking it slow wasn't a problem.

He made camp at what he estimated was 5000 feet. Already, the view was spectacular. He was in mixed clear and snow-covered terrain, and the air was clear and frigid. His thermometer read 13 degrees F. He stopped to let his system adjust to the thinner air and to rest the donkeys. He rested for a moment and decided he liked working alone.

He thought he would be full of tension once he left the base camp and company of the AFO troops, but that didn't happen. The trail demanded all his attention, and the mountains were silent and peaceful. Looking around at the beautiful high country that seemed to go on forever, he began to understand why people would choose to spend their lives here.

He was already in his role and thinking and talking in Pashto. The Pashto seemed to help with the donkeys. It provided the sounds they were used to, and even though they only responded to a few commands, they were more cooperative. He unloaded the cargo and hobbled the animals. They promptly folded their legs and snuggled close together on dry ground. Enjoy it, he thought. They wouldn't find dry ground again for a couple of days.

The trip in wasn't long in miles. His destination valley was only fourteen miles away as the crow flies, but it would take three days to reach the valley if everything went as planned. He unpacked the large pot he had for melting snow and started a fire with chemical logs. They would burn for an hour. He had enough of them for three days if he only built two fires a day.

After putting a pot of snow over the fire to melt, he got a serving of grain from the grain bag for the donkeys. He had enough grain to feed them for three days also. After that he had to find a village and purchase fodder for them. If he didn't get lost, he should find a small village at the head of the valley at about the 5000-foot level. With the animals taken care of, he opened an MRE and took care of his own needs.

When his meal was done and the trash buried, he finished melting enough snow to fill his water bag, and then enough to water the donkeys. He was set to resume his journey in the morning. He unrolled his heavy sleeping bag and sat on it to watch the sun go down. His only view was to the east over Pakistan, but the narrow slice of sky between the finger ridges that formed his draw provided a beautiful view. His eyes grew heavy and the quiet sounds of the donkeys' heavy breathing lulled him into a peaceful lethargy.

He was opening his bag to climb in when he heard a sound that snatched the idea of rest from his mind.

Chapter 54

Close and sotto voce, a voice in Pashto broke the silence. Lee reached inside his robe and lifted his pistol out. The donkeys stirred.

"Peace be upon you. Do not be alarmed. May I enter your camp?"

"And upon you, peace," Lee replied. "Enter slowly with your hands away from your body."

A dark shadow separated from the shadowy side of the trail and moved toward Lee. Soon he could see a man-figure in Shalwar Kameez with its arms spread wide. "I only seek shelter and company," the man said.

Lee put the pistol back in his robe and said, "Are you alone?"

"Yes."

"Come and warm yourself with what is left of the fire. Have you eaten?"

"A small amount of food would be welcome. Anything at all."

"Come then. What are you known by?"

"Amid."

"I am Hassan. Do you like the American food?"

"If it is Halal." Amid said.

"I have one that is eggs and cheese." *I won't miss that God-awful concoction,* Lee thought. He went to the cargo and found the MRE he wanted.

"This is the meal packet the American soldiers use," Amid said.

"Yes, some Pakistani officer is getting rich at the market and his soldiers are getting hungry, or maybe not. The Americans give them whatever they want. It is satisfying the infidels make my journey easier."

Amid laughed as he tore the packet open. Lee showed him how to set up the oven and heat his meal. They talked quietly as Amid ate. When Amid was done, Lee buried the trash.

"You are a cautious one," Amid said. "Where does your journey take you?"

"To my destination," Lee said.

Lee could hear the amusement in Amid's voice as he asked, "And what do you do in the mountains during winter?"

"I travel."

Amid laughed outright at that. "And I travel as well," he said. "While our paths are the same, would you like a companion, Hassan?"

Probably not a bad idea, Lee thought. Two sharing the struggle getting through the pass would be less conspicuous than one alone, and two could share the work. Amid could break trail and save Lee's strength.

"The Prophet, peace be upon him, always traveled with companions," Lee said. "There is no better example. Be sure you know what you ask though. There are eyes in the sky. Should I be discovered, perhaps the journey will not be pleasant. Am I correct in believing you face the same risk?"

"Insha Allah. It is not a risk. It is a destiny."

Later, Amid wrapped up in his own bed-roll next to one of the donkeys. They didn't seem to mind his presence, and he found some extra warmth. Lee slid off his boots and zipped up his heavy-duty sleeping bag and pulled the hood over his head. He kept his hand on his pistol.

He awoke several times during the night and cautiously observed Amid. He was sleeping the sleep of the innocent, at least in his own mind. Lee drifted back into a light sleep each time.

Light came to the mountain well before it reached the land below, so he had to start early. When Lee got up to melt some snow, he could see lights twinkling far below and miles away. It had snowed a couple of inches overnight and everything including the donkeys had a dusting of dry snow that flew like dust when he swatted his hand at it. He gathered snow for the pot and lit a chemical log. Then he went off in the rocks to take care of morning necessities, squatting in the Muslim fashion.

Amid arose from his sleeping roll, stretched, and shook out his blankets. He rolled them up and went back in the rocks. The Donkeys were content to remain off their feet and close together.

When Amid returned, he said, "Let me help you, Hassan. What must be done?"

"First, we will pray the Fajr. There is time for one Rak'a before the sun rises. As my guest, will you lead the prayer?"

"It is my pleasure. The snow is pure and will serve for Wudhu. We must hurry."

The Fajr should be completed before the sun rises, but If one Rak'a of prayer can be completed before the sun rises, the prayer may be completed after sunrise.

Lee completed Wudhu (ritual cleansing). He used snow to wash his right hand and then the left, three times. He washed his mouth and nose three times. His face he washed once. Next, he washed his right arm to the elbow and then the left. He ran his wet hand across his hair, then around the back of his ears and the inside. He took snow on both hands and ran it over his boots excepting the soles.

Lee used the outside of his sleeping bag for a prayer mat. Amid had a prayer rug rolled in his blanket roll. Amid recited one Rak'a before the sun rose and then continued to complete the prayer. When done, they repacked their sleeping rolls.

"If you will keep the snow pot full of melting snow, I will prepare the animals and feed them," Lee said. Then we can have a morning meal."

When the animals were fed and watered, the meal was done, and the cargo loaded, they set off up the mountain. Lee handled the bags of plastic explosives himself without saying what they were and asked Amid to load the other donkey with the camp materials. When the donkeys were loaded, Lee pushed his AK47 under the ropes that held the load on Amid's donkey. It was a show of trust Amid didn't miss.

"May I ask what you trade?" Amid said.

"Spices and other things. There are many in the mountains who long for the taste and comforts of home."

"It is so," Amid said. "There are times when the smell of the spice is all that makes life worth living. Have you been to the mountains many times?"

"No. Not many. A friend, a true brother, has taken ill and he has many obligations. There are those who will suffer if his business were left undone. I fulfill an oath for him."

Amid gave Lee a little bow.

"It is a generous thing you do. The mountains are not friendly. Many fighters make their Jihad there."

"I am not a fighter," Lee said. "But each has his own Jihad. For some, it is the battle. For me, it is fulfilling an oath. It is the struggle, not the battle."

The rear donkey chose that moment to decide he wanted to rest. Lee jerked the lead and spoke to him, but the stubborn thing just sat on its haunches and refused to get up.

"I will take this one and go on to the pass," Amid said. "The way that one looks, I will have time to establish camp before you reach the top. Come when you can get it moving. I will have the fire going when you get there. "

"Go on. It would be better to have no witnesses to my language if this stubborn one resists for one more minute."

He tugged on the lead and cursed at the donkey for ten minutes before he realized that Amid had taken the donkey with the rifle on it. He looked up the trail. Amid had only moved up a couple hundred yards, but he had taken time to pull the rifle from the bindings and was now carrying it with the butt on his hip and the barrel pointing up. Screw it. He didn't seem to be suspicious or antagonistic, and there wasn't anything to be done about it anyway.

Twenty minutes had elapsed without any success in convincing the animal to move when Lee heard a whooshing sound and then a loud explosion above him. Lee ducked instinctively and yelled, "Oh shit!" He spun to look up the trail. A plume of smoke was rising from the trail higher up just about where Amid ought to be.

Chapter 55

The explosion did what Lee couldn't do and the donkey was now standing and jerking on the lead. Lee quickly led it back into the rocks and kicked the back of its knees to make it lay down. He pushed in alongside it and waited. He had figured out what had happened.

Either an aircraft or an armed drone had fired a rocket at Amid. The rifle! The dumb ass had been carrying the rifle making him a legitimate target under the ROE. Shit! Amid had the donkey with the supplies, even his sleeping bag.

Lee listened for sounds of an engine but couldn't hear anything but the continuing echoes of the explosion. He searched the sky. Nothing in sight. Then he saw a glint. Something big high up or something small closer. He watched for the aircraft and tried to comfort the donkey with quiet talk. The aircraft seemed to be gone, but he couldn't be sure.

With slow movements, he unsnapped a compartment on the donkey's pack and found the flashlight/phone. Twitch answered after a few seconds.

"Twitch, I've been attacked. I think I lost a donkey and all my supplies. What the hell is going on?"

After a short delay. "Attacked how?"

"From the air. A rocket. I don't know if it was a drone or what."

Again, the delay. "Hold on. Let me check."

Twitch was gone for almost two minutes.

"You still there?" Twitch said.

"Yeah. Go." He expected the delay this time and waited.

"It's a royal screw-up, Igor. Were you injured? Do you need help?"

"I'm okay. What the hell was it?" The sat-phone delay didn't even seem unusual now.

"CIA drone. He wasn't even supposed to be in the area. Do you want to abort?"

"After what I went through to get here? Hell no. Is it safe to get back on the trail again?"

"Yes. You can move."

"Okay. Stand by the phone. I'm going up the trail and see how much damage was done. Maybe I can salvage something. By the way, I hooked up with a Hajj and he was traveling with me. He was leading the other donkey."

"Is he dead?"

"I'll know in about thirty minutes. I'm moving."

Lee put the phone away and yanked on the donkey's lead. It got up right away this time, and he led it up the trail. The trip took almost forty-five minutes with Lee stopping in rocks and searching the sky for any more surprises.

When they reached the site of the explosion, Lee just sat and stared. He could tell some kind of animal had been there by the blood and scattered gore on the rocks, but nothing was left that could be salvaged. He found Amid after a few minutes of searching. He was intact, but dead. The explosion had flung him a good thirty feet into the rocks. He found the rifle ten feet away from Amid. It was destroyed. He went back to the donkey and took the phone out.

A thought occurred to him. The explosion may have attracted attention and he could be under observation. He took the donkey back into the rocks and only had to kick one knee to get it to lay down. He pressed the transmit switch.

"Twitch?"

"Right here, Igor."

"I lost my supplies. I need a new sleeping bag, food, a water bag, another melting pot, and more food. That's all I can chance loading on the donkey I have left."

"I've got your coordinates. Can you move up to the pass?"

"Yes. Maybe another three hours."

"Okay. Do that. We'll figure out how to get a

resupply to you there. Make sure your chip has a clear view of the sky."

"Got it. Moving now. Just a thought. After that explosion, I may be under observation?"

"Any sign of that?"

"No. But it's a good possibility. If I am, and they come down to check me out, I think I'll be okay. My cover worked well with the Hajj I met on the trail. Anyway, the team that brings in the resupply has to take care approaching my camp. They may not be alone and I may not be either. I can't whip out my trusty flashlight-phone to let you know."

"Okay, Igor. I'll track you. For God's sake, be careful."

The next 3000 feet to the pass were agony and the last 1000 were pure hell. As they ascended above 10,000 feet even the donkey was feeling the lack of oxygen, and Lee had to stop for rest every hundred feet or so. When they stopped, the poor dumb thing just stood spread-legged with its chest heaving. The plan had been to camp at eight-thousand feet and let his lungs adjust to the lower oxygen, but he had to reach the top of the pass by dark now, and he was already fighting fatigue.

The grade was close to thirty percent and the trail bottom was littered with rock and stones like a creek bottom. Snow cover was becoming a problem, but he looked for the wind sweeps and managed to find a path that kept the snow no higher than mid-calf. He kept reminding himself that old men crossed from

Pakistan through this pass regularly. It didn't seem to help.

He fell constantly and banged up one elbow and both knees. When they had passed through 9000 feet, a brief snow storm held them up, but that was more of a blessing than a problem. He and the donkey huddled together for warmth and rested.

At the entrance to the pass at 11,000 feet, the trail widened out to a couple hundred yards across and the snow was deeper. He chose a campsite against the slope on the north side of the pass.

It was going to be a cold, hungry night until he got some supplies. The snow was now a blessing. There was snow to eat to quench his and the donkey's thirst. A wedge-shaped crevasse between two tall boulders provided a wind break, and he moved the donkey in there. He unloaded the Semtex and trading supplies from the donkey's back and they both collapsed, panting, trying to catch a full breath that wouldn't come. His blood oxygen was probably below 85%.

The pass was about 2000 thousand feet below the peak of the mountain ridge-line it passed through, but it was a relatively level and wide passage between two rugged and impassable ridges. The descent would begin 300 yards to the west.

The night was clear so far, but the weather changed hour by hour at 11,000 feet. One cloud passing could change the environment from clear night to blizzard. The night didn't get completely dark like it had far below. The sky glowed with a spectacular show of the universe. If he had been warmer and full of food, he could have marveled at the light show. He had never seen so many stars. It was as though a new sky had replaced the one he had always known.

He waited for real darkness to ascend, but real dark didn't happen. First a kind of dusk came, and then a different kind of light settled in and everything seemed to glow. The snow reflected the glow from the universe above him.

Time passes slowly when all you have to do is count your shivers and try to stay awake. Between 2200 and 2300 he heard the rotors of a helicopter far below, but that was the only thing that broke the monotony. Without his sleeping bag, he didn't dare let himself doze off. He might not wake up. He'd lost his thermometer with the rest of his supplies, but he figured the temperature was well below zero.

The time was approaching 0200 when he heard a noise near the entrance to his shelter in the boulders. Then, low and distinct, "Igor, where the fuck are you?"

The donkey snorted.

"Here," Lee said just as quietly. "In the rocks."

"Stay right there. Coming in."

A lump of snow moved into the crevasse and approached Lee.

"You've got company on the south-side slope," the snow lump said, and then AFO Sergeant Jackson lifted the white sheet covering him and shrugged out of a heavy pack. "Four Hajj. Not sure just what they are. They're hunkered down, so it's not a problem right now, but they may approach you in the morning. What do you want to do about them?"

"Nothing," Lee said. "If they're Taliban, they can guide me through the mountains. I've got to hook-up with them at some point anyway. How'd you find them?"

"Orbiting AC130 got a good thermal of the pass and surrounding terrain. In this snow, they stand out like a campfire, you too. You all are the only warm life forms in the area. What if they are bandits?"

"Probably not in this area. I'll have to risk it. Too much is going on this early in the hike. If another rocket takes out some more of the opposition, somebody is going to start wondering why it's so dangerous to get close to me."

"Okay, it's your show. Try to hang onto this gear. I'm not climbing another mountain to cover your ass. I had to stay in your tracks above the snow line and I have to follow them back out. This shit is getting old."

"I appreciate it. I'll contact Twitch and let him know you're starting back down."

"Do that. Good luck."

Taylor clipped his sheet over his back and moved back out of the crevasse. Soon Lee was left with his supplies, donkey, and silence. He inventoried the supplies before turning in. A small case with dark sunglasses. Someone was thinking better than he was, probably Twitch. An empty canteen with canteen cup.

That would come in handy. Ten MREs, a good week of food. A water bag, empty. A small bag of grain for the donkey, enough for one feeding. A melting pot, not as big as the last one. Four chemical soaked paper logs for camp fires. One cold weather sleeping bag in a Gore-Tex cover. It was enough to get him to the first village and then some.

He spread his bag, removed his boots and climbed in. His fatigue was so great even eating seemed like more of a task than he could manage. With the bag's hood tightly around his head and an Afghan scarf across his face, sleep came quickly.

Chapter 56

Lee woke-up in the middle of a blizzard. When he opened his eyes, he was in a complete white-out. He wanted to start a fire and heat some water for coffee more than anything. The fire would have to wait. It was late and full daylight somewhere outside of the driving snow. He could skip the Fajr prayer. No one could see him and it was too late anyway.

He would have to be careful to perform Zuhr and Asr, at noon and late afternoon. Maghrib, at sunset, was a good idea just to get into the habit. He would recite his verses for Isha, the night prayer. The five daily prayers were one of the five pillars of Islam and the Taliban would be strict about them. Skipping Fajr was not a good thing because he needed to make it habitual, but he was just too damn cold to get out of the sleeping bag. He wondered how the four Muj on the other slope were making out in the blizzard.

As those things go in the mountains, the blizzard blew itself out in thirty minutes and sunshine startlingly bright bathed the whole pass. Lee put his sunglasses on and set about knocking snow off the donkey and his supplies.

He fed the donkey and started a fire with one of the logs. Then minutes later, with just a small amount of snow in the canteen cup so it would melt and heat fast, he had the makings for freeze-dried coffee. He drank a cup while he gathered snow to melt for the water bag and the caffeine made him feel better immediately. While the snow was melting, he ate an MRE.

After the donkey was watered and the water bag was full, he loaded the donkey with the Semtex and spices and added the new supplies. The donkey didn't seem to mind. The poor dumb thing just panted for breath and stared straight ahead. Maybe he was mourning his buddy.

Lee noticed he could move around easier than the previous day. He was rested, fed and hydrated, and his lungs were adjusting to the altitude. It was time to get through the pass and start down the mountain to the ratline that ran along a finger ridge at 9000 feet. He wasn't sure when he started calling the donkey, Eeyore. It just sort of happened.

"Come on Eeyore, let's get down to someplace where we can breathe again."

Eeyore followed him without a complaint. As

they left the Crevasse, he noticed there was only one set of tracks, partially filled in with new snow, running back down the mountain the way he had come up. Sergeant Jackson was good.

Getting through the pass was tougher than he anticipated. Snow had drifted to several feet high in places, and the temperature was well below zero. Lee wrapped his neck and face in a heavy wool Afghan scarf that covered everything from his neck to his sunglasses, His turban insulated his head and kept Twitch informed of his location. He and Eeyore trudged through the snow for a few feet and stopped and rested, struggling to get enough oxygen in the blood to move a few more feet.

The wind sweeps along the slope provided a path he and Eeyore could struggle through, but it was hard work. Even the high-altitude dry snow dragged at his feet and the effort sucked away his oxygen. The relief from a night's rest didn't last long. His legs were heavy and his chest hurt from struggling to draw enough air in. He asked himself why he hadn't let Twitch send help to get him out of there.

Half-way to the down-slope Lee spotted the first of the Hajj he'd been warned about. A man raised up from behind a boulder on the south slope and just stood there watching without trying to conceal his presence. Another revealed himself further along toward the exit from the pass. Lee noted their presence and kept moving. It was like an old cowboy and Indian movie where the Indians suddenly appear on the ridge above the cavalry. He touched the cold grenade under his robe and then touched his pistol. The feel was reassuring.

His companions remained visible until he reached what he considered the exit from the pass. There wasn't any actual point he could call an exit. The pass just got broader and the view of the lower mountains on the other side of the ridge opened. The sight caused him to shiver and feel a renewed fatigue. Ridge after snow covered ridge stretched out to the horizon. Every step of progress would be a massive chore.

The almost level pass changed to a gradual down-slope. 2000 feet below him a two-kilometer ridgeline connected to another, lower pass through a lower mountain range. The sides of the ridge were snow-covered, but the top of the ridgeline was windswept and clear of snow. He had to transit that ridgeline on a narrow trail that ran along the top. As he started down the slope, his companions disappeared.

It took till noon to reach the ridge trail. Lee stopped and set up a temporary camp. Breathing was easier now, but fatigue still gnawed at his legs. With numb fingers, nose, and ears, he performed wudhu with snow and completed Zuhr, then gathered snow in the pot and lit a fire with one paper log. He wouldn't eat a noon meal. Until he could buy provisions from a village, he had to conserve his supplies. Damn, it was cold. Out on the ridge the wind blew without obstruction. The wind chill was well below zero F.

When Eeyore was watered and Lee had hydrated, he set off to cross the ridge. Once again, he wondered about the nature of war. Granted, this was a different kind of war, covert, and his job was to avoid contact until he was at his target valley, but even kinetic war was mostly waiting for something to happen. He wondered when the Indians would appear again. John Wayne would have looked around and said, "It's quiet, too quiet."

He was half way across the ridgeline when his escorts decided to make contact. Up ahead two men, hardly discernible at a kilometer distance, appeared on the ridge. He looked behind him. Four men were leaving the pass and entering the trail on the ridge. He looked down the slope on both sides. Steep, maybe sixty degrees and 2000 feet down. A sixty-degree slope wasn't a walk. It was a climb. On the left, the slope moderated at about 7000 feet and could probably be negotiated on foot—if you could get to it.

He put his hand under his Kameez and touched the M67 grenade in the pocket of his jacket. He let it go. He felt the cold of his pistol's steel. The ritual didn't bring any comfort this time. These guys might be just the people he wanted to contact. He had to make contact to get the information he was sent here for, but for the first time on this hike, he was truly afraid. The way they had isolated him in the middle of the ridge was slick and kind of scary. He had no place to go. Probably not an accidental meeting of three random groups crossing the high passes in the middle of winter.

Chapter 57

He decided to wait right where he was. Let them come to him. Something about this just wasn't right. If they wanted to meet with him or just check him out, why hadn't they approached his camp in the pass? Why trap him on the ridge like this? Sure, they were suspicious people and should be, but this seemed a little extreme. They were exposing themselves not only to him, but to the eyes in the sky as well.

He moved around the donkey and looked down the slope again. Damn, that's steep. It was possible, but if he lost his footing, he wouldn't stop tumbling until he reached the bottom of the mountain and he'd be dead long before then. He opened the flap on the satchel that held the real Semtex. Five kilos of plastic explosives, forty-five quarter-pound blocks. It was necessary for his bonafides Twelve pounds was a lot though. It was safe enough without a detonator in it, but he didn't want it to fall into the hands of the insurgents. He left the flap open and put his hand inside his Kameez and fingered the grenade again, then the pistol. He took the safety clip off of the grenade. Only the pin was left to keep the grenade safe.

The men approached at a steady pace keeping an equal distance between Lee and them front and rear. He leaned against Eeyore and tried to look relaxed with his hands inside his robe. His language was better than good. His manners and culture had fooled Amid. He had done nothing while he was being observed to cause suspicion. It was going to be okay. This could be the break he needed. He wondered how he could introduce the names he sought into conversation. When would the time be right without raising suspicion?

He chanced a quick glance back at the four who left the pass. He could see weapons, but they were being cautious. Each hajj had his weapon held tight against his leg so it couldn't be seen at a distance, like from a drone. They were aware of the danger and yet, they came anyway.

The men from both directions approached within hailing distance. Lee kept his eyes on the two coming from the other side of the ridge. They were new. The four coming from behind could have taken him anytime in the last twelve hours if they wanted him. He could ignore them. It's going to be okay.

Then the larger of the two coming from the

other side called out. No friendly preliminaries. "You are not Hamad. Where is he?"

"Hamad is Ill. He may be in his last hours. I have pledged to make his journey for him. Who are you, may I ask?"

Both groups were close now. The two from the far side kept coming and stopped ten feet from Eeyore. Lee heard the four come close from behind. He kept his eyes on the two.

"You should know who I am if you journey for Hamad. What have you brought us?"

As he got a good look at the two, Lee felt a burst of excitement. They fit the descriptions. Could they be Abdal and Esmail?

"I have spices." That brought a smile from the big one. Take the chance, he thought. "And for Esmail, I have a special gift."

The smaller of the two had been looking at the donkey, but now he snapped his head up. He looked at Lee intently and said, "What is it?"

Bingo, Lee thought. They found me. Now what the hell am I going to do?

"Thirty Kilos of the finest plastic and ten boxes of pencil fuses." he said

"Thirty Kilos?" Esmail said. "Hamad did well. I think we will relieve you of your burden. You may return and tend to Hamad. When can we expect the next journey?"

Lee was face to face with a bomber, an expert at blowing up innocent people. He wasn't the monster he expected. He looked like a normal young man, a trimmed beard, and he even smiled. There was no evil aura about him, but he was Esmail. He was a bomb making son of a bitch and he needed to die. The big one had to be Abdal Amit, the self-styled servant of death. They traveled as a pair. Lee's suppressed hate and anger went ballistic.

He wanted to scream, "Now, here's your fucking journey. Say hello to Allah!" But he didn't. It was all he could do to keep the hate and rage off his face.

He slowly pulled his hands out of his robe with the grenade in his right, no sudden movements. Then he quickly jerked the pin out, let the spoon fly—and stuffed the grenade into the satchel with the Semtex. He silently stepped back and dropped over the edge of the trail.

The men behind him were ready for anything suspicious, but even they weren't sure what they saw. Even so, as soon as he dropped over the edge they opened fire and green tracers flashed by Lee's falling body. They should have been running away as fast as they could.

He hit a large rock ten feet down and slipped and hit again on his back in the snow. The slope was too steep to slow him and he tumbled, picking up speed with a line of tracers following him down the slope. He tried to keep his arms and legs close to his body, but the violence of the fall whipped them out and slammed them into the snow as he turned end over end.

He was two hundred feet down the slope and

still accelerating with the men up top still firing at him when the explosion came. He hardly noticed. His brain could hardly take in the whirling scene his eyes presented until he took one flip and landed on his back thirty feet further down the slope and began sliding instead of flipping.

Buster, Jackson, and Abi were in the TOC with Twitch.

"What the hell just happened?" Buster said.

"I don't know," Twitch said. "He was stationary for several minutes and then his altitude changed rapidly."

"Can you get the AC-one-thirty up. Maybe they caught it on their image sensors."

"Hold on," Twitch said.

Twitch queried the aircraft and got a data feed from them.

"They had him on the ridge and picked up six muj closing on him from both ends. Then their screens blanked out due to a powerful flash of light. Something exploded."

"Is your drone in the area, Abi?"

"It's over Pakistan. I can re-task it."

"Do it. We need a closer look. Twitch, see if the one-thirty can get a better look, even if they have to descend to do it."

The AC130 descended to 10,000 feet and orbited the site. Their cameras got a close-up of the ridge top. Thirty feet of trail was gone and the ridge top now had a saddle in it.

"The Semtex," Jackson said. "Something blew the Semtex. He didn't have it wired, did he?"

"Only a small part of it was real." Buster said.

"Twelve pounds," Jackson said. "That's enough to do that."

"What is wrong with you two?" Abi said. "Where's Lee?"

"I'm sorry, Abi," Buster said. "If he was inside that explosion radius . . ."

"No," Twitch said. "The last thing I got on the GPS was a rapid loss of altitude and that was before the explosion. He must have jumped."

"How steep is that slope?" Jackson asked.

"I haven't got the data. It's steep though. Almost a cliff."

"Let's not get ahead of ourselves," Buster said. "Wait for the drone. We can do a close search of the whole slope."

Chapter 58

Lee regained consciousness slowly. He was on his back between two large rocks a thousand feet down the slope from the ridgeline. With awareness, came pain. He tried each limb and they all moved at his command. A small white airplane passed over him and then it passed over him again. He waved both arms over his head.

Snow was caked on his eyes and filled his ears. He cleared them and tried to sit up. It hurt but he managed to get his head and chest up to look around. The little plane was gone. A drone, he thought. Twitch was looking for him.

He tried to sit up further and began to slip down the mountain again. He dug his heels in and clutched snow with his hands. He came to a stop again a hundred feet further down the slope. The snow was a life saver. Had the hillside been clear, he'd be dead.

His head was clearing, but his body ached all over. Nothing felt broken. He couldn't be sure until he tried to stand. He scooted his butt and pulled with his heels. He began to slide again, but he could control it. He slid another hundred feet. The heavy crust on the snow hurt his bruised body, but it slowed his descent.

By scooting to get started and digging in his heels to control his speed, he made progress toward the place on the hillside where the slope eased and became flat enough to stand. Every time he moved he hurt. He had to get to that flat area and find a way to make a signal. His flashlight/phone was gone, lost in the snow above him, and he didn't have the strength to search for it. The turban was gone too. His good ear and his face were numb.

In the TOC Abi monitored the incoming from the drone control center.

"They've found a man," Abi said. "He's halfway down the slope. Oh, bugger it! I've lost the feed."

"Blackhawk on the way," Twitch said. "They can get him out on a winch."

"We don't know if it's him," Abi said.

"I'm not waiting," Twitch said. "Try to get your data feed back up."

"Just a moment," Abi said. "Oh damn. They are returning the drone to its base. It has a malfunction."

"I still have a GPS hit on the hillside," Twitch said. "It's been stationary for a while. We'll just have to wait for the Blackhawk."

They had to wait an hour for the helicopter to arrive on site and then another fifteen minutes while they searched for Lee. Twitch put the Blackhawk's relay up on speaker and everyone sat and stared at it. Finally, the pilot broke squelch.

"Positive Identification. We have Igor." Then silence.

"How the hell is he?" Abi screamed. "Will you get on with it?"

Squelch broke again.

"Status of patient," the pilot said, and the speaker went quiet again.

"You bloody imbecile, What!"

"Easy, Abi," Twitch said. "He's flying a helicopter and getting status."

The pilot broke squelch again.

"Status of patient. He is conscious, but near hypothermia. Contusions and bruises, but no apparent serious injuries. Vitals in the safe range. Returning J-bad for further transport to Bagram."

"About bloody time," Abi said. "Thank God. I need one of you guys to take me to Bagram. I don't care which one, but I need to go right now."

"Pack up," Buster said. "You won't be coming back. I'll have a Toyota at the door."

IGOR

The Bagram medical facility was a mad house. A helicopter crash had killed or injured twenty-three soldiers. Medical staff were moving from room to room. Administrative staff were overloaded and short tempered. Buster couldn't find out anything. Abi tried, but she was told to wait. Finally, a nurse helped them. Lee was in the medevac building awaiting a flight to Germany.

The little group of spooks and AFO finally found him. By then it was near midnight. He was high on pain medicine and covered with multiple blankets.

Abi stood at his bedside and examined him with her eyes before speaking,

"Lee? Are you awake?"

He opened his eyes and smiled.

"Hi, Abi. Yeah, I'm awake. A little woozy, but perfectly lucid. Hello, Buster. I'm sorry, Abi. I screwed up and didn't find out anything about your Lieutenant."

"It was a long shot anyway," she said. "What did the doctors say?"

"Just bruises, contusions, and a little hypothermia. They want to send me to Germany for an exam to make sure I don't have any internal injuries. They're worried about my spleen."

"What the hell happened back on the ridge, Igor?" Buster said.

"I got your guys."

"Abdal and Esmail?"

"Yep. Both. Blew them to hell."

"How?"

"Grenade in the Semtex."

"You did it yourself, then?"

"Oh yeah. I blew those bastards up just like they blew me up. Dropped over the cliff and rolled down the mountain. I'm sorry for Eeyore though. He didn't deserve that, but maybe he's a Muslim and enjoying his seventy-two virgins now. He sure was horny enough to handle seventy-two." Lee laughed and held his stomach.

"Is he saying Igor?" Buster said, looking around "Who the hell is Eeyore? This is getting screwier by the minute."

"The only Eeyore I know is from the Winnie-the-pooh story," Abi said. "He's the donkey."

"I think that's enough for now," an Air Force nurse said, stepping into the room. Lieutenant Toliver is on his second dose of pain medication. I doubt he'll be making much sense before he reaches Germany."

Abi was at Bagram for three days before the Air Force could get her on a flight to Germany. In Germany, she only had a ten-hour layover. She tried to locate Lee, but he wasn't even on the same base. She boarded her flight to London without knowing where he was or how he was doing.

Her search was doomed to failure anyway. About the time she were boarding a flight to London, Mallory had Lee on a C17 on his way to MacDill Air Force Base in Florida for debriefing and planned to send him back to Brooke Army Medical Center in Texas for surgery on his face.

Chapter 59

Three months after Lee's transfer to Brooke and Abi's return to England, she heard a knock at the door of her flat. She had a good idea who it was. She had been waiting. She opened the door and he was there.

"Hi," he said.

"Hi, yourself. Are you hungry?"

"I wouldn't call it that."

Abi smiled and touched his face gently.

"Umm. I think I may share your condition. It looks wonderful, Lee. They did an amazing job."

"Well, I'll admit it looks better. At least I don't have a permanent scowl now, and I can smile without scaring people."

"I've missed that smile, whatever you say. Come along. Close the door.

She walked steadily across the room, almost precisely, to the sofa. Then she had to sit down.

"Whatever they are doing to you, it's working," Lee said.

"I wanted you to see for yourself, but I've reached my limit. Tell me about your surgery. What did they do? It really is an amazing difference. Your ear is perfect."

"It's a fake. One of the surgeries implanted magnets in my scalp. They hold the ear on. Then they released the scar constrictions and that let my face relax into a more normal expression. I have exercises to stretch and strengthen the muscles, and it's already making a difference. Finally, they sandpapered my scars. Can you believe that? They sandpapered them. It was a gooey mess for a while, but it healed to what you see. Not perfect, but better, don't you think?"

"I think it's wonderful seeing you looking so full of yourself. How long do you have?"

"A month. Do you think you can stand me for that long?"

"Oh, you silly bloke. I've waited three months already. It will take a month just to catch up. With my new leg strength, I may have a few surprises for you."

"Now you're talking," Lee said and laughed. Abi looked so good walking across the room when he came in, so firm and upright again, almost like the first day he saw her.

"I believe you have an addition to your uniform." she said.

Lee lifted his coat sleeve. The broad gold band and one narrow gold band of a lieutenant junior grade were gone and replaced with two brand new equal gold bands of a full Navy lieutenant, equal in rank to a captain in the Army or Marines.

"Below the zone a year early," he said. "Commander Faulks gave me such a glowing efficiency report I made the cut. Even Mallory added a letter of commendation.

"You deserve it. Can you tell me what's next for you career-wise?" she said.

"I've been offered a job."

"Black Wolf?"

"Yes."

"Are you going to accept?" she said.

"Twitch is already working on a better way to track me. Now, weren't you saying something about leg strength and surprises?"

END

ABOUT THE AUTHOR

Raymond Hunter Pyle is a two service, two tour Vietnam Veteran. Today he spends his time enjoying life in Florida with his wife of fifty years and writing tales of war and adventure.

Made in the USA
Las Vegas, NV
22 February 2022